Also by Michelle Rowen from Gollancz:

Bitten & Smitten

Fanged & Fabulous

Lady & the Vamp

IMMORTALITY BITES

Bitten &
Smitten

Michelle Rowen

First published in Great Britain in 2010 by
Gollancz
An imprint of the Orion Publishing Group
Orion House, 5 Upper St Martin's Lane, London WC2H 9EA
An Hachette UK Company

1 3 5 7 9 10 8 6 4 2

A CIP catalogue record for this book is available
from the British Library

ISBN 978 0 575 09400 0

Printed in Great Britain by

The Orion Publishing Group's policy is to use papers that are
natural, renewable and recyclable products and made from wood
grown in sustainable forests. The logging and manufacturing
processes are expected to conform to the environmental regulations
of the country of origin.

www.michellerowen.com
www.orionbooks.co.uk

To my parents
for their love, support, and tons of patience
with a brat like me.

Chapter 1

For a dead woman, I felt surprisingly good.

I figured I had to be dead, since the first thing I noticed after opening my eyes was someone burying me in the cold ground. I was only in a few inches deep, but steady shovelfuls of dirt were landing on my chest, creating a rapidly growing mound.

The air smelled of moss and worms . . . and cheap cologne.

Cheap cologne?

I craned my neck to look around. An ornately carved gravestone stood not five feet away from my eyes. I blinked. It was dark, but I was pretty sure it wasn't my name carved on it.

The next dirt sandwich hit me squarely in the face.

"Hey!" I managed before I started to cough. I freed my right hand from under the heavy pile to wipe at my face.

"Oh, you're awake," a surprised male voice said from my left.

"What the hell is going on?"

"You're awake and asking questions." He sounded dismayed. "I was afraid of this."

Something sharp and metallic hit the ground behind my head. Sounded like a shovel. Then the owner of the voice crouched down and moved his pale, thin face close to me.

"Hello there," he said.

It was Gordon Richards, my blind date from earlier that evening, although I'd already recognized his voice. And his cologne. Whiny and nasal, it gave the impression of belonging to a very needy person. The voice, not the cologne, that is. The longer the date had gone on, the more I'd realized that the voice didn't lie.

"Hi?" I started to squirm around. "Get me out of here, you lunatic, before I call the cops."

He frowned. "But the dirt is an important part of the healing process."

"Healing process? I'll give you a healing process as soon as I get out of here."

"Sorry." Gordon began to push the dirt off me, and I struggled to pull myself free of the loose earth. He offered his hand to help me stand, but I ignored it and managed to get to my feet all by myself.

I attempted to brush the dirt off my new, not to mention very expensive, silk dress and tried not to panic. My three-quarter-length burgundy leather coat could be easily wiped off, but I knew immediately that the dress was ruined. Although, I think it was safe to say that was the least of my problems at the moment.

This guy was obviously psychotic.

I took a good look around. Just as I'd suspected, thanks to the big clue of the gravestone, we were standing in the middle of a cemetery. My blind date had just attempted to bury me in a *cemetery*. Filled with dead people. And bugs.

I shuddered, then I looked at him standing patiently nearby.

"Well, thanks so much for the date." I tried to make my voice as relaxed as possible. Calm, cool, and not ready to freak out. *Yet*. "I guess I'd better be heading home now."

"What exactly do you remember?"

I forced a reluctant smile. "That I had a lovely time. And that I'll have to thank Amy for setting this up. Yes, she won't be hearing the end of this anytime soon. I can promise you that. Anyhow, super meeting you." I made a move to leave, but he grabbed my arm and pulled me back to face him.

"What's the last thing you remember?" Gordon asked, harsher now. "It's important."

I swallowed hard. "We had a lovely dinner. Then we went for a walk"—I glanced around—"but not here. Over by the river and the bridge, the Bloor Viaduct. We were looking down at the river, and um . . . you were saying something. . . ."

"How lovely you are," he murmured as he ran a hand down my coat sleeve.

I gritted my teeth and jerked away from his touch. Why hadn't I ever signed up for that self-defense course Amy was always begging me to join with her? My eyes narrowed at the thought. *Amy*. She was so dead for getting me into this.

"Right." I tried to turn my gritted teeth into a pleasant smile. "Me being lovely. Or whatever. And then . . ."

I frowned as I tried to remember, but things seemed a bit fuzzy.

"I offered you eternity."

Uh-huh. I did remember that part. That was the moment when I decided that the date was officially over. And then—

My eyes widened as I looked at him. "Then you *bit me,* you weirdo."

Gordon looked very apologetic. "It'll heal quick. I promise."

I touched my neck and then pulled my hand away, staring with horror at the blood left behind.

"You bit me on the neck? What kind of a sorry-ass vampire wannabe are you, anyhow?"

I grabbed for my dirt-covered purse that lay by my feet. I kept a can of pepper spray in it for protection, or at least I used to. Did I still have it? Did those things have an expiration date? Didn't matter. If I had to, I'd just use it to bash him over the head.

"I'm not a wannabe." He actually had the audacity to look insulted. "I *am* a vampire."

Psycho, I thought. *Total psycho.*

"Look," I said tentatively, "you've had your fun. I'm not all that into the role-playing scene, or whatever this is, but the bite doesn't seem to be too bad. I think. So, let's just say no harm done and leave it at that, okay?"

"From the moment I saw you last month at the hot-dog stand outside your office, I knew that you had to be mine, Sarah." He smiled wistfully.

His teeth did look a little bit pointy, now that I was paying closer attention, but it was probably just the moonlight playing tricks. Still, unnerving to say the least. Also unnerving was the fact that somebody had secretly watched me getting my near-daily Italian-sausage fix. Creepy.

"You had to have me, huh?" I stared at him for a moment. "And you couldn't just do what everyone else does and try to get me drunk?"

Usually, making a joke made me feel better. At the moment, it was all I could do to keep my voice from trembling.

"It took forever to get into your friend's good graces so she'd set us up on this date, but it was worth the wait. Now you're mine. We'll be together forever."

Without another word I turned and started walking briskly away from him. Still calm. Still in complete control. Just like my panty hose.

Gordon yelled after me a couple of times and then ran, catching up to me in only two or three steps. He grabbed my elbow and spun me around to face him.

"It's rude to walk away when someone's offering you eternity." I didn't like the way he was looking at me now. Not in the slightest. And his voice didn't sound needy and desperate anymore.

I yanked my arm away from him. "Keep it. I don't want it."

He grabbed me again. Despite his scrawny appearance, his grip was crushing.

"Let go of me . . . ," I began, but then he hit me hard across my face with the back of his hand. My vision exploded in multicolor waves and my teeth loosened slightly in their sockets as the impact shook me right to my toes.

"It's too late to take it back, bitch." His snarl showed

the full length of his sharp fangs. "The bite on your neck makes you mine. It's a no-return policy."

Then he appeared to come back to his senses. His face relaxed and his eyebrows knitted together into a frown as he reached toward me. I scurried back out of his range, eyes wide, pressing my hand against my stinging cheek.

"Oh, God, I'm so sorry," he sputtered as he moved closer to me. "I didn't mean to do that. What the hell was I thinking?"

I wrapped my other hand around the cool can of pepper spray at the very bottom of my purse. My eyes were still unfocused, but I managed to yank the can out and spray him long and hard in the eyes. He howled in pain and clawed at his face.

I turned on my heels and did what any self-respecting girl with a neck wound does when she finds herself in a cemetery after midnight with a crazy guy who thinks he's a vampire.

Ran like hell.

Crazy. Yup. Definitely bipolar, and very likely in need of some serious therapy. It was probably something that happened to him in childhood that had turned him into such a loon. I'd minored in psychology during the year I spent at the University of Toronto before dropping out. Loony. That was the professional verdict. In serious need of help.

Just like I was at the moment. I ran through the cemetery. Big cemetery. Where the hell was the road?

Finally I saw the stone entry gates straight ahead of me. I heard Gordon, not that far behind, yelling for me to slow down. Yeah, like that was going to happen. Not bloody likely.

The three-inch heel on one of my black leather slingbacks chose that moment to snap off. Those shoes had cost me the better part of last month's paycheck, so it was a little disappointing, to say the least, that they couldn't take a little pressure. I crashed to the ground in a heap, but sprang up just as quickly, like one of those Bozo the Clown punching bags. The adrenaline coursing through my veins was definitely helpful, but I felt lightheaded. The loss of blood from the bite on my neck was finally catching up to me. Maybe it was more serious than I'd originally thought.

I pulled off what was left of the shoe, spun around, and threw it in the direction of my pursuer.

"Ow!" he yelled as the slingback met its mark.

Since it was impossible for me to run lopsided, I sent the other shoe sailing in the same direction like a small, expensive, Italian-leather missile. That one missed the target, so I hurled a few choice expletives behind it.

"Come on!" Gordon called after me. "Sarah, baby, we can work this out!"

I ran through the entrance of the cemetery and straight into something firm and unyielding. I looked up. It was something tall, muscular, and blue-eyed. A streetlamp shone above him like a beacon from heaven itself.

"Whoa there, miss," the unyielding stranger said. "Slow down."

I was gasping for breath after my sprint. "Oh, thank God! You have to help me."

The man's gaze slid from my neck wound over to my date from hell, who had almost reached us.

"Don't worry about a thing, darlin'," he said and smiled. His teeth were shiny white in the moonlight.

Two more men emerged from the shadows, one as thin as a rail with stringy blond hair, the other big and burly with so many tattoos that they peeked out at the edge of his neck past his dark shirt and jacket. I hadn't noticed anyone else around until they'd moved.

Hey, the more the merrier.

The man with the shiny teeth gently pushed me aside. "You wait right there, darlin'. We'll deal with you in a moment."

I nodded and exhaled deeply. Wow, it was just my luck that these fine gentlemen were out for a walk in the cemetery.

After midnight.

I frowned. What the hell were they doing here, anyhow? Seemed like quite the lucky coincidence, if you asked me. But since it was working out in my favor, I kept my questions to myself.

Gordon skidded to a halt in front of us, blinking rapidly and rubbing his eyes from the shot of pepper spray. There was a small red mark on his forehead—probably from the shoe.

I had my arms wrapped around myself to keep from shivering. I was dressed for a date, not a jog through a cemetery in late November. If I'd known that was in the cards, I would have at least worn a nice scarf. I felt ill, too: from the fear, from the loss of blood . . . and possibly from the fajita I'd had earlier for dinner.

"Why were you running?" Gordon looked confused. "I wasn't going to hurt you."

"Bite me," I told him. He was *so* going to get charged

with assault. I might even have to put a restraining order on his sorry ass. "Oh, wait a minute, you already *did* bite me, didn't you . . . you psycho!"

He rolled his eyes. "You're really going to have to get over that if this relationship is going to have half a chance."

Gordon finally noticed that we weren't alone. "Oh" was all he said as the men approached him. "Look, guys, this isn't what it looks like."

I glared at him and then tried to smile at "White-teeth." He sure was cute. Maybe my night was turning out better than I'd thought. "Look, if you guys just want to help me find a cab, I'd really like to go home. Make sure he doesn't come near me again, and I'll owe you one."

White-teeth smiled broadly. "Look what we have here, boys. Girlfriend and boyfriend vampire in a bit of a squabble."

"He's not my boyfriend," I assured him.

"I'm not a vampire," Gordon said quietly.

"That's funny. He told me he was a vampire just a minute ago. That's why he bit me." I rubbed my neck tenderly. "He's definitely crazy."

"Yeah. Crazy," White-teeth said before turning to his friends. "How many is this tonight?"

The stringy-haired guy piped up, "It's been a great night. Maybe five? No, six."

"Listen, guys"—Gordon looked scared to death—"we can work something out. I have money—"

White-teeth punched Gordon in the stomach. He clutched at his belly and fell to his knees, coughing and sputtering.

"Hey," I said, frowning hard. "I don't think that's necessary. Look, all I want is for you guys to help me get home. That's all."

"Shut up," White-teeth snapped at me. Gordon struggled to his feet, only to get punched again, this time in the jaw.

That's no way to treat a crazy person. They need supervision, not violence.

I marched over to White-teeth and grabbed his arm. "That's enough. There's no reason to be such a big bully. . . ."

He looked at me for a moment, then smiled. "Darlin', you need to learn your place." He pushed me hard enough to make me fall backward, and I yelped in pain as my ankle twisted.

Something glinted in the hands of my so-called rescuers, catching the moonlight. Some kind of metal. Knives. "Stringy-hair" held a switchblade, and "Burly" had a small ax. I also noticed they had sharp wooden spikes tucked into loops on their belts.

Then Gordon screamed. White-teeth was so close to him now that they seemed to be slow dancing, shuffling around in a partial circle. White-teeth moved back and I saw the handle of a knife sticking out of Gordon's stomach.

"But I told you I had money," he gasped.

White-teeth extended his hand like a doctor might, waiting for his next tool. A wooden spike was slapped down into it.

I opened my mouth to say something, to stop this before it went too far, but the only sound that came out was a tiny squeak.

"But, vampire, this is so much more fun than money," White-teeth said and arched his arm upward, slicing into Gordon's torso.

I brought a hand to my mouth in stunned horror and scrambled backward on the ground. A bolt of pain went through my ankle as I tried and failed to get to my feet. My heart beat wildly. All three men joined in then, taking turns hacking and stabbing and slicing my date. They were so busy with Gordon that they appeared to have forgotten I was even there. I was beginning to think that was a good thing.

Finally I was able to stand up unsteadily. But I felt frozen in place as I watched the straight-out-of-a-horror-movie scene before me. I'd changed my mind. Didn't want their help anymore. Nope. And what had he said before? They'd deal with me in a moment?

Gordon was no longer screaming or begging for his life. He'd stopped moaning. Stopped moving. In fact, he appeared to be disintegrating. The more they stabbed at his prone body, the less there seemed to be of him, until finally there was nothing but his empty clothes lying in the middle of a nasty dark stain on the road.

Then White-teeth turned to me. I shuffled backward a painful step at a time. My brain was screaming for me to run, and I finally decided that was the best idea I'd had all night. I turned around, but Stringy-hair had quietly moved to stand behind me. He grinned as he put his now-bloody wooden spike back in his belt, then grabbed my wrists to pull me closer to him. I tried to twist away.

"Where do you think you're going, vampire?" His breath smelled like rotten eggs.

I wanted to argue, to tell him I wasn't a vampire

because vampires didn't exist. I also wanted to tell him to invest in a good mouthwash. But I still couldn't find my voice. A hot tear slipped down my cheek as I looked at the other two men and took in a shuddery gulp of air. I had a funny feeling these guys wanted to add more stains to my ruined dress than the grass and the dirt that were already on it.

I wished I had another shoe to throw.

"Look at her; she's petrified," White-teeth said with amusement.

"She's new," Burly answered. "It's almost cruel to exterminate her so soon. She looks like she might be fun. Check out those legs. Can't it wait till the morning?"

White-teeth's smile widened. "Yeah. Maybe we can wait a bit. What do you say, darlin'? Want to buy yourself a little time?"

"In your dreams," I managed to hiss at him.

He laughed. "There is only one answer, darlin', and that is whatever I say it is. Now come here, or else."

I decided I'd rather have the "or else." The man who'd seemed so attractive when I'd first bumped into him, my potential hero, now was grotesquely ugly to me. His face was splattered with Gordon's blood.

I tried to pull away from Stringy-hair, but he held tight to my wrists, leering at me.

"Nice try," he said, grinning.

I shrugged at him, then kneed him hard in the groin. He let go of my wrists immediately. I glanced over my shoulder at White-teeth, then, ignoring the searing pain in my ankle, darted away from them.

While Stringy-hair moaned in agony, Burly made an annoyed noise and said, "It's never easy, is it?" Then boots slapped against the pavement as they started to chase after me.

Everything looked different late at night, and there was barely any light to help me figure out where the hell I was. I knew the Bloor Viaduct, a tall bridge that went over the Don River, wasn't too far away. If I could get to the other side of the bridge, I could find a phone, find somebody who could help me.

How much longer I could keep running was the question. My lungs burned, and with my twisted ankle I was doing more of a fast limp than an all-out run. Also, my feet, without the protection of any shoes, were screaming for me to stop. But I knew if I stopped, that would be it. They'd kill me like they'd killed Gordon. Or worse. I shuddered when I thought of how that stringy-haired freak had leered at me. I had to keep running. There was no other choice.

I was actually surprised the men hadn't caught up to me. In fact, I didn't even hear them behind me anymore. My pace slowed, but only for a moment. I braved a quick glance over my shoulder.

I was now in the middle of a park. I could hear traffic, so that meant I wasn't far from Bloor Street, but I couldn't see anything but trees surrounding me. I was all alone.

I skidded to a halt and was breathing so fast and shallow I was certain that I'd begin to hyperventilate.

They must have given up. Maybe I'd been too fast for them. I *had* been going to the gym a little more than normal lately, to get into bikini shape for my big, expensive trip to Puerto Vallarta. Amy and I had been planning it for nearly a year, and now it was just a month away. That had to be it. I was in amazing shape. Just as fit and dangerous as that chick from the Terminator movies.

Then I heard the rev of an engine and the squealing of tires. A Jeep lurched onto the road in the distance, spraying gravel under its wheels.

Outrun that, Terminator, I thought as the panic rose again in my chest.

Dammit.

I could hear them, the men I'd stupidly thought I'd escaped. They were hooting and hollering as they bore down on me. This must have been their idea of a good time.

I finally made it to the bridge. In the distance I could see the Toronto skyline.

I kept running, ignoring the pain. The concrete sidewalk that ran along one side of the bridge felt cool through my torn nylons and cut-up feet. I looked around, hoping that somebody might stop to help me, but car after car whizzed by without even slowing down for a second glance. When I stepped out into the bridge's traffic to try to flag someone down, a driver blasted his horn and swerved, narrowly missing me. I scrambled back onto the sidewalk.

It looked like it was just going to be me, White-teeth, and the boys.

And the dark shadow of a figure balanced on one of the bridge's metal suspension beams. He stood on the other side of what was called the "veil"—thin, evenly spaced metal rods put up to prevent anyone from climbing over the barrier and leaping to their death. But I saw that a section of the veil was now warped, stretched wide enough to allow someone to get through. This was where

I quickly scrambled up and squeezed through so I stood near the stranger, my back against the barrier. Behind me, I heard the Jeep skid to a halt and the doors slam as the men got out to chase after me on foot.

"Hey!" I called out to the figure. He wore a long coat that whipped about in the cold wind. He looked like an ornament on the front of a pirate ship. Or maybe even Kate Winslet flying at the front of the *Titanic*—only not as perky. And certainly not as female.

"Go away." His deep voice was sullen.

"Holy crap, this is high up, isn't it?" I inched closer to where he stood on the beam. "Help me!"

"Help yourself. Can you not see I'm planning to kill myself here?" the man said, looking down at the dark water far below us.

"Help me first and then kill yourself," I reasoned.

I was close enough to glimpse his face. He looked to be in his mid-thirties and was dressed from head to toe in black. If I actually had a moment to consider his looks in my current life-or-death situation, I'd say he was really hot. But he looked completely miserable. Whether he looked miserable because he wanted to kill himself or because he'd been interrupted, I wasn't sure.

"A friend of yours?" White-teeth's voice came from behind me, just on the other side of the veil of bars.

I braced myself and turned my head to look at him. "A *good* friend. And he's going to kick your ass if you don't leave me the hell alone."

He gave me a very unfriendly smile. "That I'd like to see."

From his perch, the stranger glanced at us without much interest. He seemed oblivious to the fact that we were hundreds of feet in the air. I saw his gaze move to my neck, and I touched it gingerly.

"Vampire hunters," he said.

"Who wants to know?" White-teeth took a cigar from his leather jacket pocket and lit it. He must have felt he had all the time in the world.

I carefully inched even closer to the stranger. Even though he was suicidal and therefore probably just as crazy as anyone else I'd had the misfortune of meeting that evening, he was currently my best bet to get out of this in one piece.

"It doesn't matter who I am," the stranger replied to White-teeth. "You are invading my personal space. Kindly take your business elsewhere."

White-teeth glowered at him. "We've just come to claim this little piece of vampire ass and we'll be on our way, so you can get back to"—he looked around— "whatever it was you were doing."

I grabbed the hem of the stranger's coat and held on for dear life. "Don't let them hurt me. Please."

He yanked his coat away from me. "I don't want anything to do with this."

"Too late."

White-teeth had started to squeeze through a section in the cement at knee level that wasn't protected by the veil, his cigar clenched between his teeth. "Here I was going to be a gentleman and kill you quick. Well, sort of quick. Now I'm going to take all the time in the world to tear you apart. You're going to feel every second of it."

White-teeth was halfway through and reached out for me. I yanked away from him, spun around, and kicked him with my bare foot. There was a sickeningly wet *squish* as my big toe met his left eye. It was the most disgusting thing I'd ever felt.

He screamed in pain and clutched at his face. The cigar fell out of his mouth and down to the river below. I lost my footing, but before I could fall, the stranger reached out and grabbed me around my waist, pulling me safely against him.

"Thank you." I barely got the words out, my teeth were chattering so hard. "I thought you weren't going to help me."

"Reflex," he said.

The two vampire hunters who weren't currently howling in pain—although Stringy-hair looked a little tender from the groin incident—pulled their injured friend away from the opening and started to climb through themselves.

The stranger looked down at the black water. "I suppose we'll have to jump."

I raised my eyebrows and clung to him as the hunters grabbed at my legs. "Wasn't that your original plan? And wasn't your original plan to kill yourself?"

"With my luck tonight, the fall won't kill me," he replied, bringing an arm around my waist. "But you just might."

He pushed off from the bridge and we fell for what felt like a very long time before disappearing into the cold black water.

Chapter 2

I struggled to keep up with the stranger after we scrambled like drowned rats out of the freezing-cold Don River and up a steep grassy hill. He walked so fast it was as if he didn't want me to follow him. But what else was I supposed to do? He'd just saved my life. The least he could do was make sure I was still in one piece. One scared, shaking, drippy piece.

So far there hadn't been any sign of the creeps who'd tried to kill me. Maybe we'd lost them. I guess they didn't want to jump into the water after us. Can't say I blamed them for that.

That was one hell of a fall. How we'd survived was another story, but it didn't really matter. I was okay. Now I was in need of a phone, a taxi, a police report, and a long, hot shower. Not necessarily in that order.

"Hey, wait up!" I called after "Mr. Tall-Dark-and-Dripping-Wet."

All I'd seen of him after our impromptu swim was the back of his head moving swiftly away from me, so I was surprised when he actually stopped in his tracks. His broad shoulders went up and down as if he'd just let out a long sigh.

He turned to face me. "What now?"

"Where are you going?"

"Home. I suggest you do the same. Go find your sire and be on your way."

"My what?"

"Your sire."

"What's that?"

He nodded toward my neck. "Whoever gave you that hickey there. You'll need your sire to show you the ropes."

I touched my neck and winced. "Those bastards killed the guy who did this." I got a lump in my throat as I said it. What they'd done to Gordon played like an instant replay over and over in my mind. A few tears made a reappearance and I wiped them away with my wet sleeve. "He was a jerk, a total nutcase, but he didn't deserve . . . that. They killed him and they were going to do the same to me. It was horrible."

"They killed your sire," the stranger repeated. He didn't say anything else. He just stared at me.

I began to feel uncomfortable. Well, more than I already was, that is. I decided that going home was an excellent idea. I could call the cops from there.

"Did you drink from him?" he finally asked.

"What?"

He sighed. "Did you drink from your sire before he was slain?"

"I had a few margaritas with dinner."

"That's not what I mean."

I blinked. "Then no. No drinking was done after dinner. Look, thanks for . . ." I didn't know exactly what to call our plunge to safety. I glanced back in the direction of the bridge. "For the thing back there."

He didn't answer.

I shoved my hands into the soggy pockets of my leather jacket. Dirt was one thing, but water was another. It was probably ruined now, too. Just my damn luck. I forced a feeble grin before I started walking away from the stranger.

"Wait," he called after I'd gone half a block. "Are you certain that your sire is dead?"

"Positive," I said grimly. I pictured the empty clothes in my mind. What had happened to the body? Probably just my eyes playing tricks on me. It was a dark night, and the margaritas with dinner had been doubles.

"What's your name?" He walked toward me.

I hesitated before answering. I'd had enough. I just wanted to go home now. "Sarah," I said. "Sarah Dearly."

His expression was tense, as if he was fighting an inner battle of some kind. *I shouldn't be hanging out with this guy*, I thought to myself. I didn't care if he did save my life. He *was* trying to kill himself, or at least that's what he had said. Not normal, sane behavior, in any case.

"Did your sire explain anything to you before he was murdered?"

"I don't know why you keep calling him my sire. He was my date. A blind date, if you want to know the truth."

"Fine. Did your . . . date . . . explain anything to you?"

"About what?"

"About your neck and what it means."

I absently reached up to touch my wound and flinched.

"He said that he was a vampire and now I was one, too."

The stranger nodded. "Well, that's a start. And then?"

"Then I sprayed him with pepper spray and ran away. He was out of his mind."

He frowned at me. "He wasn't lying."

"No, I'm sure he believed what he was saying. That's one of the signs of being crazy, isn't it?"

The stranger came nearer to me, and I studied him up close for the first time. His handsome face was very pale in the moonlight and his eyes appeared to be silver, able to reflect what little light there was the way a cat's might.

When he spoke, I noticed the fangs.

"You *are* a vampire, Sarah. He wasn't crazy."

I had the can of pepper spray from my wet purse back in my hand in a flash. I held it up to his face. "Get away from me right now."

"Your only link to your new world has been killed. You need to listen to me if you want to survive."

"Vampires don't exist." My voice was firm, but my insides felt like jelly.

"Yes, we do."

I pressed down on the spray's trigger button, but it flew out of my hand as the stranger effortlessly knocked it away. He grabbed my shoulders and I started fighting for my life, scratching and clawing at him like a wild animal.

"Stop it," he said. "I'm not going to hurt you."

It was impossible to fight him. He was so strong that I could barely move. Hot tears coursed down my cheeks and I was exhausted from fighting, from running, from denying what I was hearing.

My neck throbbed. I let my arms drop loosely to my sides. My head began to swim and I saw colors exploding as they had when Gordon hit me. I tried to focus on the stranger, his arms now the only thing keeping me from falling backward onto the cold, hard pavement.

"It's okay." His voice suddenly sounded miles away. Distant and fading. "I'll take care of you."

The world went black.

I opened my eyes. I was sprawled on a leather sofa in a dark, unfamiliar room. I sat up slowly. My head ached as if I had the worst hangover of my life.

That sure was one crazy dream.

I looked around. *Where the hell am I?*

There was a rustle to my left and a door opened. The stranger emerged from what looked like a kitchen area. He held a glass of water in his hand and he didn't smile when he saw I was awake.

Ah. Must still be dreaming. Sure felt real, though.

"Who are you?" I moved as far away from him as the sofa would allow. My voice croaked as if I'd been asleep for a while. Which was strange, since I'd never dreamed that I was sleeping before.

"My name is Thierry de Bennicoeur," he said.

"French."

"Originally."

"You don't have an accent."

"Not anymore."

"And you're a vampire."

"Yes."

"Where are we?"

"My house."

He was a man of few words. I searched my mind for something else to say. If I stayed silent too long, I might start panicking again. I didn't care if this was a dream; it was a weird one.

"Why were you trying to kill yourself?" I asked absently.

He stared at me for a moment but ignored the question. "How do you feel right now?"

"Like I went out drinking and a bus hit me. I want to go home." I made a move to stand up, but the flashing pain in my head stopped me cold. Were you supposed to feel pain in a dream? Didn't seem right.

"We need to take care of something first," Thierry said.

"What?" I glanced at him and my eyes widened when I saw a sharp knife in his hand. "What the hell are you planning on doing with that?"

He raised an eyebrow at my panicked tone. My eyes widened even more when I saw him drag the blade across his wrist.

Holy shit! He was going to finish killing himself right in front of me. That was so sick.

I felt so weak that all I could do was whimper as I saw blood flow from his cut. He held his wrist over the glass of water and let his blood drip into it. Then he produced a spoon and stirred the contents.

"If your first drink is not directly from your sire, then it's best for it to be a little weak," he explained.

I stared with disbelief at the diluted blood. Then I looked at his wrist. The wound was rapidly disappearing until there was no more than a small pink line where the cut had been.

"Drink." He offered me the glass.

I waved it away. "I'd rather have a diet Coke, if you don't mind."

He placed the glass down on the shiny black coffee table and stood up. "Let me explain a few things to you, Sarah Dearly. Number one: Your sire didn't finish making you a vampire before he was killed. The wound on your neck proves that. If he'd finished properly, it would be nearly healed by now. Number two: to finish the job, you need to ingest the blood of a full-strength vampire. Since I don't see any other volunteers around, I figured it was up to me. So don't be difficult."

"I'm not drinking anybody's blood," I said firmly.

He shrugged. "Then you'll die before the end of the night. There is a toxin in a vampire's fangs that will infect its victim when the sire drinks deeply and fully of their blood. The toxin is what makes one a vampire. If your . . . date . . . had simply wanted a small taste of you, then it would be a moot point. However, by your symptoms, his intention was obviously to make you one of us. The toxin now in your body needs to be counteracted with this." He indicated the glass of pink water. "Simple as that."

I frowned hard and touched my neck. "But why would he do that? Bite me? I don't want to be an evil, bloodsucking vampire." I looked at him. "No offense intended."

"Your experience is unfortunate, yes. Your sire didn't follow the unwritten rules, which state that one does not bring over an unwilling fledgling. And vampires are *not* evil."

"*Yes,* they are."

"*No,* they are not. Not as a rule, anyhow. Some are, some aren't. Just like humans. How one was as a human will govern their behavior when they become a vampire."

I was still frowning. "That doesn't make any sense."

He sighed. "I don't know why I even bothered trying to help you. It's obvious you won't last."

"What do you mean I won't last?" I was weak and scared and still almost completely convinced this was all just a bizarrely vivid dream, but I could still feel insulted.

He counted on his fingers. "Your sire is dead. You seem to attract hunters like a magnet. And you know absolutely nothing about vampires."

I frowned at him and crossed my arms. "I'll have you know I know loads about vampires. Anne Rice is one of my favorite authors."

Thierry grimaced. "That will get you far."

I felt a rise of anger chase away my fear. "I don't need anybody's help. I'm fine all by myself. I didn't ask for you to bring me back to your"—I looked around at the sparse decor—"subterranean love nest, mister. And for another thing—"

White-hot pain exploded through my entire body. I clutched at the side of the couch and tore at the smooth leather with my French-manicured fingernails. "Oh, God. Oh, my God," I moaned in agony. "What's happening to me?"

"You're dying," he said matter-of-factly. "But it should be over before dawn, so don't worry."

"Dying?" I yelped. I was starting to believe him. Another wave of pain hit me and I doubled over and slid down to the floor. "Help me," I managed, fear slicing through me like a knife through butter. "Why are you just standing there? Do something!"

"I can't do anything more." His handsome face was blank. "I gave you the blood. I can't drink it for you."

The pink-tinged water sat innocently on the coffee table as I suffered next to it. After another burst of agony I grabbed the cold glass, brought it to my trembling lips, and glugged the whole thing down.

The pain stopped immediately. It was like Gatorade-for-vampires. I lay on my back on Thierry's hardwood floor and stared at the ceiling for a couple of minutes. Then I pushed myself into a sitting position and took in a long, deep breath while I tried to compose myself.

"More?" Thierry offered.

"No, I'm good."

"You should go home now. It'll be dawn before too long."

I nodded with a firm shake of my head. "Can't go out in the sun anymore, right? I'll be burned to a crisp?"

He almost looked amused with me. "Is that from the school of Anne Rice? Sunlight is not good for vampires, correct. You'll feel your strongest at night. During the day the sun will make you feel weaker and it will seem at times overbearingly bright, but I promise that you won't burn up."

"Really? Well, that's good to know."

"If it bothers you too much while you're still new, I suggest you try to travel about the city using the underground tunnel system; what do they call it here in Toronto? The PATH?"

"And how long will I be considered new?"

"Fifty years or so."

"Oh." I thought about that. I'd be considered new till my seventy-eighth birthday. I'd be as old as Uncle Jim, who recently said a final good-bye to Canadian winters to move permanently down to Florida. "So it's true that vampires live forever?"

He frowned. "We don't die of the usual human ailments and we essentially stop aging from the point we are sired, if that's what you mean."

Interesting. Completely implausible, but very interesting.

"So how old are you?" I asked.

He took the empty glass away from me and returned it to the kitchen. Through the open doorway I could see him rinse it under the sink, and then place it neatly into a stainless-steel dishwasher before he answered me.

"Old."

"How old?"

"Well over six hundred."

My mouth dropped open. "Wow. I mean, you look good for six hundred. I would have thought you'd be all crusty and falling apart by that age. That's amazing."

He looked away with an odd expression on his handsome, noncrusty face. "Yes, amazing." There was zero enthusiasm in his voice.

"I guess it's just going to take me a little while to get used to being undead."

"Un-what?"

"Undead. An animated corpse. A *vampire*." I shrugged at him. "Duh."

He looked exasperated with me. "Are you breathing?"

I frowned and concentrated to make sure I was still inhaling and exhaling.

Yup.

"Of course I am."

"And, is your heart still beating?"

I put a hand over my chest. There it was, the steady thumping of my heart. A little erratic, but still beating. "Yeah."

"And my heart, does it beat?"

I frowned at him, then raised a hand to press against his very firm, very warm, and very male chest. It took me a moment before I remembered why I was touching him. Oh, yeah, the heart thing.

I nodded. "Yes."

He took a step back from me and my hand fell to my side. "So what does that tell you?"

"Not undead?"

"Correct."

I stood up. Considering what I'd endured tonight, I felt okay. "I guess I'll go. Can you call me a cab, or"—I tried to smile and actually succeeded—"or can I turn into a bat and fly home now?"

He studied me for a moment. "I'll call you a cab."

He made the call, and we waited in uncomfortable silence for ten minutes.

I was a little disappointed about the bat thing. That would have been cool.

Hands down, this was the weirdest dream I'd ever had. Even weirder than the one in which I'd married a hobbit and moved to Mars. Too bad, too, because this Thierry guy was majorly cute in a sullenly suicidal way. Maybe I'd seen him in a magazine at the hair salon the other day and he'd been burned into my subconscious for later use.

But it was definitely a dream. I mean, vampires? Hunters? My blind date being shish-kebabbed and then vanishing into a little puddle of goo? *Puh-lease.* Total "dream city." I was just surprised it hadn't occurred to me while all the drama had been in progress. I could have saved myself a lot of unneeded, wrinkle-causing stress.

When the cabdriver finally showed up, I stood up from the sofa on my shoeless feet and realized that my ankle no longer hurt. Guess it wasn't a sprain, after all. I picked up my purse from the floor and grabbed my coat that Thierry had carefully placed on the back of a chair to dry. He'd taken it off me while I'd been sleeping. Even damp, my silk dress wasn't see-through, so I had decided not to make a fuss about it.

I smiled at Thierry. "Thanks for all your help. Even though I'll wake up tomorrow and know for sure this has all been just a dream, at least it's been a very interesting one." I started to move past him, but he grabbed my arm.

"You're not dreaming, Sarah. You must take this very

seriously. Things are different for you now, whether you like it or not."

I shrugged. "I don't feel any different."

"But you are. With the hunters around, you must take your safety into consideration. You've already seen tonight what they consider fun and games." He felt around in his pockets and produced a business card. "Take this." He pressed it into my palm. "Go to that address tomorrow evening for help in starting your new life."

I slid the card into my purse without even looking at it. "Thanks, Thierry, really. Take care of yourself, okay?"

I wanted to say: "Don't go killing yourself," but figured that might be a tad rude.

His intense silver eyes flashed at me. "You too."

He held the door open, and I made my way out and into the back of the taxi.

"One-eleven Ashburn Avenue," I told the driver, and he pulled away from the curb. I turned around in my seat. The door to Thierry's high-end townhome was already closed, and the lights in the front windows went off. I'd probably never see him again.

I pulled the business card out of my soggy purse.

MIDNIGHT ECLIPSE TANNING SALON.

Must be the wrong one, I thought, and shuffled through the contents of my bag. Hairbrush, wallet, lipstick, tampon. But there was only the one business card.

Midnight Eclipse Tanning Salon was the place to go to start my new life?

I shrugged inwardly. I *was* going to Mexico next month. Now that I thought about it, it would be nice to get a base tan before I left.

Chapter 3

So, how was your date?"

I raised my head to look at Amy Smith, my best friend of the past four years and personal amateur Cupid, and attempted to lift an eyebrow at her, which, I hoped, said: "Get the hell away from my desk."

I had a headache that quite possibly would kill me in a matter of minutes. But a little death headache was no reason to use up a precious sick day from my job at Saunders-Matheson, "Toronto's foremost marketing and promotions agency"—at least according to our Web site. I usually reserved my sick days for when I felt really good.

I was the executive assistant to the "Saunders" part of the company name. Amy was assistant to "Matheson," and was the reason I had the job in the first place. She'd put in a good word for me when the previous assistant had a nervous breakdown three years before.

"Wow," Amy said. "You look like shit."

"Gee, thanks."

"I guess it was a good date, then? Not much sleep to be had, you little vixen, you?" She giggled.

If I'd been feeling 100 percent myself, I probably would have stood up, wrapped my hands around Amy's creamy white throat, and throttled her within an inch of her dumb blond life. As it was, I just tried to look like a woman on the edge of sanity. It wasn't difficult.

"You have to be kidding me. That guy was a total loser."

"No way." She shook her head. "He drove a Porsche. A *red* one."

"Hate to break it to you, but I think we've been wrong all these years about that. Cars do not make the man. He was a loser who got me drunk on double margaritas and then abandoned me in the middle of nowhere."

Amy frowned, an expression I rarely saw on her hyperpositive face. "He abandoned you? What a jerk. Okay, forget him. I have another guy who'd be perfect for you."

"Hold on there, matchmaker. Where are you digging these guys up from, anyhow? Besides, you're single, too. I think it says something that you don't want to keep any of these catches for yourself."

Amy gave me a look that could only be summed up as "duh."

"Because, Sarah, they're perfect for *you*. Not for me."

"Jerks are perfect for me?"

"You know what I mean."

"No. I really don't."

Amy was the most positive-about-true-love girl in all of Toronto, and there was nothing I could say to convince her otherwise. She went out with at least ten dif-

ferent guys a month looking for "the one." She was certain her perfect soul mate existed out there somewhere,
and by God, she was going to find him. Me—I used to
be the same way, but now I was a little more realistic
about romance. Lately my perfect soul mate was my
Visa card. We regularly had lots of fun together at the
Eaton Centre—my favorite mall.

I hadn't had a steady boyfriend since before I started
working at Saunders-Matheson, when I'd been dating a
cute out-of-work actor. Which worked out perfectly since
I was also a cute out-of-work actress. The perfect boyfriend—even though he was a bit of a mooch—until he
got a part on a soap opera in Los Angeles. I came home
one day to receive a quick dumping via the answering
machine. Throwing the answering machine out of my
window on the tenth floor did nothing to change the
situation.

"So," Amy continued, holding out her hand to inspect
her new set of pink acrylic nails, "if it was such an early
night, then why do you look like that?"

Despite the fact that any sleep I did get was filled
with this crazy dream where I was a vampire, I didn't
feel like I looked *that* bad. Come to think of it, I didn't
remember even glancing in a mirror all morning. I'd
woken up so late I barely had a chance to get dressed and
out the door into the ridiculously bright sunshine.

That's because vampires don't have reflections.

I frowned deeply at the thought. I wasn't a vampire.
It was a dream, dammit!

"Do you have a compact on you?" I asked.

Amy plunged a hand into the pocket of her pink

jacket and produced a Cover Girl pressed powder. "Here."

I opened it up and tentatively peered at the tiny mirror. For a very long time.

She was right. I did look like crap, with dark circles under my eyes and everything. But the fact that there was a reflection, however crappy, eased my paranoid mind. It was just a dream, after all. Officially.

"Oh, no. Bitch from hell just arrived." Amy snatched the compact away from me and, without another word, scurried back to her desk on the far side of the cubicle-filled room and disappeared behind her computer.

My boss had been at her Friday-morning breakfast meeting with whatever client was most important that week. Anne Saunders. But you can call her Ms. Saunders. Not Miss, not Mrs.

Ms.

She eyed me as she exited the elevator and passed my desk, but said nothing, not even a curt good morning. I could tell she was on the "Sarah looks like crap today" train. I wasn't one to normally let her lack of people skills get to me.

Doing Ms. Saunders's odd jobs, sending her e-mails, picking up her dry cleaning . . . it would have to do until I figured out what I was supposed to be doing with the rest of my life. Or won the lottery. And that was going to happen any day now.

At least I had my fabulous trip to Mexico to look forward to. It would be the first time I'd ever been out of Canada in all my twenty-eight years of life. Unless you counted shopping over the border in Buffalo. My passport photo made me look a bit like my aunt Mildred, but

I couldn't complain. Piña coladas and a nice dark tan would be coming my way ASAP.

Dark tan.

For some reason the phrase "Midnight Eclipse" popped into my head. Oh, right, the tanning-salon business card Thierry gave to me in my dream.

Vampires and tanning salons? I shook my head at the thought. Sure, that made loads of sense.

I headed to the kitchen to make a pot of coffee and realized I hadn't even had my morning caffeine fix yet. Weird. It was usually the first thing I thought about when I got to work. I must have been more out of it than I thought.

Then I went back to work. Well, back to my current game of solitaire, anyhow.

A couple of minutes later my phone buzzed.

"Sarah, I'd like to see you in my office. Stat." Ms. Saunders's words were brisk. Then she hung up.

Stat? What is this—*ER*?

I quit my game of solitaire, pushed back from my desk, and made my way through the maze of cubicles, which contained everyone from graphic designers to copywriters to administration schmoes like me. I opened the door to my boss's fancy, glassed-in office and peered inside, squinting as the light from her windows glared angrily in my eyes.

She looked up from her phone call and beckoned me inside with a curl of her finger. I entered the impossibly bright office and stood there feeling uncomfortable and hungover.

After a moment she slammed the phone down with a

"Get it done or don't do it at all!" Yup, she was a real charmer.

She looked at me. "Sarah, please have a seat."

Her voice was immediately calm and controlled. I'd seen her make this transition before. One moment yelling at an employee, the next being as sweet as pie to a walk-in client. She met my gaze directly, without blinking, a habit of hers that was unnerving to say the least. Those not able to compete in these staring contests rarely lasted long in her company. I was usually a champ, but my headache from hell was making things a little more difficult than normal. I looked away and rubbed my temples.

"Something wrong, dear?" she asked, beaming a perfect—almost too perfect—smile of expensive porcelain veneers.

"No." I sat down in the chair across from her desk. "Late night."

"You mustn't miss out on your beauty sleep. A woman's looks are one of her greatest assets in the business world, you know."

My smile held, but I did glance at her desk calendar to make sure we hadn't just time-traveled back fifty years.

She shuffled through a stack of mail and some papers on her desk. "Sarah, I know I've been unforgivably late with your review this year."

Oh, crap. That's what this was about? I was going to have an impromptu job review with zero time to prepare? Just super.

She noted my look of dismay. "Don't worry, I'll make it as pain-free as possible for you. I think you're doing a stellar job. Normally, you also look top-notch. I'll over-look today since it's the only time I remember seeing you look less than"—she eyed my outfit—"pulled to-gether."

I'd procrastinated on my laundry a few extra days this week, and because I'd woken up so late I absently reached down to smooth out the navy blue skirt I'd found balled up in the corner of my bedroom. Hey, it smelled clean enough.

"My recommendation is to keep up the good work. I'm changing your title to *senior* executive assistant, and giving you a three percent raise effective next payday. Congratulations."

Wow, three percent. I could move up that early re-tirement plan to age seventy-five now, instead of eighty. Lucky me.

"Thank you," I said. "That's very generous."

"You're quite welcome." Ms. Saunders nodded and grabbed a gold-plated letter opener to begin attacking her stack of mail.

I turned to leave. Didn't want to outstay my welcome.

"Damn it!" she exclaimed, and I turned back around. She winced and nodded at the letter opener that she'd dropped to her desktop. "Damn thing slipped. I'm prob-ably going to need stitches now. Can you be a dear and fetch the first-aid kit for me?"

She held her left index finger and frowned at the steady flow of blood oozing out. A few small drops of red splashed onto the other letters spread out on the desk.

I felt woozy. And suddenly dizzy.

I blinked.

When I opened my eyes, I was no longer standing by

the door about to leave. I was crouched down next to Ms. Saunders's imported black leather chair, grasping her wrist tightly . . .

. . . and sucking noisily on her fingertip.

I shrieked and let go of her, staggering backward. I grabbed at her desk to keep from falling, but I dropped on my butt, anyhow, taking most of the contents of the top of her desk with me.

She held her injured finger far away from her and stared at me, wide-eyed, with a mixture of shock and disgust.

I scrambled to my feet and wiped my mouth with the back of my hand.

What in the holy hell just happened?

"I . . . I . . . uh . . . I'm so sorry," I managed. "I don't know what . . . I wouldn't normally do something . . . I just . . ."

Ms. Saunders pulled her hand close to her chest, perhaps to protect it from further abuse.

"Get out," she said quietly.

"Yeah, I'll get back to work. Again, I'm so, so sorry. Would you like me to bring you a cup of coffee?"

"No, not to your desk," she said evenly, but her volume increased with every word. "Get out of here, you *freak*. I don't care what you've heard, I'm not into women. You're fired. Now get out of here before I call security."

"But . . . my job review—"

"Get out!" she yelled.

I took a step toward her, wanting to try to rationalize what just happened, but she rolled backward in her chair as if she were afraid of me. I held up my hands.

"I'm not going to hurt you. I promise. I just want to explain."

She grabbed her phone without taking her eyes off me and hit a number. "Security, this is the fifth floor. . . ."

That was all I needed to hear. I ran out of her office and back through the maze of cubicles. What had just happened? What would possess me to do something so disgusting? And was there really a rumor that Ms. Saunders liked chicks? Because that would explain *a lot*.

But there wasn't any time to think about what had just happened. I was relying on pure instinct to see me through this. And my instinct was telling me that I'd better get the hell out of there as fast as possible if I didn't want to be unceremoniously escorted out of the building by two security guards.

Back at my desk I grabbed my pink-haired troll doll that was suction-cupped to the top of my computer. Then I opened my top drawer to retrieve the little box of Godiva truffles I kept there for my daily three o'clock chocolate fix. Was I forgetting anything else?

Oh, my God. I'd just been fired.

No, couldn't think about that now. Later. Deal with it later. I nodded to myself and grabbed my bag. It was still soggy from last night.

Soggy from my plunge off the top of a bridge with Thierry de Bennicoeur, the suicidal-yet-sexy vampire. Could that have happened for real? No. I must have been so drunk that I'd taken a shower, fully clothed. And accessorized. But couldn't margaritas only be held responsible for so much?

I heard a *ding* and the elevator doors opened up.

Security got out and I saw Ms. Saunders walking toward them, holding her injured hand and gesturing wildly in my direction. I couldn't hear what she was telling them, and I didn't really want to know. The last thing I needed was all my coworkers finding out I was getting physically booted from the company for sucking on my boss's finger. The word "embarrassing" didn't even begin to cover it.

I made a beeline for the stairs, which took me past Amy's desk. She was typing steadily and looked up at me with surprise as I whizzed by. I held my thumb and pinkie finger to my ear, making the universal sign for "call me," then disappeared through the door leading to the stairwell.

I took the stairs all the way down to the parking garage. Out through a set of doors to my right and I was into downtown Toronto's PATH system—the huge maze of tunnels under the business district. I'd always loved the PATH because it helped me avoid nasty winter weather while wearing expensive footwear. Slush and heels did not combine for good results.

Actually, calling them tunnels wasn't all that accurate. They were more like the narrow halls of a shopping mall. Lined with restaurants and stores, joining together the tall, downtown buildings. Tiled floors led in all directions. Signs above and on the walls pointed toward Adelaide or King Street or Bay. The regular users never needed to look up at the signs, just forward, their lips pressed against their foamy cappuccinos, or their noses tucked into the daily *Globe and Mail,* as they traveled by foot through the commuting crowds. The tourists walked around as if they'd just entered a surreal, underground world. They were the ones who usually got in my way.

I made a quick right, pushed through large glass doors, and then got on the subway. Eyes straight forward, unblinking, my staring contest now was only with the gray stations that whipped past the window.

I got off at my regular stop and walked methodically to my apartment building. Rode up in the elevator to the tenth floor. Slid my key into the lock, then went inside and automatically locked the door behind me.

I could still taste the blood from Ms. Saunders's cut on my tongue. It tasted pretty damn good.

My knees buckled under and I dropped to the floor, just past the front door and next to the fridge. The daze I'd been in slowly lifted, leaving behind it the bizarre truth I'd been trying all day to deny.

It hadn't been a dream.

I was a vampire.

Now what the hell was I supposed to do?

Chapter 4

Falling asleep seemed the best course of immediate action. Some might call it passing out from the shock of realizing I was now a bloodsucking monster, but I'd prefer to simply think of it as a power nap.

When I woke up, it was dark in my apartment, which seemed odd since I'd left the office well before noon. I pushed myself up from the kitchen floor and flicked on a light. The clock on the stove read 7:30.

I'd just slept for nearly eight hours. Not good.

My mouth felt like a desert. I poured myself a glass of wine from a half-empty bottle at the back of the fridge and downed it while trying to organize my racing thoughts.

I'm a vampire. The words swarmed through my brain. *A neck-biting, cape-wearing vampire with a capital* V.

I began to feel woozy again.

I grabbed the phone off the kitchen counter. There were five messages waiting for me on my voice mail. The first one was from my mother.

"Sarah? Are you there, honey? Pick up." She always started her messages that way. "Just to remind you, the wedding rehearsal and dinner begin at four on Monday, but we wanted some time to visit with you first. Call us so we'll know when to expect you, okay?"

I sighed. I was to be one of the bridesmaids in my cousin's wedding back in my hometown of Abottsville, Ontario. I decided to pull a Scarlett O'Hara and think about it tomorrow. I had more pressing matters to deal with at the moment. To say the least.

The next four messages were from Amy. She was desperate to know why I'd been fired. Apparently, there were now multiple versions of what had happened circulating through the office. One had been that I'd made a pass at Ms. Saunders.

I gently bashed my forehead against the cool surface of the fridge. Great, just great. With my luck I'd probably end up getting sued for sexual harassment.

What could I tell Amy that didn't sound crazy? I decided not to call her back until I figured that out. I poured myself another glass of wine and downed that one, too, then considered having another one. But there wasn't enough wine on the planet to help me relax.

I took a quick shower and then slid into a pair of hot pink yoga pants—I didn't do yoga, but they were trendy—and a snug white T-shirt with DIVA imprinted on it in pink and purple sparkles. My comfy clothes. The clothes I usually wore when I was having an ugly night and staying in to watch *Sex and the City* on DVD.

But I wasn't doing that tonight. I needed answers and knew where I could find them. I grabbed my purse and searched through it. For a fleeting, panicky moment I thought that I'd lost what I was looking for during the course of the day, but there it was at the bottom of my purse, stuck to a loose cough candy. I pried the honey-lemon lozenge off the business card and stared at it with deep apprehension: MIDNIGHT ECLIPSE TANNING SALON.

Okay, Monsieur Thierry de Bennicoeur, I thought. *You've got some 'splaining to do.*

Less than an hour later I squinted at the business card again to double-check that I was at the correct address. I looked up at the tanning salon's exterior and made a face. It was run-down, as was the entire neighborhood in this west end part of Toronto. There wasn't a Starbucks for blocks.

But I didn't need it to be a fancy, four-star spa. I just needed answers.

My face stung from the blowing snow. It was even colder than last night had been, and there was no more fooling myself that I wouldn't be hip-deep in the cold white stuff within a couple of weeks. Thus, the upcoming trip to Mexico.

I shoved the business card deep into the pocket of my black leather coat—my backup jacket since my nicer, more expensive burgundy one was all but ruined from last night's surprise swim. I pushed open the frost-kissed glass door to the salon.

Inside there was a tall reception desk with the Midnight Eclipse logo—essentially a solid black circle bearing the words "Midnight Eclipse"—painted on the otherwise empty wall. A plastic potted palm tree stood with very little dignity in the corner. To the right of the desk was one black door and to the left were two white doors. Add to that the soggy green floor mat I stood on, and it was pretty much all the room had to offer.

I frowned, feeling tense. Where was everyone? If the place was closed, the door would have been locked, wouldn't it? This sure didn't look like a place "Mr. Tall-Dark-and-Intimidating" would frequent. Why would he send me there in the first place? What was this, some kind of joke? After the day I'd had, I wasn't in a laughing kind of mood. A crying-hysterically-and-babbling-incoherently mood, maybe. Laughing, not so much.

"You must be Sarah," a voice ventured.

"Hello?" I looked around, but still didn't see anyone. "Who said that?"

"I'm Barry." A very small man emerged from behind the desk; he couldn't have been more than four feet tall. He wore a tuxedo and had a black top hat perched crookedly on his head. "Barry Jordan." He extended a small hand upward. "I was told to expect you."

"Hi." I shook his hand automatically. No reason for me to be rude, after all. "Then I guess I'm Sarah."

"Excellent. I take it you're here for the grand tour?"

My gaze slid from the potted plant back to the desk. "There's a grand tour?"

"Absolutely." Barry's smile showed off tiny fangs. He released my hand.

A miniature vampire. Collect 'em all.

"You're a vampire?"

"Yes, of course."

I sighed. "Good. I have so many questions, I need to—"

He waved his hand. "All in good time. Are you ready for the tour?"

I stared at him for a moment. "Um. Okay, I guess."

He grinned, hurried over to the right, and opened one of the white doors into a room with a toilet, a sink, three lockers, and a wooden bench.

"The changing room," Barry announced.

"Ah."

He closed the door and moved to the other. Inside were two tanning beds, currently not in use. A dirty towel had been rolled up and discarded in a corner. Another potted palm tree sat near the door.

"The tanning room." He made a presentational flourish with his arm, as if he were showing me something very impressive. "Employees tan for free."

"Vampires tan?" I said with a frown. "But I thought—"

He waved me off again. "Please do not interrupt."

Barry Jordan was quickly outstaying his welcome as tour director in my book.

He clicked the door closed and breezed past me on the way to the last door. I held up a hand to stop him.

"Listen, I don't want to waste any more of your time. I'm really not all that interested in the inner workings of a tanning salon. No offense."

"But you'll want to see this. I'm sure you will." He looked extremely disappointed; even his bow tie seemed to wilt a little bit.

I sighed with impatience. "All right, then. Go ahead."

He nodded, straightened his tie, and reached forward to open the door.

A wave of voices, loud music, smoke, and darkness

seemed to rush into the reception area, and my mouth dropped open at what I saw inside.

"This is the real Midnight Eclipse," Barry said proudly. "Vampires only."

I blinked in disbelief. Of all the things I'd expected to see behind that last door, this wasn't it. But I suppose it made perfect sense. A nightclub for vampires. Somewhere to relax and unwind after a hard day of avoiding the sunlight and pointy wooden objects.

After a moment my eyes adjusted to the dimness. A long, black-lacquered bar hugged the wall to the left. Booths and tables flaunted sexy crimson tablecloths and small, glowing lamps. At the far side there was a stage, where, over the murmured conversations of the crowded club, a beautiful, raven-haired Bettie Page look-alike was singing a throaty rendition of "Fever."

"Have you ever waited tables before?" Barry asked.

"In college," I said, my voice barely audible. "But I'm sure it'll come back to me."

"Good."

I shut my gaping mouth. "Wait a minute. Forget I said that. I don't want to work here."

"I thought you were here for a job interview."

"No. I need to talk to Thierry."

"Thierry?" Barry sounded shocked. "You mean *the master*."

"The master?"

"Don't say it like *that*."

"Like what?"

"Without respect. The master is to be respected."

I glanced back into the club. A few eyes were now on me. Curious gazes from the gathered vampires. It was

funny, because if I hadn't been told they were all creatures of the night, I'd never have guessed it. They looked
perfectly normal to me. Not Goth, anyhow. Not one
pasty face or black Marilyn Manson outfit to be seen.

Barry took a deep breath and a smile blossomed on
his face again. "You're new. He mentioned that you were
without a sire, so any missteps are to be expected, of
course."

"Missteps?" My patience was waning. "Look, Tuxedo
Boy, is Thierry here or not?"

The smile slipped from his face again and his eyes
flashed angrily at me. Yikes. I didn't want to make him
pop a blood vessel or anything.

"Barry," a smooth, deep voice said to my left. "It's all
right. Please leave Miss Dearly to me."

The sound of his voice coursed down my spine like
the feel of your first shot of tequila on frosh night.
Shocking and unexpected, but not entirely unpleasant.

I turned, already knowing who it was.

The master.

He looked different than he had last night. More put-
together. Less suicidal. His dark, almost-black hair was
brushed off his face. He had high cheekbones, a straight
nose, and a square jawline showing a small amount of
fashionable stubble. His full lips were unsmiling, of
course, and gray eyes that seemed almost silver watched
me as if I were the only person in the room.

He, unlike the others in the club, *was* dressed all in
black. He wore a button-down silk shirt that was open at
the neck, black jacket, and black dress pants. The darkness made his face look even paler, but it wasn't unat-

tractive and pasty. It was as if he glowed with power. An inner energy that made me tingle right down to my toes.

Yowza.

"Sarah," he said. "I was not certain that you'd come."

I forced a smile. "And yet, here I am."

Barry made a sound and I grimaced. He probably wanted me to bow before the master, or something. As if *that* were going to happen.

Thierry's gaze moved to the tiny man. "Be so kind as to fetch Miss Dearly and myself something to drink."

Barry bowed, the little brownnoser that he was. Then he backed away and headed toward the bar. Thierry gently took me by my elbow and steered me over toward a booth.

"Please sit," he said.

I sat.

He took a seat across from me and met my eyes. "I imagine this is all quite overwhelming for you."

"You could say that." I leaned back and tried to look as comfortable as possible, given the situation. "I thought this was supposed to be a tanning salon."

He raised a dark eyebrow. "It is. But as you can see, it is also much more than that. The previous owner believed it to be an ironic joke. A vampire club behind the facade of a tanning salon."

"Funny."

Thierry didn't smile.

I swallowed and tried to chase my nervousness away. "So, you own this place, huh?"

"Yes."

"Cool."

Whether or not he also thought it was cool, he made no indication.

I forced a smile. "Look, I have tons of questions for you about this vampire thing."

"So, at last you believe that you're no longer dreaming?"

I looked away and concentrated on smoothing out a wrinkle on the red tablecloth. "To tell you the truth, I *did* think it was all a dream. I was positive of it. At least until something weird happened today."

"What happened?"

I was embarrassed, but anxious to move onto my real questions, so I launched into a quick retelling of the finger-sucking incident. If he found it amusing, he didn't give any sign.

"It is to be expected," he said when I was finished. "Your body craves blood now. You were simply acting on instinct."

"It's an instinct I don't want. How do I stop it?"

That comment almost earned me a smile. Almost.

"You cannot stop it."

Barry stopped at our table with two drinks on a tray. He placed a martini glass full of dark red liquid in front of Thierry. "Your usual, master. And one newbie special."

He plunked another glass of Gatorade-for-vamps in front of me. Slightly pink water. I gritted my teeth and glanced at Thierry.

"Do I have to?"

"No."

I looked back down at the diluted blood. "But if I don't, I'll get the headache from hell again, right?"

He paused before answering. "That is correct."

"Well, then, down the hatch." I gulped a bit of the drink. Damn if it didn't taste fantastic. I was so grossing myself out, but hey, at least it beat sucking on fingers.

After a moment I placed the empty glass back down on the table and wiped my mouth with the back of my hand.

"Good?" Thierry asked.

I shrugged. "I don't want to drink blood."

"Didn't look like you had much of a problem just now."

I glared at him. "You do what you have to do."

"Agreed." His lips twitched, almost smiling.

Nice to know he was finding me amusing.

"So, I'm really a vampire?" I said. "For real?"

"Yes."

"But I still have a reflection." I ran my tongue along my teeth. "And I don't have any fangs."

He shook his head. "Of course not. You are still young—barely a fledgling. These things will take time to develop."

I frowned. "So, if this is all actually happening to me, that means everything last night was real, too. Gordon really got killed."

"I'm afraid so. I'm sorry for your loss."

My bottom lip trembled a bit at the memory. "He was a jerk. But he didn't deserve to die." I touched my neck; the bite had faded to nearly nothing. "Why did he bite me?"

"He shouldn't have. Not if he didn't discuss it with you first."

"If he'd discussed it with me, I would have said no.

For that matter, I would have said no to anything else he had in mind last night, too. Definitely not a love match." I felt a shiver go down my spine at the memory of what happened. "But that still shouldn't have happened to him. Poor Gordon."

"The hunters are very dangerous."

I tensed. "Who are these hunter guys, anyhow? Do they think they're a bunch of Buffy the Vampire Slayers? What gives them the right to go around killing people?"

He brought his drink to his lips and took a sip before answering me. "The hunters think they are doing a service to the world by ridding it of a perceived evil." He smiled then, a genuine smile, but not a pleasant one. "They will never be convinced we are unworthy of their attentions. That we are not the monsters they think we are."

"How do we stop them?"

He met my gaze again, and I was suddenly floored by how intense it was, especially now, talking about the hunters.

"We don't. We simply avoid them as best we can during the hunting season."

"Hunting season?"

"Yes, the main group of hunters migrate to different parts of the world where vampires have formed communities. Like here in Toronto. There will always be stragglers that stay behind, but the main group moves every few months to another location. Right now it is our turn, and we must be even more careful than normal."

"But there has to be a way of talking to them, telling them that what they're doing is wrong—"

"No," he interrupted me. "There isn't. All we can do is stay away from them and not be careless."

"Or they'll stab us in the heart with their wooden stakes. And we'll turn into a big puddle of goo, just like Gordon?"

Thierry blinked at me. "Puddle of goo?"

"When the hunters killed Gordon, he disintegrated into a big puddle of goo. I always thought vampires turned into dust, but I guess that's just on TV. Pretty gross, though."

"How we die is determined by how long we have lived. If you are careless enough to be slain by a hunter, you will not disintegrate into goo." He grimaced at the word choice. "You will simply die. Your sire must have been very old. Only then will one decompose upon their vampire death, much like they would have in their natural human grave."

"Yuck." I shuddered. "The hunters sure went to work on Gordon, though. It was horrible. He must have been very hard to kill."

Thierry shook his head. "All that is required is a deathblow to the heart with a wooden or silver object. Anything else the hunters do is for their own perverse pleasure."

I went silent for a moment, thinking about everything I'd just heard. Being a vampire sounded incredibly dangerous. With very few perks.

But I just had to look on the positive side. Other than the hunters, being a vampire might not be so bad. There *was* the whole non-aging thing. I liked the sound of that. Everyone in the crowded, smoky club looked fairly happy to me. They were just like regular people, only they'd be young and pretty forever.

Thierry watched me in silence for a few moments. "I feel it would be best if you took a job here, at Midnight Eclipse."

I shook my head. "I'm not waiting tables."

"You don't have to, if you don't want to. There's plenty to occupy you otherwise. Perhaps as a hostess?"

"Why are you doing this? Offering me a job?"

He took another drink and made me wait. "You are currently unemployed, is that not so?"

"Yes, but who says I don't have fifty people banging on my door wanting me to come work for them?"

"What is it that you did at your last job?"

This time I was the one to pause. "Well, it's not going to sound all that glamorous, but I was a senior executive assistant."

Thierry stared at me. "You are correct; that does not sound very glamorous."

I chewed on my bottom lip. "Look, maybe I made a mistake coming here, after all."

When I stood up to leave, Thierry reached across the table and grabbed my wrist. "You must stay here. Sit down."

Something about the way he said it, as if it were a direct order from the "master" himself, pissed me off. I tried to pull away, but his grip was too strong.

"I *must* do nothing. Let go of me."

He held on for another second, then released me so quickly that I almost fell backward into the booth. "I am only concerned for your safety."

"What do you care about my safety?" I suddenly felt

very annoyed. "You don't even know me. Just because I interrupted your little suicide attempt last night—"

His eyes flashed, the expression on his face cutting me off from saying anything else.

"You will not speak of that again."

It was surprising how quickly his handsome face shifted into something scary-looking. This was not a man I wanted to be mad at me.

I swallowed hard and sat back down at the table.

"Look, I'm sorry. Whatever you want to do with your life is none of my business. All I'm looking for . . ." I paused and decided to rephrase that. "All I'm *asking* for is a little guidance."

He stared at me for a moment and I could see his anger fade away. "I thought you already knew it all from your friend Anne Rice. And this Buffy person."

"That was before I started using my boss's finger as a chew toy."

He drummed his fingertips on the tablecloth. "And what can I expect in return?"

I leaned back and presented him with my best smile. "My friendship."

He took me by surprise by throwing his head back and laughing long and hard. "Your friendship? Now why would you think I'd want, or need, something like that from you?"

I shrugged. "Just a hunch."

"Your hunch is wrong."

I wasn't about to be discouraged. "Okay, then, how about this? Those hunters were going to kill me last night. You saved my life. Therefore, you're responsible for me whether you like it or not."

That sobered him up a bit. He looked me over then, slowly, from my freshly washed, shoulder-length brown hair tucked neatly behind my ears, down my makeup-free face, along the line of my neck, and finally to my Diva T-shirt. The sparkles must have made him snap out of his sudden daze. His eyes flicked back to my face.

"There is a reason why those as old as I do not sire fledglings." His voice was serious; any trace of laughter had vanished.

"You didn't sire me," I reasoned. "But you're free to adopt me."

I tried to look cute. Then gave up. I really should have taken ten minutes to put on some makeup. I felt seriously shiny.

When he didn't say anything, I became very uneasy. Well, I *was* sitting in a secret vampire club on the wrong side of town across from a six-hundred-year-old vampire others called "master." I figured I had a right to feel a little uncomfortable.

I stood up. Better to leave of my own accord than risk any additional embarrassment.

"I guess I'll go now." I half expected him to grab me again and demand that I stay.

He didn't.

I tucked a renegade strand of hair firmly behind my ear and nodded. "I feel like I'm always saying good-bye to you."

Thierry said something, but I didn't quite catch it.

I leaned closer. "Huh?"

He looked up at me. "Then don't."

"Don't what?"

"Don't say good-bye."

He glanced around the club. The singer was on a break now, and the band just played without vocals. I waited without sitting back down or heading for the door until he decided to say something else.

"I will agree to your offer," he finally said. "On one condition."

I tried to hide my surprise. "What condition?"

He met my eyes, capturing them in his intense silver gaze. "You must leave your old life behind."

"What does that mean, exactly, 'leave your old life behind'?"

"You've seen how dangerous it is to be a vampire. You are not the same person you were yesterday. What you once knew to be reality can be no more. Find a new place to live. Part ways with your friends and family. It's best you have no contact with them at all anymore. Do what I ask, and you may succeed in avoiding the hunters."

I frowned at him. "I don't know about that. Why can't I stay where I am and just be extra careful when I go out? What difference would it make?"

"All the difference in the world." Thierry stood, towering over me. His forehead was creased from frowning so hard. I wondered if he ever let himself relax and have some fun. Maybe take a vacation somewhere warm and tropical. It was highly doubtful. "The life of a vampire and the life of a regular human are incompatible. It's too dangerous."

I shook my head. "But I feel exactly the same as I always have. Nothing's changed."

"Everything's changed. You don't feel it yet because you're too new."

"But—"

He held up his hand. "But nothing, Sarah. That is my condition. If you are unwilling to do as I request, then I can be of no assistance to you."

I didn't like that at all. My life wasn't exactly perfect, but I wasn't ready to give any of it up. It was comfortable and familiar. I was supposed to turn my back on it just because I had a new little substance-abuse problem in the form of pink water?

Then again, I knew I needed Thierry's help. If I really was a vampire, then I was positive he was the one who'd be able to help me the most. Also, he was very hot.

I probably wouldn't need Thierry's help for more than a week or two. Just long enough to learn the ropes. Then I'd find a new job and go back to life as usual. No problem. Thierry didn't have to know that part, of course.

"I agree," I said firmly, and gave him a big smile.

"Fine. Return here tomorrow night, and I will do what I can for you, Sarah, but I'm not promising anything."

"Try not to sound so positive."

He nodded with a firm motion of his head. "Now, if you'll excuse me."

And with that, he turned away and walked across the club, then disappeared through a door at the far side of the bar.

I put a hand on my hip. "Yeah, see you later, too."

We'd have to work on the warm and fuzzy. I shook my head and stifled a laugh. I had just committed myself to being tutored by a centuries-old master vampire by giving up life as I knew it.

My mother would be so proud.

Chapter 5

I left Midnight Eclipse feeling a little tense. Maybe more than a little. Sure, Thierry had agreed to help me out, but it didn't solve any of my other problems. I still had no idea what to tell Amy about why I'd been fired. Should I tell her I'd been turned into a vampire? Would she still want to go on vacation with me?

Also, should I make up an excuse to get out of being in the wedding? If I did, my cousin Missy would probably find a wooden stake and kill me herself.

I saw the neon flash of a bar sign across the street from the vampire club. After giving it a moment's thought, I walked over and went inside. I had to call a cab, anyhow, so I'd just treat myself to a quick drink of the nonblood variety while I waited.

Sounded like a plan.

The bar was called Clancy's. I'd never heard of it before. It wasn't a high-profile kind of place. Basically, it was a bar with stools, a few high tables, more stools, and a couple of pool tables stuffed in the back. All of this fine decor was covered by a thick cloud of smoke from cigarettes and something a little less legal.

I went directly to the pay phone and called for the taxi. Then I grabbed a seat at the bar. The bartender, a hulking man who must have weighed close to three hundred pounds, took my drink order. I decided on a Bloody Mary. In the spirit of the evening, what else could I order?

There was a man sitting a couple of stools away from me who was staring into his mug of dark amber beer as if it held the answers to the mysteries of the universe. He was alone. Kind of cute, actually. He wore faded jeans and a green T-shirt. His hair was dark blond and a little on the scruffy side. He had a handsome, yet vaguely boyish face. He must have sensed he had an audience because he glanced over at me with deep blue eyes.

"You look like your dog just died," I told him. I didn't normally talk to strange men in unknown bars, unless I had female backup. But I was only going to be there for a few minutes, and I felt chatty after the strained conversation with Thierry.

"Do I?" he said. "I guess it's been one of those days."

"I hear you."

He glanced down at my chest. Normally, I'd be offended, but I *was* wearing the sparkly Diva shirt. It worked like an arrow that read "Look here."

"Nice T-shirt."

"Thanks."

That earned me a smile from him. A great smile, but his eyes were sad.

"So what was his name?" I asked.

"Whose name?"

"Your dog. The one that died."

He grinned at me. "No, no dog. Just family problems, I guess. Nothing terribly interesting. I figured I'd come here for a while to try to drown my troubles." He glanced down at his beer.

"You're going about it all wrong. To drown your sorrows, you have to use tequila. Beer only magnifies them."

"Is that right?"

"Tried and true."

His grin widened. He moved over to a stool closer to me. The nearer he came, the better-looking he was. Not as drop-dead gorgeous—no pun intended—as Thierry, but definitely in a highly hot category.

He extended his hand. "I'm Michael Quinn. But my friends just call me Quinn."

I smiled back and shook his hand. "Sarah Dearly."

Quinn got the bartender's attention. "Two shots of tequila, please. With lime." Then he looked back at me. "So, what's a nice girl like you doing in a place like this?"

Ah, yes. There was a line that never got old. I decided to let it slide. "What makes you think that I'm nice?"

"Are you saying you're not?"

"Oh, I am. Very nice. To the right people, that is."

"And everyone else?"

I tried to look serious. "Not nice."

"Good to know."

I felt a cold gust of air as the door opened. I glanced

over to see three more men enter the already-crowded bar. They waved at Quinn and he waved back.

The tequilas arrived with several wedges of lime on a plate.

Quinn grabbed a saltshaker. "So this does the trick, huh?"

"I'm not promising much with only one, but we'll give it a try."

"What should we drink to?"

I thought about it. "To new beginnings."

"Sounds good. To new beginnings." We did the shot, sucked on the limes, and smiled at each other.

Ten minutes later the cab hadn't arrived yet, and we'd just done our third shot. I'd decided that Michael Quinn was going to be my new best friend. Part of my new life. In other words, I was almost completely drunk. I've always had a low tolerance for alcohol, so sue me.

"What'll we drink to this time?" Quinn slurred a little as the fourth round arrived. I had no idea how long he'd been sucking back beers before I'd even gotten there.

"To my new life," I said.

"New life?" He held his shot in his shaky right hand. "Can you elaborate on that, Sarah Dearly?"

I nodded. "Why, yes, I can. To my new life as a vampire, which quite possibly could have no end." I raised my glass. "To my newly immortal life. May my retirement-savings plan pay off big-time for me."

Quinn nodded. "To Sarah being a vampire." He clinked glasses with me and downed his shot.

"Yes!" I tried to toss the tequila back, but most of it ended up on my shirt.

"Now"—Quinn carefully placed his elbow on the bar top so he had a hand to lean against—"you really shouldn't kid about something like that."

"Like what?"

"Like being a vampire. That's nothing to joke about."

"Who says I'm joking? I *am* a vampire."

"No, you're not."

"And yet . . . I am." A wide, goofy smile spread across my features as I looked at Quinn.

He stared at me with unfocused eyes. "*You're* a vampire."

"Yup."

"You don't look like a vampire."

I frowned at him. "And how do you expect a vampire to look?"

"I don't know." Quinn leaned back in his stool to look me up and down. "More together somehow. Maybe all dressed in black. And fangs—shouldn't you have fangs?"

I shifted to cross my legs. It's true, a sparkly Diva T-shirt and pink yoga pants didn't really scream "creature of the night." I had to get to the mall as soon as possible and expand my wardrobe possibilities.

"Black makes me look too pale," I explained. "And apparently the fangs take a while to sprout."

"I see." He seemed to be mulling it over.

"So, you believe me?"

"Yes," he said, and reached into his jacket pocket and pulled out a wooden stake. He placed it in front of him on the bar counter. "I guess so."

I sobered immediately at the sight of the stake. It was exactly like the ones White-teeth and the boys had used last night to turn poor Gordon into a dark, wet puddle outside the cemetery.

Poor me.

My initial reaction was to scream my head off, but instead I forced myself to laugh—it ended up sounding a little too hysterical to be lighthearted.

"Did I say I was a vampire? That's so funny. I'm actually supposed to take this medication. It's around here somewhere." I patted my empty pockets. "Delusions, you know. Weird, fleeting images in this crazy brain of mine. Only yesterday I thought I was Marie Antoinette."

"Uh-huh." Quinn stared at me. "Delusions. Sure."

"Anyhow, it was super meeting you and all. Thanks for the drinks." I glanced at the empty shot glasses and my half-full Bloody Mary, not such a good choice now that I thought about it. "I guess I better get back to the psychiatric hospital before they notice I'm gone."

"You're not going anywhere."

"I'm not?" I grimaced as my gaze was drawn back to the very sharp stake.

Not good. Not good at all. I began to think that maybe Quinn wouldn't turn out to be my new best friend, after all. Call it a hunch.

He leaned close to me so I could feel, as well as smell, his alcohol-laden breath as he spoke. "I kill vampires, you see. That's why I'm in town. I like killing evil things, and I'm very good at it."

"Then it's a good thing I was kidding earlier. About being a vampire, that is. I'll just be on my way now."

I tried to move past him, but his iron bar of an arm blocked me.

"Let's go outside and do this proper." Quinn's eyes were narrow. Mean. The flirty friendliness that had been there only a few minutes before had completely vanished.

I looked around the bar to see if there was anyone who would help, but no one even glanced in our direction.

I turned to meet Quinn's eyes. "I'm not evil. Please don't hurt me."

He shook his head. "It's too bad. You seemed so normal. If you hadn't told me, I never would have guessed it."

"Can't we just forget the whole thing?" I asked hopefully.

"No."

Now I was freaked. This was the second time in two nights that I'd been cornered by a crazy man who wanted to kill me. I wondered if it was some kind of record. Only being a vampire for less than twenty-four hours before getting exterminated. Kind of made the whole immortal thing just a lot of hype.

"Let's go outside," Quinn said.

I shook my head vigorously. "No way. I'm not going anywhere with you."

"Then this might have to get messy."

I swallowed hard and was ashamed to admit that tears were sliding down my cheeks. "What about everyone else in here? I think they'll probably have something to say if you start manhandling me."

He glanced around and then back at me. His harsh

expression didn't flicker. Maybe he thought my tears were fake. Or maybe he was just an asshole. I was betting on the latter.

"Anywhere else, you might be right. But you were stupid enough to walk into the local hangout for vampire hunters. I know most of the guys in here."

My eyes widened at that. The local hangout for vampire hunters was right across the street from Thierry's secret vampire club? Talk about bad planning.

Quinn gripped my upper arm so tightly, I thought I might lose the entire limb. He wasn't taking any chances. For all he knew, I might have super vampire strength, or something.

Hey, maybe I did.

I focused all my strength on pulling away from him and throwing him across the room.

Nope. No superstrength.

Damn.

He turned toward the door just as it opened. An older man with graying hair entered the bar and stared straight at Quinn. "I found you," the man said. "About bloody time, too."

Quinn didn't loosen his grip, but his expression changed at the sight of the man.

The old man shook his head. "I don't want to hear anything you have to say. You sicken me, boy. The others are out doing what has to be done, and you're holed up here drinking yourself into oblivion with a local slut."

I opened my mouth to protest, but immediately shut it. Sluts didn't get wooden stakes shoved through their hearts. I decided to go with his first impression without argument.

"But, Father, I—," Quinn began.

The man held up his hand. "Shut it, boy. Shut your pathetic mouth. There's a rumor that you've turned into a coward. There is no place for scared little boys in my plan. We're here to wipe out the dark forces and clean up the evil, once and for all."

"I know." Quinn glanced at me, and I could see hatred in his eyes. "That's exactly what I'm trying to do. I'm—"

His father closed the gap between us and grabbed Quinn by his T-shirt, pushing him up against the wall. Quinn lost his grip on my arm.

"Don't make me any more ashamed of you than I already am," his father hissed. Then he glanced at me, barely making eye contact. "You. Get out of here if you know what's good for you."

"But, Father—"

"Be quiet," his father growled.

Quinn's expression was different now. It could have been shame, but to me it looked more like hopelessness. I didn't really care.

I backed away from them, feeling for the door handle behind me. At any moment Quinn could have announced that I was a vampire, but he didn't say another word. Not that his father would have given him half a chance. Looked like a real sweet relationship between the two of them. If you lived in hell.

I turned and tried to walk as calmly as possible out to the street. The cab had arrived finally and was waiting for me. I climbed into the back and almost leaned forward to kiss the driver right on the lips, since I was so happy to see him, but I managed to stop myself. He wasn't my type, anyhow.

No, my type seemed to be the ones who wanted me dead.

It had turned into one hell of a week. Thank God it was Friday.

Chapter 6

As soon as the cab dropped me off at my building, I ran for the elevator and took it up to my apartment, then locked the door behind me.

I'd been so stupid giving Quinn my real name. Stupid, stupid, stupid.

The only thing that kept me from hyperventilating about my monstrous lack of intelligence was the fact that his father had a real hold on him. He probably wouldn't let my new admirer out of his sight long enough to come looking for me.

I hoped.

I felt tense. My shoulders were in knots. I'd normally take a long, hot bubble bath while I read the latest issue of *Cosmopolitan* to help calm myself down, but this was no time for relaxation. For all I knew, Quinn had followed me home and was on his way up here to add a little more grain to my diet. Wood grain, that is.

I threw my purse into the corner of my tiny living room, but then had a thought and ran to grab it again. I searched frantically for the business card, but after a minute I gave up. It was gone. Somewhere between here and the vampire club.

I went to the phone and called information. They gave me the number for Midnight Eclipse Tanning Salon on Lakeside Drive. I wrote it down on a yellow sticky note and put it on my fridge, then began to peck out the numbers on my cordless phone.

I was calling Thierry. He'd know what I should do.

It rang once before I hung up. I couldn't call him. He'd think I was crazier than ever. No, this was my problem. There was no way I was going to bother him again. At least not until tomorrow night.

I went to sit on the sofa and turned on the television. The eleven o'clock news was just finishing for the night. I clicked around for a while, but then gave up and turned it off. I crossed my legs, grabbed one of my big embroidered pillows, and hugged it tightly to my chest like a makeshift teddy bear. If only that would help me chase all the monsters away.

Except now *I* was the monster. I made a mental note to rent all the vampire movies I could over the weekend. Research material.

Every noise, every creak through the apartment, even the sounds that carried up from the street below, made me jump. There was no way I was getting any sleep that night. I was way too wired. It was good, though. I was ready to react. By instinct. Protect myself. Fight for my life, and all that.

Nobody was going to sneak up on me. That was for sure. Just let 'em try.

But after half an hour, my eyelids began to feel heavy.

I fought for a while, but ended up closing them. I hugged the pillow tighter to my chest and drifted off to sleep.

Well, I *had* had four tequila shots and half a Bloody Mary. I was a vampire, not a machine.

———

When I woke up, the sun was streaming through the glass door to my balcony. My legs were still on the sofa, but the rest of me hung off so that the side of my face was pressed into the beige carpet. And I was drooling. It wasn't a pretty sight.

I pushed myself up. My neck was killing me from being in such an awkward position. I shielded my eyes from the blazing sun.

There was a loud and insistent knock at my door. Who the hell was it? Nobody usually knocked at my door unless they rang up from the lobby first.

Unless . . .

I stood up so quickly that I felt a wave of dizziness. I'd almost forgotten about last night. It was Quinn. He'd found me. He'd come to kill me. What was I going to do?

Defend myself, that's what. He might be a macho vampire hunter, but this was *my* apartment. I glanced around. Yeah, my tiny, six-hundred-square-foot rented apartment. There wasn't anywhere to hide, so I suppose defending myself was my only option.

The knock came again. The weight of fear felt as if it added about twenty pounds to me. I waddled over to the kitchen and opened the utensil drawer. There had to be a knife in there. A big knife.

I frowned. There was nothing. Didn't I have any big knives? What kind of a cook was I? Oh, yeah, the kind who ordered takeout.

I settled on a lethal-looking pie lifter I'd once received as a crappy gift. It was sort of pointy. It would do. Once, in a movie, I saw someone get stabbed to death with a cob of corn. A pie lifter was much more dangerous than that.

There was another knock. I moved toward the door to look through the peephole to see who it was.

If I look through the peephole, he'll poke my eye out. Stab me right through my brain. The gory visual was enough to make me shudder.

Just a quick peep. Look and move. Peek and hide.

Clutching my pie lifter, I neared the door. When I was only inches away, the banging came again, and I almost jumped out of my skin. I let out a shriek and clamped my hands over my mouth. The lifter fell and clattered noisily to the ceramic-tiled floor.

Shit.

The knocking stopped.

"Sarah?" Amy called through the door. "Are you in there? Open up!"

My eyes widened, and I let out a sigh of relief long and loud enough to wake the neighbors, if they hadn't already been woken up by all the door pounding. I unlatched the safety lock and twisted the handle.

Amy stood in the hallway, rubbing her red knuckles.

"I've been worried sick about you," she scolded, then breezed past me into the apartment. "Why didn't you answer the door, you big loser?"

"I was asleep."

"I've been trying to talk to you since you disappeared from work yesterday. I've called you, like, a bazillion times. I even stopped by yesterday before my date, but you weren't here."

"Oh." I brightened. "How was your date? The dentist, right?"

She pouted. "He thought I needed braces. He was most definitely not *the one*."

"That's too bad."

"Tell me about it." She frowned at me, the corners of her pink-lipsticked mouth going down. "Hey, wait a minute, we're talking about *you*. Why didn't you call me back?"

"I'm sorry, really. I've had a lot of stuff to take care of."

She threw herself dramatically on my sofa, and I decided to make coffee. Alcohol at night. Caffeine in the morning. The yin-yang of my life. My hands were shaking as I measured it out from the can.

I wondered if she'd had breakfast yet. And this is when I realized how long it'd been since I'd eaten. Not since that Mexican meal with Gordon. I wasn't hungry. Maybe I'd never be hungry again.

Amy watched me, silent but curious, while the coffee brewed. I tried not to make eye contact. I'd decided not to tell her about my little predicament. At least, not yet. I didn't know how she'd take the news that her best friend was a vampire. Knowing Amy—she'd either think it was cool, or she'd run screaming for the hills and I'd never see her again. The last time I'd announced that I was a vampire loud and proud, I'd nearly gotten myself sliced and diced. Not that I expected Amy to do anything weird, but . . . I don't know. It just wasn't the right time.

I poured us each a mug and topped them both off with cream and sugar—we took our coffee the same way. Her eyes didn't leave me for a moment as I handed her a mug. She was waiting for the big explanation. We normally told each other everything that happened in our lives. Unfortunately, this wasn't going to be one of those times.

"Well?" she finally asked, her eyebrow held high in silent accusation.

"Well, what?" I sipped my coffee. It tasted weak and slid unpleasantly down to my stomach. I placed the mug down on the coffee table.

"I was worried about you."

"Yeah, you already said that. I'm fine."

"Ms. Saunders isn't talking about what happened. Why did you get fired?"

I paused for a moment while I came up with something that sounded logical. "She didn't like the job I was doing. She fired me. End of story."

Amy exhaled deeply and her usual bright, shiny smile returned to her face. "I knew it had to be something like that. You would *not* believe what everyone is saying about you."

"What are they saying?"

She shook her head. "You don't want to know. Really. But I'd stay clear from Sally in accounting, if you catch my drift."

I didn't, but decided to let it go. I didn't want to catch any drift that had to do with "Skanky Sally."

"Okay, so you got fired because Saunders is a bitch."

"Essentially."

"That still doesn't explain where you've been since yesterday and why you haven't returned any of my calls. Don't you know it's rude to just disappear when people are worried about you?"

"Sorry, I . . . I've been around. But I've just been a little too upset to pick up the phone. I guess I've been feeling sorry for myself."

She drank her coffee but didn't comment on the weak taste. Maybe it was just my taste buds that were faulty this morning.

She squinted at me. "You look different."

"I do?" My hand went immediately to my hair.

"Yeah." She leaned closer. "Actually, you look amazing."

My eyebrows went up at that. "Amazing? And that's different than normal? Gee, thanks."

She waved her hand. "You know what I mean. It's like you're glowing, or something. That zit you had on your cheek yesterday has cleared up already. And"—she leaned even closer—"you're not wearing any makeup, but you don't look like hell."

I backed away from her. "I guess I must have had a really good sleep."

Her eyes widened. She stood up so suddenly that her coffee mug jerked and a little of the warm liquid splashed on me. "I think I know what it is."

"What *what* is?"

"Why you look so good. I can't believe it, Sarah. I can't believe you didn't tell me." Her bottom lip wobbled. "We're supposed to be best friends, aren't we?"

I felt what little color there was still in my cheeks

drain away. How could she have figured it out so easily? She was nice enough, but not the brightest bulb on the Christmas tree. At least, not usually.

"I'm sure it's not what you think," I said quickly.

"There's no other explanation for it. Disappearing for a whole day, not returning my phone calls. Looking so different."

She grabbed her purse and began shuffling through the contents. I stared at her with disbelief. Good God, she'd figured out I was a vampire and was hunting around in her bag for a weapon. I didn't want to fight for my life against my best friend. That would really put a damper on our trip to Mexico. Not good. Not good at all.

She stopped searching and looked at me, her eyes even wider than before. "You are, aren't you?"

Maybe I should just admit it. Get everything out in the open.

Or maybe not. Denial was a wonderful thing.

I stood up. "I don't know what you're talking about."

I got ready to tackle her, but all she ended up pulling out of her purse was her pressed powder. She held the compact loosely in her hand and sat back down on the sofa.

"You're in love," she informed me. "And you don't even want to tell me about it. I'm so incredibly hurt."

"I'm in . . . in love?"

"Who's the guy? Oh wait, I'm sure that's too much information for me, isn't it?"

I was so relieved that I almost fainted. She thought I'd disappeared for a day and looked great because some guy had swept me off my feet. Which, thinking back to the fall from the bridge with Thierry, wasn't all that far off.

I sat back down beside her as she inspected herself in the small mirror and powdered her nose. "There's no guy. I'm serious. If there was, you know you'd be the very first person I'd tell. I promise that I'm still pathetically single."

She studied me for a moment. "For real?"

"The realest."

She closed the compact and put it back in her purse. "If you say so, then I guess I believe you."

"I say so."

She grinned at me. "Then we definitely need to go to the mall today to celebrate your liberation from that dead-end job. What do you say?"

That sounded like a plan. I wanted to get out, didn't particularly matter where. After the night I'd just had, the apartment felt very claustrophobic to me.

I dressed quickly in jeans and a comfy dark blue sweatshirt with a little picture of Tweety Bird on the front. Then I slipped into my leather jacket and grabbed my purse, all in under ten minutes. Had to be some kind of a record.

The Eaton Centre was four subway stops away and accessible by the PATH. I found the skylights in the mall to be painfully bright, so I left my sunglasses on the whole time. Amy thought I was trying to be incognito in case we saw anyone from the office. I was just trying not to go blind. Luckily, it was starting to cloud over. The weather report called for snow by the end of the day.

I watched Amy rack up her credit on a pair of diamond stud earrings. I was so jealous. If I still had a job,

I might have done the same thing, but now I had to be budget girl. Had to make my money last—well, until the end of time.

We grabbed lunch in the food court. I still wasn't hungry, but I got Mexican, anyhow. Burritos with sour cream and refried beans. Diet Coke on the side. One of my favorites. But, after the first bite, it tasted so bland, and sat so heavily in my stomach, that I pushed it away.

Amy watched me absently play with my food while she chomped away on her cheeseburger and fries. Then she put the sandwich down and covered it with a paper napkin.

"You're right," she said. "We shouldn't be eating this crap. Way too many calories."

Out of the corner of my eye, I saw someone approach our table and sit down next to me. It was a crowded food court, but I didn't think we should have to share our booth without even being asked first. Some people were so rude.

I turned around to face whoever it was, and a gasp caught in my throat.

It was Quinn.

He stared at me with a smile on his face. "Do you believe in fate, Sarah? Or is this just a lucky coincidence that we've bumped into each other again so soon?"

I opened my mouth, but nothing came out.

He looked at Amy. "And you are?"

"Amy," she offered without hesitation.

"I'm Quinn," he said, and nodded at me. "A good friend of Sarah's here. Isn't that right?"

I swallowed and glanced at Amy. Her smile held, but

I could see accusation in her eyes. She thought this was my mystery man.

The real mystery was—how had he found me so easily? I felt sick. Maybe it *was* fate. He didn't have to follow me to my apartment. I'd saved him the trouble by walking right into his path.

I was so dead.

Chapter 7

I'm going to take off." Amy stood up from the table. She swung her purse over her shoulder and gave me a dirty look.

I looked up at her bleakly, but didn't try to stop her. No reason for her to get hurt, too. "I'll call you."

"Whatever." She turned her best fake smile in Quinn's direction. "Nice meeting you."

"Yeah, you too."

She was about to leave and then seemed to hesitate.

Good, Amy, I thought. *Do something courageous. Make a scene. Anything would be great.*

She turned back around and, without making eye contact with me, grabbed the rest of her cheeseburger, wrapped it in some napkins, and shoved it into her bag.

And then, my best friend of the past four years left me in the clutches of a vampire hunter whose wooden stake had my name etched on it.

Quinn watched her walk away until she was just a tiny pink dot entering a clothing store at the other end of the mall. Retail therapy to get over her friend's betrayal.

He turned back to me and presented me with a wide grin. "So, where were we?"

I breathed in slowly through my nose and let it out just as slowly through my mouth. I could remain in control here. I wasn't going to show him how scared I was.

"Before or after you decided to kill me?"

"I believe we left off at the deciding-to-kill-you part."

I took another deep breath. "Actually, I think we left off just before your daddy gave you a spanking for being a bad boy."

His grin faltered, and he took a moment before answering. "He's a man who's very hard to please."

I shrugged. "Your family problems are your own business."

"You're right, they are."

I told myself to shut up and not make things worse, but my mouth wasn't listening.

"So," I said, "does your mommy spank you, too, or just your pops?"

The grin didn't just falter this time, it slid right off his face. "My mother is dead."

"Oh." My stomach sank. "I'm sorry."

What the hell was I apologizing for? I did tend to stick my foot in it sometimes. I suppose apologizing was just my knee-jerk reaction.

"Yeah," he continued, even though I didn't want him to. "When I was just a kid, she was killed by one of your kind."

"An executive assistant?" I offered.

"A vampire. A cold-blooded, vicious, murdering monster like you."

"You have me all wrong. You don't even know me."

"I know enough."

"Look, I'm sorry for your loss. Really. But I'm not what you think."

He shook his head. "You're new. I get that. But it doesn't change anything. You're one of *them*. My sole purpose in life is to rid the world of things like you."

My eyes narrowed. "I don't much like being called a *thing*. When was the last time you had a conversation with a real live woman? When it didn't require a credit card number first, that is?"

He scowled at me. "You have a real mouth on you."

I sighed. "Look, I just want you to walk away and leave me alone. What's that going to take?"

"You not being a vampire."

"So that's the only qualification needed to end up on the wrong end of a stake with you? What about the fact that I'm totally innocent?"

"Innocent." He snorted at that. "No vampire is innocent."

"Yeah, and I used to think that vampires were dangerous and sexy. I've managed to blow that theory out of the water."

He raised an eyebrow. "You're not dangerous and sexy?"

I paused for a second and studied him. Okay, what was he doing now? Threatening me or flirting with me?

I looked around. The food court was packed and noisy. A kid had just dropped his ice-cream cone and was screaming like a banshee a couple of tables away.

"I have a question, Quinn."

"What's that?"

"Would your mother be proud of you?"

"What?" The word was like a gunshot.

"Your mother," I repeated. "Would she be proud of you hunting down helpless, innocent women and killing them all in the name of vengeance? Somehow I doubt it. She'd probably be ashamed to call you her son."

I took the moment, since I knew it was all I had. In one quick motion I threw the food at him, clobbering him as hard as I could. My untouched refried beans hit him right in the eyes. That would sting. He stood up and slipped on the spilled food and drink and fell to the floor. I grabbed my purse and ran through the crowd, out of the food court.

You'd think that with all my running around lately, I would have chosen more sensible shoes. Well, you'd be wrong. I was wearing two-inch platforms that were about a size too small. They looked great with the jeans, but it was at the price of comfort.

I pushed open the nearest door to the underground and flew down a flight of stairs and past the subway entrance. The PATH was practically deserted on Saturday afternoons, since it was mostly set up for the Monday-to-Friday business crowd. There were a few stragglers. Some window-shoppers, even though most of the stores were closed up and dark.

I looked behind me as I ran. Quinn was right on my heels, rubbing at his eyes. I hoped that he didn't know the underground as well as I did. Then again, he was much faster and probably would catch up to me before I even had a chance to lose him. Not good.

I swore, if I got out of this in one piece, I was only wearing Nikes on my feet from now on. Sensible footwear was my promise to the powers that be.

I hung a left. Directly in front of me was a set of re-volving doors leading to the lower level of a downtown business tower. I swung through them and then grabbed the door to stop it in midmotion. I'd planned it just right. Quinn didn't have a chance to stop and whacked his face against the clean glass, falling backward with a surprised yelp.

He yelled my name as if that would be enough to slow me down. I didn't even pause. I passed through an-other set of doors. Unfortunately, this time they weren't the revolving kind. The tunnels went on and on, and most looked exactly the same. I was near the exit to Dundas Street now. I passed a store that had a really nice dress on a mannequin in the front window. I instinctively made a mental note of where I saw it and kept running.

I could hear Quinn behind me, getting even closer. His breathing was labored. I sneaked a quick peek be-hind me and almost panicked when I saw the stake in his right hand. He wasn't playing around. If he caught up to me, he would kill me, no doubt about it.

The hallway coming up on my left had a sign reading UNDER CONSTRUCTION. I hurdled over the hazard tape and immediately regretted it. Only twenty feet ahead the hall was blocked off. Dead end. Well, what the hell had I thought "under construction" meant? I ran as far as I could.

Quinn appeared as he turned the corner. He looked straight at me, panting hard, and shook his head.

"Nice try."

Surprisingly enough, I wasn't winded at all. Physical endurance. Mark that down as another perk to being a vampire. Unfortunately, since I was about to die, it didn't really matter.

"Why don't we go grab a coffee and talk about this?" I said. "My treat."

"I like that you never give up. I almost wish I could say yes."

He was still moving toward me and made no move to put the stake away.

"Forget coffee." I felt myself start to panic again. I had to keep him talking. "Let's have a few more tequilas. We were having such a good time last night, weren't we?"

He paused. "Yeah, we were."

"We had a connection, don't you think?" I tried to keep eye contact with him, but that stake in his hand was extremely distracting.

"Are you saying that we should put aside our differences and be friends?"

I nodded crazily. "That's *exactly* what I'm saying."

"Tempting," he said slowly. "But no. I know what I have to do here, whether I want to or not. Sorry, but it's time to say good-bye."

I pressed up against the wall and let out a short, frightened scream. He took another step closer to me and raised the stake. I looked into his blue eyes. He didn't look maniacal like White-teeth had. Quinn was taking no pleasure from this. He felt like it was his duty. His job. Clean up the garbage, no matter how bad it stank.

I didn't like being compared to garbage, but then again, it was my own analogy.

I stared at him with wide eyes. "Don't do this."

"I'm sorry, Sarah."

A dark shape tackled Quinn from the side. He went down hard, and the stake clattered away from him. I gasped. What the hell just happened?

Somebody had Quinn pinned down on the floor, raising his arms above his head and straddling his body. The man turned to look at me. He was middle-aged with a beer belly and a full beard. He wore an expensive-looking dark gray business suit.

"Are you okay?" he asked me.

I struggled to find my voice. "Barely."

"You're lucky we were nearby."

Quinn fought against the man, but the impact with the floor had knocked the wind out of him. "Let me up. This is no concern of yours."

The man glared down at him. "It's definitely my concern when someone messes with the master's new girlfriend."

The master's new what?

Another man came running around the corner. "Dan! There you are. What the hell happened?"

Just what I was wondering.

Dan stopped Quinn's struggles with a quick bash of the back of his head against the hard floor.

"Vampire killer," Dan told him. "Picking on a fledgling in the middle of a Saturday afternoon. No damn respect."

"Monsters," Quinn moaned. "You're all monsters."

"Actually, I'm a lawyer," Dan said. "So I've been called worse."

I was surprised. "Oh? You're not a vampire?"

Dan glanced up at me. "Yeah, I'm a vampire, too. But

being a lawyer pays the bills. Can't let all that schooling go to waste, after all."

Dan's friend came closer. He touched my arm and I flinched.

"You sure you're okay?"

"I will be. Eventually, anyhow." I nodded down at Quinn. "What are you going to do with him?"

"Don't worry yourself about that."

The way he said it was filled with menace. "Don't worry yourself about that" translated into "we're going to chop him into tiny red pieces and flush him down the nearest toilet." But maybe that was just my interpretation. I hoped so, anyhow.

I looked at the friend. He flashed his sharp fangs at me in what he probably thought passed for a friendly smile. The fangs seemed longer than they had a moment ago. "Yeah, you'd better be on your way now, sweetheart."

My stomach sank. Shit. They were going to kill him. I wanted to feel nothing. After all, Quinn had tried to kill me twice, and I didn't even want to know what other damage he'd done since arriving in Toronto. But I guess that's what separated us. Even after what he'd tried to do to me, I didn't want him to get hurt. I just wanted him to leave me alone.

"This should send the hunters a clear message." Dan was talking to Quinn. "You and your friends hunted down my wife last week. We were newlyweds."

"Tough shit," Quinn spat. "I'm sure the bitch deserved it."

A deep growl emanated from Dan's throat.

I felt sick. I didn't want to leave. I wanted to help

Quinn. But even if I did, then what? Could I fool myself into believing that he'd forgive me for what he saw as an obvious tragic flaw? No. He'd just try to kill me again. He seemed the stubborn type.

Dan's friend got down on his knees beside the other vampire, grabbed the top of Quinn's head, and twisted it so his neck was fully exposed.

Then I heard it—the sound that wound haunt me. The sound of fangs sinking into soft flesh and tissue. The sound of Quinn's short scream of pain and terror. I clasped my hand to my mouth. Why hadn't he begged for his life? Why did he have to taunt them, rub in the fact that he was directly or indirectly responsible for whatever had happened to Dan's wife?

Dan looked up at me. His eyes were so dark they seemed fully black. His lips were curled back over his fangs. His mouth was bloody. I took a shaky step backward.

"Get lost," he said and then turned back to Quinn.

Not thinking anymore, I turned and ran away from them. Out of the hallway that was under construction. Away, far away from what I'd just witnessed. I wanted to block it out of my mind. Forget what I'd seen, but it was burned into my brain like a horrific Polaroid photo.

Pushing the door to the nearest public washroom open, I ran to a stall and tried to throw up, but there was nothing in my stomach to purge. I was empty.

I went to the faucet and splashed cold water on my face, then looked up into the large mirror. There was something in my eyes—a wildness, a deep fear—I'd never seen before, and I didn't like it at all. And there was something else, something not right about my reflection. I stared for a couple of moments until I figured out what it was.

The door to the stall directly behind me. I could see it.

I blinked and focused. Yes. Ever so slightly, I was able to see through my reflection to what was behind me. Even the graffiti on the door: "Joanna loves Tony."

My stomach sank even farther. But that wasn't supposed to happen yet. Not yet. I still had a reflection, but it had already started to fade.

I was a vampire. For real.

A vicious, murdering, bloodsucking monster.

My knees gave out under me, and I passed out on the dirty floor of the women's washroom.

Chapter 8

A cleaning lady nudged me with her sensible shoe. I blinked my eyes open and stared up at her.

"You need ambulance?" she asked in broken English.

I fumbled for my purse and slowly, shakily got to my feet. "No."

"You do the drugs?"

"No, no drugs."

She shrugged and got back to mopping the floor.

How long had I been out? Not long. My face was still damp from when I'd splashed the water on myself.

I left the washroom not knowing where to go next, so I let my feet choose for me. My feet decided to get on the nearest subway. But we weren't headed home. We were headed to Midnight Eclipse.

The neighborhood looked different in the late afternoon. Somehow it looked seedier, which I hadn't thought possible. I tried the front door, but it was locked. There was a sign in the window that read CLOSED. The hours of operation started at nine o'clock, and they weren't talking about the morning.

I knocked, anyhow.

I couldn't go home. I couldn't be alone. Being alone meant that I'd have to think about what I'd just seen. I'd let a man die and hadn't said a word to save him. I felt so guilty about it that it felt like it was eating me up inside.

He'd been killed by vampires. Just like me.

No, *not* just like me. I ran my tongue along my upper teeth. They still felt normal. Nothing pointier than usual. That's the way I wanted them to stay.

I knocked again, but there was no answer. I figured that there might be a back door to the place, so I went around the side of the building. There was a green Dumpster spilling its contents out on the freshly fallen snow and a sturdy red door with no handle. I knocked on it, and it hurt my knuckles. I waited for a few minutes and then knocked again.

After a few more minutes I turned away. My cheeks were wet from melting snow. Yeah, it was the melting snow. I wasn't crying. Sure.

The door made a clicking sound behind me and I spun around. It opened and Thierry looked out at me.

"Oh, it's you," he said.

I ran to him and hugged him hard, blubbering like a baby into his black shirt. He didn't hug me back, but directed me inside and closed the door behind us. I could feel his vague discomfort, but he waited patiently for me to stop wailing and clutching at him.

Finally I released him and looked up at him with puffy red eyes.

"You weren't supposed to come here until this evening," he said.

I didn't reply. I don't think I could have if I'd tried. I just looked at him with my big, soggy eyeballs until he finally nodded.

"Fine. You may as well stay, now that you're here. No one else has arrived yet, though. We don't open for six hours."

He led me to a small office. There was a couch inside, much like the one he had in his living room. I climbed onto it and laid my cheek against the cool leather. I was starting to calm down a bit. I felt safe there. With Thierry. He was staring at me, waiting for some kind of explanation as to why I'd interrupted his "alone" time, but I wasn't ready to talk about it yet. As the fear slowly faded from my body, it left behind a thick blanket of weariness.

All I wanted to do was shut my eyes. Shut it all out. Wake up later and have it all be just a horrible, horrible dream.

The pain woke me. It was like a hot knife slicing through my entire body. I sat up too fast, and the sudden movement made me double back over.

I was allowed a brief moment to collect myself before the second wave hit. I slid off the couch—déjà vu all over again—and may have let out a small yelp. Yeah, right, some yelp. No, it was more like a loud scream that caught halfway down my throat when I couldn't find the air anymore.

I decided, finally and formally while writhing in pain on the floor of Thierry's office, that being a vampire sucked. I wished that Gordon were still alive so I could kill him myself for getting me into this horrible mess in the first place.

The door to my right opened and I glanced up. Thierry entered, looking at me with concern. He had a knife in one hand and a glass of water in the other.

Newbie special.

I didn't care anymore that it was blood. Human blood, vampire blood, pig's blood—hell, even hamster blood. Come to Mama.

Another wave of pain shook me to my core and I cried out. Thierry was shaking his head, saying something like, "Too long. Shouldn't have allowed her to go for so long."

He drew the blade across his left wrist. At the first glimpse of red I clawed wildly at the leather seat behind me. He grabbed the water he'd placed on the desk just as I reached out and clutched the bottom corner of his shirt. The glass slipped from his grasp and shattered on the floor.

I pulled myself up a bit so I could grab his injured wrist and, as if by instinct, brought it straight to my mouth. He gasped with surprise as my lips made contact with his wound.

As soon as his blood touched my tongue, the pain vanished as if it had never been there in the first place. It was like a cool glass of water after being lost in the desert for a month. It was like fine champagne, strawberries and cream, Kahlúa chocolate sauce on French vanilla ice cream—ambrosia, food of the gods. Pick one.

His arm was tense for a moment, but he slowly

relaxed as I drank from him. I looked up to see that his eyes were dark and half closed, and there was an unfathomable expression on his face.

"There are reasons why those as old as I do not sire fledglings."

I ran my tongue along his wrist as the words went through my mind, his words from last night. I might have wondered what he meant by them if I'd currently been thinking straight. But I wasn't thinking. At least, not in any normal way.

Our eyes stayed locked for what felt like forever. Then slowly, very slowly, his expression changed as he regained his composure.

"Enough, Sarah." His voice was ragged.

Enough? I thought. *No, not yet. Just a little more.* I felt like Oliver Twist. *"Please, sir, I want some more."*

He groaned as he tried to pull away, but my grip on him must have been stronger than I felt.

"Enough," he said louder. He squeezed my arm and roughly brought me up to my feet. He put a hand under my chin to pry my mouth from his wrist.

I felt funny, kind of light-headed. I looked at Thierry, with the taste of him still on my lips. By his dark, intense expression I figured he would push me away from him and storm out of the room.

But instead, he grabbed my shoulders and pulled me hard against him, then crushed his lips against mine, drinking me in as I'd just done to him. I wrapped my arms around his waist and kissed him back—deeply, so deeply that I thought I might drown.

Then he pushed me away from him and stormed out of the room.

I staggered back to the couch, sat down heavily, and tried to breathe as normally as I could. I touched my fingers to my lips, feeling dazed by what had just happened.

Okay, maybe being a vampire wasn't so bad, after all. The jury was still out.

A few minutes went by before I heard a light knock on the door. I looked up, expecting it to be Thierry. I had no idea what I was going to say to him: "Thanks for the drink"? "You're a great kisser"? Nothing I could have said would have come out sounding half intelligent. Luckily, I wouldn't have to think about what to say, since it wasn't him.

A redheaded girl with a sprinkling of freckles on her nose poked her head in the partially opened door and blinked at me. She looked to be no more than a teenager.

She smiled at me. "Hi."

I checked to make sure I was the only one in the room before answering. "Hello."

"Sarah," she said.

"That's funny, that's my name, too."

I was trying to make a joke. She found it to be more than a little bit funny and threw her head back with a huge, loud cackling laugh that showed off her fangs and managed to scare me a little. I'd have to add to my growing list of phobias: "Loud redheaded teenage vampires."

"No. *You're* Sarah. I'm Zelda."

"Zelda?"

"That's right."

I didn't know what to say next. Were we supposed to

be having some kind of a conversation? I wasn't feeling all that chatty at the moment.

"Thierry called to ask me to bring some clothes in for you." The rest of her appeared from behind the door as she entered the room. She was dressed in a black skirt and an emerald green blouse. It looked as if she'd borrowed the outfit from her mother. She presented an armful of folded clothes to me, but I didn't take them. I just looked at them questioningly as I got to my feet. There was no pain anymore. Actually, I felt pretty terrific, all things considered.

"Why did Thierry ask you to bring me clothes?"

She looked uncertain. "Um, because you're on shift tonight, and . . . uh . . . jeans aren't normally part of the uniform. Cool sweatshirt, though."

I absently touched my Tweety Bird–clad chest. "You're kidding right? I'm on *shift*?"

"No. Not kidding."

I took a moment to inspect the clothes. She was a couple of inches taller than me, but we were about the same size. If the clothes were hers, then they'd definitely fit me. Black skirt, black hose. Strappy heels and a long-sleeved red blouse. Not my taste, but wearable.

I frowned at her. "What exactly do you mean when you say I'm 'on shift'?"

Zelda shrugged. "Waiting tables. Thierry said you were going to help out tonight."

My eyebrows shot up, and a hot ripple of annoyance went through me.

Of all the damn nerve. We'd made a deal. He was going to teach me how to adjust to being a vampire without getting myself killed, and in return I was going to use him for all the information I needed and then go back to my normal life. What part of that didn't he understand? Okay, maybe I hadn't been clear on all the finite details, but I'd never agreed to be a waitress at his stupid vampire club.

I shook my head. "No can do. I left my waitressing days behind a long, long time ago. Hated it then, and I'm not putting myself through it again now."

Zelda stared at me for a moment and then suddenly burst into tears. "But . . . he said . . . you were . . . going . . . to help out."

I held up my hands to try to calm her down. What the hell just happened?

"Sorry." I patted her awkwardly on her shoulder while she sobbed. "Nothing against waitressing, really. It's a fine, noble profession. It's just not for me. Nothing personal. Thanks for the clothes, anyhow."

"No, it's not that. It's just . . . just . . ."

"Just what?"

"Ralph!" she wailed.

"Ralph? Who the hell is Ralph?"

"Ralph's dead!"

I shook my head. "Okay, Zelda. Take a deep breath and tell me what you're talking about."

The waterworks eased up a bit. "Ralph was a waiter here. Until tonight. He's dead. The hunters got him."

"Oh. Sorry." There wasn't much more to say than that. Another one bites the dust.

She sniffed loudly and ran the back of her hand across her nose. "He always thought he was going to live forever."

"Well . . . wasn't he?"

"He refused to believe that anything bad would ever happen to him. But it did."

"That sucks."

"So, it won't be forever, see? Just until we find somebody to replace him permanently. Thierry said that you wouldn't mind."

"Oh, he did, did he?"

Zelda looked at me with a hopeful expression. Great. Now I'd feel major guilt if I said no. I had enough guilt to deal with today without adding any more to the load. I sighed.

"Okay. But it's just going to be for tonight."

A bright smile chased the rest of her tears away. "Thanks. I'm on bar, so we'll get to chat more later."

"Super." Any enthusiasm in my voice was forced. "So you can serve alcohol, huh? I thought you had to be nineteen to do that."

"I'm covered," Zelda said. "Since I turned three hundred and nineteen last Tuesday."

"Oh." I paused to let that little piece of information sink in. "Um, happy birthday?"

"Actually, I stopped celebrating them when I turned two hundred." She moved toward the door. "I'll be out by the bar. Any questions you've got, don't hesitate."

"Okay. Thanks."

I watched the three-centuries-old redheaded bartender leave the office and shook my head. Appearances sure can be deceiving.

So there I was. Just sucked into working the table-waiting shift of a dead vamp with the improbable name of Ralph. In a way it was probably a good thing I was filling in tonight. It would help me take my mind off what had happened in the underground. I could rub elbows with the other creatures of the night who enjoyed smoky clubs with dark-haired jazz singers. Maybe learn more about the hunters and how best to avoid the same fate as Ralph's. I might even be able to find out what the real story on enigmatic Monsieur de Bennicoeur was.

And the most important question of all: were vampires good tippers?

Along with the clothes, Zelda had been kind enough to leave her makeup bag for me. After applying a coat of bright red lipstick, I found the troubles of the day seemed to slip away. Or, at least, I was able to block out any unpleasant thoughts focusing on my slightly see-through reflection while I applied the war paint. When I was done, the memories immediately flooded back.

Poor Quinn. I got a shiver down my spine every time I flashed back to what happened. Why couldn't I be more coldhearted? Maybe that would come in time, but right now I felt like I'd aided and abetted a murder.

After a few minutes I finally stepped out of the office and scanned the darkened club for Thierry, but he was nowhere to be seen. Big surprise. I still felt embarrassed about what had happened earlier. I don't know if I felt more embarrassed about the impromptu wrist sucking or the subsequent face sucking. It was neck and neck—no pun intended.

But I was still desperate to talk to him. If I was going to wait tables, I wanted it to be worth my while. Start my tutoring deal right away. No time to waste, especially after getting myself into that unfortunate predicament this afternoon.

Barry made a beeline toward me. He was wearing a matching tuxedo to the one he'd worn last night, only tonight he had a red rose tucked into his lapel. He smiled his tiny-fanged, slightly condescending smile.

"Good evening, Sarah," he said drily and without much interest.

"Howdy," I replied. "So here I am, ready to pitch in and help out. Just for tonight. Why don't you tell me where you want me to go?"

I left it open for him, baiting him to say something rude and inappropriate, but either the line went over his head or he wasn't in the mood to play games. Frankly, neither was I.

"I don't think it will be too busy. Just make yourself available to the customers that do make it out tonight. We have a very limited menu, people mostly order drinks—a lot of us can't eat solid food as easily as others—"

"Oh, really?" I cut him off. "I guess that would explain it."

He blinked at me. "Explains what?"

"My missing appetite. Good to know that it's a normal vampire thing."

He cleared his throat. "Yes. Quite normal. Anyhow, as I was saying before you rudely interrupted me—George will be here to help out, too, but he doesn't start until eleven. I tried to get him in earlier, but he wasn't answering his phone."

"I think I can handle it." I glanced around the empty club. "Where's Thierry, anyhow? I need to talk to him."

Barry's expression darkened. "The *master* has gone out to attend to another business matter. He will return shortly."

I frowned down at him. "Why do you call him master, anyhow? Seems kind of formal."

He sighed heavily. "Like I've said before, it is a term of respect. He is the oldest of our kind that I'm personally familiar with, and I will call him master"—he searched briefly for the right words—"because that is simply what he is called."

"Uh-huh. And what's his regular drink?"

"Excuse me?"

"When you gave us our drinks last night, you gave him his regular drink. What is it? I figure I should know these things so he won't have to ask. Don't want the *master* to go thirsty." I smirked at him.

Barry stared at me for longer than was comfortable before he finally spit it out. "Cranberry juice."

I was surprised. "No blood?"

"He rarely drinks blood in public."

"Interesting."

Barry shrugged his small shoulders. "If you say so. Now, if you'll excuse me."

He nodded curtly to me and went off on his nonmerry way. Seriously, I wondered where he'd found a stick small enough to shove up his ass. Not my favorite guy in the city, but what can you do? Maybe he had one of those Napoleonic complexes. Short men with major attitude problems.

I felt a sharp tap on my shoulder and turned around.

A burly guy wearing olive green overalls and a black

T-shirt shoved a clipboard in my face. "Can you sign for the keg of O negative?"

"The keg of what?"

"O neg. Just sign right there on the dotted line." He tapped the clipboard.

Behind him was a silver keg, which I would have suspected was filled with beer. Normally, that is. I figured O neg wasn't a code name for alcohol. But who delivers kegs of blood to vampire bars?

I squinted down at the delivery form. The Blood Delivery Guys was the name of the company. Well, that made sense.

I signed on the dotted line like a good employee; then the guy snatched the clipboard out of my hands and headed for the back door. He sure was in a big hurry. I wondered how many deliveries he had that night. How many other vamp hangouts were there in Toronto, anyhow?

The customers began to filter in at the turn of the hour, none of them looking as amazed and out of sorts as I had last night. They all looked as if they'd been there many times before and were used to entering the club through a tanning salon. The band took the stage at nine-thirty and filled the smoky air with dark sexy music.

If I tried to push the thought out of my mind that all of these people were vampires, then it would have felt like any other club. Nothing out of the ordinary. None of these people wanted trouble. They'd come here to escape the troubles they had outside and be safe and secure for a couple of hours. Just like me. It was a soothing thought. For a moment. Then I remembered Dan and his buddy and what they did to Quinn. What had Thierry said? Vamps can be good or bad . . . just like humans.

"And what can I get for you tonight?" I sidled up to the newest couple to enter the club. After a couple of hours I was getting used to the job. Nobody was giving me a hard time. I got a few looks, of course. People either didn't recognize me at all, or they thought I was Thierry's new girlfriend. I didn't waste my breath trying to argue with them. Thierry hadn't shown up yet, and that was the only thing that was causing me any stress. Other than that, I felt very much at ease at Midnight Eclipse.

The man at the table smiled at me. It was difficult to call him a man, though. He looked more like a college student out after a long night of studying. He was clean-cut, with blond hair and a smooth, hairless face. He wore a short-sleeved blue-and-white-striped polo shirt and dark blue pants. "I'll have an AB positive and orange juice, please."

Big spender, I thought. AB positive was a rare blood type, and I'd learned the rarer the blood, the more expensive the shot was. It made sense in a strange Stephen King sort of way.

"Cool." I jotted the order down on a pad of paper I'd found in Thierry's office. I had a pretty lousy memory. "And for you?"

I turned to his girlfriend. Definitely not of the clean-cut variety. Of anyone tonight, she looked the most like she belonged in a vampire club. On top of black jeans she wore a deep-cut black shirt that left very little of her pale cleavage to the imagination. Her face was so white that it looked unhealthy. She wore dark red lipstick, black eyeliner, and had dark hair so long that it had to be extensions. Her nose and eyebrow were both pierced with small silver hoops.

She looked up at me with a fashionably morose expression on her pale face. "Vodka. Straight up."

"No blood?" If she said no, she'd be the first one tonight.

"Nope."

"Anything else?"

"Nope."

I turned away and headed over to the bar to give Zelda my order.

"Vodka straight up?" she asked with a frown.

"Yeah. No blood."

"Who's this for?"

I glanced over my shoulder. "Table twelve."

Zelda peered through the darkness and then shook her head. "Oh no, not them again."

I turned to follow her gaze. "What?"

"It's Timothy Langdon and his human girlfriend."

My eyebrows shot up. "*She's* human?"

"Wannabe vamp."

"So, what's the big deal?"

Zelda kept shaking her head. "If Thierry finds out they're here, he's going to flip out."

"Why? What's the problem?"

Just then, I saw a whir of motion to my left. The door to the club from the tanning salon opened wide and a good-looking guy came inside. He walked directly toward us. Well, toward Zelda. He barely glanced at me. His hair was the color of golden sand and fell just past his shoulders in a fine curtain. He was built like a Chippendale dancer and looked like he regularly made use of the tanning beds out front. His muscular pecs peeked out from beneath the thin white shirt he wore on top of tight black leather pants.

"Zelda, honey," he said. And with those two words uttered from his full, perfect lips, I realized that this grade-A prime rib of hotness was as gay as the day is long. What a waste. "What's the big emergency? From the message Barry left me, it sounded like the world is ending."

"It is, George. Brace yourself." Her expression was grim. "Maybe you should sit down."

His face stiffened. He swung his firm tush onto a stool and looked at her apprehensively. "Spill."

"Ralph's dead."

"What?" The word was a wail. "How?"

Zelda reached out her hand and touched George's arm in a comforting gesture. "Hunters, of course."

"Damn it." George's voice quavered. "Damn it, damn it, damn it." He took a deep, shuddery breath. "Does this mean I have to work a double shift?"

Zelda paused. "No."

"Thank Christ. Well, you know what? It serves Ralph right to get his ass staked. He never looked both ways before he crossed the street." George finally looked at me. "Hello there, beautiful, and who are you?"

I extended my hand a bit. "Sarah."

He took my hand, but instead of shaking it, he kissed it. "Nice to have something in here that's new and gorgeous to look at."

"Gee." I smiled at him. "That's sweet. And I assumed you were gay."

"I am, honey. I'm just not blind."

I wasn't sure if I hated this guy or if I immediately wanted to go shopping with him. Time would tell.

Zelda measured out the shot of AB positive from a nearby keg. I eyed her with curiosity.

"Where does the blood come from, anyhow?" I asked.

She poured out a glass of orange juice before she looked up at me. "The delivery service."

I frowned. "Yeah, I got that. But where do *they* get it from?"

"Donors, mostly. People paid to give over their blood. It's quite the little business. Competitive too, since there're a few delivery services around."

"There are that many donors in Toronto?"

"A lot of it comes from the States," George chimed in. "The expensive, extra-tasty blood is imported from Europe. When supplies run low, there's always the synthetic version, but that tastes a bit, well, synthetic. Or, even worse"—he made a face—"animal blood. Yech."

I tried to keep the disgust off my face. "Well, that sounds pleasant."

"You asked." George shrugged. "Where's the boss? I wanted to ask him about a raise, and since Ralph's not around anymore, this might be a good time to emphasize how much he needs me."

"He's out," I told him. "Should be back soon. I need to talk to him, too. Badly."

He eyed me. "Honey, you just started. I get the raise first, okay?"

I was about to explain that I wouldn't be competing

for a few extra bucks, but decided it wasn't worth the effort. "Sure. Whatever."

Zelda slapped the drinks down on a round tray for me. "Take these out. Tell Timothy to drink them and get out of here before Thierry gets back."

I swallowed. "I don't know if I feel comfortable doing that."

She blinked at me. "Have you ever seen Thierry when he gets mad?"

"You don't call him master, huh?"

"I'm too old to call anybody master. Answer the question. Have you seen him mad?"

I thought back to how he'd reacted last night when I'd mentioned his suicide attempt. The flash of fury and violence that went through his silver eyes. My arms were suddenly covered with goose bumps. "Does he go all green and scary like the Hulk?"

"Worse," George said.

I grabbed the drinks and went back over to table twelve. I didn't want to be rude, but God knew I was capable of it. In fact, I was quite good at it. I guess that was one tip that night I wouldn't be able to count on.

"Timothy, right?" I said as I handed him the drink.

He smiled at me. "That's right. You're new around here, aren't you?"

"Yeah. I'm Sarah."

The girlfriend made an unhappy sound in her throat.

Take it easy, sweetheart, I thought. *Not trying to move in on your man.*

I placed the vodka in front of her. "Consider these drinks on the house, okay?"

"Really?" Timothy looked surprised. "Thanks a lot. What's the occasion?"

"Your getting the hell out of here as soon as you chug them back."

"Pardon me?"

"Who the hell do you think you are?" the girlfriend snapped.

I shifted the drink tray to my other arm. "I'm the gal standing between the two of you getting physically booted out of here. You guys were told not to come here anymore."

"It's a free country." Timothy's voice rose a level.

"Maybe out there." I nodded toward the door. "In here you have to follow the rules."

"You bitch," the girlfriend spat at me.

I turned to her. "Listen, metal head, I don't want any trouble. Believe me, I've had enough trouble today to last me a good long time. So drink your drinks and get the hell out of here."

Her eyes narrowed. "Bite me."

"Yeah." I smirked at her. "I bet you'd like that, wouldn't you?"

That comment earned me the vodka, straight up, thrown wetly right in my face.

I wiped my eyes and just knew that my painstakingly applied eye makeup was running. "You did *not* just throw a drink in my face."

We'd gotten the attention of the other vampires in our area of the club. I tried to ignore their curious gazes.

She got up from the table and stood her ground defiantly. "You're not kicking us out of here. We're staying."

"Melanie—" Timothy's voice held an edge of warning.

"Come on," Melanie said to me, "just try to throw me out, you bloodsucking bitch."

She went down with only one punch. I hadn't even planned on throwing it. My fist acted of its own accord. It was the vodka that made me do it—the vodka currently dripping down my chin.

"Sarah."

The word froze me in place. It wasn't said with menace or threat, it was quite calm. Too calm. I tried to dry my face off with the corner of my sleeve before turning around. Thierry stood six feet behind me with his arms crossed.

I shrugged. "She was asking for it."

He didn't reply. He looked down at the girl and then his gaze trailed over to Timothy, whose face had paled considerably.

"I . . . ," Timothy began. "I'm sorry, master. She wanted to come here. I know I should have said no, but—"

"Leave this place." Thierry's voice was still very calm, but there was something underneath, something dark and deep and scary beyond words.

"Yes. We will," Timothy said without meeting his eyes. "Again, so sorry."

He got up from the table and pulled at Melanie. She held a hand to her nose, which was now gushing blood. I guess I was stronger than I thought. Hmm, maybe some of my vampire strength was beginning to develop. Nice.

Thierry didn't look at him; he stared straight forward, the expression on his face unreadable. But as Timothy brushed past him, Thierry reached out to grab the boy's arm and drew him near enough to say something quietly to him. It wasn't quiet enough that I didn't hear it, though.

"Return again and it will be the last thing you do." His voice was like a glint of metal, the click of a gun's safety going off. Dangerous. "You, and your human."

Timothy didn't answer; he just nodded in a short burst of movement. Then he and Melanie made for the door and the cold streets outside.

"You." Thierry was now addressing me. I felt suddenly naked, and pulled the empty drink tray against my chest as a pathetic form of protection.

"Uh-huh?"

"Clean yourself up and return to work." He turned away and went toward his corner table in the shadows.

Didn't really care for the "asshole employer" tone of voice, but I did feel kind of sheepish about what had just happened. I had to learn to control my temper. Even with potential vampire strength, I couldn't go punching out everyone who pissed me off. Well, not all of them, anyhow. It would be hell on a manicure.

Chapter 9

I hastily reapplied the eyeliner and lipstick, and tried to fix my hair as best I could, given the dissipating reflection I had to work with. I tried not to think about that too much or it started to make my chest tighten with pain and dread. What was I going to do without a reflection? It just wasn't right.

Zelda came into the washroom to check on me after ten minutes. I had to turn around to see it was her, since *her* reflection was *completely* nonexistent.

"How do you manage?" I nodded at the mirror.

She frowned until she figured out what I meant, then shrugged. "You get used to it."

"I don't think I ever will. I'm about ready to go throw myself on the next cross I see."

She studied me. "You're kidding, right?"

"Yeah. Sort of."

"Crosses don't do anything, anyhow. That's just a lame myth."

Well, that was good. I was wondering if I'd have to

avoid any churches. Not that I went to church much any-more, but it would be nice to have the option.

I tried to give her a small smile. "And next you'll probably tell me that you don't sleep in a coffin, right?"

She nodded. "Now, *that's* true. Although, I can only afford a pine box myself." She laughed at my look of surprise. "Now I'm the one who's kidding."

"Funny."

She glanced at the mirror. "If it bothers you that much, you can always save your money and buy a shard."

"Buy a what?"

"They're called 'shards.' It's a reflective surface that's just like a mirror, only it works for us, too. But they're very expensive."

"How expensive?"

"If you have to ask, you probably can't afford it. I know I can't."

I sighed. "Well, that's the story of my life."

"Well, I guess if you hate being a vamp too much, you can always go questing for the cure."

A cure. More jokes. "Yeah, wouldn't that be great." I smiled. "Nah, if I can just make it for a few more weeks, I'm off to Mexico. That's worth living for, right?"

"Absolutely." Zelda smiled at me. "By the way, I liked the show earlier."

"What show?"

She swung her arm through the air. "Knocking Goth girl's lights out. I wanted to do that the last time they were in. She's a real bitch. I don't know what Timothy sees in her."

"You know him?"

"We used to date. But that was a long time ago."

I was going to ask how long ago, but decided I didn't really want to know.

"You know," Zelda said. "Now that George is here, why don't you take off? You look kind of tired."

"I am. This whole day's been really exhausting. But I need to talk to Thierry before I go anywhere. He's my designated answer-man when it comes to this vampire thing."

"How long have you been vamped, anyhow?"

I zipped up her makeup case and handed it back to her. "Two days."

Her eyes widened. "Two days? And your reflection already looks like that?"

I glanced at the mirror and grimaced. "Yeah. So?"

She turned away. "Oh . . . nothing. Nothing at all."

"No, I think it's something. What are you trying to say?"

Zelda turned back to me and was chewing on her bottom lip. "It's just that you don't typically lose your reflection to that extent for a long time . . . unless . . ."

"Unless what?"

"Unless you've been on a steady diet of . . ." She paused and looked at me. A smile began to form on her lips. "Oh, *that* must be it."

I put a hand on my hip and glared at her. "Am I going to have to punch you out, too? What are you talking about?"

"You and Thierry," Zelda said, as if that explained everything.

"Me and Thierry what?"

"He's been giving you his blood. That stuff's like

pure gold at his age, even diluted. No wonder it's speeding up the process." She noted my strained expression and my lack of denial.. "It's okay. It's cute, actually. He needs somebody like you in his life."

"What's that supposed to mean?"

"Somebody full of life. Somebody who might be able to add a little light to his existence."

I shook my head. "Look, there's nothing between us like that."

She rolled her eyes. "If there wasn't, then he wouldn't be offering you his blood, would he? There's plenty to go around, you know, or didn't you sign for the keg earlier? He likes you. Take it as a compliment. He doesn't like very many people."

I didn't have an answer for that. There hadn't been a need for him to give me his own blood if any old blood would do. "If he likes me, he sure has a funny way of showing it."

"That's the way he is about a lot of things."

"How long have you known him?"

She crossed her arms. "A long time. He helped me out when I was a fledgling, too. My sire ran off on me, and I was in pretty bad shape. I owe him a lot"—she looked at me—"only he wasn't so generous with me. You're lucky."

I shook my head as I thought about everything she'd said. "Do vampires share blood often? Is this like a normal thing?"

"Only for fledglings. Then you move on to human blood. Kind of like a baby moving from breast milk to solid food." She glanced at the watch on her wrist. "My break's over, so I'd better get back to work. Are you leaving?"

"Yeah, I guess." I felt so exhausted. Maybe talking to Thierry could wait for another night. I was still pissed that he'd conveniently been avoiding me all evening. Maybe I could do the same in return. "Do you think you might be able to set me up with some newbie specials before I go? I don't want to get the cramps again."

"Newbie specials?" She frowned.

"Uh, yeah, the water-and-blood thing?"

"But what about Thierry—"

I held up a hand. "Let's just say that I think the well has dried up. And even if it hasn't, I still don't want to take the chance."

She nodded. "He can be moody."

"That's a word."

Back out at the bar she gave me a few bottles of newbie special to keep on hand at all times. I tucked them into my oversized purse. She told me to make sure to have a sip every four hours for the next few days. After that, I'd be able to go for longer stretches of time. Maybe if I drank the blood very diluted, I wouldn't lose any more of my reflection or develop any more *unwanted* side effects like what I was experiencing due to my two doses of Thierry's extra-strong blood. Wouldn't hurt to try.

I said good-bye to her, then walked through the darkened club toward the exit, which took me past Thierry's booth. I felt his gaze on me from the shadows.

"Where are you going?" he asked.

"Home."

"So early? I thought we would have a chance to talk."

"Another time. Maybe."

There was a lot more I wanted to say, but it wasn't the right time for it. Tomorrow was another day. Today would soon be just a distant memory. Thank God.

"Very well," he said.

I began to move past the table, but then stopped. Maybe I did have time to say a little. "This isn't what I expected, you know."

"Pardon me?"

"Last night you said you'd help me out. Well, where have you been all evening? Other than answering a few simple questions last night, you've been avoiding me like the plague. Oh, and by the way, I never said I'd work here. You didn't even ask. You just assumed I'd help."

He said nothing for a moment, just stared at me. "Perhaps it was wrong of me to assume."

"So now what?"

"I don't know what it is you want me to say."

"Nothing. Just say nothing. You're super at that." I started walking again.

"Sarah," he called after me.

I turned around again. "I don't know why you even agreed to help me. It's obvious you don't want me around."

Thierry shook his head. "You're being irrational. Please sit down."

"I don't want to sit down. Nothing makes sense in my life anymore, especially you. I honestly don't know what to make of you. First you help me, then you push me away. Then you kiss me, then you push me away. What is it?"

His mouth straightened into a thin line. "Sarah—"

"But I have to say that out of everything I can't figure out, the thing that makes the least amount of sense to me is what you were doing on the bridge the other night. You're a six-hundred-year-old vampire who can't be easily killed. But you were going to jump off and end it all? Did you honestly think that was going to do the trick? I don't get it. All the jump did was get us wet."

His eyes narrowed. "I told you I didn't wish to speak of that again."

"Yeah, yeah. I'm beginning to realize that you like to avoid a lot of unpleasant discussions. Well, guess what? You win. Discussion over. I'm out of here."

His eyes burned now like silver flames. I'd struck a chord. Well, I knew how to leave them wanting more. I pushed open the black door and left Midnight Eclipse, for what I'd decided would be the last time.

The cold night air cut into my face, but I ignored it. I glanced across the street at Clancy's neon bar sign. Nope, wouldn't be making a repeat performance in there tonight. Straight home, do not pass go.

There was a yellow cab a block away, parked at the side of the road. Finally something was going right for me. About time, too. I wobbled toward it on the heels that had been getting less and less comfortable as the night wore on.

The street was deserted. It felt a little odd, actually. It wasn't all that late on a Saturday night for it to feel this empty. Not that it was such a great party section of the city, but still. I suddenly felt very alone.

And I got the weirdest feeling that I was being watched. Or maybe I was just being paranoid after my lousy day.

No. Somebody was definitely watching me. I could *sense* it.

I groaned inwardly. *Why? Why me? Why am I such a moron who would leave the club all alone without a ride?* I noticed that the cab's NOT IN SERVICE sign was up, and the driver was nowhere to be seen.

I nervously glanced over at the local hangout for vampire hunters. *When will I ever learn? And will I still be breathing when I do?*

"Hello?" My throat was dry and I swallowed. "I should let whoever you are know that I'm a triple black belt and my boyfriend's a cop. So beat it."

There was a sound then. A moan? Or was that just the wind?

No, it was definitely a moan. Followed by a heavy sliding sound.

A hand appeared from around the corner of a building, white-knuckled and gripping the brickwork. There was blood on the hand. My eyes widened and I raised my own hand to my mouth.

"Who are you?" My voice was raspy with apprehension.

A face appeared, pale and drawn. Dark circles were under his eyes. His bloodied white T-shirt was torn. No jacket on such a cold night. The fang marks on his neck were bruised and fresh. He tried to stay on his feet, but it was no use—Quinn slid down to the sidewalk in a heap.

Frozen in place, I glanced around, but there was no one else nearby. Just the two of us. Me and the man I'd seen murdered before my very eyes earlier that afternoon.

Maybe I should have run away. Put as much distance between myself and the vampire hunter as I possibly could, but again I found my feet had a mind of their own. And they were moving me closer to the man who wanted me dead.

I crouched down at his side and reached out to push the dark blond hair off his face. He flinched and tried to pull away.

"It's okay. I'm not going to hurt you."

"You." His dark blue eyes narrowed as he recognized me.

I tried to smile. "Yeah, surprise, surprise."

When I'd met him in Clancy's last night, he'd appeared attractive but a bit boyish. He didn't seem boyish anymore. This was a man who knew pain, who had been through hell and managed to come out the other side. He hadn't died, as I'd assumed, but something about him had died. That much I could tell.

I reached out to grab his tense, firmly muscled arm. There was nothing weak about Quinn. Nothing soft. He pushed me away and scooted farther back in the shadows.

His jaw was clenched tightly, and he looked at me as if I'd been the one who bit him. "Stay away from me . . . you . . . you . . ."

"Bloodsucking monster?" I finished for him. "Look, buddy, I'm not the one who did this to you. You're lucky they didn't kill you."

He laughed—a short, wild sound that raised the hair on the back of my neck. "No . . . they didn't kill me. Worse than that. Much worse."

"You need to get to a hospital." I tried to touch him again, but the look on his face made me stop.

"Too late for hospitals. Just leave me the hell alone."

He managed to stagger to his feet, but immediately doubled over again, clutching at his stomach and moaning loudly in pain.

Oh, no.

I recognized those symptoms. Jesus, they'd done it. Dan and his friend. I thought they'd wanted to kill Quinn in revenge for killing Dan's wife. But they didn't kill him.

They made him into one of us.

They made the big, bad vampire hunter into the thing that he hated the most in the world—a vampire. It was almost poetic.

Only, as with me, they hadn't finished the job properly. He was in pain. He needed the blood of a full-strength vampire, or he was going to die for real.

"Come on." I shifted my purse to my other shoulder and reached for him again, and this time he didn't have enough energy to pull away. He leaned against me. It was either that or fall to the cement again. Our eyes met.

"I hate you," he said.

"There's that charm I remember. Come on, I know that's just the pain talking."

"Leave me. I want to die. I want to get over there."

I followed his pain-filled gaze. He was looking over at Clancy's. Filled with his beer-drinking, vampire-killing buddies.

"You think they're going to help you out?"

"No." His voice was low and deadly. "They'll kill me. Put me out of my misery."

"Well, it's just your dumb luck that you ran into me, huh? Because I'm not planning on letting you die."

However, as I half supported him, half carried him back through the doors of Midnight Eclipse, I figured that I should be more concerned about myself. As soon as Thierry saw what the cat dragged in, I figured he might kill me instead.

Chapter 10

Less than five minutes after I'd sworn never to step foot inside Midnight Eclipse again, I was back for more. And this time I'd brought a date.

Quinn had stopped being a dick for the time being. He was too busy dealing with the pain. It was almost a blessing. I quickly made my way through the tanning salon, then pushed the black door to the club open with my foot and half dragged Quinn inside with me past the fake potted palm tree.

George ran over to us. "Oh, my God! What is this? Another hunter attack?"

"Nope." I pushed Quinn toward George so I didn't fall over from bearing his weight for another minute. "Vamp attack."

George frowned as he closely eyed Quinn's neck wound. "Did someone order takeout?"

"He's a victim, not a snack, you dope. And please don't tell me you're serious."

He shrugged. "He looks tasty. I can't help it."

"Where's Thierry?"

When I turned around, my face bopped off Thierry's silk-covered chest. Hadn't even heard him approach. I took a step back from him and tried to look composed.

"What is going on now, Sarah?" he asked wearily.

I nodded toward Quinn. "Vampire attack. They turned him, but he's in major pain."

Thierry eyed Quinn, and I couldn't get any sense of what he was thinking, since his expression was the usual controlled blank one that seemed to be his trademark. "And why did you bring him here?"

"Because you can help him, like you helped me."

Thierry's gaze moved to George, who was studying Quinn as if he were the catch of the day. "Take him to my office."

George opened his mouth to protest, but then closed it. He grabbed Quinn and effortlessly swung him over his shoulder, as if he weighed next to nothing, then strode through the club.

I smiled. "So you'll help him?"

"No." Thierry didn't look at me. He went to sit back down at his nearby booth. "But it would be distracting for the customers to let him die out here."

A rise of anger flooded my body. "You're not going to help him?"

"No."

I gritted my teeth and tried to breathe normally. "You're an asshole."

He stood up and was in my face in one smooth motion. His hands were balled into tight fists. "No one speaks to me as you do. Do you have any idea who I am?"

"Yes. An asshole. I thought I just said that."

I turned away from him with a dismissive flick of my hand and tried to walk as calmly as possible to the office.

George had put Quinn onto the sofa. It was sure getting a lot of action today. Quinn was writhing and clutching his stomach.

Zelda appeared at the doorway to see what the racket was all about.

"Come on," I said to them. "Somebody help him."

George shook his head. "No way."

Zelda just shrugged. "Sorry, but the boss says no."

I felt my face flush in anger. Dammit, did I have to do everything myself? I opened my purse. I didn't need anybody's help. The bottles of newbie special were waiting there, looking pink and innocent at the bottom of my bag. I pulled one out, unscrewed the cap, and approached Quinn.

Thierry appeared behind Zelda. He raised an eyebrow at me as I knelt, like Florence Nightingale, next to the sofa.

I raised a hand in his direction. "Don't try to stop me."

"Wouldn't dream of it," he said. "Please go right ahead. Don't let me interrupt."

Good.

"Here." I pushed the bottle at Quinn. "Drink this."

He moved his face in the opposite direction and pushed at me weakly.

I frowned and poked him in the shoulder. "Do you want to die?"

"Yes." It was more of a moan than a word.

When I was a little girl, my family had a Labrador retriever. I'd named him Princess. I don't think he'd ever gotten over the unfortunate name, being a relatively macho dog, but what can I say? Little girls call things pretty names. Anyhow, Princess got sick once, and we had to give him three pills a day to cure the infection. We tried to trick him by hiding the pills in his food or wrapping them in cheese. But Princess would have nothing to do with that. He *knew*. After trying time and time again to get him to take the pills in a pleasant manner, my mother finally did what she had to do. After all, it was for his own good.

I thought I'd try a variation with Quinn.

I pinched his nose shut.

"Hey!" he protested and batted my hand away.

He was weak. I could handle him. I glanced over at the doorway. Thierry looked almost amused by my actions. I gave him a dirty look.

Then I climbed onto the sofa—pulling my skirt up high enough to be able to maneuver properly—and straddled Quinn's chest to trap his arms under my knees.

"What are you doing?" The pain in his voice wasn't hiding his surprise very well.

"Treating you like the bad dog you are," I said, and then pinched his nose shut.

I put the bottle of diluted blood against his lips and held on.

He thrashed around a bit, but I had him pinned pretty good. In fact, after a moment I almost felt as if I should be charging our audience for the show. It had been a lot different with Princess. My father pried his mouth open and my mother pitched the pill to the back of his throat. Nice and easy. Not like "Rodeo Quinn at the Midnight

Eclipse." Hey, that sounded like it could be a porno movie.

Finally Quinn opened his mouth to breathe and he choked against the water, but not before I managed to get quite a bit down his throat. I smiled at the small victory and lost my concentration for a split second.

His left arm came loose from under me and he sat up. I lost my balance and slid backward off the sofa, my legs flailing in the air. He had the water bottle in his hand now. I thought he was going to throw it away, but he tipped it back and finished drinking it down.

I straightened out my borrowed black skirt and slowly got to my feet.

"See?" I informed the onlookers. "*Exactly* like I'd planned it."

Thierry came fully into the room. "How long has he gone?"

"What?"

"When was he turned?"

"Um, it was this afternoon when he was attacked. Just before I got here."

Thierry nodded. "I see."

"You see what?"

Quinn threw the empty water bottle away as if he'd just realized he was licking a spider. "Disgusting monsters," he snarled as he got to his feet. "I want no part of your evil world."

I tried to smile. "Good to see that you're back to normal. Why don't you sit down and rest for a minute?"

"I need to find my father." He made for the door, but Thierry stepped into his path. "Out of my way, vampire."

"Yes, I thought I'd recognized you. You're one of the hunters. I saw you from afar the other night."

"That's where I suggest you stay. Far away from me. Now let me out of here."

Thierry crossed his arms but didn't budge. "So you can inform your friends of where we are? I don't think so. Besides, I doubt that you'd get very far in your condition."

"My condition?" Quinn frowned. "I feel fine now."

"More than eight hours with no intervention? We shall see." Thierry stepped aside.

Quinn blinked, uncertain about what to do, then managed to compose himself. He walked confidently as far as the door and then screamed and hunched over while he clutched at the door frame.

I made a move to go to his side, but Thierry put his arm out to stop me.

Quinn clawed at his stomach as he slid down to the floor. "No," he managed. "Not again."

"What's going on?" I asked Thierry. "I gave him the blood already."

Thierry just stood there in front of me. He turned, with the barest motion of his head, to George and Zelda. They turned and left, closing the door behind them.

I grabbed his sleeve to force him to look at me. "Come on. Tell me what's happening."

He sighed and extracted his sleeve from my fist. "He has gone at least eight hours. A mild blood cocktail will not rouse him out of this."

I felt confused by what he was saying, and then I remembered. At his townhome . . . he'd said something about vampire toxins. Like a poison in your bloodstream that needed to be counteracted by the blood of your sire as soon as possible, or—

Death. A horrible, pain-filled death that could take hours.

My bottles of newbie special couldn't compete with that.

I felt panic clutch at my chest as I watched Quinn suffer. "What can we do?"

"We do nothing, Sarah. He is a vampire hunter. He kills our kind without a moment of mercy. Do you really wish to help him?"

My entire body was clenched as tightly as my fists. "I can't just stand here and watch him die."

"Then leave."

"Thierry, *please*. Do something. What does he need?"

"He needs the blood of a strong vampire. A lot of it."

I looked at Quinn, then back at him. "*Your* blood."

He didn't answer.

"Thierry. *Please* help Quinn."

"He doesn't deserve your misplaced compassion."

I didn't have a response to that. Or did I? Quinn was one of the bad guys. I got that. But I'd seen something in him before—something that wasn't so bad. He didn't like what he did. What he was. If not for his father's tight grasp on his life, I wondered if he'd even be a hunter at all.

"I know," I finally said. "I know all of that. But please help him, anyhow."

Thierry walked to his desk slowly and then stood there, staring at me for a full minute. "We would need to keep him here until we are sure he'll not give away our location."

I nodded. "Of course."

"If I do this, you must promise to do something for me."

Quinn moaned in agony, and I glanced at him before returning my attention to Thierry.

"Okay. Anything. What is it?"

His eyes flashed at me. "Later. All I need now is your promise to help me."

"I promise."

The knife was suddenly in his hand again. I hadn't even seen him reach for it. Quinn watched him approach, his features contorted with pain. When he glimpsed the knife, I saw fear race through his eyes. He murmured something, but I couldn't hear it. He tried to back away, but he was already pressed against the wall as far as he could go.

Thierry slashed his left forearm in one quick swipe. He tossed the knife to the side and pressed his arm against Quinn's mouth. "Drink, hunter."

I watched in silence as the last ounce of fight went out of Quinn. Finally it was too much, and his body went limp. All except his hands, which clutched at Thierry's arm like a baby with a bottle. After five minutes Thierry pulled his arm away and helped Quinn over to the sofa. He fell asleep instantly.

Thierry picked up the knife from the floor and left the room without glancing at me. I followed him out into the club.

"Thank you for doing that," I called after him.

"He'll sleep for a while, I think. He won't be happy when he wakens."

"Yeah, he doesn't seem like much of a morning person."

He turned to look me directly in the eyes. "If you've endangered the people who look at this place as a refuge, I will not be pleased."

I swallowed. "I know."

"Go home now, Sarah. Rest."

"Okay." I turned to leave. "Oh, so what did I just agree to, anyhow? What do you want my help with?"

Thierry settled back into his booth and took a sip from his glass of cranberry juice. "When the hunters have moved on to their next city, and when I'm sure that you will be safe, you will assist me in ending my existence once and for all."

I took a moment to let his words sink in before I freaked out.

"You want me to help you kill yourself?" I sputtered. Maybe I'd heard him wrong.

He stared at me. "That is correct."

I sat down heavily. My face and hands felt cold. "Have you ever thought about going to see a therapist? Maybe try some kind of antidepression medication?"

He smiled, but it didn't reach his eyes. "I have given this matter much thought, Sarah. My existence has simply ceased to mean anything to me anymore. There is no longer anything to keep me here. Being what I am, I was not able to live a normal life and die of natural causes; therefore, I must choose the proper time for myself. That time is now."

"And on the bridge—"

"On the bridge I was considering my limited options more than anything. Obviously, I was well aware that the fall would do nothing. The wooden stake in my pocket was another thing."

"Oh, that was a stake?" I said. "I thought you were just happy to see me."

He frowned.

"I'm kidding." I bit my bottom lip nervously. "I didn't even know you had one on you that night. Sorry. Humor at inappropriate times, that's me."

"So you will help me?"

I took a deep breath. "I don't like it at all, but I did promise to help with whatever it is you need."

That was as far away from a yes as I could get at the moment. How could he want to die? He had everything any man would want. Long life, good looks, a thriving business . . . a hot chick across the table from him. Hmmm. Well, three out of four ain't bad.

"We will discuss this more at a later time," he said. "For now, get some sleep. I will do what I can to look after your friend."

"His name is Quinn, and he's more of a passing acquaintance, really." I looked around the busy club for a moment. "Fine, I'll go, but I'll be back first thing in the morning to make sure everything's okay."

He raised an eyebrow. "Do you think it will be?"

I bit my bottom lip again and looked away. "I'll bring donuts."

Chapter 11

First thing in the morning ended up being nine-forty-five. The alarm didn't go off. I know—excuses, excuses.

I'd slept so soundly that I hadn't even heard the phone ring. There were two messages on my voice mail at home, both from my mother. She wanted to know details about my travel plans for my cousin Missy's wedding. When I was showing up, if I was bringing a date, and that she'd made my favorite chocolate-chip cookies for my arrival.

Tomorrow.

I almost died when I remembered that little detail. How time flies when you're being hunted within an inch of your newly immortal life. I'd booked three days off work, not that that was an issue anymore. In twenty-four hours I was supposed to be on my merry way three hours north of Toronto to my hometown and the site of my cousin's second wedding. I was one of the bridesmaids. I wondered if they'd believe I had the flu.

Or maybe I could just tell them the truth. I'd been bled nearly dry and made into a creature of the night, a bloodsucking monster who barely had a reflection any-more. I wondered if that meant I wouldn't show up in the wedding photos. Or was it just a mirror thing? I should probably figure that out before I went anywhere.

I had to get out of going. There was no other way. To be a bridesmaid in my current condition would be wrong on too many levels to list. I'd have to think about what I'd say later, though. Right now I had to deal with the Quinn situation.

I swung past Tim Hortons on the way back to Mid-night Eclipse to buy a dozen donuts. I used to love donuts, but now that I seemed to be on a strictly liquid diet, their sweet, carb-filled aroma didn't make me want to gorge myself on the first dozen and buy a second dozen to cover up my binge. Not that that had ever hap-pened before. *Right.*

Strawberry-filled seemed to be a pretty good choice for your average pastry-eating vampire. Red stuff in the middle and all that.

The taxi dropped me off in front of the tanning salon. I'd decided to take only taxis everywhere now, as long as I could afford it. Walking the streets alone, even in the blinding broad daylight, was making me more nervous with every passing day.

The front door was locked, so I went around to the back. I was surprised to see George leaning against the wall outside, wearing very dark sunglasses that mirrored my own, and passionately smoking a cigarette. There were many butts strewn on the ground by his feet.

"You're still here?" I said. "Don't tell me you never left last night."

I couldn't see his eyes, but the expression on the rest

of his face wasn't pleasant. "Oh, you're back. Thanks so much for leaving us with that lunatic."

"Lunatic? Quinn? What did he do?"

"The real question is, what *didn't* he do?"

I shoved the box of donuts at George and pulled the door open all the way. I immediately heard banging—a loud, steady noise, as if somebody were playing around with a battering ram.

A tired-looking Zelda approached me. "Thank God you're finally here. He's been asking for you. Well, maybe *yelling* would be a better word."

"Wonderful," I said sarcastically. "Where's Thierry?"

"I don't know, but he wanted me to give you this." Zelda grabbed my hand and placed a large, heavy silver gun with a black handle in it. *A gun!* I'd never even held one before.

"What the hell is this for?" I sputtered.

"For protection."

"What do I look like? Dirty Harry?"

She walked wearily behind the bar, poured herself a shot of blood from what looked to be her personal flask, and drank it down. "I like you, Sarah. I really do. But you're the one who brought him here and then left. It's your turn to deal with him now. I've had it."

She grabbed her blue cloth coat from behind the bar, threw it over her shoulders, and left the club through the back door.

I swallowed heavily. Oh well, at least George was still there for support.

"I'm gonna take off, too," George said as he poked his head through the door, cigarette dangling from his lips.

I ran to the door before it closed and grabbed him by his nearly see-through white shirt and pulled him roughly back inside.

"Oh, no, you're not." I shook him by his shoulders. "You're not leaving me here all alone."

The cigarette was knocked from his lips and pinged off my thigh to the floor.

He blinked. "You're kind of sexy when you're all dominant and stuff."

"Does that mean you're going to stay?"

"Will you beat me up if I don't?" He grinned at me.

"Probably."

"Ooo."

Behind us there was a loud banging coming from Thierry's office. Gee, I wonder who that was?

"Sarah!" Quinn's voice was hoarse as if he'd been yelling all night long. "Let me out of here right now!"

I turned back to George. "Why hasn't he just busted out of there by now?"

"Reinforced door. It's stronger than it looks. Kind of like you."

"George, compliments will get you anywhere," I said. "Too bad about the gay thing."

I held the gun at my side like I'd seen cops do on television and walked toward the office. I knocked lightly.

"Quinn?"

The replying *bang* sounded like Quinn had thrown his entire body at the door, shoulder first. "Let me the hell out of here!"

"Okay, you realize that probably isn't going to happen, right?"

"Let me out now!"

I glanced at George, then back at the door. "Did you go deaf when you got bitten? Listen, nobody trusts you, especially me. If we let you out of there, you'll tell your friends and then we'll all be dead."

It made a lot more sense to me now in the harsh light of day. Maybe I'd made a huge mistake by bringing Quinn back to the club. Uh, *maybe*? Okay, I'd definitely made a mistake, I'll admit it. I didn't deal well with violence, death, and other nasty things. In fact, I normally didn't have to deal with those things at all. I guess my brain shut off its commonsense part last night and I'd been running on pure stupidity. Didn't make me a bad vampire, it just made me more likely to get dead.

But Quinn was my responsibility now, whether I liked it or not.

"Okay, Quinn, why don't you take one huge chill pill? I want to talk to you, face-to-face."

I waited for a response, but there was nothing.

"Just so you know," I continued, trying to sound as strong and confident as the commercials for my underarm deodorant said I should feel, "I have a gun. A big one. I've used it before, and I don't have a problem putting a big, gaping hole through your sorry ass if you give me any problems."

I glanced at George. He nodded with approval and even gave me a big thumbs-up.

Again I waited for a response from Quinn. Finally he said, "Fine. Come on in and we'll have a nice chat."

Why was I finding his sincerity so hard to swallow? Oh, it could be because of the extremely insincere tone of his voice.

I clutched the gun tighter. It was starting to get heavy.

"It's an automatic," George whispered. "All you have to do is point and shoot."

"Just like a camera," I said. "Listen, George, if things go wrong in there, can you tell Thierry that I'm sorry for calling him an asshole last night?"

His eyes widened. "You called him an asshole? You are *so* my hero."

I shrugged, then turned back toward the office. "Okay, Quinn," I said louder. "Move away from the door." Then added, "Or else."

George slipped a key into the lock and turned it. I tensed, ready to aim quickly. I'd shoot for the legs if I had to. Could bullets kill vampires? I didn't know for sure, although it was probably a safe bet that they'd hurt like hell.

I turned the knob and pushed the door open a fraction so I could peer inside. Quinn was now seated on the sofa, his hands clasped, head lowered. It looked like he was praying.

I took a step inside and George quickly closed the door behind me. I heard the lock click and my stomach sank. *Thanks a lot,* I thought. *Throw me in with the lions, why don't you?*

Quinn raised his head slowly, until he was staring directly into my eyes. "So here we are," he said drily. "Let's talk."

"How are you doing?"

"Great. Just great."

He stared at the gun. I raised it higher so it was pointed directly at him.

"Why do I find it hard to believe that you've ever fired a gun before?" he asked.

"Because you're a male chauvinist?"

"You don't need it. I'm not going to try anything."

"Sure. Why wouldn't I believe you? You've been so friendly before this."

He looked around. "Can I get out of here?"

"Nope."

"Why not?"

I shrugged at him. "I just want to be greedy and keep you all to myself. It's your charm. You've won me over."

He blinked at me.

I shook my head. "I'm being sarcastic."

Quinn looked down at the floor. "Can I ask you one question?"

"Ask away."

"At the bar the other night, were you planning on killing me?"

"Pardon me?" I lowered the gun a bit.

"Biting me. Making me into a vampire," he clarified.

"No." I almost laughed. "Why would you think something like that?"

"Because that's what vampires do. Bite people."

"I haven't bitten anyone yet, and I'm not planning on starting anytime soon. Do the words 'gross' and 'unhygienic' mean anything to you?"

He frowned. "You seemed so normal. I still can't believe I had no idea what you were. Are."

"Touché."

"So, what were you doing in there—in Clancy's—the other night?"

"You probably wouldn't believe me if I said I only wanted to have a drink."

"Probably not. But what did I have to do with any-thing?"

I rolled my eyes. "Wow, self-centered much? Hate to burst your bubble, buddy, but I wasn't out to get you, if that's what you think. I felt like a drink, so I had a drink. I saw a cute guy at the end of the bar, so I flirted with the cute guy."

"Cute guy?" He raised his eyebrows.

I felt an immediate flush rise in my cheeks. "I think we're getting off topic here. This is supposed to be our little chat about why you can't kill all of us."

"You thought I was cute?"

"Trust me, I'm over it now. You've been a royal pain in my ass ever since I met you, so that takes a bit away from the whole package."

"So, that man, the tall one dressed in black, is he your boyfriend?"

"Thierry's a boy and he's a friend. But not in the way you might think. What difference does that make?"

Quinn stood up. I took a step back and raised the gun, which I'd lowered almost all the way down to the floor.

"I've had a lot of time in here to think things through," he said.

I felt every muscle in my body tense as he took an-other step nearer to me. "Why don't you sit back down? It's a comfy couch."

He took a third step toward me. I didn't want to shoot him, but it was feeling as if it might be easier and easier the nearer he got to me.

He stopped then and sighed. "Look, Sarah, I know that if it wasn't for your help, I would have died last night."

"And?"

"And I know you're different from the rest of them."

"The rest of who?"

"The vampires."

"Hate to break it to you, but you're a vampire now, too."

A flash of pain went through his eyes, but it wasn't physical pain this time, that much I could tell. "I know. But I don't feel any different than when I was normal."

"See? I tried to tell you."

"But . . . I am different now. I have to be." His voice was sad. "I just can't be the same thing that killed my mother. I can't be an evil, bloodsucking, dead thing."

He lowered his head then and began to sob very quietly. The way men sob. Quiet, dry, and as discreet as possible. If I hadn't been standing right in front of him, I might have missed the signs.

I swallowed hard, but didn't put the gun down. "Quinn, it's not true. You're not like that. I'm not like that."

"Dead things," he said. "We're disgusting dead things."

"No, we're not." I closed the space between us, grabbed his hand, and thrust it against my chest so he could feel the steady beat of my heart. Immediately my heart increased to an embarrassed pounding as I realized I'd just forced him to touch my boob. I let go of him, but his hand didn't move away. His breath was ragged as he lifted his gaze to meet mine.

"You're right," he said. "Definitely not dead."

He leaned toward me with his hand still pressed warmly against my chest. I felt something tighten inside me as I stared into his intense blue eyes—it might have been desire or need or want. I didn't know. All I knew was he was so cute and vulnerable and deadly. And I was going to kiss him. I really was.

The gun dropped to the floor as I reached for him.

I felt a hand clamp down on my shoulder and I was lurched back a few feet out of arm's reach of Quinn.

"What the hell?" I turned around.

Thierry stood behind me, looking very unhappy. He turned his gaze to Quinn and pushed him up against the wall behind the desk, knocking the wind out of him.

"Thierry, no!" I yelled. "He wasn't going to hurt me."

Thierry had his hands wrapped around Quinn's neck and had lifted him a few inches off the ground. But he'd heard me. He slowly, very slowly, lowered Quinn back to the ground, where he then sputtered and coughed and sank to the floor in a heap.

"What did you think you were doing coming in here all by yourself?" Thierry said to me. "I've never witnessed such stupidity."

I felt my face redden. "I had it under control."

"Have you forgotten so soon what he is? A hunter. A hunter of your kind. Open your eyes, little girl, or you will not live long enough to reap the benefits of what you now are."

"I *said* I had it under control."

Quinn slowly got to his feet. "I won't say a word to my father or the others, I swear it. I owe both of you my life."

Thierry stared at him. "Words. Only words. I have no assurance that what you say is true."

He shrugged. "Then I don't know what to tell you."

"I will give you something more than words," Thierry said. "I will give you a promise. That if you walk out of here and it leads to danger befalling any of us, any of my customers, my employees, or Sarah herself, then I will hold you responsible."

"I understand—"

"You understand nothing," Thierry snapped. "I will hold you personally responsible. Therefore, anything in your life that you hold dear, any person you have known, any friends, lovers, or family members—I will hunt them all down and destroy them. Words are meaningless unless you have the will to back them up, so you would do well to mark my words, hunter."

Quinn's face had paled considerably, as I was sure mine had, too. Thierry could be a scary man when he wanted to be, that was for sure.

George walked into the room and looked at each of us in turn, ending with Thierry.

"Hey, boss," he said as he lit a cigarette and exhaled the smoke out slowly, "did Sarah really call you an asshole before?"

"George!" I moaned. "Now? You have to bring that up now?"

"Is this a bad time?" He didn't wait for an answer, or for that matter, a response to his first question. "I just figured that since I haven't heard any shooting in here, this might be a good time for me to take off."

"Go," Thierry said to him, but he was staring at me. I knew it even without looking because I could feel a distinct burning sensation on the side of my face.

George smiled and blew me a kiss, then he left.

It was silent for a moment until Thierry spoke again.

"Do we understand each other?" he asked softly.

"Yes, absolutely," I said.

"I was talking to the hunter."

I noticed for the first time since I'd entered the room that the fang marks on Quinn's neck had faded so much that I could barely see them anymore. Thierry's powerful blood at work again. I wondered how soon he'd lose his reflection.

Quinn didn't flinch from Thierry's fierce gaze. "Yes, I think we understand each other just fine."

Thierry studied him for a moment longer. "Then go. I won't try to stop you."

Quinn started for the door, but then turned back to look at me. "I meant what I said. I won't say anything."

I forced a smile and nodded at him. As soon as he was gone, I looked at Thierry.

"Sorry. I know it was stupid."

He sighed. "And yet you did it, anyhow."

"I had the gun you left for me."

"The gun was not meant as artificial courage. It was not so you could come in here and wave it around like you know what you're doing. Besides, the gun is now on the floor."

"Oh." I bent to pick it up and put it gingerly on the top of his desk. He opened the top drawer and placed the gun inside. "So, where were you, anyhow? When I got here, Zelda didn't know where you'd gone."

"There was a crisis at another club."

"So, you own more than this one?"

"Yes. I own three."

"What was the crisis? Did somebody quit on you?"

He slid the drawer closed and sat down at the desk.

"No, a little more serious than that, I'm afraid. Just after midnight last night they were raided by vampire hunters. Nearly everyone was killed, and the club was burned to the ground."

My breath caught in my throat.

"So," he continued, "I'm sure you'll excuse my rude behavior when dealing with your friend, as it was his friends who were responsible for what happened."

I blanched. "Oh, God, Thierry, I'm so sorry."

He shook his head. "I suppose I've been too wrapped up in my own petty worries lately, but this was enough to fully waken me to the dangers around us."

"So you've reconsidered the whole killing-yourself thing?" I asked hopefully.

"No. In fact, it makes me certain that my decision is the right one."

I opened my mouth to argue with him, but he waved me off.

"I wish to be alone for a while, Sarah, if you wouldn't mind."

I nodded solemnly. "No problem. Um, I'll go home, I guess. I've got some stuff I need to take care of." I turned to the door. "Oh, by the way, I'll probably be gone until Wednesday. I'll swing by when I get back."

"Where are you going?"

"I have this family thing to go to."

Yes, it was a sudden change of heart on my part, I'll admit it. But I'd decided the wedding was unavoidable. It would be best for me to go and get it over with. Also, getting out of the city right now sounded like a very good idea.

Well, maybe not to Thierry.

He looked at me with annoyance. "I thought I told you to part ways with your old life. That does not include attending 'family things.' How many dangerous situations do you need to be involved in before you'll do as I say?"

"It's my cousin's wedding in Abottsville. I have to go—everyone's expecting me. I'll part ways immediately after that, I promise." I smiled at him and turned to leave, wondering why I felt guilty.

"No," he said.

"Pardon me?"

He took a deep breath and rubbed his temples before answering. "I said no. You cannot go to this wedding."

I frowned deeply and felt anger rising in my chest. "You can't tell me what to do. I'll go wherever I want."

He was on his feet then, hands clutching the edge of his desk, his expression dark with anger. "Stop acting like a child. You can't go anywhere you want; you can't do anything you want. Not anymore. Your actions of the last day have jeopardized all you see around you. Don't you understand? Going out of the city will mean that I'm unable to protect you, and I have enough to concern myself with here."

I felt my throat closing up, but I wasn't backing down. He couldn't bully me, no matter how scary he got. No way. No how.

"How have you been protecting me holed up in this place planning to kill yourself? Yeah, you've been a lot of help. And sorry for saving Quinn. I guess I can't just turn my back on people dying in the street. I'm funny that way."

"I don't wish to argue with you, Sarah."

"No, you just want me to obey your every command the way everyone else around here does. Well, forget it. Not going to happen." I turned again to leave, but before I could get to the door, he was there, blocking my way. He grabbed me and pulled me closer to him. For a crazy moment I thought he was going to kiss me again.

But he didn't. He just stared down at me while his fingers bit into my upper arms. "If you leave here and ignore my warnings . . ." He paused for a moment. "Don't ever return. You'll be completely on your own." There was no more anger in his voice; it was simply a cold, monotone statement. He released me.

I stared up at him and felt a tear slide down my cheek. I swallowed hard. "That's fine with me." I moved past him and out the open door. I commanded myself not to turn around to look at him—to see if he wore any telltale expression on his face. The anger had left me as quickly as it had come. I felt sick and tired and terribly alone.

Thierry's main problem was that he was too rigid. He was black or white, there was no give-and-take with him.

My problem was that I was exactly the same way.

But what was I supposed to do? Bow my head and say, "Yes, master, whatever you say, master"? Not going to happen.

So that was it. I left Midnight Eclipse through the back door and tried to put his words out of my mind, but they ate at me like hungry termites.

Was I really fooling myself? Was it a mistake to go to the wedding? My hometown was as safe as anywhere I'd ever been. Almost too safe. And I'd be fine, just fine, without the arrogant and demanding Thierry de Benni-coeur in my life. Jerk.

Despite my unease with traveling back to my apartment all alone, I sucked it up and took public transit instead of calling for a taxi. I was in such a bad mood the hunters should be scared of me today. On the way back I stopped at Blockbuster and rented three movies to watch for the rest of the afternoon to take my mind off things. After perusing their selection I decided on the original *Dracula,* with Bela Lugosi; *Interview with the Vampire,* with Tom Cruise; and *Love at First Bite,* with George Hamilton.

The phone was ringing as I pushed open my door. I ran to it, throwing my purse and the DVDs on the kitchen counter. It had to be Thierry, I knew it. He'd apologize for the argument and everything would be okay between us again.

"Hello?" I said breathlessly.

"Sarah! I'm glad you're there."

My shoulders slumped. It was only Amy. It had been twenty-four hours since she'd abandoned me in the food court of the Eaton Centre, just before my little adventure with Quinn began. I hoped she hadn't ended up spending too much money trying to make herself feel better. She was in major credit card debt. But I had my own problems to worry about.

"Amy, about yesterday—"

"Forget it," she cut me off.

"Forget it?"

"Yeah, I think maybe I was totally being unreasonable. It's none of my business if you're seeing a new guy. In fact, I'm completely happy for you."

"You are?"

"Yeah, he's a cutie, too. Quinn, right?"

"Quinn." I felt the sudden stirrings of a migraine. Or maybe it was a brain tumor. "Yeah, that's his name, all right."

"So, how did you two meet, anyhow?"

I tried to think up a good lie, then gave up. It hurt too much to think. "I kind of picked him up at a bar and he hasn't left me alone since."

"That is *so* adorable. Who says you can't meet a great guy in a bar anymore?"

"Actually, I say that."

"Well, silly, I guess you've finally proven yourself wrong. Look, I don't want to keep you; I know you probably have your hands full getting ready for the wedding, but I just wanted to call to say thanks."

"Thanks? What for?"

She giggled. "When I left you two lovebirds alone yesterday, I went off to feel sorry for myself and ended up meeting a fantastic guy I never would have met if I'd spent the afternoon with you. And I bought the coolest new shoes. Wait till you see them."

"Oh," I said with surprise. Well, not that much surprise. This was Amy we were talking about here. "Well, that's great. The guy thing, that is. What's he like?"

She took a deep breath before she started gushing. "Well, he's sexy as hell for one thing. He's new in town, so maybe it's totally fate. I think he might be *the one*. You would love him. In fact, I'm thinking that when you get back from the wedding, maybe you and Quinn and Peter and me can get together for a double date?"

I didn't answer for a moment.

"Sarah?" Amy asked. "Are you still there?"

"Yeah, I'm here."

"So? A double date? How much fun would that be?"

I nodded, mostly from imagining how much fun that would *not* be. "Yeah, superfun."

"*Major* superfun. Why don't you give me a call the moment you get back and we'll set something up?"

"Okay, I promise." I was crossing my fingers. "Oh, and, Amy—"

"Yeah?"

"Sorry. Really. I'm just sorry if I made you feel bad yesterday."

She laughed. "Forget it. When do we ever have boyfriends at the same time? It's all good."

I hung up feeling guilty. There was no way I was going to go on that double date. For too many reasons to list. It wouldn't be the first time that week I'd agreed to something I had no intention of following through on. Besides, with Amy's track record, she'd have moved on to her next perfect man by the time I got back.

For the rest of the day I sat on my couch and watched all three movies back-to-back while feeling very sorry for myself. Every few hours I'd have a small sip from the bottles of newbie special Zelda had made for me.

I didn't learn much from the movies. Well, other than the fact that when you're a vampire, you seem to have a need to sink your teeth into any available vein. The thought made me feel a bit ill. There was no way I was doing that. Ever. Cross my heart and hope to . . .

Oh, never mind.

I packed my suitcase and went to bed early. I wanted everything to go smoothly over the next two days. I'd prove once and for all to myself that Thierry was wrong. I could still have a normal life. It would be okay. After the week I'd just had, I wasn't in the mood for any more bad stuff to happen.

But seriously, what could possibly go wrong at a wedding?

Chapter 12

The town of Abottsville is three hours northwest of Toronto. It has a population of just over eight thousand bright and cheery people who pride themselves on their town and their white-picket-fenced homes. In other words, it's hell on earth.

I hot-tailed it out of my hometown just after my eighteenth birthday to go to the university in Toronto— minoring in psychology, majoring in drama. I had big dreams of swiftly becoming a major movie star. But other than landing the lead in a local maxi-pad commercial, my starry-eyed plans fizzled pretty fast.

I'd been in such a hurry to leave home because three weeks before prom, my high-school boyfriend had surprised me by popping the question. His big dream was to take over his family's pharmacy and for me to stay at home and squeeze out four kids before I was twenty-five. Some girls might find that to be the meaning of life, but I wasn't one of them. That had been the end of our relationship. I heard he'd recently won the lottery and moved to Hawaii with a former *Playboy* centerfold. Hindsight's a bitch.

I came back to town every now and then to see my parents, though not as often as I should. The guilty feeling always wore at me about that, but it wasn't as bad as the queasy feeling I got when I passed the sign that declared WELCOME TO ABOTTSVILLE: HOME OF THE LARGEST PUMPKIN IN ONTARIO. I much preferred city living. Give me rush hour, pollution, and overpriced cappuccinos any day, thank you very much.

I'd rented an economy-size car to drive into town for the wedding. Monday was filled with happy-happy, joy-joy family reunions and a highly unpleasant final dress fitting, which only proved that my new liquid "diet" hadn't helped me lose a single pound. So damn unfair.

Bridesmaid's gowns were supposed to be ugly, but the ones Missy had picked out were guaranteed to give me a major case of post-traumatic dress disorder. It consisted of a short, shiny skirt, a wide, sparkly waistband, and a low-cut—very low—satin top. The chosen color was called "eggplant passion." I felt like a showgirl in a sleazy Las Vegas production. My cousin had obviously been dropping some serious acid.

But it was her day, after all, and who was I to complain? The other two girls who were in the wedding party looked more miserable than I did. At least I had the coolest shoes since I'd insisted on wearing my own "special occasion only" silver mules.

So, other than the dress, the day I'd spent in the town of my youth had been uneventful. I was proving to myself that I could pass quite nicely as 100 percent human. And stupid Thierry wanted me to part ways with my old life. I was proving that I could leave things exactly the same, and nobody would ever know the difference.

I stared at my barely there reflection as I tried to touch up my lip gloss in the church's powder room.

I was totally lying.

The last day had been a nightmare of epic proportions. I wasn't even exaggerating. All I wanted was to get the wedding over with so I could jump into my rented Toyota Echo and leave town.

Why was it so bad? Let me count the ways. First, the whole reflection thing. It's surprising how many reflective surfaces there are in the world. If anyone saw that I didn't have a reflection, how was I supposed to explain it? So far I'd chosen avoidance as the best course of action.

Second, at the rehearsal dinner I felt obligated to choke down some fettuccine Alfredo and garlic bread. I then learned by throwing up in the floral centerpiece what happens when certain vampires eat solid food.

Don't even get me started on when cousin Jeremy nicked his finger on a steak knife. We almost had a repeat performance of the Ms. Saunders incident. Thank God I found a raw steak to suck on. It wasn't pretty.

Now everyone was treating me very cautiously, like I was two minutes away from falling off the narrow edge of sanity, or something. They weren't far off.

On a more positive note, thanks to a rogue digital camera at the wedding rehearsal, I learned I did show up just fine and dandy in photographs. I just didn't photograph very well. No big surprise there.

"Sarah!" Missy wailed for me from the back of the church. I jumped and put my current glass of champagne down on the powder room counter before making my way over to the dressing room.

"What's wrong?" I tried to force myself to sound concerned. This was not the first time my cousin had been in tears since I'd arrived. She was either very emotional or very needy. Probably both.

Join the club.

She let out a long, shaky sigh. "I don't know if I'm doing the right thing."

I glanced over my shoulder to see if I could pass the proverbial baton to someone else. But we were all alone in the dressing room. Well, except for the two hundred people currently seated in the church next to us. Which included the decidedly creepy Reverend Micholby. Last night at the rehearsal dinner all he did was give me the evil eye. Or maybe it was the holy eye, since he was a reverend. Whatever.

"Come on." I plucked a tissue out of a nearby box and handed it to her. "It'll be fine."

"Will it? I don't know. I don't know if I'm ready."

"Richard's a great guy. You two are going to have a fabulous life together."

She sniffed. "We're very different, you know. So different, it's kind of scary."

"Hey, *vive la différence*. Opposites attract, and all that."

"But what if he gets bored with me in fifty years? When I'm old?"

"He won't. You two are meant to be together. It'll be fine. You want some champagne?" I poured her a glass. She took it from me and downed it in one gulp. I took a swig myself, right out of the bottle. The free booze was helping, although not as much as it used to.

"He is great, isn't he?" she asked.

I wiped my mouth, trying not to smear my lip gloss. "Yeah, really great."

Truth be told, I'd only spoken to Richard, the groom, for five minutes at the rehearsal dinner. He was a balding, forty-something accountant who drove a blue Volvo. He seemed fine, but I wasn't the one who was marrying him.

Missy was in her early thirties. She'd been married once, twelve years before, but it hadn't worked out due to her husband's other two wives. She'd spent the interim yo-yo dieting and collecting cats. She met Richard when he did her taxes last year. Yup, romance didn't get much more intense than that in Abottsville.

The first notes of Canon in D started up outside the dressing room in the church. That was the cue for yours truly. Time to show off this bitchin' dress.

"Saved by the Pachelbel," I said. "Get it? Pachel-*bell*?" Missy looked at me blankly. "Oh, never mind. They're playing our song."

Missy smiled and stood up.

"Thanks for being there for me, Sarah. I sure wish you could come to town more often." She hugged me lightly enough not to affect our makeup.

"Yeah, me too," I lied, and forced a big smile as I leaned back from her.

She frowned at me. "Your teeth look a little funny."

"They do?" I ran my tongue along them and felt pain shoot through my mouth. My heart sank. There they were. They'd finally sprouted, like tiny little needles, ahead of schedule because of Thierry's superstrength blood.

My fangs. Terrific.

"Um"—I tried to talk without opening my mouth very wide—"I used those Whitestrips things, that's all. I guess they're just whiter than normal. Anyhow, show-time. See you up at the front."

I scrambled away from her just as my uncle appeared in the doorway to accompany Missy down the aisle. I walked out to my fellow eggplant-clad bridesmaids. They were pulling at the hems of their dresses, but the more they pulled at the bottoms, the more cleavage popped out at the top.

"This sucks," a girl named Lana said before she began her walk down the aisle. She was first. I was sec-ond. The maid of honor, who looked ready to break out in hives, came behind me. Then it was Missy all the way.

"Breathe," I told Susan, the maid of honor. "You'll be fine."

"I feel like a big, fat whore," she said.

I didn't have a response for that, so I started down the aisle, tightly clutching my little bouquet of pink and white carnations.

Okay, I finally had my vampire fangs. Just another little thing to deal with. No problem at all. *Nada prob-lemo*.

Who was I kidding? This sucked. The Whitestrips tooth excuse was weak at best. Maybe no one would no-tice. I'd have to spend the rest of the day smiling as little as possible.

I glanced over to where my parents were sitting. I had to talk to them. Explain that I would be parting ways and wouldn't be around much in the future. That I was moving to Australia on business. They'd accept that without asking too many questions, wouldn't they?

They both beamed back at me from their pew, looking very happy. I frowned slightly. Almost too happy. What would make them look that damn happy today?

As I moved into a better angle to see them, I stopped walking right there in the middle of the aisle. My bouquet fell to the floor. Seated in between my parents, wearing dark sunglasses and a bored expression, was George.

"Holy shit!" I said aloud, and heard a gasp go through the congregation. I bent over and snatched up the bouquet, then practically ran the rest of the way up the aisle to the front of the church.

Most of the people gathered were now recovering from the shock of hearing me use the *S*-word in a house of God. I was recovering from the shock of seeing a gay, table-waiting vampire sitting thigh to thigh with my mother. My mother, however, didn't appear to mind at all.

The three-piece orchestra of high-school band students started up their mostly unrehearsed version of "Here Comes the Bride," and Missy made her way down the aisle. I couldn't take my eyes off George.

I mouthed to him, "What are you doing here?"

He seemed to be quite busy, intently staring at a tapestry of JESUS LOVES ME and trying as hard as possible to ignore me.

A million things raced through my mind. Had something gone horribly wrong? Did Midnight Eclipse get torched? Did Thierry kill Quinn while I was gone? Did

Barry find a personality? I couldn't wait for the service to be over. In fact, I wanted to say "hurry the hell up" while Missy and Richard stumbled through their vows, but I managed to restrain myself. Just barely.

As soon as the service was over, the wedding party was swept off for some photos in the painfully bright and chilly outdoors before the reception. I didn't want to be there. All I wanted was to get to George and find out what was going on. The only thing I remember about the photos was that the photographer and I got into a fight about removing my sunglasses. He lost.

The reception was held in a banquet room at the Abottsville Golf Course. I stood uncomfortably in the receiving line, shaking a multitude of sweaty hands and trying to smile without showing off my new fangs to two hundred tired and hungry people. My father finally made his way down the line to me. He looked quite dashing, if I do say so myself. His gray suit and teal tie were impeccable, although I was pretty sure the flower he wore on his lapel was bought at the nearest joke store. One of those plastic flowers that squirted water as a funny gag. I eyed it warily.

"Sweetheart," he said and gave me a big hug. "You look fantastic. If anyone could manage to wear that dress properly, it would be you."

I gave him a closed-mouth smile. "Thanks, Dad."

"I think your mother has a new boyfriend." He winked at me. "Should I be jealous?" With that, he moved on to the next bridesmaid.

My mother had George's arm clutched in her own as they shifted along the line toward me. He looked as if he would have preferred to be anywhere else. Him and me both.

"Look who I found," my mother said with a chipper smile firmly on her face. "George."

I gave George a quizzical yet dirty look. "And how do you know George?" I asked her.

"I don't, silly." She patted his arm affectionately. "At least I didn't until today. I guess this explains your odd behavior and sour mood since you got here."

"Sour mood?"

"You two lovebirds must have had a fight, and he came all the way out here to apologize. I think it's terribly romantic. We found him lurking around outside the church. You didn't even tell me you had a new boyfriend."

Lovebirds, huh? "Mom, you've always been so perceptive."

"It's a gift, dear. Don't worry, your father and I will find a place for him at our table."

She moved on to chat with Susan, who stood uncomfortably next to me.

I glared at George. "Well?"

"Well, what?" He smiled as if it were the most natural thing in the world for him to be standing in front of me at my cousin's wedding. "May I say that you look *fabulous*? That dress is simply to die for."

"You might just die for it if you don't tell me what you're doing here."

He glanced around. "Just here to apologize to my love muffin for our nasty argument earlier. That's all. Darling, please forgive me for what I said."

I took his hand and dug my fingernails into it until he

flinched. "We'll talk more later, *honey.* And you'd better come up with something a little better than that."

He bared his fangs in a half smile, half grimace, and moved on.

Oh, we'd talk all right. Thierry was behind this. I just knew it. He'd sent George to spy on me. There was no other explanation.

I couldn't take it. Both of my lives, my normal one and my vampire one, were falling apart. Neither made sense anymore. I couldn't live like this, on edge and worried all the time that something horrible was going to happen.

When dinner was served, the smell of my untouched chicken Cordon Bleu was making me feel physically ill. I pushed the plate as far away from me as possible and scanned the room for George. There was an empty chair at my parents' table, where he should have been.

I needed some fresh air. Some time to myself where I wasn't surrounded by normal people who, just by their presence, reminded me that I was horribly different now.

Outside, I leaned against the wall of the reception hall and tried to breathe. I sniffed the air, frowned, and turned to my left.

The maid of honor, Susan, had sparked up a cigarette nearby, next to the kitchen entrance.

"You want?" She indicated the pack of smokes.

"You do realize those things are bad for you, right?"

"No way." She inhaled deeply and then blew a few smoke rings into the chilly night air. "I've never heard that before. Well, nobody lives forever, right?"

I bit my bottom lip. "I used to think that."

"Your boyfriend's hot."

I opened my mouth to protest, but then closed it. "Thanks. He thinks so."

"Can you believe these dresses?" Susan shook her head. "Immortalized forever in those damn pictures. I'm going to have to get really drunk to get over this."

"The night is young. And the bar is open."

"Amen to that."

"Don't say amen. You might lure Reverend Micholby out here with us. What's his deal, anyhow?"

She took another long drag off her cigarette. "He's been away for a while. There's a rumor he had a nervous breakdown, or something. This is the first wedding he's done since he got back. I wouldn't worry about it, though. Maybe he's acting weird because of the dresses. He's morally offended by them."

I nodded. "That's probably it. I mean, if I'm morally offended by them, why shouldn't he be?"

We laughed for a moment, and I started to feel a bit better. At least until she started choking on her last inhale. I patted her on her back just as a van screeched to a halt next to us. A harried-looking guy jumped out of the driver's seat and scurried around to the back, opened the doors, and wrestled out a medium-size silver keg. He began rolling it toward the kitchen door.

"Sorry I'm late," he said to us. "I didn't realize this town was so far outside the city. I should have been here hours ago."

"Hey, I don't mind," I said. "What is that, anyhow? Beer?"

"Yeah." He laughed a little. "It's beer. Cute. Can you do me a favor and sign for this? I'm in a major hurry."

I shrugged. "Sure, why not?"

He finished rolling the keg toward the door, then came back to me and pushed a clipboard into my hands. There was a cheap pen attached to it by a piece of black string. He pointed at the last line for me to sign, and I put pen to paper.

Then I froze.

Why was I having the weirdest déjà vu? I looked up at the guy. He did look awfully familiar to me. I glanced down at the logo at the top of the delivery form.

THE BLOOD DELIVERY GUYS. YOU NEED BLOOD? WE DELIVER.

"Something wrong?" Susan asked. "You don't look so good."

I scratched my signature onto the form and pushed it back at him. He smiled at me, the moonlight reflecting off his fangs. He said thanks, then got into his van and drove away.

I felt weak. "I think I'm going back inside now."

"Yeah, me too." She flicked her cigarette butt against a nearby tree. "Now I feel like a beer."

I took my place again at the head table, feeling major stress, and downed a glass of red wine, but it didn't make me feel any better. What was going on? Why were the Blood Delivery Guys out here? Was it George? Did he send them?

Was it somebody's idea of a joke? If it was, I wasn't finding it very funny. Not even slightly.

I eyed my parents' table. Still no sign of George. Where the hell was he?

Dinner was over and dessert was served, a nice-looking chocolate torte—I loved chocolate, but I didn't want a repeat of last night, so I didn't bother touching it.

I had another glass of wine instead. By the amount I'd had, I should be feeling no pain. Instead, I felt like I hadn't been drinking anything more than tap water the entire evening.

After the speeches were given, the deejay started up the music and Missy and Richard had their first dance. Out of the corner of my eye, I saw George enter the reception hall and go to my parents' table to sit down. I beelined toward him and he raised his hands as if he expected me to hit him. I grabbed his wrist and pulled him out of his seat. Reverend Micholby was also seated at my parents' table, and he gave me a cool stare.

"Sarah!" My mother frowned at me. "Perhaps that kind of aggressive behavior is what drove him off in the first place."

I ignored her and directed George out to the lounge area and as far away from the loud music as I could get. After the first song they'd launched into "The Chicken Dance." Normally not something I'd miss, but I'd have to make an exception this one time.

"Where have you been all night?" I poked him in his chest.

"Ow. I've been around. Just checking out the town. Looking for something interesting to do." He shrugged. "Came up empty."

"Okay, George. Talk."

He smiled. "Have I mentioned that you look fabulous?"

"What are you doing here?"

"Is it wrong that I want to support Missy and Richard in their new lives together?" He squinted at me. A wide smile spread across his face. "Do you have your fangs now? Congratulations."

I ignored that. It didn't seem polite to notice a woman's fangs in public. "Did Thierry send you?"

He sat down on a rustic-looking sofa and sighed heavily. "Do you honestly think I'd be in this place if he hadn't?"

"He told me he never wants to see me again."

"He's a hard man to understand. But you know what they say—a hard man is good to find." He grinned.

I was trying to be patient. I really was. "But he didn't come. He sent you to spy on me instead."

"He's super busy. Another club was hit."

"The hunters?" I raised my eyebrows.

George nodded grimly. "Normally, they only pick off the vamps in the open, but this year they're finding our hiding spots, too. I don't know how."

"Thierry sent you to keep an eye on me," I said suspiciously. "To make sure I was okay?"

"Yeah, he likes you."

"So everyone keeps telling me. He sure has a funny way of showing it." I took a deep, slightly shuddery breath and looked at him. "It's been bad, really bad being here, George. I feel like my entire life is falling apart. Don't tell Thierry, but I think he was right. I can't pretend to be normal. Well, not as normal as I used to be, anyhow."

"Why be normal? Normal is boring."

I glanced up as one of Richard's groomsmen emerged from the reception hall. He smiled at me and headed off toward the kitchen.

"He's cute," George said.

"Hello? Focus, George." I frowned at him. "You didn't happen to have a keg of blood sent here, did you?"

"No."

"Seriously. You can tell me if you did. I just signed for it out back."

He shook his head. "Seriously, no, I didn't."

I leaned back in the sofa. "Then I don't get it. Why would they make a delivery all the way out here?"

"Probably for the groom," George said.

I sat bolt upright. *"Excusez-moi?"*

"The groom. He's one of us. Didn't you notice his fangs?"

"I don't inspect the mouth of every person I come across, you know. Besides, fangs are small, hardly noticeable unless you're right up close and personal." I shook my head so hard I felt dizzy. "No way. He's from Abottsville, for Christ's sake. He's a bloody accountant."

"And?"

"And . . . ," I sputtered. "He's not a vampire. No way. Not a chance."

Just then, the groomsman reappeared dragging the silver keg behind him. He disappeared into the reception area after giving me another grin. Staring after him, I had my mouth so wide open that small children might have been tempted to throw things into it. I turned to George.

"And so are his buddies," he said.

Chapter 13

No way." I shook my head. "Richard's not a vampire. Neither are his friends. You're being ridiculous."

George stood up from the sofa. "Whatever. Doesn't matter, I guess."

I grabbed his brown-leather-clad leg and stared up at him. "Of course it matters. This is important. Why would you think something like that, anyhow?"

"Other than the keg of blood he just rolled across the dance floor? I just know. It's a Spidey-sense kind of thing. Since you've got your fangs now, I'm surprised you don't feel it, too."

"Spidey-sense? No. No way."

"Anyhow"—George rolled his eyes—"let's move on, shall we? The boss wants me to escort you personally back to Toronto. So, let's say, noonish tomorrow?"

I stood up, feeling tense—from my ugly purple beaded earrings to my nice silver three-inch mules. "You can't just tell me my cousin married a vampire and then change the subject."

"Why?"

"Because"—I flailed my arms, looking for a reason I could pinpoint—"because he's a vampire, that's why. Missy's a human. Hello? And from what I've gone through in the past day, I can vouch for it being a mondo bad idea. Unless . . ." I put a hand to my mouth to stop a gasp. "Unless Missy's a vampire, too. Is she?"

"She is *so* not a vampire."

I let out a long sigh. Lucky Missy. "Then I need to tell her what she's gotten herself into. The wedding's already happened, but she can always get it annulled." I paused. "I just hope she doesn't end up with more cats because of this."

"Yeah, you go tell her." George sounded as if he couldn't care less. "And I'm going to go dance."

We parted as soon as we walked back into the reception hall. George took over the dance floor, dragging my mother up with him for a rousing rendition of the Macarena, and I scanned the room. Before speaking to Missy, I needed to confront Richard. Find out what the hell he thought he was doing marrying my poor naive cousin. But he was nowhere to be seen. For that matter, neither were his buddies or the newly delivered keg of blood.

I spotted Missy on the dance floor with Lana and Susan. They'd sidled up to George and were flirting madly with him. They beckoned for me to join in, but I gave them the bottoms-up signal to make them think I was looking for another drink.

So, George could sense other vampires, huh? I wondered if I could do it, too, this sensing-vampires thing. I was losing my reflection earlier than normal, thanks to Thierry's extra-caffeinated blood. My fangs had sprouted early, too. Maybe this was the same sort of deal.

Worth a try, anyhow.

I closed my eyes and tried to block out the music and voices around me. I breathed in deeply through my nose, then let it out slowly through my mouth and concentrated as hard as I could.

Then I opened my eyes, walked directly to the tiny coat checkroom just past the bar on the right-hand side of the reception hall, opened the door, and flicked on the light.

Richard and his two buddies looked up at me in surprise. They were seated cross-legged next to a row of coats with the keg in between them. Each held a shot glass.

I raised my eyebrows. Hey, my Spidey-sense worked. Who knew?

"What the hell is going on in here?" I demanded.

"Shhh." Richard grabbed my wrist and pulled me down to the floor. Then he wheeled a rack of coats between us and the door, so we were partially hidden, and got up to flick off the light. My eyes adjusted surprisingly fast to the dimness.

"Drink?" his blond-haired buddy asked—he'd been the one George had thought was cute. He didn't wait for a response and handed me a shot of the strangely appetizing red liquid. All things considered, it sure looked good.

"Well, maybe just one." I wagged my index finger at him. "But then I want to know what the hell is going on here."

The red-haired, pug-nosed friend raised his glass. "To Richard and Missy."

We clinked glasses and drank. I wasn't sure what blood type it was, but it tasted delicious. Then they passed a half-empty bottle of vodka around and all took a drink from it. I waved it off when it was my turn.

"That stuff has no effect on me anymore."

Richard shook his head. "No, it wouldn't normally. Alcohol only gives you a buzz when you use it as a chaser to the blood."

"Oh. Good to know." I grabbed the bottle and took a swig, then passed it back to him. "What the hell is going on in here?"

They eyed one another. "What do you mean?" Richard asked.

"You're a vampire."

"And so are you." He shrugged when I gasped. "Sorry, but it's kind of obvious. The whole raw-steak thing last night was a dead giveaway. So, yeah, I'm a vampire. What's your point?"

What is *my point?* I frowned. The shot of vodka was already making things a bit blurry.

"You're not supposed to mix with humans. It's wrong and dangerous, and many other words I can't think of right now. Bottom line is, you can't be a vampire and live a human life, too. It's just not done."

"And who told you that?"

"A master vampire."

The three of them looked at one another. "Oh, a *master* vampire," "Blond Buddy" said. "I'm sh-sh-shaking."

"Very scary," "Red-Haired Buddy" said, straight-faced. He adjusted his bow tie. "I'm closing my bookstore tomorrow and moving underground with the other monsters."

"There are monsters living underground?" I said, eyes wide.

"Have another shot."

I did. And then another. And then I was feeling no pain whatsoever.

"Look, Sarah, it's great of you to be so concerned for Missy." Richard tipped the vodka bottle back and finished it off. "You're right. It's not easy trying to combine two very dissimilar lives. But sometimes it's worth the effort. Missy's worth it."

I poked him in the shoulder. "And you're not just trying to bite her?"

"Only when she misbehaves." At my look he waved me off, laughing. "Just kidding. Here's the thing, Sarah. Back in the day, me and the guys here used to be college roommates. It was too stressful in the city, dodging the hunters all the time. In a small town like Abottsville, things are quieter, easier to manage. Sure, there's been a few"—he paused to search for the right word—"*incidents* from time to time. But we've made it work."

"Incidents?"

Blond Buddy lit up a cigarette. "There have been a few misguided souls who imagine themselves to be 'vampire slayers.'" He actually made air quotes. "It's that damn television show. With the skinny blond chick. So we keep to ourselves as much as possible. If everyone found out the truth, they might come after us with pitchforks and torches."

"Pitchforks." I snorted with drunken laughter at the

mental image. "That's funny. In a bizarrely scary sort of way."

"So, Sarah, how are you enjoying your new life?" Richard asked.

"Me?" I quieted down and made a sour face. "I think it's safe to say that becoming a vampire is the worst thing that has ever happened to me. In fact, I have a strange desire to throw myself off a bridge."

"That's not good." Red-Haired Buddy shook his head solemnly. "Besides, that would be a total waste, since you're way hot. Even after the whole puking thing last night."

"Gee, thanks."

"You know," Richard said, "if you feel that strongly about it, maybe you should try to find the cure."

I blinked at him. "Huh?"

"The cure."

I got to my feet in a flash and managed to bang my head on a coatrack. I sat back down. "I don't think I heard you right."

Richard sighed. "The cure for vampirism. I've heard some scientists have been working on it in Europe for years now."

A cure? My mind raced. Well, as fast as a mind dulled by blood and vodka could race. Hadn't Zelda mentioned something about a cure? I thought she'd just been kidding around.

"You're serious? There's a cure?"

"It's really just a rumor I've heard here and there, but if you really hate being a vampire so much, you should try checking it out further. Seriously, though, Sarah, give it some time. It's not as bad as you think."

"You guys are great." I leaned over and kissed Richard noisily on the cheek. "Missy's so lucky to have you." I grabbed him around the neck and hugged him as only a drunken woman in a low-cut eggplant-colored dress could do.

"Am I?" Missy said from behind me. I jumped and banged my head against the rack again. I rubbed my now-tender scalp and turned around. Missy was peeking through the mass of coats, watching me drool all over her shiny new husband.

"Missy! Um, this isn't what it looks like."

"That's funny, because it looks like the weekly meeting of Vampires Anonymous is going on in the coat checkroom of my wedding."

I reached up and grabbed her by her pearl necklace to pull her down to the floor next to me. She shrieked and I clamped my hand over her mouth.

"First of all," I said, "shhh! And second of all, that was kind of funny."

She pulled my hand off her mouth, then stood back up, brushing the front of her wedding gown off. "Geez, Sarah, I just wanted you to know I'm almost ready to throw my bouquet. Now I have to go fix my makeup. Thanks a lot."

"Sorry. But this means you know? About"—I pointed at the guys—"you-know-what?"

"Of course I know."

"Don't you care?"

Missy's bottom lip wobbled. "Of course I care. Like I told you before, we're very different, Richard and me. I'm worried that in fifty years when I'm old and he's exactly the same handsome man—"

"Missy, baby," Richard said. "We've discussed this."

She sniffed. "I know."

Richard glanced at me. "I offered to sire her—make her a vampire, too—but she decided against it. I respect her decision, and I'll love her always."

That was so sweet. But I've always been a hopeless romantic. Emphasis on the "hopeless" part.

"And you, cousin of mine"—Missy turned to me—"what in the holy heck happened to you?"

I sighed. "Bad blind date. Looks like I may have eternity to recover from it."

She nodded. "I *knew* it. As soon as you flashed those fangs at me. Teeth-whitening strips, my hiney. Anyhow, let's get this bouquet-throwing thing done. I'm ready to start my honeymoon." She leaned over and kissed Richard. "Eww. Make sure you brush your teeth. You have blood breath."

"Yes, dear."

One by one we exited the coat checkroom, while trying to look as casual as possible. Back in the reception hall the reverend stared at me from the corner of the dance floor. He had a black tote bag over one shoulder. I gave him a big grin, then slapped my hands over my mouth to cover it. *Must remember not to flash the new fangs around.* Talk about an awkward moment. I straightened out my skirt by pulling it down over my knees and nearly had a nipple make an appearance. The reverend blinked and looked away.

I felt nicely drunk from the blood/vodka combo. It felt pretty good. Come to think of it—in my current state at least—this might be the perfect time to "part ways"

with my parents. I figured I had a few minutes before
Missy got back from the bathroom. Why waste them?

Part ways. Get it over with. Break the news to them
that they wouldn't be seeing me for a while. Hopefully,
they wouldn't take it too hard.

I felt a tap on my shoulder and I turned around.

"Sarah," my father said. "Your mother and I are leaving."

"You're leaving *me*?" I yelped. "Why?"

He shrugged. "Too much free white wine. Your
mother's drunk."

"Am not!" my mother slurred from ten feet away at
the table, her coat hanging off her shoulders. Then she
let out a loud hiccup.

"But, Dad, I—"

He chucked me under the chin. "See you later."

"But I—"

Without another word he and my mother . . . parted
ways with *me*. At least for the remainder of the evening,
anyhow. Feeling stunned, I watched them leave the banquet hall. I suddenly felt like an orphan. Like a Little
Vampire Orphan Annie.

"Okay," the deejay announced after Buster Poindex-
ter's "Hot Hot Hot" ended. "May I have all single ladies
on the dance floor now for the bouquet toss?"

I trudged over to the dance floor and glanced at
Missy.

"Whoever catches this will be the next to get married," Missy said. "Isn't this fun?"

I elbowed into position. Missy turned around and,
after psyching out the gathered crowd of ten single
women with two fake throws, launched the bouquet into

the air. It sailed way over our heads and directly into the hands of Reverend Micholby, who was standing directly behind us. He stared at the bouquet for a moment, then dropped it onto the ground in front of him.

Before I could make a comment about him making a lovely future bride, he opened up the black duffel bag he'd been carrying around all evening and pulled out a wooden stake and a large silver cross.

"May I have your attention, please," he said calmly. "It has come to my attention that there are several vampires here. Could you kindly accompany me outside so I can kill you? Now, please?"

I gasped and ducked down in the middle of all the single women. Unfortunately, everyone else immediately cleared the dance floor, and I was left sitting on my butt looking up at the reverend-by-day, vampire-hunter-by-night. Nervous breakdown, my ass.

He stared down at me with cold, determined eyes.

"Very well, we'll start with you."

Missy approached him. "Reverend, what's going on here?"

"Monsters," he said matter-of-factly, as if he were discussing a slightly distasteful item at the buffet table. "That's what's going on. I had a feeling about this one, and when she bared her fangs, I knew I had to do something. I have a sacred duty to keep my town safe from Satan's spawn."

"Satan's spawn?"

Missy laughed but eyed me nervously. "I think you've been watching too many movies. There are no such things as vampires, of course."

The reverend didn't shift his gaze from me and instead shook the cross in my direction. It was a nice cross. Looked like real silver. Didn't bother me at all. It was the sharp stake in his other hand that troubled me.

"She is one," he hissed, pointing at me with the cross. "An evil bloodsucker. There are more, too. I'm sure of it. I will find them and destroy them all."

The hall was completely silent. Nobody was taking the initiative to rush forward to save me. Maybe they all figured that this was an odd little piece of dinner theater.

"I'm not a vampire." My voice was squeaky and strained.

"Silent, evil vixen. Dressed to seduce and kill."

I scrambled to my feet. "This outfit was not my idea, buddy."

"What's going on?" somebody said from the crowd of onlookers.

"He's crazy," I shouted, loud enough for everyone still in the reception hall to hear. "And drunk. Crazy, drunk, and I think he might be high, too."

The reverend took a step toward me, but Missy was still in his way. He pushed her and she cried out as she fell to the floor. Richard ran to her side and pulled her away from danger. The reverend got closer to me, and I kept backing up until I could feel the deejay's table behind me.

All of a sudden, George was at my side. He was supposed to protect me, after all. Damn well took him long enough.

"Sorry." He put an arm around my shoulder. "Nature called."

The reverend took a moment to reassess the situation while he stared daggers at us. Then he raised the stake high above his head and arched it down directly at George.

George let out a high-pitched squeal of pain as he looked down at the stake, which now protruded from his chest. He fell to his knees and smacked his face on the dance floor before rolling onto his back. I was in shock, frozen in place. The reverend then moved close enough to press the silver cross hard against the side of my face.

"Hey!" I yelled. "Stop it."

"Burns, doesn't it, demon?"

"Not really." I gritted my teeth. "But this probably will."

I brought my knee up sharply against his groin. He screamed, doubled over, and I heard the cross clatter to the dance floor. I rubbed my bruised cheek and collapsed to my knees next to George. I foggily registered that everyone at the reception was collectively screaming and running for the exits.

"George!" I pushed his long hair off his forehead. "George, sweetie. Are you okay? Talk to me!"

George stared glassy-eyed at the ceiling. "Ow."

I forced myself to look at the stake. It was surrounded by a dark red, wet patch on his cream-colored shirt. I studied it for a moment. "The stake isn't in your heart; it's mostly in your shoulder. You have to be staked in your heart to die, right? You must have moved just in time." I let out the breath I hadn't even known I'd been holding. "That's good, right?"

George turned his head and blinked up at me. "Ow."

I shook my head. "Your shirt is definitely ruined, though. Was it real silk?"

He shifted his gaze to behind me, then made an attempt to get up but failed. "Ow," he said again and pointed weakly.

I turned. The reverend was rising to his feet with an expression of unadulterated hatred on his face. Crushed groin or no crushed groin, he was going to tear me apart with his bare hands. And by what I could see of the reception hall, there was nobody left to help me.

With one hand against George, I held the other up to try to stop him as he staggered toward me. Good luck there.

I heard a loud crash and the reverend stopped in his tracks. His eyes glazed over and he fell to his knees, then face forward down to the floor, his head ending up mere inches away from me. I looked up with wide eyes.

Thierry stood behind him, holding the remnants of a broken wine bottle.

George looked up at him. "Ow."

I couldn't speak, so I just stared at him with probably a very stupid look on my face.

"So"—Thierry turned around to glance at the empty reception hall—"was it a nice wedding?"

I swallowed. "Lovely. You should have been here."

He crouched down and raised a dark eyebrow at George. "Brace yourself. This will hurt."

George was about to protest, but Thierry gripped the wooden stake and pulled it straight out of his chest before he could. It made a sickening *smuck* sound.

George shouted out some swearwords I'd actually never heard before. I added them to my vocabulary as I watched the blood gush from his wound. I knew I should be completely grossed out, but my stomach actually growled with hunger at the sight of it. I decided to keep this disturbing revelation to myself.

"Will he be okay?" I asked.

"Yes." Thierry tossed the bloody stake off to the side. "In time."

I glanced over at the reverend. "Is he . . . is he . . ."

"Dead?" Thierry finished for me. "No."

He pulled a cell phone from his inside jacket pocket and called the police, who showed up ten minutes later. After speaking privately with Thierry, they handcuffed the slightly conscious reverend and took him away as the wedding guests milled about.

"What did you say to them?" I asked.

"You needn't concern yourself with that." He had George on his feet and was helping him to the door.

"Thierry," I called to him. He turned around, letting George lean against him for support. "Why are you here, anyhow? George said that you sent him because you were too busy. Not that I expected anyone to come after . . . well, after our little discussion the other day."

He took a deep inhale of breath. "Are you telling me I shouldn't have come?"

"No, I'm not saying that. In fact, talk about perfect timing. It's just . . . George told me you were busy because there was another hunter attack. Did they"—I swallowed hard—"kill anybody?"

"Happily, no one was injured in their last attack; however, another of my clubs has been damaged enough for me to shut it down." He met my gaze, then looked away. "I simply felt that you needed me."

I waited for further explanation, but there was nothing. "Are you heading back to Toronto now?"

He shook his head. "George is not well enough for a long car ride. We will pick you up tomorrow morning at eight. Please be ready. Unless, perhaps, you were planning on staying here longer?"

"No, no. I'll be ready."

He continued toward the door.

"Thierry," I called again. He stopped walking, but he didn't turn around. "Um . . . thanks."

He left without another sound, except for a last gasp of pain from George as he hit the door frame. Abottsville is well known for its narrow doors.

I went outside to watch Missy and Richard leave for their honeymoon. A little anticlimactic now, but it would do. I heard the murmurings of the crowd as they talked about Reverend Micholby finally going off the deep end—an event that apparently had been predicted for years. Why didn't that make me feel any better?

Missy gave me a quick hug.

"You're going to be okay," she told me.

I nodded, but I knew she was lying to make me feel better. "Yeah, sure I will be. Us bloodsucking monsters always land on our feet."

She opened her mouth to say something else, but I stopped her.

"You'll be okay, too." I smiled at her. "Richard's a keeper."

She nodded, and Richard winked at me from inside the limo. Missy got in and the door closed behind them. Nobody had any rice or confetti, so we all just waved good-bye. Attached to the back of the limo was a sign in the shape of a red heart with two suspicious-looking puncture marks. It read TILL DEATH DO US PART HAS A WHOLE NEW MEANING. RICHARD + MISSY FOREVER.

Funny. Then why wasn't I laughing?

I tried to swallow the big lump in my throat as I watched them drive away.

Chapter 14

Mom insisted that I stay in my old room at the house. This was my second night tucked snug as a bug in a rug in my single bed with the frilly pink canopy. I stared at my old Madonna poster for a very long time. I used to want to be Madonna. Instead, I just became a "Material Girl." I guess it all worked out.

There were lots of signs of the "me who used to be" scattered around the room. My old diaries tucked in their secret hiding places, my old teddy bear without any eyes because I gnawed them off in my sleep. I guess I had an oral fixation even as a kid. In my closet were all the clothes I'd bought with every last cent of my McDonald's pay. Not much different from now. Spending all my money on frivolous things. Pretty things to make me feel better. To make me feel special. What a joke.

It wasn't even midnight yet, the wedding reception having wrapped up earlier than originally planned. I kicked around in the sheets for a while, but I wasn't tired. I figured that I'd read the issue of *Cosmopolitan* I'd brought with me until I got sleepy. I slid out of bed.

I was wearing my Roller-skating Mama nightshirt. Very retro.

I sat down at my little vanity, where I used to dream about becoming a grown-up. I'd apply the makeup I'd stolen from Mom's bathroom drawer and imagine being a world-famous model, or actress, or flight attendant. Any of the above would have done just fine. Little did I know back then that I would never amount to more than a senior executive assistant. And I wasn't even that anymore.

Yes, I was feeling sorry for myself—what else was new?

The worst thing about sitting at my childhood vanity was seeing that my reflection was now completely and utterly gone. Kaput. I'd never get used to that. Out of absolutely everything that sucked about being a vampire, not having a reflection was the thing that sucked the hardest.

Material Girls should be able to see themselves in mirrors. That was just a given. But it was over. I may as well stop wearing makeup altogether. What was the point anymore?

Okay, I knew it wasn't just the lack of reflection that started the tears flowing down my cheeks. It was everything that had been happening—the mirror was just the proverbial straw on the camel's back. I hated everything about being a vampire, and the list was getting longer by the day.

And the cure that Richard had talked about?

I was sure that was just another lump of bullshit to add to my already-full bullshit collection.

So, being that I was all alone, in the room that had

been filled with so many optimistic, wonderful dreams of my imaginary future, I allowed myself to cry like the little girl who used to live there. May she rest in peace.

"Sarah," a deep voice said.

I sniffed and raised my head. I looked at the mirror, but it only reflected back the dark, empty room. I turned around. Thierry was sitting on the inside of the window-sill next to my open window.

"What are you doing here?" I tried to wipe my tears away.

He stood up. "I wanted to check on you."

"I'm fine," I said, but my voice was shaky. "Can't you see that I'm fine? Just peachy keen, jelly bean. Never better."

"You could have fooled me." He took a deep breath and didn't say anything for a moment. Then, "About what happened at the club the other day—"

"Don't worry," I said, stopping him. "I said I'd never go there again and I won't."

"No, it's not that. Well, actually, it is that."

"What?"

"I was wrong to say those things to you."

My eyebrows shot up in surprise. "*You* were wrong?"

"Please, let me finish. I will admit that since I first agreed to help you in your new life, I haven't been there as I said I would be. If I had, you wouldn't have crossed paths with Quinn. Your unfortunate decisions were made as an innocent fledgling in need of an attentive sire. And for me to demand that you leave the only life you've known without having any support was wrong of me. I shouldn't have been surprised when you decided to go against my wishes." He crossed his arms and looked away. "I sent George here to keep an eye on you—make sure you were all right. I did hope he would be able to do it a little more subtly, but what's done is done."

I blinked. "Is he okay?"

"He'll be fine for the drive back to the city tomorrow morning, yes."

I was allowing the fact that Thierry had just apologized to me to sink in. I didn't need anyone to tell me that this was a rare event.

"Why were you crying?" he asked after a moment.

I shrugged at the empty mirror. Then I pointed at it, afraid that I might make a weird sound if I tried to talk over that big lump in my throat.

"Oh," Thierry said. "That reminds me, I brought you a little something." He stood up and moved closer to me and reached into his pocket.

He pulled out a medium-size blue box wrapped with a white ribbon and placed it in front of me on the vanity.

I looked up at him. "What's this?"

"A gift."

Thierry had gotten me a gift? I picked it up, pulled off the ribbon, and looked into the box. There was a silver oval inside. I took it out and looked up at Thierry in confusion. He seemed amused.

"Open it up," he said.

The oval was about four inches in diameter with a release mechanism at the bottom. I pressed the button and up popped the top. It was an antique silver compact, like one you'd use to powder your nose in the old days.

"It's very pretty," I said as I stared at my red-eyed reflection in the small mirror.

Wait a minute. My reflection? I watched my eyes widen with the growing awareness. It was a shard. Thierry had given me a shard—a special mirror like Zelda had told me about. Of the highly expensive variety.

I raised my wide eyes to look at Thierry.

"Do you like it?" he asked.

I started crying again, but now for an entirely different reason. Thierry was going to think I was a complete basket case, but I didn't care. He looked dismayed as I gently put the shard down and got to my feet.

"If you don't like it," he said, "I can—"

I squeezed his words off with a huge bear hug, pressing my nightshirt against his black suit.

"I love it, Thierry. Thank you so, so much." I looked up at him, my eyes filled with tears of happiness. He smiled down at me. He looked great when he smiled. He pushed the tears off my cheeks with his thumbs and gently held my face in his hands, just staring at me with his silvery eyes. His smile slowly vanished.

My heart was pounding hard as I looked into his eyes. He leaned closer to me, and I could feel his warm breath glance against my face. He was breathing faster than he should have been, and his heart was beating against my own.

He pulled me to him and our lips met, softly at first but slowly growing in intensity, until we were battling each other for who could kiss deeper and sweeter and longer. I traced my hands down his back, under his jacket and lower still, pressing his body even closer against my own.

His hands moved down to the backs of my bare

thighs and he lifted me up, turned us around, and we fell down to my messy single bed without his lips leaving mine for even a moment. His weight pressed me firmly against the narrow mattress, and he began to kiss down my neck with a growing hunger.

The fleeting thought of *Why did I have to wear my Roller-skating Mama nightshirt to bed tonight?* went through my mind, but I pushed it away.

Thierry traced his mouth back up my neck to claim my lips again, and I forgot all about the stupid nightshirt. But I'd definitely go shopping for some sexy new lingerie as soon as I got back to the city. Oh, yeah.

I ran my tongue along the inside of his mouth and then lightly across his fangs. He let out a low moan and pulled back a bit to stare down at me, with dark eyes.

"Is this the way you always say thank you for a gift?"

"Absolutely." I grabbed the back of his head to pull him down to me again. "Now shut up."

His mouth curled into a smile and he kissed me again.

There was a sharp knock at my door.

"Sarah?" my mother's voice said. "What's going on in there?"

"Oh, shit," I murmured against Thierry's lips. I gently pushed his face away so my voice wouldn't be muffled. "Nothing, Mom."

"You don't have a boy in there with you, do you? Is it George? I said he could stay in the guest room, young lady. We have rules in this house."

Thierry looked down at me and raised an eyebrow.

"Um . . . nope. Nobody's in here, Mom. Just little ole me."

"Can I come in?"

"Uh . . . yeah, just a sec." I squirmed out from beneath Thierry and straightened out my nightshirt. I cleared my throat and tried to compose myself as best I could. Why did I feel guilty having a man in my room? I wasn't fourteen anymore, for Pete's sake.

Thierry slowly pushed up off the bed. He moved toward the open window, and I gave him a sheepish look. Sheepish yet sexy. At least that's what I was striving for.

He cleared his throat quietly, ran a hand through his tousled dark hair, and smiled back at me. "We'll pick you up tomorrow at eight."

"Make it nine?"

"Eight-thirty. Good night, Sarah." He climbed out the window and, with a last look, was gone just like that.

I took a few deep breaths and tried to look calm before I opened the door. My mother stood in the doorway wearing her bright green housecoat and looking a little worse for wear. Maybe her hangover had kicked in early.

"Yeah, Mom? What is it?"

"Do you want eggs for breakfast?"

I blinked at her. "You just wanted to know if I wanted eggs for breakfast?"

"That's what I just asked you, didn't I?"

I sighed. "Sure, eggs would be great."

"Scrambled or over easy?"

"Scrambled." *Much like my life.*

"Okay, honey, have a good sleep." She blew me a kiss and turned to walk down the hall.

"Yeah," I said under my breath. "Thanks to you I'll be getting lots of sleep tonight."

She turned around. "What was that?"

"I said, you have a good sleep, too."

"Okay. Good night."

I closed the door and stood there with my back pressed up against it for a few minutes until my racing heart slowed down to a relatively normal pace. Then I went back to my little bed, got in, and pulled the covers up high. I leaned over and felt around for my old diary I'd always kept in the secret hiding compartment of my bedside table. I opened it up to a blank page, grabbed my strawberry-scented, pink-inked Hello Kitty pen and wrote:

Mrs. Sarah de Bennicoeur.
Thierry + Sarah = Tru love 4ever.

I drew a heart around it. With an arrow and everything.

Then I came to my senses enough to scribble on top of it. I absently chewed the end of the pen while wondering what tomorrow would bring.

The morning came extremely bright and damn early. I got dressed in faded jeans, hot pink T-shirt, and my black leather jacket. I happily used the shard to help put on my makeup. It was simply the coolest thing ever. Then I choked back half of the scrambled eggs my mother made, so as not to seem rude, and said my goodbyes, praying I wouldn't throw the eggs up all over the interior of Thierry's sleek black Audi.

Dark sunglasses firmly in place, I gave my mom and dad one last hug each—they were still stunned from the breakfast conversation of, "Oh, by the way, Reverend Micholby tried to kill me last night and now he's in jail." So as not to freak them out any more than they already were, I'd officially decided not to part ways with them till the next time I saw them. At Christmas dinner. Or maybe it could wait until Easter. I'd have to play it by ear.

I climbed into the backseat of Thiery's car on the dot of eight-thirty. Thierry was driving. George was in the passenger seat, looking pale but alive.

Thierry turned around and smiled at me. "Good morning, Sarah."

I smiled back and felt my cheeks redden as I remembered the feel of his incredible body pressed against mine. "Good morning to you, too. And how are you feeling today, George?"

"Like someone should take me out back and shoot me," he said very seriously.

I patted the top of his sandy-colored hair that was currently back in a messy ponytail. "Sounds like somebody needs some caffeine."

The three-hour drive back to the city was relaxed and mostly comfortable, except for the fact that I badly wanted to climb into the front seat and straddle Thierry. I managed to control myself for the time being. But the heat I was feeling between us would have to be handled very soon. I might just explode if it wasn't, or at the very least I'd get a very bad sunburn. I busied myself looking out the window at the passing countryside. Tree, barn, horse. Horse, barn, tree.

Finally the barns and horses gave way to pavement

and traffic. The city enveloped us and I began to feel relatively normal again.

I wondered if Amy would mind if Thierry came along on the double date. I'd tell her that Quinn was out of the picture. Way out. Then again, I couldn't exactly imagine Thierry tolerating dinner and dancing with my best friend and her new man of the moment. Time would have to tell on that one.

"I've shut down Midnight Eclipse for a couple of days," Thierry said as we neared the club. "But I need to pick up some files and invoices."

He parked around the back of the club and got out of the car. I got out, too. George stayed put in the front seat, his cheek pressed against the window. Thierry raised an eyebrow at me as I approached him from the other side of the car.

"I'll only be a moment," he said.

I grinned up at him. "And your point is?"

"Oh, nothing at all." He smiled as we turned toward the back door.

There was a woman sitting with her back against the red door, her knees up against her chest. She was—hands down—the most beautiful woman I'd ever seen in my life, at least in person. She had raven-colored hair, which was long and wavy, perfectly pale white skin, and full burgundy lips. Big, dark Gucci sunglasses covered her eyes. She wore a dark blue shift dress that swished against her trim body as she got to her feet. Standing, her legs were as long and shapely as any swimsuit model's I'd ever had the misfortune of seeing. I felt the sudden urge to get back to the gym as soon as possible.

"Finally," she said and placed an elegant hand on her slim hip. "I've been waiting here for ages."

I glanced at Thierry. He took a deep breath and didn't seem as if he was going to say anything back to the woman. How rude was that?

"Hi." I extended my hand. "I'm Sarah."

She smiled, showing off perfect white teeth, fangs included, and shook my hand. "Veronique," she said. "Thierry's wife."

Chapter 15

Veronique de Bennicoeur was slightly over seven hundred years old, though she didn't look a day over thirty. She and Thierry had met during the Black Death plague in Europe. She'd been a vampire first and Thierry's sire. She currently lived in France, but word had reached her through the grapevine that there was trouble in Toronto, and she thought she might be able to lend a hand. Her favorite drink was a martini on the rocks.

I listened to her give me the Cliffs Notes on her life with the poorest excuse for a smile frozen in place on my face. I was trying to decide, while listening to her go on about her fabulous life, who I wanted to kill more. Her or myself.

"So, what do you think?" Her voice was as beautiful as she was. She could have been a deejay. Or a phone-sex operator.

I decided. I was going to kill myself.

"Hmm? What was that?" I stood behind the bar, bracing the edge of it for support. I'd originally gone behind it to get myself a shot of whatever blood type was on tap, and Veronique had sat down across from me and ordered a martini. I only gave her one olive.

She smiled. "I just asked if while I'm in town, the two of us could go out for a girls' lunch. It's so rare that I find another woman I feel I can really talk to. You're an excellent listener."

"Yeah? Wow. That sounds great." Even I couldn't coax enthusiasm into those words.

After a quick two-cheeked European-style kiss and a few words of greeting to Veronique, Thierry had disappeared into his office shortly after he'd let us in the club. George was lying down in a nearby booth concentrating very hard on healing, but I was pretty sure he had a curious ear open for our mostly one-sided conversation. What I was still doing there was beyond me, although I was sure that the bone-jarring shock had something to do with it.

Thierry had a wife.

Not something that had come up in casual conversation.

I was trying very hard not to freak out. It was difficult, but so far I was succeeding. He had a wife. Okay. He wasn't currently living with this wife; that much I'd figured out. Well, I suppose when you're married for six hundred freaking years you need a little time apart to help keep things fresh.

I'd done four shots of B positive with vodka chasers since we got back. They weren't making me feel better. I guess B positive didn't live up to its optimistic reputation. I was starting to feel way claustrophobic. Since Thierry hadn't said a word to me to explain what was going on, I was getting the distinct, stomach-churning impression that I wasn't needed anymore. Gorgeous European *über*-wife had returned.

"I should go," I said.

"No, dear girl, stay. I like you. And you make an excellent martini." She ran a French-manicured finger along the edge of her glass.

"Thanks. Um, no, I really have to take off."

"Very well, if you insist. And listen, I know Thierry wants to shut down the club. Don't worry at all. We will open for business tonight as usual. I know how hard it is to be a working girl in the big city."

She thought I was only a waitress there. *Kill me. Somebody, kill me.*

"Great." I smiled at her through clenched teeth. "I'm just going to say bye to Thierry now."

There were a few other choice words I had in mind for him, too. But I was going to try to be mature. That was me. Mature with a capital *M*.

I knocked lightly on his office door and then pushed it open. Thierry sat at his desk, staring intently at some papers. He didn't look up.

"I'm leaving," I said.

He still didn't say anything.

"Hello? I said I'm leaving."

He finally glanced up as if surprised to see me standing there. "I thought you'd already left."

I felt heat rise in my cheeks. "Oh, did you?"

He shrugged, then looked back down at the papers. "Doesn't matter, I suppose."

I stepped farther into the office and closed the door behind me. I could prove I was mature. Just watch me. "Veronique is very beautiful."

"Yes, she is."

I counted slowly to ten in my head. "I didn't know you were married."

He blinked. "And now you know."

"Um, she seems very nice."

"Didn't you say you were leaving?"

This time I counted to fifteen. I knew without a shadow of a doubt that I had said nothing to piss him off. I'd even thought about what I was going to say before I let the words leave my mouth. That rarely happened. There was no reason for him to be acting like a jerk to me, especially after . . . well . . . after everything that had been happening between us.

"There's no reason to get snippy with me. I guess I'm just trying to understand."

"Understand what?" He stood up and pressed his palms against the desktop.

"It's just that I thought . . . well, about what happened in Abottsville. I just figured—"

"I guess you figured wrong," he said cutting me off. "I don't mean to be rude, Sarah, but perhaps you read more into the situation than you should have. I have agreed to help you adjust to the life that has been thrust upon you, yes. But please, do not mistake a potential fling for something more meaningful."

"A potential fling?" I sputtered. "Are you kidding me?"

"No, you're right. To call it a fling would be exaggerating. It was only a few kisses, after all."

His words felt like a slap in my face. For the last twenty minutes I'd wondered who I wanted to see die more, myself or Veronique. I'd just revised that list to include Thierry. And he was officially at the top of it.

I took a deep breath and concentrated on erasing the stunned look from my face. "You know what? I think you might be right. It *was* just a few kisses." I forced a smile at him and didn't try to make it look friendly. "And now you can kiss my ass good-bye."

"Ah, yes." The corner of his mouth raised into a half smile. "The refined wit of Sarah Dearly. It has been so refreshing this past week."

Turning the doorknob, I looked back over my shoulder. "Oh, and by the way, if you happen to get the urge to throw yourself off another bridge anytime soon, don't bother waiting for me to help you out. Just go for it."

My reward was seeing a frown spread over his features before I slammed the door behind me.

I saw the club through a foggy daze. I absolutely had no idea where that fight had materialized from. The only thing that echoed in my mind were the words "potential fling." Was that really all he thought of me? And why did the idea of that cut me deeper than finding out he had a wife?

I knew why. Because I'd been a silly dope and sort of fallen for him. But I wasn't completely stupid. You didn't have to hit me over the head, over and over, for me to see the truth. Not when it was sitting at the bar with its long, lean legs crossed, seductively sipping a martini.

Veronique waved good-bye to me. "Lunch. Soon."

I walked around to the other side of the bar toward George. "Bye, George. Get well soon."

"Sarah," he said, his voice was still weak, but not as

weak as it was earlier. He was healing up very nicely; another asset to life as a vampire.

"Yeah?" I leaned over.

"If it's any consolation . . ."

"What?"

"You're way cuter."

I bent over to kiss his forehead. "You are now officially my favorite person in the entire world."

I stopped at Holt Renfrew on my way home and bought a new pair of shoes. Hot pink, expensive stiletto pumps I'd seen a couple of weeks ago in *Vogue*—same pair Charlize Theron wore to a recent movie premiere. Did I mention expensive? The fact that I had no money except for twenty bucks left over from the tips I made the other night did occur to me. But I needed to buy something in the worst way—retail therapy.

When I took the shoes out of the box at home, I realized I didn't even like them. I cried over those pink shoes for a whole half hour. I was crying over the shoes. Really.

I didn't call anyone. I didn't talk to anyone. I'd decided to officially become a hermit.

My hermitivity lasted exactly three hours. I did some laundry, took a shower, and paced around my small apartment. Finally I was so bored I was climbing the walls, and I decided to go out for a walk. Danger be damned.

I walked past a small park about two blocks from my apartment complex. In it, there was a girl arguing with a

young guy. I squinted at her familiar black hair, black
clothes, and pale face. She looked over and saw me
studying her and then I recognized her.

It was Melanie. The Goth chick I'd clocked the other
night at the club. The human girlfriend of Timothy, the
vampire. Her eyes narrowed as she recognized me, too.
She poked the shoulder of the guy she was with—not
Timothy—and pointed at me. Then she started to march
right toward me, and she didn't look friendly.

The guy followed dutifully behind her.

"That"—Melanie pointed at me—"that's one."

"What?" I asked. "Somebody who's kicked your
ass?"

Melanie scowled at me. Her friend just blinked a couple of times. Maybe he had even less of a clue what she
was talking about than I did.

"No, bitch," she snapped. "A *vampire*."

I sighed. "Wow, alert the media. You know, Timothy
should really invest in a leash and muzzle for you."

"Timothy and me are through," she spat and grabbed
the arm of the timid-looking boy. "*This* is my new
boyfriend."

He blinked at me again.

"My condolences," I said and turned away.

"Where do you think you're going, bitch?"

I raised my eyebrows and turned around. "You have
a lot of hostility, Melanie. But at least your glowing personality makes up for it."

"Vampire," her friend finally spoke. His voice was
small and nervous. He struck me as the kind of guy
who'd be better off wearing a polka-dot bow tie, sitting

in a small office, adding lists of numbers together, than out on the town with "Miss Congeniality."

Melanie nodded. "That's right, Eugene. A *vampire*. And what do we do with vampires?"

His forehead creased in concentration. "Uh."

Melanie rolled her eyes. "We *kill* them. Come on, get your stake out and kill her."

"*He's* a vampire hunter?" I asked, my voice devoid of any panic. I mean, come on.

"That's right," Melanie said proudly as Eugene searched his pockets. "I'm training him, based on my knowledge of your kind."

Eugene finally found what he was looking for. He held a stake tightly in his trembling right hand, but it slipped away from him and clattered to the sidewalk.

I bent over to pick it up and handed it back to him. "I should let you know that I'm in a very bad mood right now. It's been one of those days."

"Kill her," Melanie prompted, her black-rimmed eyes shiny with the prospect of violence.

Eugene raised the stake.

I kicked him in the shin.

He dropped the stake again, blinked painfully up at me as he rubbed his leg, and then ran away in the opposite direction.

I shook my head as I watched him flee. "Honestly, Melanie, I think your taste in men may be even worse than mine."

I turned to glance at her just in time to see her lunge at me, the stake now in her hand. Instinctively, I grabbed her wrists to prevent her from plunging it into my chest. Her momentum knocked me backward and we fell in a heap on the ground, my dark sunglasses knocked off my face. She was stronger than she looked, plus she'd taken me by surprise. Not a good combination.

"This'll teach him for dumping me," she shrieked. "He thinks I'm not good enough for him, huh? We'll see about that."

It never would have occurred to me, after facing off against legitimately deadly vampire hunters, that I had anything to be afraid of with Melanie. But as I wrestled with her—her jilted-girlfriend rage tripling her normal strength; her seeing me as the reason for all of her problems—my life flashed before my eyes.

And it wasn't pretty. I hadn't lived a very interesting life.

I felt the sharp tip of the stake nick my chest. The pain brought me out of my mental slide show and back to reality.

With my hands busy fending off her attack and my legs trapped under her, I knew I'd have to use my head if I wanted to get out of this one. Literally use my head.

I smacked my forehead against the bridge of her nose. She screamed but didn't budge.

"Let go of me," I yelled.

"No way. You're dead meat!"

"What about Eugene?" I managed. "Don't you want to make sure he's okay?"

"Screw Eugene!" she yelled.

"No thanks!"

We rolled around on the ground. The girl sure had spunk, I'd give her that. When she set her mind to something, she didn't give up. Unfortunately, I didn't feel that killing me was a very good thing for her to set her sights on.

Then I saw somebody out of the corner of my eye. Thank God. Somebody was going to rescue me.

The somebody wasn't moving. While I held Melanie's hands away from me, I glanced over.

Quinn looked down at us wrestling on the ground. He wore dark sunglasses.

"Hey," he said.

"Hello," I replied.

"How's it going?"

"Not so good." I bashed Melanie in the upper lip this time, giving me the opportunity to maneuver myself on top of her. I was going to need some Tylenol after this was over. Either that or a mortician.

"Who's your friend?" Quinn still wasn't making a single move to help me out.

"Oh, this is Melanie," I said, after I narrowly avoided the stake hitting my jugular. "Melanie, Quinn."

Melanie wasn't in the mood to meet new people at the moment.

It was quite obvious that Quinn was trying to keep from smiling at my predicament. If I weren't fighting for my life, I would have been extremely annoyed.

"Need some help?" he finally asked.

"Oh, no. I've got it all under control."

Melanie rolled over, so she was on top again, and let out a Xena-like war cry.

"Okay," he said. "I guess I'll see you later, then."

"Quinn!" I yelled after he turned his back. In this position the bright afternoon sun was blinding me. "Welcome to the land of sarcasm. Help would be nice."

He grinned and, with one hand, snatched Melanie by the back of her black sweatshirt and hauled her off me. She clawed at him, the air, and everything in between. I slowly got to my feet and brushed off my jacket. There was a patch of red over my heart, where she'd grazed me with the stake. I rubbed it tenderly and pouted. She'd ruined one of my favorite T-shirts.

Quinn gently shook Melanie until she dropped the stake. She didn't seem scared; she just looked pissed off that we'd been interrupted. Quinn held her arms firmly against her sides so she couldn't budge.

I grabbed my sunglasses off the ground and put them back on. Then I walked over to Melanie and slowly looked her up and down. "Now is the time when I'm supposed to say that I'm sorry about how things went down with you and Timothy. And that vampires aren't all bad. Also, that in time you'll be okay; you just need to give your feelings a while to heal."

She blinked at me, and I could see the rage slowly fading from her eyes.

"Let her go," I told Quinn. He released her and she turned to walk away without saying another word.

"Oh, just one more thing, Melanie," I said.

She turned around and I punched her in her already-injured nose.

I smiled at her. "Come near me again, and I'll bite you."

Her lower lip quivered and she turned and ran away.

I rubbed my throbbing hand. "Ow, that hurt."

Quinn just shook his head at me.

I frowned at him. "What?"

"You just made me remember one of the first things you ever said to me."

"What's that?"

"That you're not a nice girl."

"Oh, right! That was after your pickup line from hell." I smiled, and then stopped myself from looking too friendly. "What are you doing around here, anyhow?"

"Looking for you."

"Is that right?" I was immediately on my guard.

"Relax," he said. "I'm not going to hurt you. Besides, after what I just witnessed, I don't think I'd be able to hurt you. You're pretty tough."

I crossed my arms. "Then what do you want?"

He began to say something and then stopped. He opened his mouth again and met my eyes. "I wanted to apologize."

I raised an eyebrow. "Apologize. For what?"

"For everything. Mostly the nearly-killing-you part. Yeah, I wanted to apologize for that, and then thank you for saving my life."

"You know, Quinn, even though I haven't known you that long, I hope you're not insulted if I doubt your sincerity."

He shrugged. "I know. I guess it's been one of those 'walk a mile in someone else's shoes' things for me. I've been raised to believe that va—that vampi—" He stopped and frowned deeply.

"Bloodsucking, murderous monsters," I finished for him. Again with the sarcasm. It was a gift.

He sighed. "It's hard. I've always been raised to believe that they're evil. Now I'm one of them, and I don't feel any different than I ever did. It makes me wonder if I've been in the wrong all of this time."

"You think?" I rolled my eyes. "Let's just leave it with your apology and my saying no big deal. I hope you have a good life, Quinn, I really do."

When I turned to walk away, he grabbed my shoulder. "It's not just that, Sarah. Ever since I met you, I . . . I don't know. I just can't think about anything else."

I looked up into his blue eyes. "Come again? Can't think of anything else but what?"

He turned away, rubbed his forehead hard, then turned back to me. "I can't stop thinking about you."

"Me?"

"I know it's stupid. I know that you and Thierry . . . well, whatever. That guy wants to kill me as it is. I don't know what this is between us. But it's something."

I didn't say anything for a moment. He couldn't stop thinking about me? My brain temporarily stopped working. Finally I found my voice.

"Are you nuts?"

"What?"

"You have a hell of a lot of nerve, you know that?"

Quinn stared at me blankly.

I shook my head. "I'm just supposed to forget everything that happened before, now that you suddenly realize I'm not as evil as you thought I was? If it hadn't been for your father at the bar, I'd be dead right now. If it hadn't been for Dan and his friend in the PATH, I would be dead again. No way, buster. I'm not about to give you a third kick at the can. I helped you out because I felt guilty about what happened to you. That's it. That's all. So, why don't you find some other girl to stalk?"

He rubbed his forehead again. His face was a little red, either from all the rubbing or from embarrassment, I wasn't sure. "You're right. All of it. You're absolutely right. I don't deserve your forgiveness. I've done nothing to prove myself to you. I'm sorry to have bothered you."

He shook his head hard, as if that might erase everything he'd just said to me, and turned to walk away. After my little outburst I'd be surprised if he ever came near me again.

And that was a good thing, right? I don't care if he'd seemed like a nice guy when I first met him, that we hit it off really well. He'd been nothing but a problem since that moment.

But still . . .

I was in a little bit of shock. Mr. Vampire-Hunter-turned-Vampire had just basically admitted that he had a crush on me? The last damn thing I needed was another complication in my life.

I chewed my bottom lip. Not that that had ever stopped me before.

I swallowed hard. "Quinn!"

He stopped and turned back around. "Yeah?"

"How do the words 'double date' sound to you?"

Chapter 16

Amy was thrilled when I phoned her at work. She immediately put me on hold so she could call to make reservations. She got right back to me.

"Tonight. Top of the CN Tower," she said. I could tell she was grinning from ear to ear at the prospect of our mutual date. "In the 360 Restaurant."

"Isn't that expensive?" The CN Tower was Toronto's landmark tourist attraction, a huge tower that rose high above all the other downtown skyscrapers and had a world-class rotating restaurant on the top floor. Fancy schmancy.

"So?"

"Yeah, I'm unemployed, remember? I was thinking more along the lines of McDonald's."

"Don't worry about money. This is a special occasion. You are *so* going to love Peter."

I was already regretting agreeing to this. Why did something sound like a great idea one moment and a horrible mistake the next?

But it was just dinner. It didn't mean anything. It

would give me something other than my vampire problems to focus on for a while.

I returned my overdue monster movies and begrudgingly paid the late fee. Then I returned the designer shoes and went shopping for a dress to wear to dinner. After seriously shopping for two hours I finally found it. Short, tight, and a gorgeous shade of violet. Plus, it was on sale. Buying it triggered my happy shopping endorphins. Maybe the day was turning out better than I thought.

I went back to the apartment to get ready. I'd decided I was going to have a good time and forget all about Thierry and his magical mystery spouse.

It was working until I had to put on some makeup. As soon as I pulled the shard out of my purse, I got a little misty-eyed. I had the overwhelming urge to throw it against the wall and watch it shatter into a thousand pieces. But I wasn't that crazy. Not yet, anyhow.

Quinn had given me his cell phone number and I called to tell him when to show up. At seven-thirty I pushed open the glass door to my apartment building and strode out into the chilly night air on my three-inch heels.

He was waiting for me. When he smiled, I could see his brand-new fangs. Guess we were in the same boat when it came to developing early, thanks to Thierry's full-strength blood. He looked good, too. Some men clean up well, and Michael Quinn was one of them. He wore a dark blue suit with a crisp white shirt underneath, open at the collar. The color of the suit brought out his gorgeous blue eyes. His sandy blond hair was combed back off his face, and as I got closer, I noticed he was wearing my favorite Calvin Klein men's cologne.

Still didn't excuse him for almost killing me twice. But it was a nice start.

We took a cab to the CN Tower, then gave Amy's name at the reservation desk and were ushered past the tourist crowds to the elevator reserved especially for restaurant patrons. I'd been there a few times before, so it was all no big deal, but Quinn looked amazed as the elevator rose high into the sky.

The hostess showed us through the busy restaurant to Amy's table, which was against the curved window that looked down at the city lights below. She sat there all alone, napkin in lap, sipping a glass of white wine. When she saw us, she got to her feet and gave me a hug. She wore a sea green sparkly dress and the earrings she'd bought the other day at the mall. Her light blond hair was pinned back from her face with matching sparkly green clips.

"You look amazing," she said. "And, Quinn, it's good to see you again."

Quinn smiled back at her. "You too." I'd told him to be on his best behavior since Amy didn't exactly know about my secret identity as one of Toronto's best-dressed monsters.

"Peter's still at work. But he said he'd get here as soon as possible."

"Overtime?" I glanced down at my watch. "Dedicated guy. What does he do for a living, anyhow?"

"Um." Amy frowned. "Not totally sure about that. I think it has something to do with pest control."

I nodded. "That sounds sexy."

We sat down at the table.

"So, what do you do for a living, Quinn?" Amy asked.

"Coincidentally enough," Quinn said, "I used to do a little pest control myself."

"Really?"

I kicked him under the table.

"What is it about that business that makes you work such long hours?" Amy asked.

Quinn ignored my dirty look. "Dedication to a job done right, mostly."

"Did you find it dangerous?"

"Dangerous?"

"It's just that Peter keeps getting hurt. I'm worried about him. Every time I see him, he has a new bump or bruise."

"Accident-prone," I said. "Or a really badass cockroach. Hey, let's change the subject, shall we? Talking about work is depressing for an unemployed slob like myself."

"Sure, no problem," Amy said. "Quinn, have you lived in Toronto long?"

The waiter arrived to take our drink orders and brought a basket of various breads for us to pick at. I ordered a tequila sunrise and ignored the bread. Quinn asked for a beer.

"Not long," Quinn said when the waiter left. "Only a few weeks so far. Actually, I was planning on leaving soon, but things change. I may end up staying here permanently."

"Well, I hope for Sarah's sake that you do." Amy grinned and grabbed a sesame-seed bread stick. She crunched on it thoughtfully. "Peter's new in town, too. You guys sure have a lot in common."

And that was about the point I began to feel an odd sense of dread concerning Peter, the mysterious pest controller. I started putting two and two together, but instead of adding up to four, they added up to a gnawing, sick feeling in the pit of my stomach.

Amy glanced up. "Finally! Here he is." She leaned over the table toward me and grabbed my hand. "Try not to look at the eye patch too much," she whispered. "He's very sensitive about it."

I swallowed the huge lump of dismay that was forming in my throat and slowly turned around in my seat.

Amy was right. Peter was very attractive. He wore a dark suit with a T-shirt underneath that, along with his blond hair, gave him a vaguely *Miami Vice* look. He wore a black eye patch over his injured eye. He gave Amy a wide smile of sparkling white teeth as he approached the table.

The smile drained from his face as he noticed I was sitting across from his new girlfriend.

My last memory of White-teeth had been feeling my big toe making squishy contact with his left eye. Just before Thierry and I had jumped off the bridge nearly a week ago.

Now he was walking toward me at least a thousand feet above street level.

I wasn't planning on jumping from that height, but the night was still young.

He hesitated. I could practically see his brain churning out different scenarios, different reactions to seeing me. His eyes flicked to Quinn, and he immediately seemed to relax at the sight of a fellow vampire hunter.

He approached the table and leaned over to give Amy a quick kiss. His good eye never left me.

"Hey, darlin'," he said to Amy. "Sorry I'm late."

He sat down directly across the table from me. I felt like I might melt into a puddle of goo right there on the floor of the 360 Restaurant with the intensity of hate in his single eye.

Amy, perhaps blissfully, remained unaware of the bad vibes shooting over the top of the bread basket.

"Peter," she said and took hold of the sleeve of his jacket, "this is Sarah. I've told you so much about her that you probably feel like you already know her, right?"

"Yeah." Peter's voice was low and gravelly. Barely restrained. "Feels like I already know you . . . Sarah."

"And," Amy continued, "this is Sarah's boyfriend, Quinn."

Quinn glanced at me after hearing Amy's choice of introduction. Then he looked back at Peter and smiled. "Small world, man."

Peter grinned at that and clasped Quinn's outstretched hand. "You can say that again."

"You two know each other?" Amy asked with surprise.

"We do," Peter said.

"See?" Amy smiled at both of them. "I knew you had a lot in common with the whole pest-control thing, but it never occurred to me that you might already know each other."

I sat there as quietly as I could. Maybe I could just slide under the table, crawl through the crowded restaurant, past the bustling waiters, toward the elevator. No one would even notice.

Then again, what was I so worried about, anyhow? We were in the middle of a restaurant full of well-dressed, potential witnesses. Also, he wouldn't dare murder me in front of Amy. It would be doubtful she'd date him after that, or at least I'd like to think so.

"Pest control, huh?" Peter said to Quinn as he raked his eye over me. "Looks like you have some work ahead of you tonight."

Quinn's closed-mouth grin held. I noticed he wasn't taking a chance of showing his fangs. "You can say that again."

An uncomfortable hush fell at the table, and I felt everyone staring at me. I grabbed a piece of bread for lack of anything else to do and buttered it violently.

"So, Peter"—I felt the sudden and overwhelming urge to break the silence—"what the hell happened to your eye?"

All five eyes at the table shot to me.

"Sarah!" Amy said, appalled.

"Sorry." I shrugged. "I'm just curious. So sue me. I simply want to know if my best friend is dating someone with a real injury or if it's just some weird pirate fetish."

The seething rage came off Peter in hot waves. I cocked my head to one side and tried to give him a friendly smile. It would have worked better if I hadn't felt as if I'd just had my lips Botoxed.

He stroked the patch tenderly. "An unfortunate work-place accident. But you know what they say, don't you, darlin'? 'An eye for an eye'?"

Amy frowned. "I thought you only called me 'darlin'.

I thought that was our thing, like when I call you 'pooky.'"

"Pooky?" Quinn asked.

Peter gritted his teeth. I was honestly surprised that he hadn't reached across the table and attempted to kill me with my butter knife yet.

"What are you going to order?" Amy asked me as she glanced down at her menu. She had drawn a little away from Peter, her annoyance about the pet-name faux pas obvious.

"I'm fine with the drink," I said.

Amy closed her menu. "Don't be silly. Order whatever you like. Peter said he'd pick up the tab this time, didn't you?" She nudged him.

Peter clenched his jaw.

I gave him a closed-mouth smile. "Gee, that's so nice of you, Peter. In that case"—I scanned the menu for the most expensive item—"I think I'll have the prime rib. And maybe we should order another bottle of wine."

"That sounds great," Amy said. "I'll have the same thing."

I turned to Quinn. "Okay, why don't you tell me all about how you two know each other?"

"It's not a very interesting story."

"No, come on, Quinn," Peter prompted. "Let's tell your new *girlfriend* all about it."

Did he think I was completely oblivious to the fact that Quinn was a vampire hunter? Well, ex–vampire hunter. He said it as if it would come as a complete shock to me when the truth finally came out. What a moron.

"We've worked together on occasion," Quinn said

after a long swig from his bottle of Heineken. "We're more acquaintances than close friends, actually."

"Come on, Quinn," Peter said with an unpleasant grin. "We've done a whole lot of *pest control* together over the years. Long days, even longer nights. The search, the hunt, and then the incredible kill. The satisfaction of knowing you've snuffed out an evil creature with your bare hands."

Amy made a squeamish face as she probably imagined her handsome new boyfriend killing cockroaches and spiders in the palm of his hand.

"That's true," Quinn said with a glance toward me. "But I'm thinking it may be time for a change in careers."

"You're kidding, right?" Peter said. "Even after what happened last night? Taking down that"—he looked at Amy—"uh, that nest of disgusting insects? Come on, that was a rush. Best time we've had in months."

My eyes widened at that. Last night? I stared at Quinn, wanting him to deny it, but he wouldn't meet my gaze. My heart was jumping inside my chest.

Quinn was going about business as usual, even though he was now a vampire himself? Even though he had acknowledged to me that he no longer believed vamps were all evil? The thought of him joining the other hunters on a raid made me feel sick. I wanted to hit him, slap him so hard that his ears rang. I wanted him to say it wasn't true, even if it meant he had to lie to me. How could I keep on being such a bad judge of character? Was I honestly that stupid? Don't answer that.

Peter was still grinning at the memory of whatever had gone down last night. The waiter came to take our order, but Amy told him we needed a few more minutes. He brought us more ice water instead.

Quinn finally looked at me. He didn't share Thierry's ability to have an expressionless face. Every emotion he was feeling, every thought he was thinking, was etched into his features.

Unless he was just an amazing actor. Maybe that would be easier for me to stomach.

"I didn't kill anyone," he told me quietly.

"Don't be so modest," Peter said. "You know, Quinn, I think your father's all wrong about you. I think you'll make a great leader one day. You're not afraid to make the hard decisions, go after the difficult kill." His gaze slid over to me. "No matter how good she is in the sack."

Amy poked Peter in the arm with the rest of her bread stick. "I honestly don't know what you're babbling about, pooky, but did you just insult my friend? I don't think I like that very much."

"Amy . . ." I rose from the table. Quinn was staring out the window again. Either feeling major guilt or major denial. He could sort that out on his own. I was through. "I'm going to the bathroom."

"Okay." Amy stood up and grabbed her bag.

I'd slipped the butter knife into my small beaded purse just in case I needed a weapon later. I know, my choice of weapons did lean toward the nonlethal culinary variety, but it was better than nothing. I made a mental note to invest in another can of pepper spray.

I swung the ladies' room door open and we went inside. I did a quick stall check to make sure we were all alone.

"I don't really need to pee," Amy said. "I just wanted

to apologize for Peter. I don't think he's going to be *the one,* after all. I don't know why he's acting so weird."

"I know why." I felt tense and watched Amy inspect her makeup in the mirror while I stood with my shoulder against the door to prevent anyone from entering.

"You do?"

"Yeah. I need to tell you something, Amy. Something I should have told you already."

"What?"

I took a deep breath. "I'm a vampire."

Amy stared at me for a moment. "Huh?"

"A vampire. A creature of the night."

She continued to stare at me blankly.

I sighed heavily. "Dracula, Lestat, Angel, you know? Blood drinking, no other food, live forever and still look good . . . slightly pasty, pointy-toothed . . . *vampire.*"

After a moment of silence she nodded and smiled patiently at me. "I told you to lay off the Anne Rice books for a while. And buying every season of *Buffy* on DVD? It was only a matter of time before you'd start thinking this way."

"No"—I shook my head—"this has nothing to do with any of that. Besides, those DVDs were on sale. But forget all that. I really am a vampire."

She smiled and nodded at me. "Whatever you say, Sarah."

Amy tended to be frustrating at the best of times, but this was just annoying.

"Okay, I'll prove it to you." I bared my teeth. "Look. I have fangs."

She leaned closer to inspect them. "Cute. But Halloween was over a month ago. We shouldn't leave the boys at the table much longer. They'll end up eating all the bread."

I thought I was going to have to bite her to prove it. No, wait, there was a better way right in front of me. I grabbed her upper arms and moved her around to look in the mirror. When she stared at her reflection, that's all she saw. Just her. Not me. She looked at herself, then turned to me. Then she looked at the mirror again. Then turned to me again.

This went on for a while.

Finally her eyes bugged out in shock.

"See?" I said, feeling slightly triumphant that I'd finally gotten through to her. "What did I tell you?"

Amy opened her mouth and started to scream.

Chapter 17

I clamped my hand over Amy's mouth before she'd let out more than a second of the bloodcurdling sound.

The door swung open and a gray-haired older woman entered the bathroom holding the hand of a little girl, about six years old, probably her granddaughter. She took one look at me, clutching Amy tightly from behind, and her eyes widened. A look of disapproval came across her features and she shook her head gravely at us.

"Honestly," she said. "I'll never understand you lesbians."

She covered her granddaughter's eyes and turned to leave.

Amy strained to move and face me, my hand still firmly across her mouth. She said something, but it was too muffled for me to hear.

"What?" I asked and removed my hand.

"*You're* a vampire." Her eyes were wider than the bread plates at our table.

I nodded. "Good to see you're finally catching on.

Now please don't scream again. I'm not going to hurt you or anybody else."

She looked at me for a long moment, then ran into the closest toilet stall and locked it behind her.

"Amy—"

"Go away! Leave me alone!" Her voice trembled.

I crossed my arms and paced around the small bathroom nervously. "There's no reason to be scared. Seriously. I'm not going to hurt you."

"Why did this happen? I don't understand! Does this have anything to do with why you got fired? Did you try to bite Ms. Saunders?"

I thought about that for a moment. "No."

Finger sucking and neck biting were two entirely different things. Finger sucking being the less disgusting of the two. Marginally.

"Then what happened to you?"

"Come out of there and I'll tell you."

"No! Tell me first and then I'll come out."

I let out a long sigh. "It's all your fault, you know. You should be feeling bad instead of freaking out."

"My fault?" I saw her look through the narrow space at the side of the stall door.

"Yeah. This whole thing is because you set me up on a date with Gordon Richards. He was a vampire and he bit me."

"You're kidding! He seemed so normal."

I let the fact sink in for her without saying anything else.

"That asshole," Amy said, louder now, a bit of the fear and shock leaving her voice. "I'm going to kill him the next time I see him."

"Yeah. You do that." I decided not to tell her that the deed was already done, and by her date, too. It might put her right over the edge.

There was a long pause, and then . . .

"So, are you trying to say that you're a good vampire?"

"Yeah. I'm a good vampire." I paused. "Like Angel. With a soul and everything."

"But Angel wasn't always good. Do you turn all evil when you have sex?"

I rolled my eyes. In the name of all that was holy, I shouldn't have lent her those *Buffy* DVDs. "You're just going to have to trust me on this one. I'm good Angel. All the time."

I waited for another minute in silence.

"Amy," I finally said. "Are you okay in there?"

I heard the toilet flush. Then the latch clicked and the door opened slowly. Amy peered out at me nervously. Her bottom lip quivered. "I'm so sorry I set you up with that jerk!" She staggered out and hugged me tightly.

I patted her back. "Me too."

She sniffed, then backed away from me. "I can't believe you didn't tell me! That's not very nice."

"I've been hoping I could get back to life as usual before anyone noticed anything different about me. Unfortunately, it's not turning out to be that simple."

"Why would you want that?" Her voice was getting stronger, and her wide smile was making another appearance. "My best friend is a vampire. I am so completely jealous."

"Don't be. Trust me on that."

"So, what about Quinn?"

"What do you mean, 'What about Quinn?'"

"Does he know?"

I took a deep breath. "That's one of the reasons I wanted to bring you in here to tell you. Quinn's a vampire, too."

"Get the hell out of here!"

"Wish I could. Long story short, Quinn used to be a vampire hunter. He even tried to kill me a couple of times. Then he got turned into one of us."

"And you two fell in love." She sighed. "Oh, my God, that is so romantic."

"I'm not in love with him," I said firmly.

"But you two are so cute together. The wedding pictures would be amazing."

"Not enough of a reason to fall in love, I'm afraid. But there's something else I have to tell you. Something bad."

Her breath caught. "What?"

"Peter's a vampire hunter."

She gasped. "But he said he was in pest control."

"Yeah, let's put it together now, Amy. *Pest control*. As in killing vampires. They think vamps are evil, but take it from me on this one, we're not. He's the bad guy."

"Do you think he hurt his eye out hunting vampires?" Amy looked so confused that I felt sorry for her. It was usually hard enough for her to follow the plot of *The Young and the Restless*, let alone *The Fanged and the Fashionable*.

"That's the thing, Amy. I was the one who did that to his eye last week. I had to. He was trying to kill me, and I was just protecting myself. I haven't seen him again until tonight. There's no way he's going to let me out of here alive. And to top it off, he has no idea that Quinn's been turned. He just thinks that he's still one of the boys. Ready to go out later tonight and do some more hunting."

"Peter tried to kill you." Her voice was full of disbelief that her shiny new boyfriend would be capable of anything so unsavory.

"Yeah."

"And you think he's going to try to kill you again."

I shrugged. "He's a vampire hunter. That's what he does."

"But you're my friend."

"I don't think he sees things quite that simply, unfortunately."

"Well, that's not good."

"Major understatement. I just can't believe that out of all the guys in Toronto, you ended up dating him."

"Sorry."

"Don't apologize." I sighed. "It's not your fault. Just fate giving me a swift kick in the ass."

"So, what's the plan?" she asked.

"Plan?"

"The plan to get you out of here safely."

"We'll have to kill Peter," I said.

Amy gasped and put a hand to her mouth.

"Kidding." I patted her shoulder and tried not to laugh out loud at her reaction. Maybe I *was* evil, after all. "Just kidding. Sorry, I couldn't resist. I don't know how to get out of here. There's no way he's going to let me go this time, after what I did to his eye."

Amy opened her purse and pushed through the contents. "I think I might have an idea."

There was always a first time for everything.

"What are you looking for?" I said.

"I know I have them in here somewhere. Oh, good, here they are." She pulled out a bottle of pills.

"Are those sleeping pills?" I suddenly imagined Peter curled up in a corner of the restaurant, dozing away while we safely slipped into the elevator. "Because that would be perfect."

"No," she said. "They're muscle relaxants. For cramps."

"Sorry to spoil your brilliant plan, but I don't think it's Peter's time of the month."

She shook her head. "Trust me, they'll do the trick."

"So you're willing to drug your boyfriend to help me out? You are such a good friend."

She hugged me. "You'd do the same for me."

Would I? Yeah, sure, why not?

"Peter will be mad at you after this. I don't want to ruin your relationship."

She threw the bottle of pills back into her purse. "Forget it. Besides, this makes up my mind for sure that he's not the one for me. My real Prince Charming would never mess with my best friend. Peter deserves what he gets."

We went back to the table. Quinn and Peter seemed involved in an intense discussion. They stopped talking as soon as we approached the table.

"Everything okay?" Quinn asked as I sat down.

"Peachy," I said without looking at him. I was still fuming that he went out hunting last night.

"Good." He downed the rest of his beer.

"We went ahead and ordered dinner," Peter said. "Couldn't wait forever."

"Speak for yourself," I said under my breath.

"Quinn and I were talking about what we should do after." Peter was staring at me intensely. "Amy wanted to go dancing, but I'm thinking about something a little more intimate. I'd like a chance to get to know *Sarah* a little better." He said my name like it was a four-letter word. "Maybe even introduce her to a few of my other friends."

That was *so* not going to happen. But I smiled at him, anyhow.

"Only if they're all as incredibly charming as you are."

The appetizers arrived. Peter had ordered salads all around, and had gotten himself an order of escargot. Amy would grab him and kiss him every so often to distract him as she slipped a tiny blue pill in with the snails. He tossed them back without even flinching. Quinn was too busy staring out the window or down at his refilled glass of beer to notice what was going on.

When dinner was served, I picked at it nervously, noticing that Quinn did the same. I wondered if solid food made him throw up, too. I didn't want to take the chance tonight. I had too many other things to think about.

I glanced over to see Amy push a blue pill into Peter's mashed potatoes. He scooped them into his mouth without a moment's hesitation. What if Amy's plan didn't work? What was I supposed to do then? I attempted to make some kind of vampire telepathy happen between Quinn and myself, trying to get a message to him about a potential escape plan, but it didn't seem that telepathy was one of my new talents. He was barely even meeting my eyes anymore.

It would have to be something a little more out in the open if I wanted to get his attention.

I jabbed him in the hand with my fork.

"Ouch." He snatched his hand away and finally looked at me.

"What do you think about Peter's plan?" I asked. "Meeting his friends after dinner. Do you think that sounds like a good idea?"

"They're my friends, too."

"And your point is?"

"I don't have a point."

"No, you really don't." I was so frustrated with him. Had he forgotten that he was a vampire, too? Or was he completely delusional? I'd almost believed it when he'd told me that he couldn't stop thinking about me. Obviously, he'd meant that he couldn't stop thinking about ways to piss me off.

I frowned and looked across the table at Peter. He ate his dinner with a vengeance. Hunting vampires must be hungry work. His finesse with the fork and knife didn't show any sluggishness, no awkwardness that would hint at successful muscle relaxation. Did that mean the pills weren't working? I didn't know what to do next. He was going to take me to meet his friends, and Quinn was going to go along with it all, living "*la vida* denial." I wasn't happy with that plan at all.

The waiter came to clear away the plates and took our dessert orders. I ordered a Spanish coffee. I liked things that reminded me of the trip to Mexico. It was like my shiny finish line. If I could just make it till then, everything would be okay.

I tried to be patient while I sipped on my after-dinner drink and waited desperately for Quinn to stand up and defend me. To punch Peter's lights out, or something. Anything would be nice, instead of sitting there acting like he was afraid to make waves.

"Peter, I want to tell you something," I said suddenly, desperate for a way out of this.

He didn't look up from his dessert—a multilayered slice of moist chocolate cake.

"What?" he snapped, and I noticed he had a little chocolate icing on his black eye patch.

"It's very important. You could at least stop shoveling food into your mouth for half a second."

He pushed his plate away. "What." It was a statement, not a question this time.

I took a breath. "What I'm going to tell you is going to change everything."

He cocked his head to one side. "Is that so?"

"Yeah, it's so."

"Then spit it out, darlin'." He hesitated and looked at Amy. "I mean, *Sarah*."

I glanced at Quinn. "It has to stay a secret."

"You have my word of honor." He grinned at me. His word of honor was worth less than squat in my books. Squat minus twenty.

I took another deep breath. *Here it goes.* "Quinn's a vampire, too."

"Sarah!" Quinn knocked his water glass over, gaining us the momentary attention of a couple of neighboring tables. The entire restaurant went silent for a split second, but then the noise picked right back up again. He desperately tried to dry the tablecloth with his napkin, and looked at me with astonishment.

"What in the hell did you say?" Peter hissed.

"Vampire. Quinn is one. Just like me. Has been since the weekend. So that means if you're planning on killing me, you'll have to make it a two-for-one deal. It's only fair, after all."

"I can't believe you," Quinn said, and his voice sounded strangled.

"Believe it, buddy boy. I'm not going down alone."

Peter shook his head slowly with disbelief and then, after a moment, began to laugh. "You're funny. But your lies won't work on me."

"It's not a lie," Amy said. "She's telling the truth."

He turned to her. "And let me guess, you're a vampire, too?"

"I wish!" She pulled her purse up to her lap and zipped it shut. I guess she was finally out of pills. Dammit.

"Quinn," Peter said, "say something to this bitch."

"I . . . ," Quinn began. The look on his face was desperate. "I don't know what to say."

"It's not true, is it? It *can't* be true."

"It's true," I said and put an arm around Quinn. "That's why we're together. Show him your fangs, honey. Yup, we're vampires. Both of us. Vampire lovers, together for all eternity."

I kissed Quinn fully on the lips, then turned to smile widely at Peter, fangs and all.

I watched Peter's expression turn from confusion to

rage as he stared at his old hunting buddy. He grabbed his steak knife, his one good eye full of fury. "That bitch did this to you. That bitch made you an evil bloodsucker."

Amy stood up and stomped her foot. "I won't let you talk about my best friend like that."

"I'll talk about her any way I damn well want to," Peter snarled. "Quinn, I am sorry, I truly am. If you were me, I know you'd want me to do the same thing and end your life. Please don't make this more difficult than it has to be."

Quinn was still in shock by what I'd said. I couldn't help but feel slightly guilty. In one sentence I'd basically screwed his life up beyond repair. But I only did what I had to do. Anything to take attention off myself. Unfortunately, it seemed like it was going to work in reverse. Peter's attention was now fully on me, his rage multiplied by the thought I'd ruined his friend in such a monstrous way.

"Please don't tell my father," Quinn finally said, his voice weak. "I beg you."

Peter raised an eyebrow at that and clutched the knife tighter. "I will only tell him that you died with honor at the hands of one of these evil creatures. It would be better for everyone that he never knows the truth. Now let's go."

He rose to his feet. He was taller than I remembered, must have been at least six foot five. He was a tall, imposing man, built like a Mack truck, easily able to crush me with his bare hands as any good pest-control career man could do.

He took a step toward us, and his legs crumpled beneath him. He fell in a heap to the floor, regaining the stares of the restaurant patrons. A waiter narrowly missed stepping on him as he went by with a tray full of drinks for a nearby gawking table.

"What the hell?" Peter tried to brace himself against the table, attempting to get up but failing. "What the hell have you done to me?"

Amy let out the breath she'd been holding. "Thank God. I didn't think the pills were going to work. But I figured twenty of them should probably do something."

Quinn leaped to his feet, and I grabbed his arm to stop him from getting too close to Peter. "You poisoned him?"

"Don't worry, they're only muscle relaxants," I told him. "But, come to think of it, twenty is quite a lot." I leaned over toward Peter, who tried to lift the steak knife at me, but it fell uselessly out of his hand. "If you don't feel very good in ten minutes, I'd ask one of the waiters to call an ambulance, okay? Oh, and thanks for dinner; you're a sweetheart."

"Sorry, pooky." Amy bent down to kiss his cheek. "But I can't have you trying to kill my friends. It's just not nice. I think we should probably see other people."

I grabbed the arm of a passing waiter. "Our friend has had a little too much to drink and he's saying silly stuff. Just ignore him. He'll be okay in a minute, I'm sure, but he probably shouldn't drive."

"Would he like some coffee?" the waiter offered helpfully.

I nodded. "What a good idea. Yeah, lots of coffee."

"We'll take care of him for you," the waiter said.

"Bye, Peter." I patted the top of his head. "Thanks again for dinner. It was great meeting you."

Quinn stood by us in stunned silence. I grabbed the sleeve of his jacket. "Come on," I said. "Let's get the hell out of here."

Chapter 18

We made it to street level and out into the cold night air before I finally let out the breath I was holding. I suppose I'd almost expected Peter to come after us, even if it meant that he'd have to drag his highly relaxed body behind him like a walrus or a mermaid.

Outside the CN Tower, Amy fumbled through her purse to light a cigar, then inhaled deeply on it, resulting in an immediate fit of coughing.

"I didn't know you smoked," I said.

"I don't. This is Peter's. But it seemed like a good time to start."

Quinn hadn't said a word all the way down in the elevator, but I was not going to feel guilty. I wasn't.

Okay, maybe just a little bit.

"Quinn." I approached him. He'd sat down heavily on a snow-covered bench. "Are you going to be okay?"

He stared off into space. I waved my hand in front of his face. "Anyone in there? Look, I only did what I had to do to get out of there in one piece. He would have found out, anyhow. They all would have, eventually."

"You're right."

"See? I knew it."

He looked at me with angry, narrowed eyes. "They would have found out. But they would have found out from *me*. Not from you making it into a big joke."

I felt anger rising up inside me. "Do you see me laughing? It's not a joke to me. And you know what else isn't all that damn funny? You going out last night and killing more vampires, as if none of this means anything to you. That doesn't make you a hero, Quinn; that makes you a murderer. You're not exactly gaining my confidence when I hear about stuff like that."

He shook his head, then suddenly sprang to his feet and was in my face. "I didn't ask for this, in case you didn't notice. Every moment of my life now is torture knowing that I'm the same thing that killed my mother."

"You have to stop dwelling on that."

"I'll dwell on it if I damn well want to," he said through clenched teeth. "I did what I had to do."

"Yeah, killing vampires. That sounds like something you had to do. Couldn't you have taken the night off? Would that have been too much to ask?"

"I tried to." He slumped back down to the bench.

I glanced over at Amy. She was keeping her distance, puffing away on the cigar and pretending that she wasn't listening. Wise girl.

"What do you mean, you 'tried to'? Tried not to kill anything for a few hours?"

He sighed and it was a deep, shaky sound. "I didn't know what else to do."

"What are you talking about?"

"I needed the blood of a full-strength vampire. I

heard you all talking the other night. I understood the rules. When the pain came again, I didn't know what to do. It was excruciating. I wanted to let it happen. I wanted to let it kill me, but self-preservation kicked in. I wasn't going back to Thierry. There was no way. But, damn it all to hell, I knew if I wanted to live, then I needed blood. So, I . . ." His voice trailed off, as if too disgusted with himself to finish the sentence.

"So you went along on the raid to find a vampire who was willing to help you," I finished for him.

He sighed. "It didn't actually matter to me if they were willing or not. When Peter and the others were done, there was plenty of blood to be had. I hid until they'd left and did what I had to do."

I felt the color drain from my face. "After they'd been killed."

"One of them wasn't dead yet. But, yeah." Quinn's face was tense in the moonlight. "The older the vampire, the less there is left. The young ones stay solid after death; the old ones disintegrate."

Right, Thierry had mentioned that to me before. So, what Quinn was trying to tell me was that he went along on the raid, not to participate in killing vampires, but to feed from them. Like a macabre McDonald's drive-thru. I looked at him, expecting to feel revulsion, but instead I felt sorry for him. He'd been all alone in this. He didn't have any other options. I'd been all alone, too, but at least I'd found Thierry. What would I have done in Quinn's place?

"I'm sorry," I finally said. "Nobody should have to go through what you have. And now I've outed you."

He shook his head. "Like you said, they would have

found out sooner or later. I was fooling myself if I thought I could pretend nothing has happened to me."

"So now what?" I felt the overwhelming urge to hug him, to hold him close, and to tell him that everything was going to be okay, but I stopped myself. Mostly because I wasn't sure that everything was going to be okay. For either of us.

"I don't know. I just don't know."

"If you need anything, don't hesitate to ask."

"Yeah," he said. "Anyhow, I'm going to go. You two shouldn't stick around here long, either. Peter will be coming for you."

"He does seem the stubborn type, doesn't he?"

"He told me something while the two of you were in the bathroom, and I . . . I wasn't going to say anything, but . . ."

"What?"

"He said that there's something major going on. That before they move on this year, they'll have wiped out nearly every vamp in the city."

"I thought that was their plan to start with. The whole hunting-season thing. Kill as many vamps as possible, then go drink beer at Clancy's to celebrate."

He frowned and shook his head. "No, Peter was talking about something different. We . . ." He paused. "*They* do try to take out as many as possible, usually out in the open, but not a complete massacre of every vampire within a hundred-mile radius. This is bigger than anything I've ever heard of before."

My breath caught. "Do you think he was just bragging? Blowing some hot macho air?"

"I thought so myself, but he went on about it for a

while. Like there's some master plan this year. Something even I didn't know about, not that that surprises me. My father has never been all that forthcoming with his plans. I think this is for real, though. He said that they have an insider."

"What's that supposed to mean?"

"An informant. Sounds like it could be a vampire who's giving up names and locations."

A vampire traitor willing to sell out his peers. How horrible was that? That must be why some of the secret clubs had been hit this year. For all I knew, Midnight Eclipse might be next on the list. And Veronique *had* said they'd be open for business as usual tonight. I had to tell Thierry to be careful.

I looked at Quinn. "Will you be okay?"

"I'll be fine," he said. "Be safe, Sarah."

He held my gaze for a few moments and then turned to walk away.

"Bye, Quinn," Amy called cheerily after him. "It was nice seeing you again."

"You," I said to Amy, "should go home."

She smiled at me. "Yeah, as if *that's* going to happen. Where are we going now?"

"Nowhere I'm taking you."

She frowned. "When did you get all serious?"

"Serious situations call for serious facial expressions. Now go home."

"No." She crossed her arms.

"Go home or I'll bite you."

She bared her neck. "Go ahead, I'd like to see you try."

I scrunched my nose. "Gross. Fine, be that way.

Come with me. Just promise to be quiet and well be-
haved. Don't say anything, and look as mean as you
can."

"I can do that."

I snagged the first cab that came along and gave him
the address to Midnight Eclipse. I didn't want to go
there. I didn't want to see Thierry again after our ex-
change this afternoon, but I could do it. I had to. I'd just
march right in there and tell him what Quinn had told
me. Then I'd leave, job done, and never have to see him
again. Sounded simple enough.

But then I had a flashback to what it had felt like
when he'd kissed me in my bedroom in Abottsville. So
wonderful, so perfect, so incredible. And then to have it
all dashed against the rocks so fast. It was difficult. All I
wanted him to do was take me into his arms and tell me
that it had all been an elaborate practical joke. There was
no wife. That he only said the cruel things to me to find
out how I really felt about him. And everything was
wonderful and perfect, and we'd ride into the sunset together, dark sunglasses firmly in place, in his gorgeous
black Audi. And we'd live happily ever after.

But I wasn't that stupid. Happily-ever-after was just
for fairy tales. I'd never read a fairy tale with a vampire
in it. Those were horror stories, and nobody lived happily ever after in those.

"You're quiet," Amy said in the back of the cab.
"What's wrong?"

"Nothing." I wiped a stray tear away.

"Sarah!" she exclaimed. "Tell me what's wrong!"

I looked at her and revised my answer. "Everything."

She nodded as if she understood and didn't prod me for any more answers.

When the cabdriver pulled in front of the tanning salon, Amy fished into her purse to pay. She looked confused by our location but dutifully followed me through the front doors like a good friend.

Barry was at the front desk in his usual small black tuxedo. He sprang to his feet and walked over to block the black door.

"Oh," he said disdainfully. "*You're* back."

"Yes," I said. "And you're short. I need to see Thierry."

He was about to to reprimand me for not calling him "master" for the thirtieth bloody time when he looked past me to Amy. His mouth dropped open, exposing his tiny fangs.

I turned to see Amy staring back at him.

Then I could have sworn two cupids appeared above us and shot arrows into both of their hearts. Strange but true: it was love at first sight.

I raised my eyebrows. "You have got to be kidding me."

Barry practically ran to Amy and took her hand in his, kissing it gently. "My name is Barry Jordan, and I am at your service, lovely lady."

"Gag me," I said.

She shot me a look. "Amy," she offered, blushing prettily. "Amy Smith."

"And I thought I was going to be sick before." They didn't respond to me. "Okay, forget it. You two keep each other company. I won't be long."

I pushed open the entrance to the club. It was busier than I'd expected. Nearly every table was full. The band was onstage; the music almost too loud for conversation. From behind the bar Zelda spotted my entrance and motioned for me to come over.

"Hey," she said with a fanged smile as I approached. "Long time no see."

"In the grand scheme of things, it hasn't been all that long." I wearily swung onto an empty bar stool and looked at the crowded, smoky club.

"You're more philosophical than you were three days ago." She pushed a shot of blood toward me. Hopefully, it was on the house, since I currently had about fifty cents to my name.

"I guess it's been a philosophical kind of week. The kind of week that makes you consider taking a bath with a plugged-in toaster. Busy in here, huh?"

Zelda glanced around as she made another round of drinks and arranged them on a serving tray. "Fewer clubs are staying open these days, so the ones that are get the overload."

George appeared next to me and flashed me one of his fabulous Chippendale smiles. "Hey, gorgeous. I was worried I wouldn't be seeing you around here tonight after your dramatic departure this morning."

I smiled back at him. If he was working this evening, it meant he was healing up quickly. "Every time I come in here, I say I'll never come back. But here I am again."

"You want me to find you-know-who for you?"

"If you mean Thierry, I think I'll track him down myself. But not just yet."

Zelda grabbed my hand across the bar. "Sorry about our new arrival. I had no idea she was going to be visiting."

I tried to play dumb. Wasn't all that hard. "Whoever do you mean?"

" 'Queen Vee,' of course."

"Oh, *her.*" I forced myself to laugh. "Why ever would I have a problem with *her* being here?"

Zelda studied me for a second. "Oh, no reason." She and George shared a look. "No reason at all."

"Speaking of Veronique"—I glanced around the dimly lit club again—"any word on how long she's planning on staying in town?"

"Haven't asked," George said. "She doesn't like me that much, don't ask me why. But it seems indefinite."

"Her visit or her not liking you?" Zelda laughed.

"Probably both."

I smiled. "It's nice that she's come for a visit. She seems to be a very interesting person."

They shared another look. "Come off it, Sarah," Zelda said. "You don't have to pretend with us. We know you're jealous as hell."

I just raised my eyebrows at them and drank my shot a little quicker than necessary.

"Jealous? Why ever would I be jealous?"

George glanced at Zelda. "She's totally jealous. And can you blame her? Thierry is to die for. Believe me, if I had a chance . . . I'd . . . well, I won't get into any details until I check your IDs to make sure you're old enough to hear what I'd do."

"Actually," I said, "I'm not all that interested in married men, especially the ones who leave that little piece of information out about themselves. So, you're welcome to him."

"Ah." Zelda poured me another shot, this time vodka.

"Do I see our little fledgling's shields are slipping a bit, the more we talk about this?"

My lip quivered. "No. Just forget it, okay? I don't want to talk about it. I don't want to talk about anything." I let out a long, shaky sigh. "Unless, of course, you two happen to know anything about this cure for vampirism I've been hearing about."

"A cure?" George played with the salty rim of one of the drinks he had yet to deliver. "Doesn't ring a bell for me."

"I know about it," Zelda said simply. "Didn't I mention it to you?"

I was surprised. "I thought you were just joking around. So, how? What? Where?"

She laughed. "One question at a time, okay? First of all, yes, there is a cure, if you want to call it that. Very hard to come by, and not everybody knows about it. It's some kind of secret experimental thing."

"Are you sure?" George said. "How come I've never heard of it?"

"I guess you're just not hanging with the right people, Georgie. When you've been around as long as I have, you get to know a lot of people. Add to that my current vocation as an underpaid and overworked bartender, and everyone is practically tripping over each other to tell you things."

I was stunned. "Have you ever tried to find out more about it?"

She shrugged. "Why would I? I'm not interested in being cured. I like being a vampire. It makes life so much more interesting."

"How about you?" I said to George. "Would you want to be cured?"

He thought about it for a moment. "Maybe once upon a time. Not anymore. I mean, look at me. If I wasn't a vampire, I'd be in my eighties by now, cooped up in an old-age home praying for a clean bedpan. Besides, how much fun could it possibly be to tan wrinkled skin?"

Zelda leaned against the bar counter. "Are you saying that you're looking for a cure?"

"Maybe." I frowned. "It was one thing before I knew there really was a cure, and now I'm not sure how I feel about it."

"This doesn't have anything to do with finding out Thierry's married, does it?"

"No," I said quickly. "All I know is, nobody tried to kill me before, or called me a monster. I could see myself in a mirror, and my teeth were a normal, nonpointy shape. My life was a whole hell of a lot less complicated, that's for sure."

"Life's no fun without complications," Zelda said.

"I guess that depends on your definition of complicated."

I watched a large, pale man approach George and tap his shoulder roughly.

"We've been waiting for our drinks for a long time. You want a tip, or what?"

George picked up the tray full of drinks and handed it to the man with barely a glance. "Here you go. You can keep the tip."

The vampire grumbled about lousy service, but then dutifully carried the tray back to his table while trying his best not to spill anything.

"You see, Sarah, honey?" George put an arm around my shoulder. "Things are only as complicated as you allow them to be."

"You know what? I think you might be right. I *am* making too much of a big deal out of all this stuff. I'm going to stop caring at all. And the next time some big, self-important asshole decides to play with my emotions, I'm going to wipe the floor with his ass . . . ," I trailed off. Zelda's and George's faces had blanked and they weren't looking directly at me anymore. In fact, they were trying to look anywhere else but at me.

I slowly turned around. Thierry stood directly behind me, his head cocked to one side and his expression neutral—although I could have sworn I saw a trace of amusement slide behind his silvery gray eyes.

"You've come back," he said blandly, as though he hadn't just overheard every word of my little rant.

"Just like a bad penny." Then I frowned. Where did that expression come from, anyhow? I'm not sure I even used it right.

"Did you want to see me?"

"Not particularly." I was recovering my composure. Hey, it came and it went. Mostly, these days it went. "But I do need to speak with you."

"Then perhaps you could have simply used the telephone."

I sighed. "Hindsight is twenty-twenty. Now, not to sound like Joan Rivers or anything, but can we talk?"

"Of course." He motioned toward his booth in the corner.

I shook my head. "In your office? I'd prefer something a little more private." He raised an eyebrow and I glowered at his amused expression. "Not *that* kind of private."

"Unfortunately, my office is in use right now for another private matter."

Then I guessed the booth would have to do. I didn't want to debate conversation locations for much longer. Just talking to Thierry was making me nervous, and not particularly in a good way. I wanted this over with as fast as possible, so I slid into the booth and George brought us over a couple of drinks. He winked at me before he left us alone.

"So," Thierry said after a moment, "what is it you wish to speak with me about . . . in private?"

Was it wrong that I wanted to kiss him, even after everything that had happened? Rain kisses on his beautiful face and down his neck and along the edge of his oh-so-black silk shirt. Tuck his stray dark hair behind his ear and whisper how I felt about him, loud enough so only he could hear it?

Yes, it was wrong. It was very, very wrong.

"It's about the hunters," I finally said.

"What about the hunters?" He seemed surprised, as if he'd expected me to bring up another subject. What other subject could I possibly have to talk to Thierry de Bennicoeur about? Hmm, let me think.

"They're planning something this year. Something big. Big enough that they believe that they can kill every last vampire in the city this time around."

He pursed his lips. "Yes, I already know all of that."

"You do?" Of course he'd know that. He was the master, after all. He probably just knew things through osmosis or that vampire telepathy I'd been hoping for.

"Was that all, Sarah?"

"No, that's not all. I also have it on good authority that there's a vampire who's selling the rest of us out. Feeding information to the hunters."

He took a sip of his cranberry juice and then placed it back soundlessly on the table. "And who are you getting *your* information from, if you don't mind my asking?"

"You don't believe me?"

"It's not simply a matter of believing or not. It is a harsh accusation to say that there is a traitor in our midst. I simply wish to know who is telling you these things and what proof they may have."

I felt the sudden urge to lie, or make up some outrageous story about where I'd heard the rumor. But I didn't. "Quinn told me."

Thierry leaned against the back of the booth. "Quinn."

"That's right."

"The hunter who is now a vampire."

"Thanks for the recap. Yes, that's him."

"When did he tell you this?"

This time I took a sip of my own drink before answering. George had been nice enough to bring me over a newbie special, heavy on the "special" rather than the "newbie." I guess I was officially ready for the grown-up vampire drinks.

"Tonight," I answered after a moment.

"Tonight."

"You don't have to repeat everything I say."

"It helps me to understand you better. And when you saw Quinn tonight, where were you? Did he search you out to give you this piece of questionable information?"

"No." I struggled to keep my face as blank as his. "Actually, we were on a date."

His expression gave nothing away, not that I expected it to. What, did I think he was going to leap out of his seat in a rage of jealousy? Not bloody likely.

"I didn't realize that the two of you were dating."

I shrugged. "You know what they say about opposites attracting."

"Yes, that is very true. So, the two of you, is this serious? This relationship between vampire and ex–vampire hunter?"

"Well, we're not planning on getting *married,* or anything like that," I said with special emphasis on the married part.

"And you trust this . . . Quinn?"

Good question. Did I trust him? Not particularly. Did I think he was lying when he told me about the hunter's plans? No, it was the truth. That much I had faith in.

"I believe him."

"I didn't ask if you believe him. I asked if you trust him."

I narrowed my eyes. "Frankly, Thierry, I'm having a little trouble trusting anybody these days. Call me crazy."

"And you decided that you needed to tell me this news. Why come to me?"

I shrugged again. "You seem to be the man everyone answers to around here. They call you *master,* for God's sake. Like, what century is this? Anyhow, I just figured that you would be the one to tell something like this to. So consider yourself told. My job is done. I don't want anything to do with it. In fact, if I can move up my trip to Mexico, I'll be out of here before any of this even goes down."

"You're planning on leaving the country, are you?"

"The tickets have been bought for three months. Amy and me, that's my best friend, not that you care, we've been planning it for ages. I was thinking about canceling, but now I think that it's the best idea ever to get out of this city."

"Perhaps you should invite Quinn to accompany you."

I raised an eyebrow. "You seem quite obsessed with that little tidbit of information, huh? That I and Quinn are together. Well, can you blame me? He's so incredibly hot. And dangerous. And sexy. What girl could resist?"

The corner of his mouth raised into a slight resemblance of a smile. "My, my, he sounds like quite a catch."

"He is," I said. "And, hey, to top it all off, he's not suicidal or married."

His jaw tightened.

I saw George approach to my left. "Sarah, sorry to interrupt, but you have a phone call."

"I do? I mean, of course I do. Yes, I will be right there. Thanks, George." I turned back to Thierry. "Well, I think I've said all I came here to say, and a dash extra. Now, if you'll excuse me, I have an important phone call to take."

I turned away.

"Sarah," Thierry said, and I turned back.

"What?"

Our eyes met and I felt the fight go out of me. He

stared at me for a long moment. "Nothing. Take your phone call."

I walked blindly to the bar while working on reducing the big lump in my throat. The phone was off the hook, and I picked it up and held it to my ear.

"Hello?" I noticed my voice was a little funny.

"Sarah?" Amy said. "Is that you? Your voice sounds a little funny."

We were always on the same wavelength, Amy and me. Well, almost always.

"Yeah, it's me. Where are you?"

"I left. Sorry I didn't say anything to you first."

I sighed. "It was Barry, wasn't it? He is such a little prick. Did he insult you?"

"No, nothing like that." She giggled. "He's with me right now."

"You're with Barry? The little freak from the front?"

"Don't be mean." Her voice was stern. "I'm so glad you introduced us."

"I didn't introduce you. Don't blame me."

"Blame you? I want to thank you! I thought Peter was wonderful, but Barry is spectacular."

"Spectacular? Are we talking about the same guy? The Napoléon Bonaparte of Toronto? Did he drug you, or something?"

"Sarah," she scolded. "You need to learn to look past the external. You're so superficial."

"Yeah, that's me. Superficial Sarah."

"You know, I never believed in love at first sight before, but, Sarah, he's got such beautiful eyes. I could die."

"You're making me feel sick to my stomach. Where are you?"

"Never mind about that. I'm having a good time, and I just didn't want you to worry about me."

I simply didn't have enough time or energy to worry about Amy. I had so many of my own problems that I was thinking about alphabetizing them. "Can you do me a favor?"

"Sure, anything."

"Can you give Barry a message for me?"

"Mmm-hmm. Let me grab a pen."

"You don't need a pen for this. Just tell him that if he hurts you in any way, I'm going to kill him, varnish him, and stick him on my parents' front lawn. He'd make a fantastic garden gnome."

"I'm not going to tell him that! You're horrible."

"Love you, too. Have fun."

"I'll call you. Maybe we can go out on another double date."

I paused. "I think I'd rather throw myself on a bed of sharp chopsticks."

"Oooh, great idea. We'll have Chinese food next time."

I hung up the phone. The lump in my throat had relocated to my stomach. Maybe I should rethink my choice of best friends. Anyone who would be romantically interested in Barry had to have some serious mental issues. And it wasn't just the fact he was short. He was just so . . . so *Barry*. That was some serious ick factor at any height.

I figured I'd just go home. No reason to stick around the club any longer. I'd said all I wanted to. Come to think of it, I'd said a lot more than I'd wanted to. Not that any of it mattered.

I saw a flash of long, wavy, dark hair out of the corner of my eye. It was Veronique, and she was making the rounds, stopping at the tables to do the schmooze thing. I didn't want her to spot me. She must have just arrived, since I hadn't seen her until now. She was sort of hard to miss.

I moved to the far side of the bar and into the hallway that ended at Thierry's office. She hadn't spotted me, and I breathed a slow sigh of relief. Maybe I'd just duck out the back door. No reason I had to go out the same way I came in.

Just then, I heard a loud crash. I almost didn't hear it over the music. The band hadn't stopped playing since I'd gotten there. Right now, they were doing a cover of the Rolling Stones' "Sympathy for the Devil"—only with a female singer and a jazz feel. I wondered fleetingly if the band members were also vampires. Had to be. There was no way Thierry would hire them if they weren't.

The sound came from Thierry's office. I moved toward it, straining to hear anything else. What did he say was going on in there? A private matter of some kind?

My eyes widened as I heard someone yelling indiscernible words and then another crash. My hand found the door handle and I turned it. I put my hand flat on the door to push it open slowly.

You know what they say about curiosity killing the cat? Well, I was hoping that curiosity didn't keep any wooden stakes on hand.

Chapter 19

I recognized one of the men immediately. It was Dan, the lawyer, the one who'd saved me from Quinn and then turned him into a vampire. There were also three other men in the room. Two I'd never seen before, but when they moved out of the way, I recognized the third. It was Melanie's new boyfriend. I think his name was Eugene, the apprentice vampire hunter.

He was tied to a chair in the middle of the room and he stared at me with wide, frightened eyes. His glasses were broken and hanging off his face.

Dan turned to me as I opened the door, and his expression lit up. "Sarah." His voice was warm and friendly. "So good to see you again. Guys, this is Sarah."

"Hi, Sarah," the other two said in unison.

"What the hell is going on in here?" I managed.

"I thought that door was locked," Dan said. He didn't seem too concerned about it.

"Yeah," one of his friends said. "I thought so, too. Weird, huh?"

I felt my face flush with anger. "Does Thierry know

what you guys are doing in here? Maybe I should go get him."

"Yeah, you do that, sweetheart," one of the other guys said. "The thing is, the master told us to do this. That's why we're in his office." He turned to the other. "She's cute, but kind of dumb. Just the way I like 'em."

My eyes widened. "He *told* you to do this?" I backed up a step and felt someone behind me. I turned around.

"Why did you come back here?" Thierry's voice was calm.

"You . . . you told them to do this? How could you?"

"You shouldn't have seen this."

"Untie him right now," I said quietly. "And let him leave."

"I can't."

"You can't or you won't?"

"Very well, I won't. He is one of the hunters. We need to extract information from him about their master plan."

I snorted at that. "From *him*?"

"You know him?" He raised a dark eyebrow. "Ah, perhaps you are dating him as well."

I ignored that. "Eugene isn't one of the main group of hunters. He's only a wannabe. He could barely hurt a fly, let alone a vampire. He's harmless."

"I am! I'm harmless," Eugene squeaked, but was silenced by Dan cracking his knuckles loud enough for everyone to hear.

Thierry turned his gaze to me. "That does not mean he wouldn't know anything that could help us."

"Has he told you anything yet?"

Thierry glanced at Dan.

Dan shook his head. "Nothing useful."

"That's because he doesn't know anything," I said. "Just stop messing around and let him go. Please."

Thierry paused before he answered, "No."

"Why not? Give me one good reason why you won't let him go when you know bloody well he's not going to tell you anything that you don't already know. All you're doing is scaring him half to death."

"I don't need to justify my decisions to you, Sarah. But, very well. I won't let him go because I refuse to have another human out there who knows the location of this club."

I frowned so deeply it hurt. "So, if you're not going to let him go, then what does that mean? You can't keep him here forever."

"We shall do what needs to be done to protect our kind."

I felt cold at his words. "Oh, my God. You're planning on killing him, aren't you? You're no better than the hunters themselves. I won't stand by and let this happen."

"Then you had best leave."

Thierry turned away from me. I couldn't bare to look at Eugene again. I knew Thierry's decision was final. If I continued to argue with him, all I'd end up doing was wasting my breath and looking like a whiny brat who didn't care about the fate of "her kind." Whatever the hell that meant.

I left the office and slammed the door behind me, wishing that Thierry's head had been caught in the middle. I was so furious I couldn't think straight. I took a moment before I went back out to the club and walked through the crowd directly to the bar.

Zelda smiled at me. "I thought you'd left already."

"Do you know what's going on in Thierry's office?"

"No, what?"

I studied her for a moment. "Never mind."

"Are you okay?"

I shook my head, feeling stunned and damaged by what I'd just seen. "No. I haven't been okay for nearly a week. I hate this. I hate all of this. Listen"—I looked up to meet her gaze—"about that cure thing we were talking about earlier, do you have any information for me? Maybe somebody I could talk to about it?"

She stopped mixing the margarita she was working on. "Are you serious?"

"Deadly."

She appeared to think about it for a moment, then grabbed a napkin that had the Midnight Eclipse logo on it. "Do you have a pen?"

I opened up my little purse and pushed past the two quarters and the shard that lay inside. "Yeah, here." I handed one to her.

She scribbled a name and number down. "Last time I heard anything about it, this is the guy you needed to contact. I don't know if he's still around, but it's a start." She pushed the napkin across the top of the bar to me. I picked it up, folded it, and tucked it into my purse.

"Thank you."

She grabbed my hand and squeezed it. "It's not that bad. Being a vampire. You've hardly given it a chance at all."

"I just like to have options. Thanks again, Zelda. You're a real friend."

I stood up and began making my way toward the

exit. I was going to go home and, if I could get any sleep tonight, I was going to sleep on it. I knew that all I'd be able to see when I closed my eyes was Eugene, tied to the chair and looking like a helpless, geeky puppy.

"I know how you must feel," a cool, soothing voice said. I looked up through my teary, blurred vision. Veronique leaned against an empty nearby table. Her long hair was pushed past one shoulder like a dark waterfall. "It is unfortunate what men do in the name of war."

"You can say that again."

"I have witnessed many wars in my time, and it is always the same. There are those who fight and those who get hurt. In the end both sides lose, even if it's just a piece of their souls."

I blinked at her. "Yeah, whatever you say. I'm going home."

"You aren't waiting tables this evening?"

"I'm not a waitress."

"I thought that you were an employee here."

"You thought wrong. I helped out the other night, but that was it."

"When you showed up at the club with Thierry early today . . . you are friends, yes?"

"Friends." I snorted at that. "Yeah, we're friends. At least I thought we were before I just saw the little piece of male posturing in his office."

"If it's any consolation to you, Thierry rarely—if ever—does his own dirty work."

"That's not much of a consolation, Vee. But thanks."

She narrowed her eyes. "What did you just call me?"

Oh. Oops.

"*Vee*. Sorry. It won't happen again."

"No." She smiled. "I like it. *Vee*. I don't remember the last time I had a nickname. What shall I call you?"

"Um, just Sarah will do nicely. Plain old Sarah."

She shook her head. "There's nothing plain about you, my dear. But I can see you're upset about what you've just seen. May I buy you a drink to help ease your mind?"

"It would have to be a very large drink. But I don't want to be here anymore, anyhow, so no thanks."

"No, not here." She took a moment to gaze at the crowd of gathered vampires. "I thought we could go to another club. A human one, perhaps."

"Living on the edge, are you?"

"Just living, my dear."

Let's see, did I want to go out on the town with Thierry's gorgeous wife? Not so much.

"Okay," I said. "Let's go."

Then again, I was never one to turn down a free drink.

We left the club through the tanning salon. Veronique nodded across the street at the Clancy's neon sign. "How about that one?"

I eyed it warily. "That, Vee, is the local hangout for vampire hunters. Probably not such a good choice."

She started to cross the street, and I had to jog to catch up with her. She had really long legs.

I grabbed her arm. "What part of *vampire hunter hangout* didn't you understand?"

"It's just a drink." She gave me a big smile. "Has it been so long since I last visited that Canada is no longer a free country?"

I hadn't planned on setting foot in Clancy's after what had happened the last time, for, oh, the next thousand years or so. But Veronique marched right across the street on her four-inch heels as if she owned the street and every business on it.

I felt suddenly delegated to the role of shorter and slightly less gorgeous sidekick as I quickened my pace to keep up with her. Maybe I just should have said, "No, there's not a chance in hell that I'm going in there." But I didn't. So much for speaking up for myself.

Veronique pushed the front door open and entered the busy bar without pausing for even a moment.

"Ah, yes." A wide smile touched her full lips as she surveyed the smoke-filled, wall-to-wall vampire hunter pub. "This reminds me of a tavern in Germany I once frequented. I haven't been there for over fifty years."

"Okay, Vee," I said as a huge man brushed past me. He wore a leather jacket with KILL written in metal studs on the back of it. "If you insist on being here, you might want to *ixnay* on the *ampirevay alktay*."

She turned to me. "Is that pig Latin?"

"Yup."

"You are the most charming girl."

It's true, I was. But compliments weren't going to get us anywhere if she kept talking the way she was. I didn't want any unwanted attention. I'd had my fill of drama for the evening. One drink and I was out of there. I tried subtly to scan the rough-looking crowd. I didn't recognize anyone who'd tried to kill me lately. That was a good start.

I took a seat on the very same stool where I'd been sitting when I met Quinn. Seemed like ages ago.

The bartender glanced over at me.

"Tequila," I said meekly. "Pretty please."

Veronique sat next to me. "I'll have a mimosa."

"What's that?" the bartender asked.

"A mimosa? Well, it's champagne and orange juice, of course."

"Don't have any champagne, Your Majesty." He stifled a laugh. "Does this look like the Ritz to you?"

"Of course not," she said. "The closest Ritz-Carlton is in Montreal."

"Just give her another tequila," I told him. The longer she took to order, the longer we'd be there.

Veronique didn't argue, and instead smiled at me sweetly.

I hated that even in this light, much harsher than the soft lighting at Midnight Eclipse, she still looked gorgeous. I was hoping that the more I stared at her, the more I'd notice some flaws coming to the forefront. Maybe a stray facial hair or a freshly sprouted zit. I'd even be happy to see an oily T-zone, but I couldn't find a damn thing. She was like a magazine-cover model after they'd been retouched. Flawless.

Actually, the only flaw I could find about her was that she was married to Thierry. But, I guess, that was a pretty big one.

"So, Sarah, dear," she said after a ladylike sip of the tequila. "Why don't you tell me all about yourself?"

I downed my shot in a decidedly unladylike manner, and ordered another one. I couldn't get drunk from just alcohol anymore? Let's put that to the test, shall we?

"What do you want to know?"

"Let's see." She thought for a moment. "How did you come to be friends with my Thierry?"

I grimaced at "*my* Thierry."

"He's become sort of my adopted sire. He helped me when I'd first been made into a vamp"—I glanced around. Better rephrase that—"An *executive assistant of the night*. He saved me from the, uh . . . mean people in human resources."

"He *saved* you?" Thankfully, she seemed to be following my line of thought with an amused nod of her head. "Interesting. What about your natural sire?"

"He was transferred to the big company branch in the sky, if you know what I mean."

"Oh, dear." She shook her head and made a *tsk-tsk* sound. "How horrible for you. And how long ago was that?"

"A week tomorrow night."

She looked surprised. "Truly? I would have taken you for much older than that. You glow with an inner energy one normally only sees in much older . . . *executive assistants*."

"Yeah, that's sort of what Zelda told me, too. She said it's because I've had Thierry's blood . . . er . . . coffee. Yeah, Thierry sure does make a strong cup of coffee. More like espresso, if you ask me."

She nodded. "Of course that would be it. Yes, his *coffee* would be strong by now."

I sighed. "I can't deal with the office analogy any-more. Can we talk about something else?"

She studied me for a moment. "I'm beginning to think that your friendship with my husband is more than I originally thought."

I shook my head. "No, don't think that way, because it's not true. We're just friends, and after tonight I'm not sure I even want to be that."

"What do you mean?"

"Sorry if this comes off as extremely naive to some-body like you, but I didn't like what I saw tonight. That he would do something like that, it's just so horrible. Even if he feels that he's doing it for the right reasons, I'll never understand it."

"It is true." She took another tiny sip of her drink. At the rate she was going, we were going to be there all night. "It is more his style to hide when danger appears and not come out until it's gone." She laughed then, and her voice sounded like delicate wind chimes.

"Excuse me?"

She smiled. "I'll tell you one thing, my dear, you are very brave to go through all you have in the past week and come out on the other end looking no worse for wear. Truly admirable. But then there are those who would rather hide their heads like ostriches in the sand and hope no harm befalls them."

I blinked at her. "Are you trying to say that Thierry's an ostrich?"

She had to be mistaken. Were we talking about two different Thierrys? Maybe I'd blanked out at that part of the conversation earlier. Could happen.

"He once was. Oh, I could tell you stories."

I ordered another drink. "For example?"

"No, no. I should say no more. I wouldn't want to ruin his facade as a brave and powerful leader of the . . . *executive assistant community*."

I spotted an empty booth in the corner, which would afford us some privacy. My heart thudded in my chest at the thought of learning something about Thierry he'd prefer I didn't know.

Veronique followed me as I moved through the wall of muscled beer-drinking men—and a few muscled, beer-drinking women—to the new table.

"I told you the other night that we met during the Black Death in Europe centuries ago, yes?" she said as she flicked her dark, gorgeous hair so it draped perfectly over one pale shoulder.

I glanced over to see a large, hairy man crack his pool cue into the next game so hard that several of the balls went flying off the table.

I leaned forward so I wouldn't have to raise my voice to be heard. "Yes, you mentioned that."

"Before the plague, it was a glorious time in France. I was the daughter of nobility, living on a vast estate." She sighed. "Good times, let me tell you."

"No indoor plumbing," I said.

"Excuse me?"

"No indoor plumbing," I repeated. "I couldn't have handled that. I can't even deal with going camping. Okay, uh, never mind. Please continue."

"One day my family entertained a very rich, very handsome gentleman. I fell immediately in love with him."

I nodded. "Thierry."

She laughed at that. "No, silly girl. Decidedly not Thierry. His name was Marcellus, and he was a powerful vampire. He took a liking to me and made me what you see before you today."

Annoyingly perfect? I hoped I hadn't said that aloud.

"We were together for twenty glorious years. I was so happy. And, might I add, he was a magnificent and insatiable lover."

I signaled to the bartender to bring me another shot. Immediately.

"Alas, my happiness was not to last, for one day he did not return to our homestead. I didn't know if he'd been murdered, or if he simply felt that it was the right time to move on. I would have liked to believe that he was murdered."

"Of course." I nodded.

"By this time, the plague had befallen Europe. Without Marcellus's money to support the way in which I was accustomed to living, I had to take to the streets. There were no servants to bring me my blood in a silver goblet anymore. I had to fend for myself. But during such a time of illness, there was plenty to drink just lying around."

The bartender brought us three shots of tequila each. That would do for a couple of minutes.

Veronique continued when he walked away. "This was a terrible time for me. The sick would drop at your feet and die in a stinking mess right in front of you. It was rather unsavory. And unclean. No wonder they were all so ill. They can blame it on the rats all they like, but a proper floor scrubbing does no one any harm. Except perhaps the scullery maid."

I glanced at my watch. It was nearly eleven o'clock. I hoped this wasn't going to be a long story. I'd been the only one I knew who'd fallen asleep during *Titanic*.

"So, how did you meet Thierry?" I asked wearily.

"I'm getting to that, dear girl. But first I must set up the background of the story. So there I was, a beautiful, helpless—yet immortal—woman in the middle of plague-ravaged Europe. Wandering aimlessly, searching for more of my kind who might take me in.

"Finally I came upon a small town called Le Vieux Cochon. Most of the peasants had left, but their homes were still fairly intact, so I decided that I would stay there for a while. Wait out the plague, for I knew I had the time to be patient. I set myself up in a small but quaint cottage, and hoped not to be disturbed."

She frowned. "But disturbed I was. One day there came a knock at the door and when I opened it, there was a wild-eyed man outside. Dirty, long-haired, and desperate. He begged me to take him in, that there was a mob after him. You see, then, those who were still healthy ran off those who were ill. If they couldn't run them out of town, they simply killed them, burned their bodies in large piles in an attempt to prevent the spread of the disease."

"So the man," I said. "*That* was Thierry."

"Yes. Not quite the same man you see before you today, but time can be an interesting thing when it comes to change and evolution, *n'est-ce pas*?"

"So you helped him."

There was a big, boisterous cheer from behind us and I glanced over my shoulder. A man the size of a small elephant had just sunk his eight ball in the corner pocket to win the game. The loser broke his pool cue over his knee in anger.

Nice place.

I turned back to Veronique, who didn't seem to notice anything unusual about our surroundings.

"No, of course I didn't help him," she said as if that was a stupid thing to suggest. "I shut the door in his face. I wanted no part of his or anyone else's problems. Ah, I see the look of surprise on your face. Trust me, you would have done the same thing. There is no comparison to what was going on then, the sheer paranoia running rampant. There is nothing to compare it with today."

She waited to see if I had anything further to say, and when I didn't, she continued.

"The mob caught up to him finally. He tried to hide on his own, but it was to no avail. The amusing part of it all was that he wasn't ill. Not yet, anyhow. I'm sure it would have been only a matter of time before he became so. The crowd captured him, and they ran him through."

"Ran him through? What does that mean?"

"Killed him," she said as though she were discussing no more than the weather outside. "At least they believed him to be dead. His bloodied body was thrown upon a pile of corpses nearby, and lit on fire."

"Then what?" I yelped.

"Sarah, dear, you must learn patience. Being what you now are, you have the luxury of time. Use it well, for sometimes it is all we have."

I gritted my teeth. "Sorry. Please go on."

"By this time the crowd had dissipated. They'd seen enough death to hold them, and they found no reason to stay behind and watch the fire burn away the illness they so despised. I, at this time, was feeling rather peckish. I left my house and walked amongst the dead, stopping here and there to have a small taste, most of which was quite unsavory."

I felt a cool breeze as the door, a short distance away from our booth, opened up and a group of about ten men entered the already-crowded pub. I tried to ignore them and focus on Veronique's story.

"I came upon the man . . . although he seemed more of a boy to me. At this time I was nearly fifty years of age, though I appeared much as you see me today. I believe my hair was a little longer."

I was trying for the patience thing. I really was. My knuckles were white, gripping my knees under the table to keep from punching her in her perfect face.

"He was still alive," she said. "But barely. His injuries great, his blood loss high. He wasn't to be much of a meal for me. But then he opened his eyes and stared at me from the top of the burning pile of bodies. His eyes are the most extraordinary shade of gray. Especially as they flickered in the firelight.

"Suddenly I felt quite taken with him, despite the grime and sweat. I dragged him from the top of the pile and carried him to my cottage. I cleaned him up as best I could and then I sired him. It was silly for me to do such a thing after only finding his eyes attractive, but I suppose I was lonely. I desired companionship. By the next day I regretted my actions, as I was not interested in looking after a fledgling. I required someone to look after me, but it was done and I have never been one to turn my back on any responsibility that befalls me.

"He awoke the next day terribly confused. He had never heard of what I am, what he was now, and it took much explaining for him to understand. He was very scared. Hid from me much of the time." She laughed softly. "Called me a devil. Ah, the memories."

She took another sip of her first tequila as I downed my fourth.

"But in time he came to accept what had happened, even cherish the second gift of life. We hid in the town for several years before moving on to Paris. There we came into contact with our first hunters—even I was ignorant to their existence until that time. Marcellus had not mentioned that we were so reviled there would be those who would wish to do us harm. We wore our immortality on our sleeve, proud of what we were, and spoke of it to many, looking for others of our kind. We were married in Paris, and I thought for a while that I could be as happy as I had been with Marcellus."

I saw her grip the edge of the table and her knuckles whiten.

"Until that one day when I saw him again. Across the River Seine. He was with another woman, a young girl of no more than sixteen, with fresh marks upon her neck. I then realized that Marcellus had left me because"—she stopped talking and took a shaky sip of her drink—"because I was too old."

I shook my head. "But you looked exactly the same. You'd stopped aging."

"Men," she said simply, as if that explained everything. Actually, it did.

"Thierry and I went to an opera that night. I was trying to take my mind off seeing Marcellus again after so many years. But he was also there. He spoke with me privately, giving me compliment after compliment, attempting to ease my hurt feelings. His charm was so compelling, and perhaps I was a fool to believe him, but I forgave him everything in no more than a blink of his beautiful eyes."

She stopped talking again as the men who had entered the club a few moments ago walked past our booth toward the pool table with drinks in hand.

"He took us with him to a secret club, and it opened up a whole new world to us. That night Marcellus was the man I remembered. Charismatic, engaging, electric. I felt more alive than I had for the ten years since I'd last seen him."

"What about Thierry?"

"He watched me from the other side of the club. I could sense his jealousy, but what was I to do? My true love had at last returned to me. But it was not to last, for that night the club was raided by hunters. It was chaos. They came in like the plague itself, attempting to wipe out everything in their path. Marcellus fought bravely, but . . ." She stopped talking.

I waited.

Veronique sniffed and drew a nearby white paper napkin to the corner of her eye. "He was killed. They surrounded him and killed him with swords carved from wood. Our eyes met as he disintegrated before me. Gone forever. My true love, Marcellus."

She sobbed into the napkin for a moment.

"What about Thierry?" I said again.

She looked up at me sharply. "If I did not know any better, I would say that the only thing you care to learn about is Thierry. Thierry's life, Thierry's fate. But it's my story. *My* story. And my love was dead."

She was feeling such pain for something that had happened more than six hundred years ago that my heart bled a little for her. Just a little. I decided not to provoke her, to make the pain any worse. I waited until she was ready to continue.

"When it finally registered with me that he was gone for good, rage filled my soul. Such rage, such vengeance— but they gave me strength. I, who had never fought anything in my life but perhaps a light cold, took to arms and fought back against the hunters. But I was not the only one. Others in the club fought back. It was a true moment of glory for me as I fought, shoulder to shoulder, with those I'd never met before but now considered as close to me as my own family.

"In the wee hours of the morning, when it was finally over, I looked around for Thierry. He was nowhere to be seen and I felt a sharp pain go through my heart."

"You were stabbed?"

She looked at me. "It was a metaphorical stab of pain. Not literal, dear. I was concerned, for I thought that my young charge—not to mention, loyal and devoted husband—had met the same fate as my beloved Marcellus."

She shook her head. "It was not for two days that I found him. At the first sign of trouble he had left, hid himself away from danger. He had not come out until he felt that it was safe.

"I did not greet him with the open arms he perhaps expected. I was angry with him. Marcellus had fought bravely and died, and he had hidden like a coward and lived."

I let her story settle over me. This was her proof that Thierry was a big, fat coward because more than six hundred years ago he hightailed it out of a fight to the death? Didn't seem like the Thierry I knew nowadays, a man who came off as brave and strong and impenetrable. But I was pretty sure that six hundred years could change a lot of people.

Veronique smiled at me, though her eyes were a bit red from thinking about this Marcellus dude. Yeah, the man who cheated on her and left her without a word. I could see why she was still in mourning. Sounded like a great fellow.

"You've lived a very interesting life."

She nodded solemnly. "Yes, I have."

"How long have the two of you been apart?" I asked. "At least I got the impression that you and Thierry didn't live together anymore."

"That's a rather personal question, isn't it? But I feel as if we're old friends now. I don't mind personal questions from old friends. Our marriage has been in name and memory only for over a hundred years. It was patchy before that. Ever since the incident at the Paris club, I have not felt the same toward him."

"If Marcellus had lived, would you have left Thierry?"

She blinked. "Goodness, what a question! He was my

husband; how could I have left him? I simply would have taken Marcellus as a lover."

"Oh."

I saw someone approach the booth and figured it was the bartender wondering if we wanted more drinks. I looked up, and my breath caught in my throat as I saw Quinn's father staring down at me.

"Hi there," I squeaked.

"I recognize you." He wagged a finger at me. "You were in here with my son before."

"Uh, that's right."

He frowned. "Have you seen the boy? I cannot find him anywhere tonight."

I swallowed hard. "No. Haven't seen him."

He shook his head. "I have reached the end of my patience with him. He'll receive no more mercy from me."

"Roger?" Veronique said, and Quinn's father glanced over at her.

"Veronique?" He raised a bushy eyebrow. "It can't be you."

She stood up. "But it is."

His eyes tracked down her tight black dress. "Stunning. A vision of beauty, just as I remember you from so long ago."

"You have a few more lines in your face," she said with a smile. "But it suits you. You are as handsome as I remember as well."

He smiled back at her, and it was almost a leering grin. "And how long ago was that?"

"Thirty years? Perhaps more? Sarah, dear, would you excuse us for a moment?"

I nodded, since I couldn't find my voice to speak. I

watched Veronique follow Quinn's father, the leader of the vampire hunters, into a dark and smoky corner of the bar. Their faces grew close, and they whispered and laughed and touched each other like old friends.

Did he know that she was a vampire? He had to. I think he was smart enough to figure out if someone hadn't aged a day in decades that something was up. He was acting a little different than I would have expected him to in a situation like this, not that I knew him at all. All I knew was what I'd overheard when he reprimanded Quinn as if he were a naughty toddler. Quinn had been bullied all of his life by this zealot of a father who despised vampires and had devoted his life to wiping them off the face of the planet.

Then why was he giggling with Veronique like a schoolboy with a crush? It just didn't make sense.

Unless . . .

A thought so horrible went through my mind that I immediately pushed it away. But it came back and poked me, insisting that I give it more consideration.

Could it be that Veronique was the vampire traitor? Was that why she'd shown up in the city just before the hunters had come up with their new and improved annihilation plan? Veronique gave me the impression that she cared about one person and one person only—and it wasn't Thierry. It was herself.

Then it *had* to be true. It just made sense. *She* was the informant. She was giving the hunters information on the secret clubs' locations and then turning her pretty, dark-haired head in the other direction when they went in and slaughtered everyone in sight.

I slipped out of the booth and left the bar without letting Veronique see me. I thought briefly about going back across the street to tell Thierry my suspicions, but didn't. I didn't want to be near him, either, after what I'd witnessed earlier. Veronique's story hadn't changed my opinion of him or softened my judgment that what he was planning to do to poor Eugene was wrong, wrong, wrong.

Instead, I went back to my apartment. I was so tired that I just wanted to sleep and push the conscious world far away. Maybe everything wouldn't seem so hopeless tomorrow, although I had a feeling that was just wishful thinking.

I fiddled with the key for my lock and slid it in, turned the handle, and pushed open my door. I tossed my purse and keys on the kitchen counter and sighed long and hopelessly in the darkness. It did feel good to be home. Something normal after such a crazy day. Here I could still pretend that nothing in my life had changed. That I was still the same girl who watched *Sex and the City* while eating Häagen-Dazs ice cream right out of the carton. Who talked with Amy over the phone for two hours straight about a cute guy one of us was seeing, even though we'd already just spent the whole day working together. Whose closet was color-coordinated for ease of wardrobe choices.

Yes, my apartment was my own space. My rented safety zone. My Ikea-decorated oasis.

I flicked on the overhead light.

And screamed.

Quinn was sitting on my sofa. He blinked at the sudden harsh light.

"What the hell are you doing here?" I managed, my

heart beating wildly in my chest. "How the hell did you get in here?"

He got to his feet and held out his hands to calm me down. "Easy. Take it easy. I'm sorry, I just . . . It wasn't that hard figuring out which unit was yours. *Dearly* isn't that common of a last name, you know."

I felt in my purse for the knife I'd stolen from the restaurant. It was only a butter knife, not very sharp at all, but I bet it would hurt a lot. At the very least, it would cause a bad bruise. I held it up in front of me.

He glanced at it and almost grinned. "Are you going to start singing something from *West Side Story*?"

"I don't sing. What the hell are you doing here?"

"I thought we left things off pretty well earlier. I thought you trusted me now." He took a step closer to me.

I took a step backward.

"*Trust* is not in my vocabulary when it comes to you, Quinn. Besides, you just broke into my apartment when I wasn't here. Not exactly a way to build my confidence in you."

"But I didn't have anywhere else to go."

"Ever hear of the Holiday Inn? There's one just around the corner. You get a free continental breakfast and everything."

He sighed. "That's not what I meant, and you know it. I needed to see you. And you did say if I needed anything, I shouldn't hesitate to ask."

"I meant you should ask somebody else. Someone who gives a shit. Now I suggest you get the hell out of here before—"

He closed the space between us before I could do

anything about it and snatched the knife right out of my hand. I heard it clatter to the floor at the same time I felt his strong, warm hands on either side of my face as he pulled me to him, taking my breath away with a passionate kiss.

Chapter 20

We made it to the bed before I came to my senses. Even then, I was still kissing him back, clutching at him like a life preserver for the drowning woman I'd become.

"No." I broke off the kiss and pushed at him weakly. "We can't do this."

He wasn't listening very well and ran his mouth down my neck. I let out a quavering little moan before I gathered all the willpower I could manage.

"Quinn, *no*." I pushed him harder this time, and he stumbled backward to the floor. He lay there looking up at me. His eyes were dark.

"Why not?"

"Just because, that's why. Isn't that good enough?"

He shook his head. "You want me, I can tell. Don't try to deny it."

I stood up and straightened out the dress I'd bought for our double date tonight. I noticed that there was a fresh tear in my panty hose. Just perfect. "I think you should leave."

He got to his feet and came closer than I would have liked. "Sarah." His voice was low and sexy, and it made my stomach tighten. But I backed away from him and refused to meet his eyes. He stopped moving toward me.

"It's him, isn't it?"

"Him who?"

He sighed. "Thierry. You're in love with him."

I frowned. "Just because I don't want to put out on the first breaking and entering doesn't mean that I'm in love with Thierry."

He sat down heavily in the purple beanbag chair in the corner of my bedroom. "He doesn't deserve you."

The very mention of Thierry's name had made my heart pump loudly and painfully against my ribs. "Go away, Quinn."

I heard him swallow, and his eyes grew shiny and moist in the darkness. "I thought . . . I thought that you and I had a connection. I feel something when I'm with you. You feel it, too. Forget him. We're a much better match, anyhow."

"I don't want to talk about this anymore. Do you know the kind of day I've had? All I wanted to do was come home and blank it all out, even if it was just for a couple of hours. I don't need any more complications."

"That's all I am to you? A complication?"

"Do you really want the truth?" I saw his face start to crumble. He'd had a pretty hard day himself, and I was just being a bitch to him. "I'm sorry, Quinn. I'm so sorry." I moved toward him and took him in my arms. He began to sob against me. We sat like that for a while, nothing sexy about it anymore, just comforting.

After a few minutes he looked at me. "I'm a vampire."

"I'm afraid so."

"I hate this. I want things to be the way they used to be. I knew what to do then. I knew how to behave, how to think. I don't want to be a vampire."

"Neither do I." Now I was crying, too. Yeah, we made a good pair, all right. The overly emotional monsters of the greater Toronto area. How fierce, how scary, how much in need of a box of tissues.

Wait a minute. I pulled back from him as a thought tweaked at me. We both hated what had happened to us. Neither of us wanted to be vampires.

I stood up and left the bedroom. I grabbed my purse on the kitchen counter and picked through it to find the napkin. Clutching it in my hand, I went back to Quinn.

"Here's the answer."

"The answer?" He looked up at me. "To what?"

"All of our problems."

"The answer to all of our problems is a cocktail napkin? Maybe your problems are a little different than mine are."

"Nope, same problem." I handed it to him and knelt back down next to the beanbag chair. "That's the phone number for a guy who knows about a cure for vampirism. We don't have to be vampires. We just need to talk to him and convince him to help us."

He stared at the napkin. "There's a cure? I didn't know there was a cure."

"Then I guess it's a good thing you know me."

"Have you already called him?"

"Not yet."

"Who did you get this from?"

I took the napkin back from him and folded it gingerly. "Zelda, at the club."

He just sat there, stunned, as the information slowly sank in. "There's a cure."

"Yes." I smiled. "We can be normal again."

"It's too good to be true. There has to be some sort of catch."

"Can't you just be happy about this?"

He smiled at me and stroked the hair off my forehead. "Okay. I'm happy. But what does this mean for you and me?"

"What do you mean?"

He glanced at the bed.

I raised my eyebrows. "It means we'll both be human again. It also means that I have a very comfortable sofa in the living room." I stood up so I could grab one of my pillows and throw it at him. "Sleep well."

I thought I was tired. I really did. But I lay awake for most of the night with thoughts racing through my brain. This was it. I was going to be cured. Being a vampire was a disease, and I was going to get the medicine that would make me all better. I could be normal again; I wouldn't have to worry about being hunted within an inch of my life; I could lose the fangs and get my reflection back.

I should have been happy. It was everything I wanted. Why, then, couldn't I sleep? I tossed and turned, the events of the past week going through my mind like a midnight monster-movie marathon.

After a while I must have dozed off, because when I opened my eyes, it was light outside. I pushed back the covers and pulled on some powder blue sweats. I hadn't forgotten for one moment that Quinn was sleeping on my sofa, not ten feet away.

I pushed open my bedroom door and peeked out. He was on the phone in the kitchen. When he saw me, he quickly said good-bye to whomever he was speaking with and hung up. I saw the cocktail napkin on the countertop.

He looked at me. "I called him."

"Already? Couldn't you have waited for me?"

"How long did you want me to wait? It's noon."

"It is?" I glanced at the clock on the stove. He was right. "Okay, so tell me all about it."

"He's agreed to meet with us. We can leave now. It sounds like it's on the up-and-up. There is a cure, and we're going to get it. So get dressed."

"I am dressed."

"Those look like pajamas."

"And yet, they're not." I rolled my eyes. "Sorry that I don't dress up in short skirts and heels all the time. Welcome to my real life. I just need to wash my face and brush my fangs first and we can get out of here."

"Whatever." Quinn turned away from me.

Okay. Fine. Was he in a shitty mood because of my rejection last night? I could almost see the tiny construction workers hovering around him, helping to build up the walls that kept his male ego safe from harm. I wondered how he would be acting if I hadn't made him sleep on the couch. Not that I was having any regrets. I was extremely attracted to him—sure, I'd admit that. But that was no reason to complicate further my already-too-complicated life.

If things had been different . . .

Oh, I don't know. I wasn't even going to think that way. Besides, starting out a relationship after a failed murder attempt was not a good foundation to grow on.

And it had nothing to do with Thierry. Absolutely, positively, *almost* nothing.

The mystery scientist guy lived forty-five minutes away on the outskirts of Grimsby. The cab was going to cost a fortune. I insisted on stopping for coffee at the first Tim Hortons we saw. Just because the caffeine didn't have any effect on me anymore was no reason to give up one of my very favorite bad habits, provided it didn't make me want to throw up. Quinn got one, too. Black, no sugar. No big surprise there.

After a while the cab made a left, off the main road, and drove for a few miles into the rough. I became nervous.

"Where does this guy live, anyhow?"

He shrugged. "Along here, I guess."

Great. The cure doctor and Bigfoot. I should have brought my camera.

The cab came to a stop outside a run-down trailer home in the middle of nowhere. Quinn got out of his side of the car, paid the driver, and asked him to stick around for a bit.

I opened my car door and stepped out directly into a big, slushy puddle of mud. I grimaced as the dampness soaked through my shoes. Great. At least today I'd decided on the Nikes.

Quinn didn't wait for me. He strode right up to the door of the mobile home and knocked sharply. And waited. There was no answer.

I put a hand on my hip. "You're sure this is the right address?"

"Yes," he hissed.

"Quinn, save the attitude. We're in this together, remember?"

He turned to glare at me, then his eyes got wide. "Don't move."

I froze in place. "What?"

"Just don't move. I'm serious, Sarah."

I heard something. Close. Twigs breaking on the ground. Loud breathing in and out. Sniffing.

Sniffing?

I glanced down. There was a large—and I mean *large*—dog staring at me from only inches away. It growled, low and menacing, and bared its teeth.

"I don't like dogs," I whispered. "Go away. Shoo."

"Be nice," Quinn warned.

"Uh . . ." I could feel sweat dripping down my back. "Nice doggy? Yeah. Good doggy."

The growl increased and it took a step closer to me. I couldn't tell what breed it was. Big, black, and probably rabid. The kind of dog that rips your throat out now and asks questions later.

"Nice dog—"

It jumped at me, muddy feet on my chest, knocking

me to the ground and into a big pile of wet snow. I screamed and saw Quinn leap toward me.

Then I heard the gunshot.

And I felt the hot, wet tongue of the dog licking up my left cheek.

"Ew." I tried to push its muzzle away.

There was another gunshot, but the dog didn't budge. Who was shooting?

"Barkley," a coarse voice commanded. "Get off the lady. Now!"

Barkley whimpered and, with a last affectionate swipe of its tongue, moved away from me. I was too stunned to stand up yet, so I just lay there on my back. Quinn came into view above me, a look of concern on his face. Then another man appeared. He was tall, skinny, and had sparse, longish white hair plastered to his head. He wore a ratty burgundy housecoat. If crazy had a look, this was it.

He pointed the gun at me. "Get up, vampire."

He backed away as Quinn helped me to my feet and motioned with the shotgun for us to go toward the trailer.

"You're Dr. Kalisan?" Quinn asked.

"Shut it. Get."

We turned toward the door, and he pushed the gun into each of our backs to nudge us forward.

"Listen," I said. "We can just go. Don't want to bother you or anything. Our cab . . ." I glanced behind me. Where the cab used to be were two dark tire tracks in the light covering of snow. I shook my head. "Oh, never mind."

Kalisan pushed us into the trailer and shut the door behind us. Immediately we were plunged into darkness.

"Down," he said, and I felt the gun jab me in my spine again.

I clung to Quinn's arm and found that we were making our way down a long flight of stairs. Down and down. It was so strange. I stumbled a couple of times, but finally ended up on flat ground.

Fluorescent lights flickered on. We were standing in a large living room: couches, television, stereo system, weird embryos in glass jars on the bookshelf. The trailer must have been just the tip of the iceberg. This was a whole underground lair. Well, suburban-style lair, anyhow.

Kalisan still had the gun on us, his eyes narrowed. Barkley sat next to him, large and foreboding, but panting, with his tail wagging happily.

"Why don't you point that gun somewhere else," Quinn said, holding on to my sweaty hand.

"What do you want, vampires?"

I frowned. "The cure, of course. We called for an appointment."

"You think it's that easy? Just call for an appointment and come on over?"

"Well, yeah."

His eyes narrowed even farther until they were such tiny slits I couldn't believe he could see out of them at all. "Who are you? What are your names?"

Quinn glanced at me and squeezed my hand. "I'm Michael Quinn. And this is Sarah Dearly."

Kalisan frowned and lowered the gun a fraction. "Quinn, eh?"

"Yeah, so?"

The doctor moved backward, without taking his eyes

off us. He grabbed a framed photo that sat on a table next to his television and brought it back to us, thrusting it in Quinn's face.

"Who's that, then?"

The photo was of a much younger Kalisan. He wore a bright yellow leisure suit and a tie so wide I would have thought it was a Halloween costume if my father hadn't owned the exact same outfit. On either side of him was a much younger Roger Quinn and a pretty blond woman.

Quinn snatched the photo away from Kalisan. "Those are my parents."

Kalisan eyed him for a moment. "Your father is the great vampire hunter, Roger Quinn?"

Quinn stared back at him. "Like I said, I'm looking for a cure."

"I see." He lowered the gun to the floor. "Your father is an admirable man. Someone who would be disappointed to find out what has happened to you. He doesn't know, I presume?"

"You presume correctly."

Kalisan glanced at me. "And what's your story?"

Barkley had come to sit next to me, and I patted his head absently. "I'm just a girl in need of a cure."

He glanced down at the dog. "I suppose you can't be all that bad if my werewolf likes you."

I removed my hand. "Were-*what*?"

Kalisan smiled. "Ah, so you are a vampire who doesn't believe in werewolves?"

Barkley licked my hand, and I immediately wiped it on my pants. "Gross."

"His rude behavior isn't his fault. He's been stuck

that way for a very long time. He forgets normal human manners. I've been working on a cure for him as well, but alas, the university's grants for this sort of research are few and far between."

I glanced down at Barkley. "Bad dog."

He licked my hand again.

Kalisan turned to Quinn and took the photo back. "You truly want the cure?"

Quinn nodded. "Yes."

"I'll give it to you." He handed the gun to Quinn. "But first you must shoot the woman."

I heard a whimper, and I wasn't sure if it was Barkley or myself.

Quinn frowned down at the gun in his hands. "You want me to—"

Kalisan pointed at me. "Shoot her. She's a vampire; you're a hunter. This should be no problem for you."

I backed up a step. "Quinn."

"Shut up," Quinn said. Then to the doctor, "You're saying that all I have to do for the cure is to shoot her. Right here. Right now. And you'll give it to me."

"That's correct."

Quinn raised the shotgun toward me, and I backed up against the wall. I was barely breathing, barely thinking. Just the word "no" going through my head over and over again. And the thought that I shouldn't have made him sleep on the couch last night. Big mistake. Huge.

"Just shoot her," Quinn said to himself as he aimed the gun at my forehead. "Easy as that."

Then he turned the gun toward Kalisan.

"Sorry, Doc. Things stopped being that easy for me a while ago. Now about that cure?"

The doctor stared at him for a second and then laughed and pushed the gun away. "Blanks. Just blanks. I was only testing you."

I hadn't moved. I'd been seconds away from needing adult diapers and was trying to make my brain work again. *Guns are bad. Very bad. Especially when they're pointed at me.*

"Sarah," Quinn said. "You okay?"

"Sure, no problem." My voice was squeaky.

"Come," Kalisan said. "I'll make coffee."

Five minutes later I was sitting in the doctor's expansive kitchen trying to make my near-death twitches go away. He'd given me a coffee mug that read RESEARCHERS DO IT BY THE BOOK. I think it was supposed to sound dirty, but I wasn't in the mood to find it amusing. We'd already called for a cab. Being where we were, it would be better to have one waiting outside than be stuck here forever. To put it mildly.

"You two are an item?" Kalisan asked after biting into an apple Danish.

Quinn glanced at me. "No. Just friends."

"May I ask why you want to be cured?"

"It's simple," Quinn said. "We want our old lives back."

"Then perhaps you should have thought twice before being sired."

I shook my head. "We were both turned against our will."

He studied me for a moment, perhaps trying to decide if I was lying or not. "You'd allow yourselves to be my guinea pigs?"

I didn't particularly like the sound of that.

"Has the cure been used successfully before?" Quinn reached under the table and squeezed my hand.

"Yes, of course. But, in the grand scheme of things, it's still a new technology."

He nodded. "We're interested."

Kalisan went to refill his coffee mug, topping it off with a lot of cream and several spoonfuls of sugar. "Then there is only the matter of price."

I'd expected that. You can't get anything good for free anymore, even when you volunteer to be a guinea pig. I could sell my sofa. There were those commemorative Princess Diana plates that were probably worth a pretty penny on eBay. And I still had a bit of money my grandmother had left me in her will. It was only a few thousand, but it was nice to know I had it for a rainy day. And it was very rainy.

"Okay," I said. "How much?"

"One million dollars." Kalisan took a sip of his coffee. "Each."

My Princess Diana plates couldn't go up that much, even if there was a last-minute bidding war.

"What?" I managed. "Are you kidding me?"

I looked over at Quinn. His face was red. "That's excessive. There must be another way."

"Unfortunately, that's the going rate," Dr. Kalisan said, almost apologetically. "It's not as though I have a lab here and am able to mix up the ingredients easily. It is a long, expensive process. Components have to be gathered from the four corners of the earth. Dark magic is involved, too, and you would not believe how much the going hourly rate is for a wizard these days. Working wizards have such huge egos, you have no idea. I don't care what the movies would have you believe."

I grabbed Quinn's arm. This was bad news. We weren't going to get the cure. It existed, but it was all about money, like everything in the world. Money talked, bullshit—and vampires—walked.

"Thanks for your time." I pulled at Quinn. "We'll hold on to your number in case we win the lottery. Come on, Quinn, let's wait for the cab outside."

That was it, then. It was over. I was stuck as a vampire forever.

"Just a moment," Kalisan said. "If you truly have no money, I think there might be another way."

We turned back around.

"You're from Toronto, isn't that so?"

Quinn crossed his arms. "That's right."

"There is a much-sought-after vampire who is reportedly living in your city. He is old, very old, and impossible to kill. He's a legend. There is a price tag on his head, which would more than cover your fees. If you were to give me his location—information I could sell to those who wish to find him—then I think we could come to an understanding."

"You'd give us the cure for this information?" Quinn said with disbelief.

"Yes."

I didn't say anything, but my mouth had gone dry. He wanted information for the hunters to capture and kill a vampire who was old and powerful enough to be considered a legend? There was only one vamp living in Toronto I was aware of who fit that bill. Gee whiz. What a small world.

"Who is it?" Quinn asked.

"His name is Thierry de Bennicoeur." He smiled. "To bring the great Thierry de Bennicoeur down would be a feather in anyone's cap. A feather that they'd be willing to pay quite dearly for."

I dug my fingernails into Quinn's arm before he had a chance to say anything.

"We don't know him," I said.

"Perhaps not. But I am quite sure he is in the city. I am confident that you are sufficiently motivated to find his location, his hiding spots, for such a reward as the cure."

Quinn inhaled deeply. "I don't know about that."

I could have kissed him.

Kalisan nodded. "Ah, loyalty. I respect that. Misplaced loyalty, but loyalty nonetheless. Protecting your own kind, whether or not you wish to remain one of them, is an admirable gesture."

Quinn didn't say anything, and I knew it was a struggle for him. It wasn't as though he liked Thierry very much, but he had saved Quinn's life. Quinn was honorable, and that counted as something to him.

"There has to be another way," Quinn said.

"I wish that there were. But I am not the only one involved in the process. If it were up to me, I would hand over the cure to you happily, for free. But I'm afraid that's not the way it works."

"Then I'm sorry we couldn't work this out." Quinn's voice sounded strangled.

The photo of Kalisan with Quinn's parents had been placed for the time being on the shelf behind the doctor. He glanced at it. "Your mother was a wonderful woman.

Beautiful, charming, a marvelous wife and mother. I had the honor of meeting her on several occasions. A shame about what happened to her."

"I didn't come here to discuss my family," Quinn said sharply. "Sarah, I think you're right. We should leave."

Dr. Kalisan nodded. "A painful memory. Yes, I understand that."

"You have no idea." There was no more friendliness in Quinn's eyes. He looked at Dr. Kalisan as he once looked at me. Emotionless, murderous, without compassion or feeling. He grabbed my hand and steered us back in the direction of the stairs without another word.

Kalisan cleared his throat. "I see that you have no idea that it was Thierry de Bennicoeur who was responsible for your mother's death, or I can't imagine that you would be protecting him so fiercely."

Quinn froze in place.

"Yes, he murdered her," Kalisan continued. "It is well known in the hunting community, but I would assume your father has shielded you from the unfortunate details. I saw the papers, the reports. I know what he did to her before her death, and if I shared with you the grisly details, then you would be having no second thoughts about handing him over on a silver platter."

I was screaming inside at what I was hearing, though I tried not to show anything on my face. I couldn't think about what was true and what was not. I only knew that I had to get Quinn the hell out of there before he did something crazy.

He was still in the same spot, hadn't moved an inch. I touched his arm and he flinched.

Quinn glanced over his shoulder. "I'll think about your offer." His voice was dead.

"Yes, you do that." Kalisan took a sip from his mug of coffee. "You have my number. Would you please be so kind as to close the door behind you?"

Chapter 21

The entire ride back to the city was in silence. But it wasn't just uncomfortable silence, it was torture.

I didn't know what to say. I didn't know what to think. It felt like some sort of a nightmare come to life. Thierry killed Quinn's mother? It couldn't be true. Dr. Kalisan was lying, he had to be.

The cab pulled up in front of my apartment building. I turned to Quinn.

"What are you going to do?"

He didn't meet my eyes. "I don't know."

"Where are you going now?"

"I don't know."

"I can come with you. We can talk about this. There has to be another way."

"I want to be alone."

"But . . . you're not going to . . ." I swallowed. "Are you going to call Dr. Kalisan back?"

He looked up at me, and his eyes were full of pain. "I don't know."

"He's lying to you . . . to us. He has to be."

"Of course *you'd* think that." His voice was scornful. "I don't know, Sarah, I can't think straight. I need to be alone. If what the doctor said is true—if Thierry really did that to my mother—" His voice broke off. "I still don't think I'd tell him."

I let out a breath.

He gritted his teeth. "I'd rather kill Thierry myself, even if it costs me the cure."

"Quinn . . ."

"Get out of here, Sarah."

"But—"

He leaned over to open the cab door and practically pushed me out onto the sidewalk. "Get out."

I struggled to keep my balance, and by the time I was ready to say something else, the door slammed shut behind me and the cab drove away.

If only I'd never tried to find out about the cure. Opening that can had let out too many worms. And I hated worms.

I didn't know where to turn. I didn't know where to go. I thought briefly about just going up to my condo and crawling back into bed, but that didn't seem like something I should do.

A sign. I was lost and didn't know what to do next— I needed a sign to show me the way.

Looking up, I saw a billboard for the Toronto stage production of *Mamma Mia!,* surrounded by glowing reviews from a bunch of newspapers.

I frowned. I meant a different sign. Not that one.

Somebody bumped my shoulder as they walked briskly past me.

"Hey!" I yelled after him. "Watch where you're going, jerk."

The man turned to glance at me and my breath caught in my chest. It was Eugene, looking nervous and jittery, but he was alive and well.

"Eugene!"

Fear crossed his expression when he saw me. "Leave me alone," he said in a quavering voice. "Don't hurt me."

I ran to catch up with him and grabbed his shoulder. He backed up against the wall and held his hands up to protect his face.

"I'm not going to hurt you. What are you doing here? Did they let you go last night?"

"Y-y-yes," he stammered. "They released me when they finally decided I was telling the truth."

"They just let you go? Just like that? Even now that you know where the club is?"

"The dark-haired man, the scary one, he let me go. The others didn't want to."

The dark-haired, scary one had to be Thierry. Everything I expected to happen last night, all of my crazy imaginings of what Thierry would do—letting Eugene go was not one of them.

I cocked my head to one side and tried to look mean. "And you aren't going to say anything about where you were?"

"Nothing! Not a word. I promised him. Scout's honor!"

"What about the other hunters?"

"I don't know any other hunters. This was all Melanie's idea. She wanted some kind of revenge on her old boyfriend. I didn't want to hurt anybody. I'm leaving town, so I won't be speaking with anyone. I'm leaving the country and going back to Wisconsin."

I let him go. "Good. You do that. And, uh, have a nice trip."

He scurried away up the street like a scared mouse who'd just escaped from a hungry cobra. It was highly strange to have someone look at me like they were afraid I might hurt them.

Thierry hadn't ordered Eugene's death. He'd let him go. I let it sink in.

Then I took a streetcar to Lakeside Drive. I didn't have enough money for a cab, so public transit would have to suffice. It was three o'clock. The club wouldn't be open yet, but I tried the front door, anyhow. Surprisingly, it wasn't locked and swung inward at my touch.

I walked into the tanning salon just before I was attacked.

Well, "attacked" might be too strong a word. It was more like a fierce hug that seemed to come from nowhere.

I pushed away from whoever it was and looked at them, my eyes wide. But it was only Amy, smiling bright and shiny back at me.

"Hello, sunshine!" she said. "How are you on this fine day?"

"Amy." I tried to compose myself, then realized it was impossible. "What the hell?"

"I have had such a great day, you would not believe it. And last night? In-freaking-credible."

Oh, yeah. Amy and Barry's little romance from hell. Spare me the details.

She frowned at me. "You don't look so good."

"I don't?" I said with mock surprise. "That's funny, 'cause I feel like a million bucks. That reminds me, you wouldn't happen to have a million bucks I can borrow, would you?"

"Sorry, no. Oh, dear, I guess I shouldn't be acting all happy in front of you then, if you're having a lousy day."

"Try lousy decade."

She laughed then and flicked her light blond hair off her face. I spotted something odd on her neck. It couldn't be what it looked like, could it? I grabbed her and pulled her hair off to the side to inspect the fading fang marks, like two tiny hickeys over her jugular vein.

She clasped a hand over her neck and smiled sheepishly at me. "I didn't want you to see that."

I waited, not saying anything.

"I have news," she said.

I raised an eyebrow. It wasn't a happy eyebrow by any means.

She held up her left hand. She was wearing a ring with a tiny diamond in it.

"I'm engaged."

I still didn't say anything. Her smile faltered.

"Aren't you happy for me?"

I felt the headache/potential brain tumor arrive right on schedule. "Amy, don't you think you're taking things a little too quickly? I don't want you to get hurt. He's probably just doing this so he can feed off you. Disgusting, but true."

She looked shocked. "Feed off me? How dare you say something so horrible about my Barry. He didn't just feed off me . . ." She paused and then met my eyes directly. "He made me into a vampire just like you!"

She said it with such enthusiasm, such pure joy, I almost felt happy for her. She made it sound as though she'd just won an all-expenses-paid trip around the world. But she wasn't going anywhere. Except to hell in a handbasket, that is.

Her smile slowly faded when I didn't jump up and down with excitement about her "wonderful" news.

"I'm so sorry, Amy." I felt tears rising in my eyes. "I dragged you into this. This never would have happened if I hadn't let you come here last night. It's all my fault."

She frowned at me. "What are you talking about? This is the best thing to ever happen to me."

I shook my head. "You're delusional. I can't believe you, Amy. Wake the hell up! Being a vampire is horrible. If the hunters don't kill you, you're in constant pain if you don't have blood regularly. You grow fangs and lose your reflection. It's not normal, and it's definitely not fun. Why would you want this for yourself?"

Her expression turned cold. "You're just jealous."

"Jealous? Yeah, I'm so jealous."

"You are, you just don't know it." She crossed her arms in front of her, defensively. "I'm engaged to a wonderful man, I'm happy, and now I'm a vampire just like you. You thought you could be the only one? Well, I've got a news flash for you: the world doesn't revolve around Sarah Dearly."

"You know something? Just three weeks ago you went out and bought the same skirt as me because you thought it was cool. You are such a follower, Amy. Well, hate to break it to you, but this isn't exactly a piece of clothing you can just return tomorrow if you don't like it. This is your life, and you've just gone and ruined it."

"What has happened to you, Sarah?" Her disappointment in me was palpable. "You've changed so much. I barely recognize you anymore. I mean, you look the same, but you don't act the same."

I snorted at that. "Yeah, I suppose I used to act like an ignorant bubblehead just like you. Funny how a week of running for your life can change a girl."

"It's your own fault that you can't see the positive side of things. Maybe that's where we're different. I'm sorry that you can't be happy for me. But *I'm* happy for me. *Barry's* happy for me. And that's all that matters."

I held up my hands, totally exasperated with her. "Whatever. I don't want to deal with this."

"Then don't." Her bottom lip quivered. "Just don't. Now, if you'll excuse me, Barry said I could use the tanning beds for free this afternoon."

She turned away and went into one of the rooms; then she slammed the white door shut behind her.

I stood there for a minute in stunned silence. I couldn't believe it. She was such a dope. Was that really the way I used to come off to people? Like there wasn't anything more in my brain than what I was wearing and how pretty other people might think I look? It was sickening.

But a part of me wanted to go after her and talk. We'd been friends for so long. We'd shared so much, and it hadn't just been surface crap. I hoped our friendship could survive this. I really did. I just wasn't so sure. Then again, by the sound of things we might have a long, long time to make up.

I shook my head. I wondered where I should throw the bachelorette party.

Maybe I was overreacting. Who, me? I took a few deep breaths. Maybe I just needed to take a little time and relax, do some deep yoga breathing. Find my zen. I think I'd lost my zen about the same time I got fired last week. That's assuming I ever had a zen in the first place. Come to think of it, I wasn't even sure what a zen was.

I pushed open the black door to the club and walked inside. It was empty, but I'd expected that. It wasn't due to open to customers for another six hours. It felt eerie being in there all alone, the chairs up on the tables, the lights off. Everything was so still and quiet.

I went to the bar and helped myself to a few shots of blood. It's amazing how good such a disgusting thing made me feel. Funny how you can get used to the craziest things if given enough time.

Thierry's office was empty, too. There was no one there but me. And Amy out in the tanning bed. It would be good to have a little peace and quiet for a while. I had to think through everything I wanted to talk to Thierry about.

I needed to know if he had anything to do with Quinn's mother's death. I wanted to know why he'd let Eugene go when he'd given me the impression that he'd die.

Sitting down at Thierry's booth, I laid my head on the table. After a while I must have dozed off.

I awoke to a sharp pain on my shoulder. Somebody was poking me.

"What the hell?" I looked up.

"Hey," Zelda said.

I rubbed my eyes. "Hey yourself."

"What are you doing here?" She slid into the other side of the booth.

"I wanted to talk to Thierry, but he's not here yet."

"How did you get in?"

"Amy was out front using the tanning bed."

"Oh, right." She smiled. "Our little bride-to-be."

"Yeah." I rolled my eyes. "Can you believe that?"

"I think it's kind of cute." She pushed a newbie special across the table. "I made this for you."

"Oh, thanks." I took a sip. The diluted blood tasted weak, now that I was used to the real stuff. "You seriously think it's cute?"

"Why not? Love is always cute."

I laughed. "Yeah. Love. Right. I think it'll take me a while before I'm convinced that they're in love. And can you believe it? He actually turned her. I'm going to give him a piece of my mind the next time I see him. Maybe a piece of my fist, too, while I'm at it."

She smiled back at me. "Barry's harmless. Your friend could do a lot worse."

"If you say so."

She looked at me for a moment. "You seem a little down."

"Do I?"

"Yeah. What's wrong?"

I sure wanted somebody to confide in. Normally, it would have been Amy, but it didn't look as though she was going to be much help. I still needed someone's opinion about everything. Somebody I trusted.

Zelda waited for me to answer. It was funny, but looking at her across the table, I felt like I could be looking at my younger sister. If I had one, that is. Zelda appeared to be only in her late teens, and even though I knew she was three hundred years older than that, the illusion was still pretty persuasive. Maybe we could braid each other's hair later and talk about boys. Maybe not.

"I went to see that guy," I said. "The cure guy. Met with him and everything."

"Really?" Her expression was guarded. Maybe she didn't know how to react, if it was good or bad news that I went to see him. I was still trying to figure that part out myself.

"And it's true. There is a cure."

"You went there all by yourself? Wow, that's brave."

"Actually, I took Quinn with me."

Her eyes widened. "The guy who practically remodeled this place the other night? The hunter?"

"That's the one. He's calmed down a bit, though. He wants the cure, too, so I took him with me."

"Well, that makes sense. So, what happened?"

I sighed. "You'll never believe how much the cure costs."

"There's a cost? Oh, I never even thought about that. I guess it makes sense. Okay, how much?"

"Try one million bucks on for size."

Her eyebrows shot up. "Holy shit. That's a lot of money."

"Yeah."

"And he wasn't able to come down at all? He wouldn't lower the rate?"

"Why would he?" I shrugged. "He doesn't know me. Why should he do me a favor?"

"God, Sarah. I don't know what to say. I know you were counting on it."

I chewed my bottom lip while I tried to decide if I wanted to tell her any more. It was eating at me like ants on a moldy egg-salad sandwich—I wanted to get it all out on the table.

I looked at her. "He did say there was another way to get the cure. I'm not going to do it, but there is another way."

"Did he want you to sleep with him?"

I made a sickened face. "God, no. Ew. You should have seen him. Not the cream of anybody's crop. No. He wanted to know where to find Thierry. Said he'd be able to sell the info to the hunters for big bucks. That he'd be some kind of a trophy kill because he's so old and legendary and shit."

"You're kidding." Zelda's eyes were so wide I probably could have seen my reflection in them if I still had one. "And what did you say to that?"

"I played dumb, of course. Wasn't hard."

"And Quinn?"

"Same deal. He didn't say anything. But then the guy said something about how Thierry was responsible for Quinn's mother's death. It was terrible."

"He said that? What did Quinn do then?"

"I think he had a small stroke. But he still didn't say anything. I think he was in too much shock. But all bets are off now. I don't know what to do, Zelda. Tell me what I should do. Should I tell Thierry that this guy is spreading lies about him?"

She was quiet for a moment. "Why do you think it's a lie?"

I blinked at her. "Because it has to be. Thierry's not a murderer. He couldn't have done it; there's no way."

She didn't say anything to confirm that I was 100 percent correct. In fact, she wouldn't even meet my eyes anymore.

"Zelda." I felt panic rising in my chest. "Talk to me."

"Thierry's always been kind to me," she said. "I told you he helped me out when I was a fledgling, right?"

I nodded.

"Not that he shared any of his blood with me"—she eyed me for a moment—"but I owe him, okay? He's been good to me, and I've always felt a sense of obligation to look out for him and not do anything to cause him pain directly. I don't want to say anything that'll make things worse than they already are."

"Things couldn't possibly get any worse than they are." My voice had turned shrill. "Please, Zelda, tell me what you're thinking about."

She shrugged a little and shifted around in her seat. "Don't you ever wonder why there are vampire hunters at all?"

"Just to make life interesting?"

She shook her head. "They all do what they do because, for the most part, they honestly think they're doing the right thing. That they're the good guys and we're the evil hell spawn."

"But they're wrong. We're not evil."

She paused. "It hasn't exactly always been that way."

"Okay, Zelda, stop beating around the bush. Tell me what you're trying to say."

Her face was grim. She didn't want to tell me whatever was on her mind. I wasn't sure I even wanted to hear it, but there was no going back now.

"First of all," she said, "try to remember that things haven't always been as easy as they are now."

"What the hell does that mean?"

"Look around. You're in a vampire bar. For a few bucks you can get all the blood you need, with or without alcohol. We can live normal lives, interact with regular people, hold so-called normal jobs if we need to. Nobody has to know what we really are, unless we tell them."

I clenched my fist. I wasn't going to hit her, but it helped ease my stress a bit. Or maybe it added to it. I don't know. "Still beating around the bush. Move away from the bush."

"Hundreds of years ago things weren't so simple. We need blood to survive. Not that many people are going to say—hey, you can have my blood. Sure, just sink your teeth in my arm or neck and have at it. When we feel the pain of true hunger, and I believe you've felt it yourself, we'll do whatever is necessary to get what we need."

My fists were so tight my nails dug painfully into the palms of my hands. "You're going to have to spell it out for me, Zelda. I'm a slow learner."

She sighed. "I'm not all that old, in the grand scheme of things. It was hard for me. Still is, actually. But before was much worse. The vampires took what they needed, and sometimes they took too much."

"And bled people to death by accident," I said numbly.

"Hunger is a terrible thing. Accidental deaths happened. And after a time it became accepted. I guess they had to rationalize it or they would have gone crazy."

"What does this have to do with Quinn's mother?"

"Nothing. But it tells you why vampires are now considered monsters."

"Because they once were," I finished, my heart thudding in my ears.

"Mostly, it was a select group that originated in Europe who gave us the bad name we still have. They were the partiers of that age. Drinking all they wanted and, after a time, not really caring if they took too much. A great deal of blood can be intoxicating, and if you're constantly drinking . . . well, you get the idea."

She took a breath and waited to see if I had anything to say. I didn't, so she continued speaking. "So the vampire hunters gathered to rid the world of this group of murderers. Chased them out of Europe, but all it did was scatter them through the rest of the world. Most of them were killed over the next couple of hundred years, but I know of two that survive to this very day."

"Let me guess," I said dully. "Veronique and Thierry."

She nodded. "They're legendary. Oldest vamps I know personally, anyhow."

"So you're saying that Thierry may or may not have had a bit of a drinking problem in the old days. But that was then and this is now. Quinn's mother would have been killed only around twenty-five years ago. Sorry, but I don't buy that explanation."

"You're sweet," Zelda said. "And so young. You look at him with rose-colored glasses because he's so handsome and powerful. But don't fool yourself. He's also very dangerous and always has been. Anyone who gets in his path isn't usually in his path very long, if you get my meaning."

I felt my frown deepen. I wasn't enjoying story time very much today. "Veronique told me about their lives back in the old days. She called him a coward. Somebody who'd hide at the first glimpse of danger. Doesn't sound like somebody who's all that dangerous."

"Veronique told you that?" She laughed softly. "Well, consider the source, would you?"

"Huh?"

"Veronique has always loved to tell stories that make her shine and everyone else pale in comparison."

"Are you saying that she was lying?"

"Hundreds of years can color a story. Just like an old photograph, the details fade, the edges get worn. I don't think Thierry is, or ever has been, a coward. But I don't know. All I know is the Thierry from today, and that's nobody you want to mess with. I also know that he hates the hunters. Beyond that, I suppose I'd just be guessing."

I leaned back in my seat. I'd always hated history in high school. Too many dates and people's names to memorize. Now I hated it for an entirely different reason.

"Why did you tell me this?" I wasn't crying. I just felt sort of numb.

She reached over and touched my hands, which were clasped together on the tabletop so tightly, I couldn't feel them anymore. "Knowledge is power. But please don't tell Thierry I told you any of this."

"I won't."

"I'd better go get the bar ready. We're opening up in a little over an hour."

I nodded but didn't look at her. She moved away from the table, leaving me there alone.

And I'd never felt so alone.

Thierry was a bad guy. A storybook vampire who bit necks, drank blood, and left dead bodies in his wake. The kind of monster who is hunted down and killed, after which the townspeople cheer his death.

The kind of man who could kill a loving wife and mother and not look back.

I found myself on my feet. I wanted out of there. I wanted to go home. No, I wanted to find Quinn. Yes, find Quinn. I had to talk to him. Tell him . . . tell him what? That everything he'd heard was true? That we should sell Thierry out so we could get the cure? Did he deserve to die for the crimes he'd committed in the past? And if so, did we deserve to profit from his death?

I put my thoughts on hold. I couldn't deal with them right then. I needed some fresh air. No, what I really needed was to wake up and have it all be a dream. Everything. Every last piece of it. I wanted it all to go away.

Practically running for the back door, I pushed it open and felt the cold air sweep the hair back off my shoulders. Maybe if I started running, I could leave it all behind me. Put some serious distance between me and the monster I'd become. Run far, far away. I noticed the tears on my cheeks now as the temperature made them feel like streaks of ice. Christ, I'd cried more in the past week than I had in all of my twenties. I hadn't even cried this much when my senior-prom date dumped me and stuck me with the limousine bill.

I felt someone grab my upper arm and stop me in my tracks. He pulled me around to look at him, to make me stare directly into his strange silver eyes.

"Sarah," Thierry said. "What's wrong?"

Chapter 22

Thierry, I . . . I was just leaving."

"Did you need to speak with me again?"

"No." I didn't know what to say to him. "I have to go." I could see my breath in the cold air in front of me. His warm grip on my arm didn't loosen.

"I didn't like how we left things last night," he said. "There are things that must be addressed between us."

I shook my head. "I saw Eugene. I know you let him go. Thank you for that."

He studied me. "Then why are you acting this way?"

"What way?"

"As though you can't bear to look at me."

I swallowed and glanced up from the ground, forcing myself to meet and hold his gaze.

"Why don't older vampires like to sire new ones?" I asked.

I don't know where that came from. The question surprised me as much as him, I think.

"Pardon me?"

"The night after we first met, you told me that there

are reasons why those as old as you don't sire fledglings. I just wondered what they were."

"Please come inside, and we'll talk about it."

"No . . . I don't think I will. I just wanted to know."

He sighed. "The older the vampire, the more powerful his blood. This can have certain side effects on the young ones that are not always desired or wanted."

"Such as?"

"Such as many things you have experienced yourself. Your reflection, for one. It faded many months before it normally would have. Your fangs also grew early. I suppose they're inconveniences more than anything, but it is sometimes sad to lose touch so quickly with what you once were."

"And that's all? Just a fast-forward button on the vampire VCR? I already know all that."

"No." He paused and moved closer to me so his face was only inches from mine. "It is said that the psychic and emotional bond between an older sire and fledgling is stronger and deeper in some ways. However, I wouldn't worry too much about this, as I am not your original sire. You will not be bonded to me any longer than you wish to be."

"Oh. Well, that's good, I guess. I'm not into bondage that much, psychic or otherwise, no matter what you've heard." I stood there without knowing what else to say. And normally I was a blabbermouth. Thierry had turned into the one man, the one person in the world, who had me perpetually tongue-tied, especially when he stood so close to me.

There was the smallest trace of a smile on his lips. "I think I shall miss you."

"Why? Where are you going?" His answering silence told me all I needed to know. I shook my head again. "Oh right. How could I forget about that?"

"It's not something to be sad about. It is simply an event whose time has come."

"Who said I was sad?" My words were harsher than I meant them to be. "I did promise to help you, didn't I? Just name the place and time and I'll be there. That's what us fledglings are good for. I don't seem to be good for much else around here."

He finally broke off our staring contest and put his hand on the partially open door I stood against. He pushed it wide open and moved away from me. There was still a smile on his face, but it felt like that was the wrong word. There has to be a better word to use than "smile" when it's done with no joy or humor behind the expression. When it's only a position your mouth chooses to be in at that particular moment.

I realized then that if I didn't know him—if I just saw him on the street and didn't know he was a vampire or anything other than human—I wouldn't assume there was anything unusual about him. Anything old and legendary. Anything evil, murderous, and cold-blooded. He simply looked like a very attractive man in his mid-thirties. A little sad, but perfectly normal.

But as the old cliché goes, you can't judge a book by its cover. Thierry was a many-paged, leather-bound book with a mint-condition cover—but the pages were worn and faded. And the story inside would keep you up at night, afraid of what might be lurking in your closet.

"Till then, Sarah," he said before he disappeared into

the club. The door slowly closed behind him and locked with a click.

I stood there for a long time while large flakes of snow landed in my hair and on my face, melting thickly against my skin.

I headed home. I couldn't do anything by staying at Midnight Eclipse other than feel crappy, and I figured I could do that just as easily on my sofa curled up in the fetal position. There would possibly be some thumb sucking involved, too. The infantile kind, not the boss's paper-cut kind, that is.

I got off the bus in front of my apartment complex and walked steadily toward it, placing one foot in front of the other. If I concentrated on the easy things, maybe the difficult stuff wouldn't feel so overwhelming.

One foot in front of the other. One deep breath of cold-evening air after another.

And a hand clamping down roughly over my mouth. I was so surprised that I didn't even try to scream. Whoever it was had me locked tightly against him, with his arm around my chest like a safety harness on a carnival ride, the other hand pressed tightly against my mouth.

He was strong, whoever he was, and he dragged me around the corner into a deserted alley. Then he let me go.

I spun around to see who it was, a scream rising in my throat.

Why wasn't I all that surprised to see that it was Quinn? He was dressed all in black and wasn't wearing a smile.

"I am so going to kick your ass for that." I wiped my

mouth with the back of my hand. "Just what in the holy hell do you think you're doing?"

He reached into his pocket and pulled out a length of rope. I eyed it uneasily.

"What's that for?"

He met my eyes. "I know you'll protest what I'm going to do, but I need you to come with me."

"I'll come." I held my hands up to ward him off. "No need to go all psycho on me. Now, why don't you tell me what's going on before I freak out?"

He paused, wrapping the length of rope around his wrist in the same way a potential strangler might do. It wasn't doing much to ease my mind.

"We're going to get the cure," he said. "Tonight."

"No way." My voice was firm, yet ever-so-slightly hysterical. "No, Quinn, you can't do this."

"I'm doing it. It's the best decision and it will benefit both of us. I'm going to get you the cure, whether you like it or not. Now, we can do this with or without the gag, Sarah. It's entirely your decision."

Needless to say, the gag was required. As soon as he came toward me again, I started screaming, more from reflex than fear. Not that anyone came to help. Weren't there any good Samaritans in the city anymore? Maybe they'd all headed south for the winter like birds do.

In less than a minute he'd trussed me up like a Thanksgiving turkey. He didn't hurt me in the least doing it, though. Made me wonder how much practice he'd had tying women up in dark alleys.

There was a car parked in the shadows. I thought for a second that this was going to be a mob-style kidnapping. He'd throw me in the trunk of an ominous black sedan or something. Turned out it was a rented silver Volkswagen Beetle, and I got to sit in the front seat. Lucky me.

For a while I made as much noise as I could, calling him every name in the book, even though it was muffled by the gag, and the sounds I was making were more along the lines of "Mrrrghhh!" I struggled against the ropes. I probably could have thrown my body against his, but the best I could hope for by doing that would be his losing control of the car and possibly ending up at the side of the highway in a fiery, mangled mess.

So, I ended up sitting still, with my eyes facing forward, and tried to relax. I knew he wasn't going to hurt me. But I couldn't promise I wasn't going to hurt him when he finally untied me.

He was going to tell Dr. Kalisan about Thierry and where to find him so the hunters could go and make vampire mincemeat out of him. And he was doing it because Thierry killed his mother. After all that Zelda had told me, I didn't have much of a leg to stand on if I wanted to argue in Thierry's defense. I'd like to believe he didn't do it, that he'd never hurt anything larger than the odd spider. But I couldn't.

Quinn pulled up to the doctor's trailer and put the brakes on so hard that the car lurched forward. Luckily, he'd made sure I was properly seat-belted before heading off on our little road trip from hell.

He leaned over to unfasten me and finally met my angry gaze in all its intensity.

"I know what you're thinking, but this is for the best.

And it's not just revenge." He paused as he unclicked me, and then with emphasis added another, "It's *not*."

Right. And I bet he almost believed that himself.

He came around to my side of the car and tried to help me out, but I wasn't budging. He gave me zero choice about coming along, and I wasn't about to make things easy for him.

He groaned with obvious annoyance and then bent down to throw me over his shoulder.

Okay, if I'd known he was going to do that, I might have agreed to walk on my own. He carried me to the doctor's front door like an industrial-size sack of potatoes. If I weren't already steaming mad, I'd be embarrassed.

He knocked on the door so hard it shook in its frame, I could feel the reverberations going through me. A couple of minutes went by before Dr. Kalisan appeared. I'm not sure what the expression was on his face when he saw me—well, the back of me, anyhow, at eye level, but he quickly ushered us inside.

Quinn carried me down the flight of stairs and put me down on the couch in the doctor's living room. Then he finally removed the gag from my mouth. He probably expected me to unleash an immediate tirade of expletives, but I didn't say a word.

He didn't make a move to untie me further. He just pushed some hair that had fallen across my face back and tucked it behind my left ear.

"Are you okay?" he asked with concern as he knelt down beside me. "I'm sorry I had to do it this way."

I turned my face away from him. I'd officially decided that I wasn't speaking to him.

"This is simply the only way." There was no joy in his voice. No excitement at the prospect of getting the cure.

Perhaps I could save the silent treatment for a more opportune time.

"There *is* another way," I said.

"What? Tell me."

I took a deep inhale of stale subterranean trailer air. Not so surprisingly, the scent of wet dog was mixed in with it. I briefly wondered where Barkley was today. "I don't know, but I'm sure there is one. There has to be. If we had a few days—"

"But," Dr. Kalisan interrupted me, "in a few days hunting season will be over, and the more affluent hunters will have moved on. They'll still desire the information, of course, but it will be worth much less by then. Time is of the essence, I'm afraid."

Quinn stood up. "So, how does this work?"

"Quinn!"

"Sarah, I'm going to do this whether or not you want me to. I'm going to cure both of us, and when it's all over, if you never want to speak to me again, well, I guess that's just something I'm going to have to live with."

"There has to be another way. There has to be. I won't let you do this."

"Look"—his voice was harsher this time—"I know you and Thierry are . . . close. He's helped me, too. But I'm not damn well going to feel guilty about this. He killed my mother. Do you know what that woman meant to me?" I shook my head and lowered my eyes. "I was only five years old when she died. Even I don't know how much she meant. But I remember a woman who'd give anything for me, for our family. By giving his location over, I'll get my revenge and get us both the cure. There is more good to be had from this situation than bad."

I sighed, a slow, shaky noise. I wished I could argue with him, but the fight was draining from me. If Thierry had killed his mother, then he had every right to seek revenge. I wasn't stupid; I got that. It's just that the world wasn't quite as black and white for me as it was for him. Whatever Thierry might have done in the past, I didn't think he deserved to die for it now.

The thing is, though, Thierry *wanted* to die. He was sick of living, and was possibly planning his suicide at this very moment. So, then, would it be so bad to do this? Well, not do it, but let Quinn do it without making it into a bigger deal than it had to be? After all, Thierry might beat the hunters to it in the end. What a disappointment that would be for them. Or perhaps they'd just believe that he'd vanished, safely keeping his reputation as a legendary master vampire intact.

"It's very simple," Kalisan said. "You will give me the location of where he can be found, and I will get the cure for you. In a matter of moments all of this unpleasantness will be over."

That gave me an idea. What if Quinn went ahead and told him where Thierry's location was? Then we'd get the cure immediately, like he'd said. Next thing you know, I'm on a phone warning Thierry to clear out. Yes, it made perfect sense. Nobody had to get hurt. We could all get what we wanted out of this. But I had to play it cool.

"I have to know one thing," Quinn said. "You have to assure me that no one else will be harmed. The place where you can find Thierry is populated by other innocent people."

"Don't you mean populated by other vampires?" Kalisan laughed under his breath. "My, how things change. The mighty hunter becomes one with his former prey."

Quinn scowled. "It's not that. It's just that there's no need for additional violence. Promise me that no one else will get hurt."

"I'll do what I can. But I'm afraid once the information leaves my hands, the control does also."

There was silence then, and I glanced at Quinn. His forehead was set in deep furrows; he was bothered by this. But that was the price he'd have to pay. Did he really think things would go completely smoothly?

"Untie me," I said, and Quinn's gaze flicked to me. "I promise I won't do anything."

He seemed to welcome the delay and began working on the knots he'd made. After a minute the ropes dropped loose and I rubbed my wrists. He met my eyes.

"Remember, you promised."

"I know." I felt a dull fog hanging over me that had been building for an hour. Hell, who was I kidding? That fog had settled in days ago, around the same time I realized that my being a vampire wasn't just a crazy dream.

So, we were going to be cured. Why didn't I feel happier? Plan or no plan, this situation sucked. I decided that after it was all said and done, after I was back to normal—not that I was even sure what normal was anymore—I was going to move away. Start fresh somewhere else. Maybe I'd head out to Vancouver. I went there as a kid, and I remembered being thrilled by the mountains and the ocean. I'd be thrilled to be thrilled by anything again.

Quinn turned back to Dr. Kalisan and took a deep breath. "Okay, here it goes. You can find Thierry de Bennicoeur at 217 Lakeside Drive in Toronto. He owns the tanning salon there called Midnight Eclipse. There's a secret vampire club in the back."

Dr. Kalisan nodded. "Good. Very good."

I wiped a tear away. So, that was it. Hardly took any time at all. I wondered how much longer I could play it cool as a cucumber before I totally freaked out and ran for the nearest phone. The countdown began.

"Now, the cure?" Quinn's voice was strangled, fighting back some serious emotions of his own. "Please?"

Dr. Kalisan nodded curtly. "I'll go get it for you. I happen to have it on hand. I had a feeling that you'd be back this evening."

He turned and left Quinn and me alone in the living room. Quinn looked at me.

"I'm sorry."

I couldn't answer him, so I just shook my head. I felt terrible. I felt like I'd just shoved the first of many stakes into Thierry's chest. I'd decided my plan was stupid. Even if Thierry got out alive, the club was a write-off. Shit. It was all my fault. I should have done something to stop this. I didn't know what. Anything.

"Sarah." He touched my arm, and I flinched. "Say something."

"How about don't talk to me? Ever again."

"Fair enough."

A few minutes passed in silence. Long enough for me to have second, third, and fourth thoughts about what we'd just done. I was about to turn and leave, but Dr. Kalisan reappeared at the doorway that led to the kitchen. He had a self-satisfied smile on his face.

"You have it?" Quinn asked.

"What makes you think that the cure is an *it*?" the doctor said.

Another person appeared in the doorway from behind him. A familiar face, lined and worn with age and experience. A well-kept graying beard adorned his face. His eyes were similar to his son's, but much less friendly and compassionate.

"Yes." Quinn's father stared at the both of us, but he was speaking into the cell phone held to his ear. "Midnight Eclipse. That is correct. I shall meet you there." He closed the phone and tucked it into his inner jacket pocket.

Shit. Double shit. My stomach dropped.

"Father?" Quinn's voice was barely audible.

Roger Quinn shook his head, an obvious motion of disappointment. "Why am I not surprised? My only son has sullied the family name. I can smell your vileness from where I stand."

"I'm sorry." Quinn took a step forward. I wanted him to do anything but apologize. I had a feeling that he'd spent his life apologizing to this man, even for things he hadn't done.

"Don't waste your breath. I have nothing more to say to you."

"But, Father, I've come here to get the cure. I don't

want to be what I am. I don't want it! And now I won't be. Dr. Kalisan said that he has the cure for this. That's why we're here."

"Stupid boy," Roger Quinn said. "There is no cure."

Chapter 23

My mouth dropped open as I heard his words fall on the air. *"There is no cure?"* He had to be kidding. He just had to be playing a game with us. Any moment people were going to spring out from behind the couch and tell us where the hidden cameras were.

It was a joke. It just had to be.

Then why wasn't anyone laughing?

I looked at the doctor. He shrugged slightly at me. "I'm sorry, my dear, but he speaks the truth. There is no cure for vampirism. Never has been, never will be."

"But . . . but why did you lie to us?"

"A means to an end, I suppose. It was a rumor originally started by the hunters, a ruse to draw out some of your kind. Clues had been scattered, here and there. Mostly as an experiment. My name was leaked due to my background as a scientist and my friendship with Roger. It's what I do to help fight the evil in any way I can."

I tried to frown, but my face felt frozen. "How many times do I have to tell people that I'm not evil?"

"It's in a vampire's very nature to be evil. I don't blame you any more than I could blame a lion for stalking her daily meal."

"You used us," Quinn said, his voice still soft. "To find out Thierry's location. That's all this was about."

"The opportunity presented itself. That particular result wasn't planned, it was just a happy coincidence."

"But he killed my mother." Quinn glanced at his father.

Roger smiled a thin, unpleasant smile. "How you remind me of her right now. She protested her innocence right until the end as well."

"What are you talking about?"

Roger sighed and shook his head. "I never told you the truth about your mother. And now, now I feel as though I'm living those horrible days all over again."

"Her murder—"

"Her punishment," Roger corrected. "It would have been better if you'd been led to believe from the beginning that de Bennicoeur slaughtered her. But, instead, I told you nothing. I assumed you'd try to find out more on your own and was disappointed when your curiosity didn't lead you any further than it did."

"Father, what are you talking about?"

"Your mother was a whore." Roger spat the words, his anger as palpable today as it must have been twenty-five years ago. "An adulterous whore who cavorted with vampires."

"What?" Quinn's eyes were wide.

"When I found out, I confronted her—demanded the truth. She didn't deny it for a moment. She said she was in love with one of them." He laughed, and it wasn't a pleasant sound. " 'Love,' as if a vampire could know the meaning of such a word. At the time I was still in love with her, and ready to forgive her indiscretions, but she'd already been turned, the marks still visible on her pale white neck. She was planning on leaving me, leaving *you*, boy, without a word of explanation that very night."

I could feel my heart beating loudly and violently in my chest. I wasn't liking this tale one little bit, and I can't imagine that Quinn was, either. He stared at a spot on the wall just to the side of his father's head. His hands were clenched into tight fists, but he made no sound that might stop the truth from being told finally.

"Your mother," Roger continued, "was a whore vampire, her black heart filled with the joy of deserting those she promised before God to love and obey till death do us part."

"You were the one who killed her." It was my voice that said those words. I didn't mean to; they just came out all by themselves. Roger looked at me directly for the first time.

"I did only what had to be done. And knew that from that day forward, it was my sacred duty to rid the earth of scum like her."

It wasn't Thierry. He didn't kill Quinn's mother. This news should have made me happy or, at the very least, relieved, but I was numb. I waited for Quinn's reaction. What was he going to do? He'd just learned after two and a half decades that his father murdered his mother for being the exact thing he was now.

"You didn't seem to be having much of a problem with Veronique the other night," I said. But then, I already knew why. She was the traitor. Roger Quinn liked vamps as long as they provided him with the means to kill other vamps.

A strange smile twisted across his wrinkled face. "Veronique is a special case. A rare rose in a garden of snakes. But I wouldn't hesitate to tear her heart from her lovely chest if she provoked me."

He glared at me, his narrow gaze doing its hardest to intimidate me. It was working. I looked away first.

"Well, this is rather uncomfortable, isn't it?" Dr. Kalisan said after a moment. "Perhaps I should put on a pot of coffee and we can move this discussion to the kitchen?"

"Unfortunately, my friend"—Roger reached into the jacket pocket opposite to the one with the cell phone and pulled out a long, sharp wooden stake—"there's no time for that."

Quinn's eyes narrowed. "Just what do you think you're going to do with that, Father?"

"What I have to," he said simply. "Do not think that for one moment I shall take any pleasure from your death. I had great hopes for you. Great hopes. But they are not to be anymore."

"Yeah, quite the disappointment I've been to you, haven't I?" The anger and bitterness in Quinn was so strong it was like a thick, dark aura surrounding him. "Trained me to hunt and kill all of these years, and look what happened to me."

"Yes." Roger tested the sharpness of the stake with the tip of his finger. Looked pretty damn sharp to me. "It is unfortunate, but a risk with the life of a hunter. At least to the weaker ones."

"You never gave me any credit for all the work I did."

Quinn's voice was getting stronger, fueled by the truth he just heard. "What I thought was right. You raised me to believe that vampires are evil and need to be killed, as if they're no better than insects."

"They aren't, son. Please don't make this harder than it has to be." Roger took a decisive step toward Quinn with the menace of the practiced hunter he was.

"No!" Quinn's arm moved almost faster than I could see, and in the one motion he snatched the stake right out of his father's hand. "I'm not evil. Sarah's not evil. I've spent all these years murdering vampires in the name of good. And all of that time, I never knew I was one of the bad guys. Snuffing out innocent lives because of your personal vendetta. You lied to me. Lied to me. *You* killed my mother. It was you, all of this time."

"Yes, it was me. Doing what had to be done. Protecting my only son from the hurtful truth. I feel no guilt over your mother's death. She deserved it. She deserved worse than that, but unfortunately she died much too quickly for me to inflict the quality of pain I had planned."

"I hate you." Quinn's voice was uneven and pitchy now, just short of hysteria. "I think I've always hated you."

Roger leaned over to his side and pulled a long blade from his boot. "Silver," he said and moved it so it reflected the light in the room. "Works just as well as wood on monsters like you."

He rushed Quinn before I could move or even scream. Quinn tried to hold him off, keep the knife away from his throat, his chest. The wooden stake, Quinn's only weapon, was knocked to the floor. His fist flew out, catching Roger's chin. I saw a streak of red as the blade caught Quinn across his cheek.

Then I heard the gunshot. And the body slumped heavily to the floor.

Quinn stepped back from his father's body. He was shaking. I was shaking. I looked over toward the kitchen. Dr. Kalisan held a smoking gun in his hand and shook his head sadly.

"I never knew the truth. If I had, I would have wanted no part in this. Please forgive me." He turned around and disappeared into the kitchen.

I staggered toward Quinn and grabbed ahold of his arm, tried to stop his shaking.

He was in shock. I could see it in his glassy eyes as he turned to look at me. "He's dead."

I nodded.

Quinn fell to his knees in front of his father. He was crying. Crying over this man who'd killed his mother in cold blood. Who'd made his life a living hell for the ensuing years. He cried because his father was dead.

Then he wiped his face on the sleeve of his shirt and took a deep and shuddering breath.

I got down on my knees and hugged him. I expected him to push me away, but he didn't. He didn't hug me back, he just let me hold him.

I felt a nudge at my arm and jumped. It was Barkley. He'd come into the room to see what the noise was all about. He sat next to me, panting. I gave the werewolf a small smile and looked back at Roger.

It was usually at this point in a horror movie when the bad guy would sit up, unhurt by his injuries and keep coming, focused only on getting the job done.

But Quinn's father wasn't going anywhere. He stared at the ceiling with blank, unseeing eyes.

The doctor must have come back, because after a few minutes I heard him speak.

"Excuse me," he said, and I looked up to see he had poured himself a very tall glass of amber-colored alcohol—probably Scotch. He took a healthy chug of it and wiped his mouth with the back of his hand. "I don't mean to interrupt."

I just blinked at him. I could barely register what end was up, let alone what to say or do next.

"I feel very responsible for what has transpired here," he continued. "But I don't know who to call to stop them. I only knew Roger."

Quinn didn't look up. "What are you talking about?"

"The information you gave me. It doesn't feel right that the hunters should have it, now that I know the truth."

I let go of Quinn and got to my feet in the space of a heartbeat.

Thierry.

I remembered what Roger said to his friends over the telephone. *"I'll meet you there."*

"Shit, he's already told the other hunters. We have to leave right now."

"My apologies will never be enough," Dr. Kalisan said. "Only know that if you should need my assistance in any way in the future, I'll give it to you without hesitation."

Quinn and I ran out to the Beetle. It felt like hours had passed since we arrived there, but I knew it had only been a matter of minutes. The big, life-changing stuff always tends to happen quickly.

"I need a cell phone."

Quinn handed his over without question. It would take us a while to drive back to Toronto, but I could at least warn Thierry—tell him to get the hell out of Midnight Eclipse before it was too late.

That meant I'd have to tell him what we'd just done. Sold him out. It didn't matter. He could hate me, but at least he wouldn't be dead because of me.

I dialed the number from memory. While it rang, I glanced at the clock on the dashboard. It was 9:15. The club would have been open for fifteen minutes already.

"Come on," I said into the phone as Quinn pulled the car away from the trailer. "Answer, dammit."

What if it was already too late? What if the hunters had all been at Clancy's bar drinking beer and playing pool when they got the call? They could have just marched across the road and taken the whole place down within minutes. It was too horrible a thought to consider.

On the fifth ring someone finally picked up.

"Midnight Eclipse," Zelda's voice rang out over the phone, and I let out a long sigh of relief.

"Is this some kind of pervert?" Zelda asked as she listened to my long exhale.

"No. It's Sarah."

"That's too bad. I was hoping for a pervert. Sarah, what's up?"

"I need to speak with Thierry. It's urgent."

"Sorry, sweetie. He's stepped out."

"Where did he go? When will he be back?"

"Hey, take it easy. He went to talk to some people. I

don't know. Something to do with finding the traitor. What's the problem?"

"The traitor," I repeated. "But I already know who it is."

"You do?"

"Yeah. God, why didn't I tell you earlier? Thierry has to know this, too. It's Veronique."

"Veronique? Are you serious?"

"It's her. I'm positive. When I went out for a drink with her, she ended up schmoozing with the hunters. Just be careful. She's probably dangerous."

"Where are you?"

"Just turning onto the QEW, coming back from Grimsby."

"You were in Grimsby? What the hell were you doing there?"

I glanced at Quinn, but his eyes were focused on his driving. He probably needed every last ounce of concentration to keep the car on the road.

"I've done something terrible, Zelda. Quinn and me—we went after the cure. Thierry's in terrible danger. Tell him . . . tell him to go and hide somewhere safe. I feel so horrible. I don't know what to do!"

Zelda was quiet for a moment.

"You sold him out," she finally said. "For a cure that doesn't even exist?"

"I know. I'm stupid. I'll admit it. But if the hunters aren't there yet, then there's still a—" I stopped talking. The sick feeling in my stomach was spreading all through my body now. "Wait a minute. How do you know the cure doesn't exist?"

There was silence before I heard Zelda laugh lightly.

"I guess I should have just let you keep talking. At least that's something you're good at."

"You knew that it didn't exist?" My brain felt like it was about to explode. "But you're the one who gave me the phone number to get it."

"Yes, I did."

A chill went down my spine. "My God. It's not Veronique at all, is it? It's you. You're the traitor."

"Those in glass houses, honey. I believe you're the one who just screwed Thierry over. As far as I know, it wouldn't be the first time you screwed him, but that's your business, not mine."

"How could you?"

"The real question is, how couldn't I? We all do things for a greater purpose, Sarah. You did yours to get the cure. I did mine for simple monetary gain."

"For money?"

"I've lived a long time. Never had a goddamned penny to my name. I'm a three-hundred-year-old bartender, for Christ's sake. You've had it so easy and you don't even realize it. Thierry never helped me as much as he's helped you, and even then I never would have sold him out like you just did. Then again, I didn't know he was worth so much until today. Still, nobody but him ever lifted a finger to help me. Well, now I'm lifting a finger. My middle one—and I'm finally going to get what's coming to me."

My grip on the cell phone tightened. "Yes. You'll get exactly what's coming to you. As soon as I get there."

"Gonna have to let you go, sweetie. The boss just got back, and he doesn't look happy. It's funny, him being worth all that money. Makes me look at him in a different light. That kind of cash would have been sweet, but I guess you beat me to the punch on that juicy little piece of information. *C'est la vie.*"

The phone went dead.

I screamed into it and smashed it hard on the dashboard. It broke into pieces in my hand.

I glanced at Quinn. "Oops. Sorry. I'll buy you a new one."

"Forget it. What the hell was that all about?"

My numbness was going away. The fog was pulling away and leaving behind a hot line of rage.

"Zelda's the traitor. I can't believe it. I thought she was my friend."

"Who's Zelda?"

"The bartender at Midnight Eclipse. Looks like a teenager." I stared out the window at the road ahead. "And as soon as we get back there, I think I'm going to ground her for life."

Chapter 24

Quinn was gunning it all the way back to Toronto, but it still felt as though we were moving at a snail's pace.

"What's the plan?" he asked as we saw the CN Tower ahead and the shimmering lake to our right.

I shook my head. I wasn't going to panic. There wasn't any time for a luxury like that. "I don't know. Hope we're in time to even have a plan."

"I'm sorry."

"So am I. I'm sorry about your father. Maybe the two of you just needed some time to work through all that stuff."

He laughed, but it wasn't a pleasant sound. "I think that's the only thing I'm not sorry about. He killed my mother. He treated me like I was shit on the bottom of his boot for nearly thirty years. Is it wrong to be happy he's finally dead?"

I didn't know how to answer that, so I didn't.

Finally we got to the club. It was just after ten o'clock. Quinn didn't bother trying to park neatly, so we left the car with one tire up on the sidewalk. I ran to the front door and pushed it open, Quinn at my side.

It was empty. Nobody at the front desk. The sound of recorded Musak-like tunes filled the air. I went toward the black door that led to the club and pushed it open.

An entirely different kind of music filled my ears now. The black door must have been soundproof, because in the tanning salon there was zero indication that anything else was going on only a few feet away. The usual band was onstage, the Bettie Page–like singer belting out a tune. At the moment she was singing "Goldfinger," the James Bond theme song.

At first glance, the only thing out of ordinary about the club was that it was filled way past capacity. There had to be at least a hundred vampires in there. It struck me as odd for a moment, but then I realized that other clubs were closed, either burned to the ground or shut down to prevent being burned to the ground.

And here I thought Veronique wanted to keep things trucking because she was the traitor and wanted to give the hunters easier access. Now I knew it was simply a business decision. It took a lot of greenbacks to pay for her designer wardrobe. And with that many thirsty vamps filling the club, she must have been raking it in tonight.

"Sarah!" George raced up to me. His hair was sweaty and plastered to his forehead. "Am I glad you're here!"

My eyes widened and I grabbed his muscled arms. "What's wrong? Where's Thierry?"

"Who cares where he is! Romance can wait, sweet pea. Do you see this crowd? I'm going nuts. Grab a tray and start taking orders." He glanced at Quinn. "And you, too, handsome."

I grabbed his shirt. "I'm serious, George. *Where's* Thierry?"

He raised his eyebrows. "He's around. I saw him just a minute ago, okay?"

I let him go and glanced toward the bar. "Where's Zelda?"

"She's gone. It's just me and the new guy, and he's a total waste of space. Come on. Help me out. I'll owe you a big one, and you can take that any way you want to."

"I thought you said you didn't sweat the small stuff?"

"I lied. I'm sweating. Look at me, it's disgusting." He looked over at the bar to see a young vampire reaching over to refill his mug of blood. "Hey! Hands off!" He ran off to stop him.

I looked at Quinn.

"I'm not exactly in the mood to wait tables tonight," he said.

I grabbed his shirt. "We have to find Thierry."

We threaded our way through the busy tables until I felt a hand reach out and grab my arm. I spun around, ready to punch or kick whoever it was.

"Sweetheart," a dark-haired man slurred. He was with a busty blonde, and both of them were obviously drunk. "Can we get a round of O pos and gins here? Actually, make them Rusty Nails, would you, toots?"

I turned away, ready to ignore him, but he pinched my ass hard enough for me to spin back around. I had to clench my hand at my side to stop from slapping him.

"Look, dickweed, do I look like a waitress to you?"

"You were the other night."

"Oh. Well, I'm not now. And hands to yourself, buddy."

"I'm going to complain to the management."

But I'd moved far enough past him not to care. I glanced at Quinn. Considering the horrible night it had been, especially for him, he actually had the audacity to look amused.

"What?"

"Dickweed?"

I shrugged. "And your point? He was one and I call 'em like I see 'em."

"I can imagine what you want to call me right now." His amused expression faded.

"Don't get all melancholy on me. I need you to keep it together."

"You *need* me?"

"Yeah. Now don't go getting any ideas, though."

"A discussion for another time?" He looked at me hopefully.

"You're impossible."

"Is that a yes?"

"It's a yes, you're impossible. Other than that, I'm not promising anything."

"You know we're perfect for each other, Sarah."

"I can't believe you want to discuss this right now after everything that's happened. This is *so* not a good time."

He smiled at me. "I like the fact that you're not turning me down flat. I guess I just don't understand what your objection is to the two of us getting together."

"Did I mention that you're due for a serious ass kicking?"

His smile widened at that. "That sounds like it might have interesting possibilities."

I made a frustrated noise loud enough to be heard over the music. "You tried to kill me, dumb-ass. Twice."

"And now all I want to do is kiss you. Just give me one reason why we shouldn't be together."

He was nuts. And this was such a bad time for this discussion. I turned away from him because my face was growing warm. My gaze moved over the dozens of vampires enjoying the night out, drinking with their friends, families, lovers—despite the lousy service tonight. My gaze finally reached Thierry's booth.

He was leaning against it, staring directly at me.

"Thierry." I let out a long sigh of relief and immediately began walking toward him.

"Oh, right," I heard Quinn say dully. "*That's* the reason why."

I got closer to Thierry, pushing my way past the clubgoers until I was finally standing right in front of him.

"Sarah." His lips moved slowly into a half smile. "Good to see you." His silver-eyed gaze turned toward Quinn, who had swallowed his hurt pride enough to stay by my side. "I see that you've brought a date tonight."

My mouth opened to deny it, but I closed it. There were more important and urgent things to discuss than petty jealousies. Was he jealous? No, I couldn't think about that right now. I couldn't get distracted, but he was so distracting. And now I knew that he hadn't killed Quinn's mother. So did Quinn, but it didn't keep the loathing from radiating off him in waves.

"You have to get out of here," I told him.

"It is my club," he replied. "Why should I go any-where?"

"You have to. It's not safe."

He studied me for a moment, then motioned for the two of us to sit down. I slid into the booth despite my brain screaming at me to tell him everything as quickly as possible. I just didn't know where to begin.

"It is not safe anywhere, Sarah. That doesn't mean that we should hide ourselves away like cowards."

I cocked my head to one side at his words. They sounded awfully familiar.

He smiled at me. "Yes, Veronique told me about your little 'girls' night out.' She fears that she may have scared you away, or made you think less of me, as you left with-out saying anything to her. I know she told you stories of my earlier days. I now realize why you were acting so odd earlier."

"I didn't believe her."

Quinn remained silent beside me, hands folded in front of him on the table, saying nothing.

"Why not? After all, she was telling the truth, but that was a long time ago. And you needn't think I'm the same man today I was then."

"I needn't. I mean, I *don't*."

"Then why do you ask me to hide like a child afraid of a thunderstorm?"

I was about to let it all spill out of my mouth. Tell him that I'd been terrible, sold him out, and now the hunters were after him. In other words, the truth. But Quinn beat me to it.

"It's all my fault," Quinn said. "The hunters now know where this place is, and they're after you in particular. I sold them the information to buy the cure for me. For me and Sarah. I wanted us to be human again."

Thierry studied him for a moment. I half expected him to kill Quinn where he sat, or at the very least to scream at him, threaten his life. But he was calm, stoic, like a statue.

"There is no cure."

"We know," Quinn said. "Now we do, anyhow. But it's too late. They tricked us, and now you have to get out of here."

"I'm not going anywhere."

"But, Thierry," I heard the hard edge of panic in my voice, "you have to. They're going to kill you."

His eyes slowly tracked to mine, where they held for a moment. "Yes, they will."

I shook my head. "You don't care?"

"No, I don't. As you well know, Sarah, it is a time long overdue. If I am to die tonight at the hands of the hunters, then I will accept my destiny. It is fate. I am not afraid."

His voice sounded so loud suddenly, or maybe it was just his words, hopeless and despondent. I wanted to slap him hard across the face. Make him wake the hell up. There was no reason for him to die tonight. No damn reason at all.

I could hear my heart pounding, the blood rushing through my ears. Everything seemed louder suddenly. But why?

No. It wasn't just me. The club was silent. The music had stopped playing. Conversation had halted throughout the smoky room.

I looked over at the band. The dark-haired singer

clutched the microphone on the stand in front of her, standing there, unmoving, unsinging. There was an odd look on her face. Surprise? Shock? But before I could figure it out, her expression faded, and a large red stain spread across the front of her white blouse. And then she fell—it seemed to take forever—face forward off the stage.

Peter stood behind her, holding a bloody stake in his right hand. He grabbed the wobbling microphone and pulled it close to his mouth and raised an eyebrow. The one that wasn't covered by the patch.

"Is there a Sarah Dearly in the audience tonight?" he said, loud and clear. "If there is, could she please come up to the stage?"

Chapter 25

The silence in the club was deafening. I slumped down in my seat. How did Peter know I was even there, or was he just guessing? Hoping I was there so he finally could exact his revenge on me for what I'd done to his eye.

Thierry made a move to stand, but my hand darted out to catch his wrist. I squeezed it as tightly as I could.

"Sit down," I hissed across the table. "Please!"

He met my gaze and shook his head. He placed his other hand on top of mine and pried my grip off him. He stood up and turned to face the stage.

"Leave this club. You're not welcome here."

"You're not Sarah," Peter said but then smiled. "But I'm betting that you're this Thierry dude, right?"

"That is correct. My name is Thierry de Bennicoeur."

"Pretty faggy name, man. I hate the French. Don't worry; we'll get to you in a minute. The boys and I got all night for this. Now, where are you hiding that bitch? Give her up and maybe I'll let a few of you live."

There were several other rough-looking guys flanking Peter. I recognized a couple of them from the night I was sired, and a few more were from the pub across the street. The others I'd never seen before. But they all looked out to the audience of frozen vampires like lions who had their pick of weak, helpless prey.

I felt the press of a warm body join me and Quinn on my side of the booth. It was George. He looked petrified.

"What the hell?" he whispered "Why do they want you?"

"It's hard being so popular," I whispered back.

"You," George said to Quinn "They're your friends, right? Do something!"

Quinn's expression was bleak. "Not anymore. There's nothing I can do."

"Then come on." George pulled on my arm. "Let's sneak out the back."

I shook my head. "No. There're too many people in here that will be hurt. And Thierry's going to get himself killed if we don't do something to stop this."

I scanned the crowd and spotted Amy sitting with Barry at a small table near the stage. She gave me a quick wave of her hand and mouthed, "What now?"

She clung to the small frame of Barry as if he were the only thing keeping her from falling into the abyss. He stared up at the stage with a fierce, brave expression on his face.

I shrugged at her. I honestly didn't know what to do next. All I knew was that I couldn't just slither out of here on the floor, saving myself but no one else. It just wasn't polite.

"Any dealings you need to have," Thierry said to Peter in a commanding tone, "you can have with me. Sarah has nothing to do with any of this."

Peter took the microphone off the stand and pressed it against his lips so the words came out slurred and extra loud. "Sa-rah. Sa-rah. Come out, come out, wherever you are. I think I'll start with your eyes and work my way down that luscious little body. Come on now. Don't keep me waiting."

Quinn climbed over me to stand next to Thierry.

"Peter," he yelled up to the stage. "Don't do this."

Peter smiled at his former acquaintance. "Well, if it isn't Michael Quinn. Glad you're here. Wanted to say thanks a bunch for leaving me at the restaurant like you did. They had to take me to the hospital and pump my stomach. I almost died."

"Kill or be killed, man. Times have changed."

"Yes, they have. Look, Quinn, I'll do you a favor because we have a history. I'll let you walk. Leave now and I'll look the other way. Doesn't mean I won't hunt your ass down another time, but all I want tonight is that bitch."

Quinn was blocking me so Peter couldn't see I was sitting right behind him. He shook his head. "Can't do that. You've made this my fight now."

"Stupid decision. Maybe your father's been right about you."

"My father is dead."

Peter's eyebrows shot up. He took a moment before speaking again. "Then I guess you really have made your decision. Okay, people"—he turned from Quinn to survey the rest of the crowd—"let's get this show on the road. Time is money."

He jumped off the stage and snatched Amy right out

of Barry's arms. He dragged her back up to the stage with him, his arm tight around her neck.

"Hey, darlin'." He kissed her cheek with a sloppy, wet sound. "Good to see you again."

I didn't even feel myself move, but suddenly I was on my feet. "Hey, asshole," I called up to the stage. "Let her go right now."

Thierry turned around to glare at me for making my presence known. Quinn too. My two handsome protectors. I sure was a lucky girl.

Peter smiled at me but didn't loosen his hold on his ex-girlfriend. "I'd be happy to let her go. Why don't you come up here and take her place?"

"No, Sarah!" Amy's voice was strangled.

Thierry, Quinn, and George grabbed my arms to try to stop me from moving forward, but I was determined. I marched through the crowd, which now parted before me like the Red Sea, and then I was standing in front of Peter.

"Here I am, you one-eyed bastard."

"Come a little closer. Don't be shy." Peter stared down at me, and raging fires burned beneath the furious gaze of that one good eye. He was going to kill me. For what I'd done to him in self-defense.

I hesitated. After all, I didn't want to die. Maybe I was all talk, no action. Come to think of it, that's what they used to say about me in high school. But I didn't want anyone else to die tonight, either. What was up with these hunters? Didn't they realize what they were doing was wrong? We weren't evil. We weren't monsters.

But that's how they saw us.

A breath caught in my chest. They saw us as evil,

bloodsucking monsters that needed to be exterminated like insects.

That was it. That was the answer.

I tried to make my voice as calm as I could. "You can have me, Peter. Do what you want to me. But could I say a few last words to everyone first?"

"You're kidding, right?"

"A condemned person on death row gets to say their last words. They also get a last meal, but I'm not hungry. All I want is my moment in the spotlight. Come on, be a sport."

He studied me for a moment, then sneered. "Sure, why not? Go ahead, darlin'. Say your fill. After that, you're all mine."

The smile he gave me then was full of the promise of all the horrible things he'd do to me if this didn't work. I suddenly wished for a Plan B. You can never be too prepared.

I stepped onto the stage. He released Amy after giving her a last disgusting lick up the side of her face and pushed her hard out into the audience. A few people caught her so she didn't get hurt or land on top of the dead singer.

Peter's smile widened as he moved away from the microphone, waving his hand at it to indicate it was all mine. I was now close enough to him that if he'd wanted to reach out and snap my neck, he could have easily. But he'd promised to let me have my say. I guess he was a man of his word, even if that word was "asshole." He sheathed his stake and crossed his arms.

I tapped the microphone. The lights were painfully bright up there, and the faces in the audience were darkened now, but I could tell I had everyone's undivided attention. At the back of the club I could see two more hunters guarding the black door so no one could escape. That made, I counted in my head, twelve hunters in total.

I looked over to Thierry and Quinn. George had stood up next to them so he could see me better. They all watched helplessly. They had no idea what I was going to do, other than get myself killed.

"Hi, everyone," I said into the microphone. "I don't have much to say. I know Peter here's in a big hurry. Men, you know. The thing is, he's just doing what he thinks is right by killing me and maybe killing the rest of you before the night is through. That's what the hunters do. They kill vampires. I mean, look at what Hollywood has done to us. Made us into bloodsucking, murderous monsters. Ugly, white-faced bat creatures. Scary, icky night stalkers. Or, on the other hand, you have the hot, steamy vampire lovers. Those are my favorites, of course, but they're still mostly evil."

I pulled the microphone off the stand so I could hold it closer to my mouth.

"And evil things should be killed, right? If we were all just regular folks—doctors, lawyers, and school-teachers—going about our daily business . . . well, that would be another thing. We wouldn't deserve to die because of that. These hunters would be the murderers then, wouldn't they? But we're not those normal, every-day, boring things."

I took a deep breath. "We're monsters. Evil, scary, fanged monsters. Strong and dangerous, able to look after ourselves and our nasty friends and families. We give the hunters a run for their money, don't we? We'd never make it easy on them or they might enjoy it too much. Might look at killing us as a game, a hobby—big fun. Something they can do to feel powerful and important.

"They have the weapons, sure. They have the teamwork, okay. But at the end of the day—in the wee hours of the night—take a look around, my monstrous friends . . . we have the goddamned numbers."

I heard a rustle through the crowd as they looked around at one another, whispering about what I was saying and the point I was trying to get across. I hoped to God I was making that point loud and clear.

Out of the corner of my eye, I saw Barry climb up on top of his chair.

"She's right," he said loudly. "We are monsters! And there's a hell of a lot more of us than there are of them."

There was silence for a moment, and then another vampire rose to his feet. And then another. And then another. In the space of a few heartbeats, the entire club of a hundred-plus vamps were on their feet, staring up at the hunters, their fangs catching what little light there was in the club. I heard a growing growl, which got louder and louder, and I felt my grip on the microphone increase along with the tension in the room.

I turned to look at Peter. His eye was very wide and white, and I could see a shiny film of sweat on his face now. I smiled at him.

"Thanks. That's pretty much all I wanted to say."

Chapter 26

My army of monsters took a collective step closer to the stage. I placed the microphone back on the stand and shaded my eyes from the bright lights. I glanced at Peter again.

"Now, where were we?"

"Smug little bitch," he said under his breath, but I could taste the fear that covered his words like a candy coating.

The vampires never had thought to fight back collectively against the hunters. They considered themselves victims that were going to be picked off one at a time. They didn't know what to do except to try to avoid it. Well, avoidance didn't get you much in life. Except in this case, it might get you dead. I figured, if the hunters thought they were dealing with evil monsters, then let them have to deal with evil monsters. See how long they still found it fun and games.

Peter took a step toward me, but I felt strong arms come around my waist and pull me off the stage. I turned to see Quinn behind me.

"Good plan," he said.

"Thanks. Worked on it for all of thirty seconds."

Peter grabbed the microphone. "Yeah, great plan, bitch. Well, we've got more than one way to kill you pieces of shit. This was just a small part of it. You'll all be dead in the next couple of days, and you'll never even see it coming."

"Now, how are you going to kill us in your current position?" I asked him sweetly.

"I'm not." Then he laughed and it sounded just this side of insane. "You're already killing yourselves. Just being here. Just drinking here. It's so simple, too. You're all so stupid to not see it coming."

I felt Thierry's hand on the small of my back. I looked up into his eyes; then he turned his gaze on Peter.

"Do you mean how you've poisoned the blood supply?"

A gasp went through the club.

Peter raised an eyebrow. "Very smart. Yes, all your blood has been tainted. My idea, might I add. We've had the Blood Delivery Guys working with us, under duress, for more than a week. By now, you all have enough poison in your systems to drop dead in agony within days. And there's no antidote." He laughed.

I stared at Thierry. *Oh, my God. Poisoned blood?* Everyone I was aware of got their blood by buying it. Nobody got it the old-fashioned way anymore—it just wasn't done. Even after finally standing up for ourselves, we still were all going to die.

Thierry nodded. "It *was* a brilliant plan. However, I recently stopped using the Blood Delivery Guys. I now use the Blood Drivers—a little more expensive, but well worth it, don't you think? Perhaps the shared uniforms I arranged threw you off a bit. No, the Blood Delivery Guys haven't personally made a delivery in over a week. Everyone in the city has also made the change. I personally made sure of it."

Peter's face had gone a medium shade of crimson. "You knew. How?"

"Perhaps you are not the only one who has informants."

"Zelda," I said under my breath to draw Thierry's attention away from Peter. "Zelda's the informant. Well, *their* informant."

"I know."

"You do? What are you, like freaking Kreskin?"

He smiled at me. "No. Simply a good judge of character. Also, she stopped drinking the blood that was delivered here. She'd brought her own supply in and kept it under the bar. Little things say a lot."

"Where's Zelda now?"

"In my office." He paused. "With Veronique."

I raised an eyebrow. "Poor Zelda."

"Indeed."

"Shut up!" Peter screamed. "Both of you. Shut up! I don't care what you've done. I don't care how many of you there are. Do you know my kill count? Neither do I, because it's so bloody high! I can take half of you out tonight with my eyes closed." He glanced at his friends. They were all looking a little less sure of themselves than they had when they first got there. But each hand held a sharp weapon. A weapon meant to slice, to dice, to kill. And they had the power of desperation and rage fueling them.

Peter leaped out at the audience that rose to meet him. Then all hell broke loose.

It was one thing to say to the vamps that they could hold their own, but when push came to shove, a lot of them bailed and ran to the exits, pushing past the petrified, overpowered hunters who blocked their way. I got swept up with the crowd and pulled away from Thierry and Quinn.

I tried to fight my way back, but I was pressed on all sides. People were going crazy. Either fighting against the dozen hunters or trying to get the hell out of Dodge. A hand reached out from beneath a table and pulled me under. It was George.

"Just stay here," he said. "It'll be over soon."

"But Thierry—"

"Thierry wants to die. Everybody knows that. Save yourself, sweetheart."

He didn't mean to be cruel. He was trying to be helpful, and I knew it. I grabbed him and kissed him hard on the cheek.

"Don't get stabbed again." I slipped out from underneath the table.

"I'll try," he said sadly. "You too."

I tried to find somebody I knew, but I was surrounded by unfamiliar faces that were filled with rage or fear or confusion. Where were Quinn and Thierry? Why couldn't I find Barry and Amy?

Did Veronique even know what was going on? I had to get to the office and warn her. I was close to the bar at that moment, and I used it to pull myself along through the crowd going in the opposite direction. I ran down the hallway and opened up the door, slipped inside, and closed it behind me. I looked around.

Zelda was right in front of me, smiling sweetly.

"Hey, Sarah." She backhanded me across the face. "Glad you could join us."

White stars exploded in front of my eyes. I fell to the floor and tried to scramble away from her, stunned by the pain from the blow. What just happened? I thought Veronique was looking after her.

I looked up. Veronique was sprawled on the sofa, unconscious. There was a wooden stake protruding from her ample chest; her designer dress was ruined, and one expensive shoe was off, the heel broken and flung across the room.

I crawled along the floor until I got to Thierry's desk. Using it, I pulled myself up to my feet. My ears rang from the hit I'd just received. I never knew girls could hit that hard, but Zelda wasn't a girl. She was a three-hundred-year-old vampire with a chip on her shoulder.

We weren't the only ones in the room. Peter emerged from the corner and smiled at me.

"Nice little scene out there, darlin'. Didn't see that coming."

"Yeah, well, I guess you don't see much coming these days." I noticed the familiar taste of blood in my mouth. "At least not out of your left side, that is."

His smile vanished and was replaced by a scowl.

"Got anything to say to me?" Zelda asked.

"Nope." I wouldn't give her the satisfaction of getting any more of a rise out of me. "Not a damn thing."

She almost looked disappointed. Then she shrugged.

"Okay, Peter, I'm leaving now. I've done everything you've wanted."

He stared at her. "Thank you. You've been most helpful. Although, I can't say that I'm too thrilled about how this night is going so far."

"Not my fault. So, how about my payment?"

"Your payment?"

"That's right," I said. "After all, our dear little Zelda only wants what's coming to her."

I almost felt that Peter and I shared a moment, but that was impossible because he was a psycho and the last time I checked—I wasn't. A wide smile spread across his face.

"She wants what's coming to her, does she?"

"Come on," Zelda said impatiently. "I don't have all night."

Peter pulled out his stake and sank it into her chest. I scrambled farther behind the desk as I watched her expression change from greedy to surprised.

"But"—she looked up at him—"that's not what I meant."

She fell forward, mimicking the poor singer earlier. Her face smacked against the carpeted floor. But unlike the singer, who must have been much younger since she stayed in one dead but solid piece, Zelda slowly shrank and darkened, until there was nothing left of her but a pile of clothes, a stake, and a gross stain on the carpet that would probably require professional steam cleaning to remove.

Peter bent over and picked up the stake. He looked down at the stain and shook his head. Then he took a step toward me and flicked his eyes absently at Veronique.

"She's a hot one. I'm glad she's not dead yet. I plan on having lots of fun with her."

I'd slowly worked my hand into Thierry's top drawer, praying that I'd find what I was looking for. It had to still be in there. It just had to be. If it wasn't, I was seriously screwed.

I let out a little sigh of relief as I wrapped my hands around Thierry's gun, the one he'd given me only a few short days ago to protect myself from Quinn.

Peter came closer until he was standing on the other side of the desk. "Yeah, we all get what's coming to us sooner or later, don't we, darlin'? Now it's your turn." His grin widened as he reached for me.

"You first." I pointed the gun at his chest and squeezed off a shot. The sound was deafening, and the recoil sent me crashing backward against the wall.

Peter took a step backward, too, and looked down at himself. Just like the singer he'd murdered earlier, a red stain blossomed out from the center of his chest. He dropped the stake and pressed his hand against the wound, as if that would make a difference.

"Sorry," I said. I actually meant it. First his eye, now this. He really should have known just to leave me the hell alone.

"You bitch." His voice was so surprised it was almost sad.

"Sticks and stones, Peter."

He took another step back and then his knees gave out. He collapsed in the middle of the puddle that once was Zelda, and I heard the last breath leave his body with a hiss.

With shaking hands I put the gun back in the drawer

and went to Veronique's side. She was still breathing. Thank God for that.

"Veronique." I glanced at Peter every couple of seconds, just in case he was planning on making another appearance, but he was pretty much as dead as he was going to get. Wooden stakes in the hearts of vampires, lead bullets in the hearts of humans—they worked every time. I swallowed hard. I'd leave the freaking out about killing somebody, no matter how much they damn well deserved it, for another time.

"Veronique," I said again and slapped her face.

Her eyelashes fluttered open and she stared up at me. "Sarah. What happened?"

"Don't move. You're hurt."

She looked down at the stake and her eyes widened.

"I'm going to have to pull it out," I told her.

I touched the stake, but she pushed my hands away. She wrapped her own hand around the base of the wooden weapon and pulled it out of her chest in one quick, sickening motion. She didn't even scream. She gingerly sat up on the sofa.

"If I had a nickel for every time I've been staked"— she glanced at me wearily—"well, I'd only have about twenty cents. But still, it's never a fun experience."

"You're going to be okay?" I was surprised she'd been able to remove the stake all by herself. She was one tough cookie.

"No, I'm not." She looked down at herself. "This dress was one of a kind. I'm very upset. Let's shoot the hunter again, shall we?"

"You saw me shoot him? I thought you were unconscious."

"I was, but I see him lying there with a hole in his chest. It's obvious what happened."

I smiled and helped her to her feet. We stepped around the mess that once was Peter and Zelda, and I opened up the door to peek outside. Everything was quiet. Too quiet.

"Maybe you should stay here," I told her.

She shook her head. "No. Let's go."

We slowly made our way out to the main club area. It was mostly cleared out. The fight was over. There were a few bodies on the ground. Some vampires, a few hunters. Some were moving, some weren't. It looked like a dimly lit, smoke-filled war zone with makeshift nurses and doctors tending to the injured.

George rushed toward us with a huge smile on his face. "You're okay!"

"Yeah. And you, too." I smiled back. "You stayed safely under your table?"

"No. I got out and kicked some ass. It was more fun than I thought it would be."

"Good for you."

"Sarah." Quinn made his way over to join us at the bar. He was limping, and there was another cut on his forehead to match the one his father had given him earlier on his cheek.

He grabbed me and hugged me tightly. I was so glad he was okay that I almost burst into tears.

"You look like hell," I told him.

"You look like heaven."

I rolled my eyes. "You honestly have to start working on your pickup lines."

He grimaced. "I don't think I'll be picking anything

up for a while, but I'll keep it in mind." He glanced at Veronique. "Who are you?"

"Veronique." She extended her hand and then winced in pain.

He took her hand but didn't shake it. "Nice to meet a fellow battle-scarred soldier."

She shook her head. "I'm not planning on scarring. My injury should heal up fine."

He let go of her hand. "It was just an expression."

Amy and Barry joined us. Barry was cut up, too, but smiling. Amy hugged me.

"Glad you're okay," I said to her.

"You too."

"No hard feelings?"

"None. We've been friends too long. I just want you to be happy for me."

I looked at Barry and he met my gaze. "I love her. I know it seems fast, but sometimes life's just like that."

"Fine." I smiled at him. "Then congratulations, you two. When's the big day?"

"We're leaving tonight," Amy said. "We're going to elope to Niagara Falls."

"You're going to Niagara Falls for your wedding? That is so cheesy. I love it."

Amy paused. "This means I won't be able to go to Mexico with you."

"I kind of figured that. After everything that's happened, I might just skip it myself. I mean, a vampire in Mexico? How weird would that be?" I glanced around. "Where's Thierry?"

George turned around in a circle. "Don't know. Haven't seen him since the battle royale took place."

My breath caught in my throat and a tear streaked down my cheek. "Shit. Please don't tell me that they killed him."

Quinn touched my arm. "No, he's not dead. He fought hard against the hunters, but he's not dead. I saw him leave through the tanning salon five minutes ago. He didn't say where he was going."

I let a long, shaky sigh out slowly and wiped my face. I tried to smile.

"You care about him, don't you?" Veronique said. "You've denied it before, but you can't fool me."

I bit my bottom lip. "Look, I know he's your husband and—"

She waved me off and laughed until it hurt so much she had to stop. "It's okay. We were married a long time ago, but we haven't been man and wife for so long, I forget even what it was like. I have had many lovers since then, and I certainly don't expect that Thierry has remained faithful to me. Now, dear girl, answer me. Do you care for him?"

I sniffed. "Yes. But I just figured that since you came back after all this time, you were interested in getting back together with him."

She smiled, but it didn't hold. Her expression turned serious. "I came here because it was requested of me. Thierry asked me to come."

"Why?"

"There's something you need to know," she said gravely. "Thierry plans to end his life; he's weary of living. There's nothing in it for him anymore. Six hundred years is a long time."

"I know that already. But why did he ask you to come?"

"He knows I have an excellent head for business. He asked me to look after the clubs he owns, to either run them myself or sell them to another who will keep them open. He didn't want his employees or clientele not to have a place to count on being here. I agreed, because I feel a sense of responsibility to him. I sired him, after all, and he was my husband at one time. I'm also searching for direction in my own life now. I, too, am weary, but not ready yet for it all to end. I don't know if I'll ever be. This seemed like the perfect answer."

"But you didn't say anything to try to talk Thierry out of what he wanted to do?"

She paused. "No. It's his decision. I don't think anything I could have said would have swayed him otherwise."

"I need to talk to him. I need to know where he went."

No one said anything.

Anxiety filled me, spreading evenly through every part of my body. "He's gone to do it tonight, hasn't he? Where? Where did he go?"

They all glanced at one another.

George shook his head. "Sorry, he didn't say."

I exhaled and it sounded shuddery and hopeless.

"I can't deal with this. After everything that's happened, I can't lose him. I just can't."

I felt a hand on my shoulder. It was Veronique. She smiled at me, and there was more warmth in her perfect features than I'd seen before. Or maybe I just hadn't been looking hard enough. "If there is one thing I've learned after all of my many years, it's this: when the world has gone mad and you feel the most lost—that is when you must trust your heart to lead you where you need to go."

I blinked at her through my tears. "That is the lamest thing I've ever heard."

It may have been lame, but I knew it was the truth. The one thing I'd trusted during all that had happened to me was what my heart told me, be it right or wrong, and at that moment my heart was telling me it wasn't too late.

"There is a reason why those as old as I do not sire fledglings."

I closed my eyes. Thierry had said that sires and fledglings have a bond, sometimes heightened by age. Okay, he wasn't my real sire, but goddamn it, this had to work. I cleared my mind. I focused. It was like being at Missy's wedding again searching out the other vampires. A Spidey-sense.

But there was nothing. Nothing.

Nothing.

And then . . .

I opened my eyes.

"I think I know where he is. I need somebody to give me a lift. Right now. There's no time to waste."

Barry stepped forward. "My car's out back. Amy and I were going to leave now, anyhow. We'll drive you anywhere you want to go."

I let out the breath I'd been holding. "Thanks. You're growing on me. A little."

"The feeling's mutual."

Amy and Barry went to the black door to leave. I turned to the others.

"Thanks, guys. For everything. Wish me luck."

Quinn grabbed my wrist. His eyes were sad, but he was trying to smile. "Good luck. I mean it."

I kissed him, just a quick kiss, but I meant every bit of it. I wanted him to know how much he meant to me. If things had been different, then who could say? But they weren't. I wanted to be with Thierry. And I had to stop him from what he was planning on doing. I blew another kiss to the others as I backed away toward the door; then I turned around and followed Amy and Barry out to the car.

I directed them to the Bloor Viaduct—the bridge where Thierry and I had first met. Where the hunters had chased me. The Don River raced underneath, cold and dark and foreboding.

I got out and slammed the car door. I quickly scanned the bridge. I couldn't see him, but I knew he was there.

"Should we wait?" Amy asked.

"No. I'll be fine. You guys go."

"You're sure?"

"Positive." I turned away, then glanced back. "Thanks, guys. Sorry I've been such a bitch."

"You can't help what you are," Barry said, and then the little bugger winked at me. "Good luck. Bring the master home in one piece."

I nodded and watched them drive away; then I turned to focus my attention on the bridge, scanning the length of it.

For a moment I thought that I'd made a mistake. He

wasn't here at all. I'd put all my eggs in one basket and I was wrong. He was lost to me forever.

But then I saw him. Halfway down, past the protective bars and on a suspension beam, just standing there surveying the night that surrounded him. He didn't look at me as I approached, but he must have known that I was there.

"Thierry!" I called to him.

I saw he had a wooden stake in his hand. So he was serious this time. This was it. If I couldn't find a way to stop him, he was going to do it, once and for all. End a life that had spanned more than six centuries. Seemed like an event that the papers and the six o'clock news should cover. An event of great importance. But how did they know? He'd just be another jumper. Nobody to lose any sleep over.

He glanced at me and shook his head. "You shouldn't have come."

I climbed up on the cement barrier and crawled out to meet him through the opening in the metal bars he'd made last week. There was a time when being this high up would have paralyzed me. I wouldn't have been able to function—scared of falling, scared of dying. But the first time I'd been chased out there was for fear of my own life, and this time it was out of fear for his. My fear of heights seemed to vanish in times of great stress.

Finally I was standing, balanced on a metal slat a little more than an arm's length away from him. His eyes didn't look silver now, it was too dark. They were expressionless, dark pools that matched the water so far below us.

"Nice view," I said.

"Leave here, Sarah. You can't stop me."

"Who said I wanted to stop you?"

"Pardon me?" He looked surprised.

"I said that I didn't come here to stop you."

"That is a surprise, Sarah. But you have never stopped surprising me since we first met. So tell me, why, then, are you here if you did not have it in your industrious mind to stop me?"

I pulled Peter's well-used stake out from the back of my powder blue sweatpants. I'd put it there for safekeeping. Definitely not a comfortable thing to carry around, especially when sitting in the back of Barry's car—but you do what you have to do.

I blinked at him. "I've come here to join you."

"What?"

"I'm going to kill myself, too."

"Please, Sarah, be serious. I am in no mood for your jokes."

I shook my head. "Neither am I. I'm through with jokes. I'm serious. Deadly serious."

I now had his full attention. "You can't do this."

"Why not?"

"You're young and beautiful. You have a long and exciting life before you. There's so much you have yet to experience. You can't end it all tonight."

I shrugged and studied my stake. "I'm not happy. I thought being a vampire might be sort of cool. Well, it's not. I thought there was a cure. There isn't. I fought against the image of being a bloodthirsty, murdering monster. Well, let's see, I just killed Peter. I'm a little parched, and I just happen to drink blood now."

He stared at me. "And for this you wish to join me in my watery grave?"

"No." I blinked back tears. I was trying to hold it together, really I was. But it was getting harder, the longer I was out there. "What I'm trying to say is that being a vampire sucks. This has been the worst week of my life. And now I know there's no out. No magic pill that's going to make it all better. Being a vampire is hard enough with you being around, Thierry. I don't want to face it without you."

"Sarah—"

"Shut up. Just let me finish. Dammit. You could have turned your back on me last week and let the hunters have me. It would have caused you a lot less grief. But you didn't. You helped me."

"Of course I did."

"You're still talking."

"Sorry."

"I thought you were a jerk. A real pompous, know-it-all asshole. I believe I expressed that sentiment to you several times."

He opened his mouth to reply, then shut it. Good for him. He was learning.

"But the whole time, I knew I was falling for you. And it wasn't just the gorgeous exterior, the power, the money, although I won't say those things aren't nice perks. It was *you*. I could see you underneath it all, and I liked what I saw. I liked it a lot. But then your bloody wife shows up out of the blue. I didn't know what to think. And then you froze me out. Made me feel like you didn't think I was anything more than a potential fling. Actually, I think those were your exact words."

He looked away. "She reminded me of what my plans were. I wanted to keep you from being hurt further."

"Yeah, now I know that. But then I thought she was everything I could never be. Gorgeous and powerful, with a vast history with you. How was I supposed to compete with that?"

"So you began dating Quinn," he said bitterly.

"Quinn and I were never dating. I just said that because I wanted to hurt you back. But who knows? Maybe in a different place, a different time, a different life, we might be together. But not now."

"Why not?"

"Because, stupid, I'm a little bit crazy about you."

He blinked those dark, dark eyes at me. "Perhaps you're just a little bit crazy."

"That's a definite possibility. But here's the thing, Thierry. I think I love you. I don't care if you don't feel the same way about me. It's the truth. I love you. And if that means nothing to you, if you're just going to jump off this bridge because you feel that there's nothing in this life to keep you here, then go for it. Just know I'm going to be right behind you."

Silence fell as I ran out of things to say. Tears streaked down my face. There it was. Everything I was feeling was out in the open. *I love him.* I hadn't even realized it myself until I heard myself say it. A crush? Yeah. Infatuation? Definitely. But love? No wonder I couldn't be happy with Quinn, even though I cared so much for him, so deeply it hurt.

But I *loved* Thierry.

"Sarah—" His voice, choked with his own emotion, caught on the wind that had just picked up. A storm was brewing. The first major snowstorm of the year. I could taste it in the air, sense it was coming with every fiber of my being. Plus, I'd heard about it on Barry's car radio on the way over. We were expecting twenty inches of cold white stuff between now and tomorrow.

He took a step toward me and I tried to move a step closer to him, but my foot slipped and, with a surprised scream and scrambling at the empty air—I fell.

Thierry dropped his stake and caught my wrist, holding me dangling high over the Don River. I looked up at him frantically.

"Pull me up!"

He cocked his head to one side. "But I thought you wanted to jump?"

"I've changed my mind! Pull me up!"

"What about the other things you said? That you love me? Have you also changed your mind about that?"

I gulped, looked down, then back to his face. "No. I love you. I do!"

"Then perhaps I shall pull you up."

"Stop being a jerk and do it right now!"

He smiled. He was strong enough to hold me this way all night if he wanted. "You do need to work on your manners. But very well, Sarah." He braced himself against the bridge to haul me up, but a gust of wind hit him before he was fully secure. He wobbled a bit, casting a worried look down at me. Then he lost his footing and slipped off the side of the bridge.

"Oh, shit!" I yelled as we made our second plunge together into the ice-cold, dark water.

Chapter 27

Three weeks later I was reclining on a beach in Puerto Vallarta. My big, floppy hat and dark sunglasses were firmly in place. I'd packed four bikinis. I was presently wearing the red one. Looked pretty good against my white skin. I hadn't bothered with a tan. The sun was way too annoyingly bright for that, and I just couldn't be bothered with the messy self-tanning creams. And don't even start with me about tanning salons. Not going to happen.

I sighed contentedly as I watched the red sun leisurely slip beneath the horizon. Mexico was so beautiful. I felt the cool sand between my toes and listened to the ocean lap softly at the shore.

The beach was mostly deserted at this time of the evening. Most vacationers were inside eating dinner or starting their drinking binges, since, after all, this was an all-inclusive resort. But they also served out on the beach at this time of the day if you requested it. A bit begrudgingly, but they did have a policy of the customer always being right.

I hadn't planned on going there. After everything that had happened, it hadn't exactly felt right just to pick up and go on vacation. But I needed to get away. Clear my mind. Get over the drama, the sadness, the pain. I figured that I deserved it.

The waiter gingerly made his way over with the drink tray balanced in his hands. He smiled politely and handed me a tequila sunrise. I took an enthusiastic sip.

"Delicious. *Muchas gracias.*"

"*De nada*. And your cranberry juice, sir?"

Thierry reached out to take the drink from him. *"Gracias."*

"Hope you're both having a wonderful vacation," the waiter said.

"Oh, we certainly are." I smiled at Thierry. We clinked glasses as the waiter wandered away.

"What shall we toast to?" I asked him.

He met my eyes and smiled back at me. "To new beginnings."

We drank to that, and I snuggled against his fully clothed body. I hadn't convinced him to go the swimsuit route yet, but just give me time.

Amy and Barry were still on their extended honeymoon in Niagara Falls. Thierry had shut down the club for a few weeks and given everyone—well, Barry, George, and the new waiter—time off with pay. The place was up for sale, since the location was well known by the hunters who had ended up escaping. Thierry was looking into some property for a brand-new vampire club in the Beaches area of Toronto. Very chic.

Quinn was happy that Thierry and I were together. Or, at least, that's what he said. In private he told me that one day he'd win me back. Which was kind of funny, since he'd never really had me in the first place. I just nodded and told him he should find someone else in the meantime. I didn't know he'd take that advice to heart. To get over me, he'd launched into a passionate romance with Veronique. He'd even learned to speak some French, at least the dirty words, anyhow. Believe it or not, they were coming down to Mexico to join us for the weekend. Weren't we just the happy little family?

Yeah, things were good. I gazed at Thierry as he watched the multicolored horizon, and then he met my eyes. I was doing my very best to keep him happy to be alive. And so far I'd received no complaints, thank you very much.

I took another sip of my drink as I watched the rest of the sunset. Maybe after all was said and done, vampires actually could be the stars of fairy tales and get the chance to live happily ever after. Who knows?

Then again, maybe that was just the tequila talking.

Acknowledgments

Many thanks to:

Jim McCarthy, my wonderful agent. Your insights and encouragement will never be forgotten.

Melanie Murray, my fabulous editor. You have made my first novel a completely positive experience, and it has been a pleasure working with you.

And last but never ever least, Bonnie Staring, my amazing friend, beta-reader, and cheerleader, who can Simon Cowell my work any day.

Turn the page for a sneak peek at the next novel in the Immortality Bites series, *Fanged & Fabulous*

Chapter 1

Jogging is great exercise. Running for your life—even better.

At least that's what I tried to tell myself.

It was the new jogging suit that did it. I felt all *J. Lo* in my fuchsia velour (admittedly a little outdated, but happily purchased for half price) out for a quick, late-afternoon jog. Feeling good in the cold but fresh February air with my newest pair of very dark sunglasses firmly in place.

I guess I shouldn't have smiled at the cute young guy by the hot dog cart outside of my apartment building. Firstly, because, hello? I'm *taken*, thank you very much.

Secondly, because of the whole "fang" situation.

Fangs never seem to go over very well with vampire hunters.

Next thing I know, instead of getting a modest workout—surprisingly enough, a diet of diluted blood is *not* calorie-free—I was hightailing it through a nearly deserted park with a hunter on my Reebok-clad heels.

I shot a look over my shoulder. "Leave me alone!"

"Stop running, vampire!" he hollered.

I eyed the wooden stake he had in his right hand, and then picked up my pace, darting past a couple of speed walkers who didn't bother to give us a second glance.

Almost an entire month had gone by without seeing a single hunter. A *very* good month. Enough for me to let down my guard way too much.

Not good.

"I'll catch you!" the hunter shouted from a few steps behind me. "So why don't you stop running and save me some time?"

I jumped up as we passed an overhang of evergreens and grabbed at the nearest icicle. Then I stopped abruptly and spun around to face him with the sharp piece of ice clenched in my hand.

He skidded to a halt, almost slamming right into me, and looked at me with confusion. "You stopped."

"I'm trying to be more proactive these days. Come near me and this—" I indicated my drippy weapon "—is going through your eyeball."

My heart was beating so hard and fast I thought it might burst out of my chest like the slimy creature in *Alien*. Vampire hearts beat just as hard as human hearts. I never thought they did before I became one. I used to think that vampires were undead. But they aren't. They're just another kind of alive. Heartbeat mandatory to stay that way, otherwise what difference would that famous wooden stake make?

Hunter-boy was actually kind of cute. Probably in his

early twenties, with fashionably shaggy dark hair, a thin but attractive face, and brown puppy-dog eyes. He wore a black leather jacket over . . . beige Dockers?

I could totally take him.

"Proactive?" He raised an eyebrow and shifted the stake to his other hand. The frozen air puffed out of his mouth with every breath he took.

I shivered, and it wasn't just from the temperature. "Yeah, that's acting in advance to deal with an expected difficulty. I looked it up. It means that instead of running like a chicken with my head cut off—pardon the cliché—I will confront my attacker and deal with the situation in a calm yet forceful manner."

"You're smart for a vampire," he said.

I raised my eyebrows at that. "Really?"

"A vampire who's about to die."

I tensed and curled my other hand into a fist. I'd been going to self-defense fitness classes with my best friend Amy for a couple of weeks. It was true that only a few hour-long lessons probably weren't going to earn me any major ass-kicking awards, but I felt a little more confident about my current woman-in-jeopardy situation. A *little*.

Proactive with a capital P. That's me.

Okay, now I was shivering *and* sweating. I take it back. I wasn't confident. Not in the slightest.

Hunter-boy was going to stake me. Easily.

"What's your name?" I blurted out.

"Chad."

"Seriously?"

"Yeah. Why?"

"Is that short for anything?"

"Yeah, it's short for 'I'm going to kill you now.'" He frowned. "Why are you still talking?"

He kicked the icicle out of my hand. It hit the ground next to me and shattered. I blinked at it.

I held my shaking hands up in front of me. "Look . . . Chad, just walk away now. You *do not* want to mess with me." What was I going to do to get out of this alive? To defend myself? I'd go for the groin. Always a good place to start. And end.

"Let me tell you a little something . . . " he paused expectantly and raised his eyebrows.

"Sarah," I offered, without thinking. *Stupid*.

"The only reason you're still talking, Sarah, is because I'm allowing it. I might not look it, but I've dusted over a dozen vamps, this year alone."

I swallowed hard and felt a trickle of perspiration run down my spine.

"Well, if you've killed that many," I said, even less confident now if that was possible, "you should know it's not really dust. It's more like goo."

"Whatever." He looked down at the stake, ran his thumb along the sharp tip, and then glanced over at me. "Now let's get this party started."

Hell, he looked fairly harmless what with the Dockers and all. Guess you can't judge a man by his casual, stain-resistant pants anymore.

I turned and tried to run farther into the park along the snow-covered, cobblestone path, but before I got more than a few steps, I felt his hand clamp down on my shoulder, stopping me in midflee. He spun me around, then shoved me so hard that I stumbled back and fell to the ground in a heap. I scrambled back a few feet on my butt and looked around frantically. We were all alone. Why were we all alone? Where were innocent by-standers when I needed them?

"I'll make it quick." Chad winked at me. "If you stay nice and quiet for me."

Yeah, like that was going to happen. "Are you aware that you're the bad guy?"

That stopped him, but his stony expression didn't change. "What?"

I shuffled back a little more, feeling the cold snow against my bare hands. "Vampire hunters are evil, homicidal bastards who kill for the fun of it. They're the bad guys. Vampires are completely harmless. Like adorable, pointy-toothed bunnies."

He laughed a little at that and stepped closer. "Yeah, right."

I held a hand up in front of me to stop him from getting any nearer and slowly and shakily rose to my feet.

Keep him talking, I told myself.

I tried to smile and felt my cheeks twitch nervously. "Let's talk big picture here, Chad. Do you know what you'd be doing if you murder me?"

"*Slay*, you mean."

I shook my head. "Don't try to make it sound all Hollywood. You'd be *murdering* me. Just because you think I'm a monster. But I'm not a monster. I'm just a little dentally different than you."

He studied me for a moment, his expression growing uncertain. "You drink blood, don't you?"

I made a face. It sounded so gross. "This is true. But it's provided by willing donors. There's kegs of the stuff, hopefully sanitized and homogenized or whatever they do to make it clean and disease-free."

"You're an undead creature of the night." He frowned and jabbed the stake in my general direction.

I looked up and pointed at the sky. "Sun's still up, isn't it? And I'm breathing. Heart's going all pitty-pat. Seriously, you need to read up a little on the topic. Take some notes."

Chad sighed heavily. "You're saying that everything I've been told all my life—everything I've ever believed—has all been a lie. That I haven't been doing my job as a protector of mankind by ridding it of bloodsucking monsters, I've actually been killing innocent people."

I nodded enthusiastically. "Bingo!"

He stared at me for a moment and then snorted. "You're funny. That's almost enough for me to let you live, but you know what? Not going to happen."

Bingo denied.

I tried to scramble away from him, but he grabbed my fuchsia-covered leg and pulled me back until he was completely on top of me, pinning my arms under his knees so all I could do was thrash from side to side like a wounded seal. He grabbed my face and squeezed, making my mouth open up so he could inspect my fangs. He ran a thumb over one of them.

"I usually take these from the young ones I slay. Got myself a nice necklace now."

I sank my teeth (fangs included) into his hand as deep as I could, and he pulled away with surprise and a sudden yelp of pain.

He smacked me across the side of my face. "Shouldn't have done that, vampire."

"You touch me again and my boyfriend is going to rip your lungs out," I hissed.

"Yeah?" He smirked and looked around from his position on top of me. "I don't think I see your boyfriend anywhere. Or anyone else for that matter. It's just you and me."

"He's a master vampire and he's not a big fan of hunters. Lungs? Ripped out? Do I need to repeat myself?"

That got his attention. "A master vampire? In Toronto? There's only one that I've heard of."

"That's him. Do I need to mention the ripping out of lungs again?"

His raised stake lowered slightly, and his brow furrowed. "Did you say your name was Sarah?"

"So what if I did?"

"Sarah *Dearly*?"

I struggled to get out from under him but he had me pinned too firmly. "Get off me, you bastard."

Surprisingly, he did. As if there were wires attached to his body like a marionette, he sprang to his feet and stared at me with a deep frown while I slowly got up and brushed myself off.

"Sarah Dearly," he repeated. "The master vampire's girlfriend."

I glanced at him warily. "How do you know my name?"

His eyes widened. He breathed in a deep breath of cold air and let it out slowly before he spoke again. "Everyone knows about you."

"Everyone?"

"The Slayer of Slayers." He said it under his breath and took a step backward.

"The what of the what?"

"Last month . . . the massacre at the vampire lair. You killed so many hunters . . . so many . . . " His voice trailed off and he brought a hand to his mouth.

What in the hell was he talking about?

He took another step backward and hit the thick trunk of a tall oak tree next to a park bench. "I . . . I . . . should never have . . . " His eyes shifted back and forth and I noticed the hand that held the stake was now shaking. "Please, spare me. That whole thing earlier, me acting all tough . . . that was just an act. The other hunters . . . they're so mean, and they all think I'm weak. I was just out for a hot dog and a Coke, that's all. Please, don't hurt me. I was kidding about the fang necklace! Really!"

Last month, there had been a hunter/vampire showdown at the Midnight Eclipse, my boyfriend (sounds like a silly thing to call a six-hundred-year-plus-old vampire, but that's what he was) Thierry's secret vampire bar.

It was true that the night in question was a major deal, that a lot of people got hurt, both hunter and vampire, and that I may have . . . possibly . . . *sort of* . . . had to kill a hunter named Peter, jerk that he was. But that had been pure self-defense—and something I was still feeling great gobs of greasy guilt from, even though he'd majorly deserved it. And it had been with a gun, not with my bare teeth as Chad seemed to indicate with the fearing-for-his-life expression on his now-sweaty face.

Now everyone knows my name?

The theme song from *Cheers* suddenly began to play in my head.

I took a step toward him and he fell to his knees, the stake falling to the ground. He put his hands together and began to pray in barely coherent whispers. With a trembling hand he reached inside his shirt to pull out a heavy silver cross, which he then held up to ward himself against me.

I sighed. *Let's just nip this in the bud, shall we?*

I closed the remaining distance between us, reached forward, and grabbed the cross to show him that it didn't hurt me at all. It was quite pretty, actually. And shiny. His eyes widened in fear.

Then I grabbed his shirt and pulled him up to his feet—easy to do since he was like a rag doll now—then brought him close enough that our eyeballs were only inches from each other.

"I will let you live . . . *today*," I said, calmly and dangerously. I used to aspire to become a world-famous, well-paid actress, so I just called on that questionable ability to give my words a little extra weight. "But if you or your friends come near me again, I shall bathe in your blood."

Ew. Did I just say that? How disgusting.

But it seemed to get my point across. Chad was now the one scrambling backward, nodding like a lunatic, saying, "Yes, yes, I promise," over and over again. Then he got shakily to his feet, and with a last look of fear—

the intense kind one might have just before losing total bladder control—he turned and ran from the park like the proverbial bat out of hell.

I leaned over and picked the stake up from where Chad the Vampire Slayer had dropped it and studied it for a moment. I had to go find Thierry, tell him what had happened here, and ask him what I should do about it. If anybody would know, he would. He just wasn't going to be too happy about it.

Slayer of Slayers, huh?

I threw the stake into a nearby garbage can.

That new little nickname was *so* going to come back to bite me in the ass.

I first tried calling Thierry's cell phone, but it immediately took me into voicemail, which was frustrating at the best of times. He wasn't at his townhome, either. So I'd gone back to my apartment to change, then paced back and forth impatiently until eight o'clock when I knew somebody would be at his new vampire club. It didn't open for another hour, but some of the staff would already be there setting things up.

It had only been one week since Haven opened. I didn't like the place as much as Midnight Eclipse. Instead of being hidden behind the façade of a tanning salon, the entrance to Haven was a plain-looking door located along an abandoned alleyway. No bells, no whistles. Just an ugly, three-hundred-pound vampire bouncer named Angel (unfortunately, no relation or even a passing resemblance to David Boreanaz) who sized up vamps who came a-knocking.

Typically the entrance was also monitored by Barry Jordan, the manager of the club. He was extremely short and usually dressed in a tuxedo as well as a sour and annoyed expression. The guy hated me with a passion. Can't say I was all that thrilled with him either. Unfortunately he recently married my best friend Amy, who seemed to like him just fine for some odd reason.

Barry had a really annoying habit of calling Thierry "the master," which was very Renfield, and kind of creepy. And he seemed to have a big problem with those who did not refer to him that way. Namely, *me*.

Barry wasn't at Haven tonight. It must have been his night off.

The club was small, intimate, with dark walls, ornately carved cherry wood tables and chairs. A splash of color came from the blue and teal ceramic tiled floor, which had a swirling pattern like a whirlpool. Actually it looked more like a flushing toilet, if you ask me. Modern chandeliers dripped from the ceiling, filling the club with a soft, flickering light that filled me with anything but ease. I was way too stressed out by the time I got there.

"Where's Thierry?" I blurted out as I entered the club.

George was lighting a candle on a nearby table and he looked up at me. "Do you realize how often you enter a room saying that?"

I blinked at him.

"You could come in here with a 'Hi George, how are you doing George,'" he continued. "But, *no*. It's all about Thierry."

I felt a wave of anxiety. "I need to find him. I have a major problem."

He rolled his eyes. George was a waiter at the club. He'd also worked at Midnight Eclipse, and I considered him one of my very best fanged friends. Totally gorgeous, too. He had shoulder-length sandy blond hair, a square jaw, high cheekbones, full lips, and bedroom eyes. A body like a Chippendales dancer, or one of those hottie male models on the covers of romance novels. Yeah, George was damn hot.

Too bad he played for the other team.

"Marco dumped me," he announced.

"Who's Marco?"

"My boyfriend." He frowned. "You knew that already."

I shrugged, feeling too distracted to fully concentrate on what he was saying.

"He was one of the construction workers who worked on the club," he said.

"Oh. Well, I'm sorry. I'm sure you'll . . . I don't know . . . meet somebody else." I glanced around the dimly lit club. "So where's Thierry?"

He sighed and leaned against the table. "Your lack of compassion for my acute depression is duly noted. What's your *trauma du jour*, anyhow?"

I quickly explained what had happened, starting with the jog and ending with my new nickname. George whistled.

"Well, that explains all these crazy rumors I've been hearing," he said. "About some badass vampire in town. I never realized it was you. No offense."

My anxiety increased another notch. "There are rumors? Already? What am I going to do?"

He appeared to think about it. "You should probably talk to Thierry."

"Well, *duh*."

I felt a rough tap on my shoulder and I turned around. A husky man wearing a dark blue ski jacket presented me with a fang-filled grin. "You Veronique?"

I stared at him blankly. "Not even remotely. Who are you?"

"I'm her ride to the airport."

There was a sudden change in the air and I knew without a doubt the woman in question had just entered the room. The scent of expensive perfume wafted under my nostrils. I'd been turned into a vampire exactly seven weeks ago and my sense of smell had been growing daily. This was sometimes a blessing and sometimes—depending on where in the city I was walking—not so much.

I turned to watch her glide through the club.

Veronique eyed the driver and her red lips curved up to the right. "If you could give me one moment to say goodbye to my friend I would greatly appreciate it."

He nodded, immediately intoxicated by the gorgeous woman with long raven hair, flawless skin, and remarkably white and sparkly fangs.

She glanced at the leaning tower of George and her eyes narrowed. "Shouldn't you be working?"

"I was . . . I was just going to . . . " he stammered, then gave me a stricken look. "Um . . . I'll go find Thierry." He scurried away.

Well, her charms didn't work on everyone.

But I liked Veronique. Actually I liked her a lot, but there was one big thing about her I wasn't terribly fond of.

She was Thierry's wife.

I had been assured that their marriage was in name only after more than six hundred years. Frankly, I couldn't imagine knowing somebody for thirty years, let alone six hundred. But I still wasn't thrilled with the situation. Dating a married man, even though the wife was fine and dandy with it, just seemed . . . *extremely* wrong.

I'd recently summoned enough courage to ask if she'd ever considered getting a divorce. Veronique had waved off my question with a laugh and said, "After so many years, why would I want something like that?"

Yeah. I'd managed to refrain from digging my fingernails into her perfect eyeballs. Barely.

So, as I said, I liked Veronique. But her recent decision to go back to her fabulous life in France wasn't the most heartbreaking news I'd heard all year.

She gave me a tight hug, followed by a brief kiss on each of my cheeks. "*Au revoir*." She leaned back. "Are you all right, my dear?"

I forced a smile. "I'm fine. Have a nice flight. Bye now."

"Are you quite certain? You look a little . . . *malheureux*."

"I failed French in high school. But I feel fine." I shrugged. *Well, other than narrowly escaping death only hours ago*, I thought. *Again*.

I looked over my shoulder. Where the hell was Thierry?

"I think I know what it is." A smile played at her perfectly outlined lips. "You are afraid to admit how much you will miss me. I understand. But the time that I was needed here has passed and yours has just begun."

My eyebrow perked up at that. Was she talking about Thierry? Maybe she'd given the divorce thing more thought. I shifted my feet, which now, instead of the Reeboks from my near-death jog, sported low-heeled, rubber-soled Tender Tootsies that looked okay with my black jeans. My trendier footwear was currently piled up at the back of my closet to make way for that which was consistently comfortable and easy to run in.

Proactive = Me.

Veronique reached into her tiny Fendi bag, pulled out a business card, and handed it to me.

"That is the number to my home in Paris. If you ever need to talk to someone, please don't hesitate to call me. I know things will soon be difficult for you."

I glanced at the card and then tucked it into the pocket of my jeans. "So you've heard about the hunters' special new interest in me, too? Wow, rumors sure spread quickly, don't they?"

Her forehead creased prettily. "No . . . though that is certainly cause for concern. I was referring to how distraught you will be when my Thierry leaves you."

"Huh?" My forehead creased less prettily, and I scanned the nearly empty club again. "What? He's leaving me? When did this happen?"

She shook her head. "No, not yet, my dear. I'm simply saying that when it does happen, please feel free to call me. I can dispense invaluable advice to help mend your broken heart."

My eyes widened with every word.

The driver approached her. "We should be leaving now to catch your flight, ma'am."

I just stared at Veronique. "Did Thierry say something to you? Is that why I can't find him tonight? Is he avoiding me?"

She smiled patiently at me. "It is so sweet how taken you are with him. I am not saying this to upset you, but it is quite obvious that this will only be a short-term relationship."

"Short-term?"

"You have known him for what . . . less than two months, yes? I know he feels a great sense of responsibility for your safety. From the attention he has paid you, it is understandable that you would become greatly smitten with him."

"Smitten?" I sputtered. "You think I'm *smitten*?"

She frowned slightly at my words. "Thierry is almost seven hundred years old. You are . . . what? In your mid-thirties?"

"I AM TWENTY-EIGHT!"

"There is no reason to shout, my dear. I am trying to be a friend to you and tell you how things truly are, so you will not be shocked by how things inevitably turn out. I have known Thierry for so, so many years. I know him better than anyone else. I am simply warning you to prepare for his interest to wane." She touched my arm. "I am sorry."

The driver cleared his throat loudly. "If we don't leave soon, ma'am, I'm afraid you'll miss your flight and then I'll—"

I spun around. "And then you'll *what*?" I snapped.

He took a step backward. "Never mind. Take all the time you need."

Veronique shook her head. "*Mon dieu.* I should not have said anything. It is simply my desire to see those I care about happy. Being in love with a man such as Thierry will not bring you happiness. He is too old for you. There are too many secrets. Simply too much against you. I apologize for being blunt, but I have only done so as a friend."

It was difficult to be friends with somebody who had been effortlessly perfect for seven centuries. She'd seen everything and done everything at least once. Plus, she had really great hair.

She also had a nasty habit of being right.

I ran a quick hand under my nose, sniffed, and tried to compose myself. "You'd better go. Don't want to miss your plane."

Veronique nodded. "Of course. Take care, my dear."

She looked at me with concern for a moment longer. Then, with a single glance at the driver, she left the club without another word.

I took in a deep breath and let it out slowly and shakily as I tried to compose myself.

"*When my Thierry leaves you.*" Her words kept repeating in my mind like a bad burrito. "*It is quite obvious that this will only be a short-term relationship.*"

I shook my head. No. Thierry wasn't going to break

my heart. Our relationship was on solid ground. Rock steady.

Even though he was absolutely perfect and I was far from it, I wanted us to work out. I'd do whatever it took to prove to him that I was the right woman for him. Long-term.

Sure, he'd been a little distracted lately with trying to open the new club in record time. I'd barely seen him at all for the last couple of weeks, but that didn't mean a thing.

Not a damn thing.

It was only a little over two weeks ago that we'd gotten back from a fantastic trip to Mexico. Romance. Margaritas. Sunscreen.

It could have been better, I suppose. Even while staying mostly out of the blaringly bright sun, I'd still managed to get a serious burn on my back that made it difficult to move without screaming. Thierry warned me about staying out of the sun, but I hadn't listened to him. Vampires are not killed by sunlight as is the popular myth. However, it still makes us a bit weaker physically and annoyed by the brightness of the "big ball of fire death" in the sky, which is what I call it now, ever since the sunburn from hell. Especially after going through vats of Noxzema during the healing process. Talk about putting a major crimp in your love life.

After getting back, Thierry focused all his attention on the club. But now that it was open . . .

I glanced around. Where in the hell was he, anyhow?

No. I couldn't think about this right now. I had rumors to worry about. Hunters to hide from. Etcetera.

Veronique was crazy. Thierry and I were just fine. Sure he was a little distant, but that was just the way he was. We had a deep, romantic *connection*.

Well . . .

Except for the fact that we hadn't had sex since Mexico. Oh, didn't I mention that? Yeah. Might be a problem.

I swallowed hard.

Maybe Veronique wasn't so crazy.

"Sarah—" a deep, familiar voice said from behind me. "George says you're looking for me?"

Michelle Rowen was born in Toronto, Ontario. As a child she decided that when she grew up she would become a flight attendant, a jewel thief, and a writer. One out of three ain't bad. She is a self-confessed bibliophile, the proud owner of an evil cat named Nikita, a Reality TV junkie, and has an unhealthy relationship with anything to do with *Buffy the Vampire Slayer*. She currently lives in Mississauga, Ontario.

Visit Michelle's website at www.michellerowen.com.